What the critics are saying…

"TOP PICK! 4 ½ Stars! Agnew's paranormal suspense, next in the Special Investigations Agency series, is hot and very, very exciting. …The adventure is nonstop and the sex hot and heavy. New readers will definitely want to look up the earlier books in the series." ~ *Romantic Times Bookclub Magazine*

"JERR Gold Star Award! I do not know where to begin my praise of Primordial!!! Ms. Agnew has done a wonderful job…Every page was a juicy discovery for my mind and libido….If you like a good story line and plot mixed in with your action, adventure and love, I strongly suggest getting this Primordial (why are you still here, go and get the book!), I promise you will not be disappointed." ~ *Faith Jacobs Just Erotic Romance Reviews*

"PRIMORDIAL is a hot trek into the rainforest where two people encounter danger at every turn, and legends that will raise the hair on the back of your neck…The story moves quickly and smoothly and readers will hasten to turn the pages to find out what will happen next…PRIMORDIAL is full of fiery passion, bewitching characters, and a boatload of danger. Grab your copy today!" ~ *Sinclair Reid Romance Reviews Today*

"The writing talent at Ellora's Cave just keeps growing by leaps and bounds. A prime example of this talent is found in Denise Agnew's PRIMORDIAL. Words like adventurous, sexy, exciting and suspenseful all come to mind when thinking about this paranormal treat… PRIMORDIAL was an edgy, erotic and adventurous paranormal treat. Definitely worth the read." ~ *Love Romances*

Primordial

Denise A. Agnew

PRIMORDIAL
An Ellora's Cave Publication, March 2005

Ellora's Cave Publishing, Inc.
1337 Commerce Drive Suite #13
Stow, Ohio 44224

ISBN #1419951726

Edited by: *Martha Punches*
Cover art by: *Syneca*

Warning:

The following material contains graphic sexual content meant for mature readers. *Primordial* has been rated *E-rotic* by a minimum of three independent reviewers.

Ellora's Cave Publishing offers three levels of Romantica™ reading entertainment: S (S-ensuous), E (E-rotic), and X (X-treme).

S-*ensuous* love scenes are explicit and leave nothing to the imagination.

E-*rotic* love scenes are explicit, leave nothing to the imagination, and are high in volume per the overall word count. In addition, some E-rated titles might contain fantasy material that some readers find objectionable, such as bondage, submission, same sex encounters, forced seductions, etc. E-rated titles are the most graphic titles we carry; it is common, for instance, for an author to use words such as "fucking", "cock", "pussy", etc., within their work of literature.

X-*treme* titles differ from E-rated titles only in plot premise and storyline execution. Unlike E-rated titles, stories designated with the letter X tend to contain controversial subject matter not for the faint of heart.

Primordial

Dedication

Always to Terry, for his never ending love and support. You are my secret agent man.

Acknowledgements

Special thanks goes to Mireya Orsini for her invaluable assistance with the Spanish in this story. I couldn't have done it without her. Thanks so much, Mireya!

Prologue
Cairo, Egypt

Zane Spinella watched the bustling market square, taking in the sights and sounds like a predator stalking his next meal. A woman's beautiful singing voice undulated on the stifling air, lulling the senses with sensual promise. But he couldn't afford to relax, to take pleasure in the haunting sound as it drifted around him with seductive allure.

Sequestered near an alcove, he observed the comings and goings with anticipation. Sweat rolled down the back of his neck and into the collar of his desert khaki camp shirt. A shiver passed over his body despite the stifling heat. He knew what the sensation meant. The telltale quiver forewarned of trouble.

His sixth sense never lied. *Yeah, trouble in spades and then some.*

He squinted in the hot sun. Even his wraparound sunglasses couldn't cut this burning light. *Nothing like being baked alive.* He took two deep swallows of his bottled water and returned it to the loop on his belt. At the very least he should be prepared, because if Aloysius Makepeace showed up this time, he would act fast.

Zane had prowled Cairo for two days and not a sign of his quarry. Maybe the intelligence he'd received from his contacts in Egypt and the message traffic from SIA didn't jive. As he raised the digital camera and adjusted the telescopic lens, he sucked in a deep breath and regretted it. The alcove stunk to high heaven of dog feces and urine. He could handle it, and it didn't distract him from his primary focus; capturing damaging photographs of old man Makepeace with international artifact thief and terrorist Darren Hollister was more important.

There he is.

Aloysius moved into position in the square, the noonday sun glaring down on his tall body. Like clockwork a shorter, well-built blond man stepped up to him. Dressed in a short-sleeved green polo shirt and brown dress pants, Hollister looked so out of place it should be laughable. Sunburned and Nordic as hell with his thick, straight long blond hair, Hollister drew attention to himself in this country.

Makepeace moved forward, smiling and shaking Hollister's hand. *Prove me wrong, old man. Don't do it.*

Zane snapped a few shots, pausing between each frame. The sophisticated device, which Zane once heard described as the secret squirrel camera, zeroed in on the two men, ready to capture damning evidence.

With his sun-weathered, wrinkled face and prominent features, Aloysius blended with the locals. Zane knew the robe hid the skinny body of an eighty-year-old. No one would ever suspect him of being a criminal. A linguistics scholar like old man Makepeace, with a genius IQ, should have more brains than this, but Zane had seen it happen before. Greed could drive a man to do horrible things.

Zane's heartbeat quickened, his breathing coming fast as the thought of bringing down the enemy sent adrenaline surging into his body. He'd done surveillance like this so many times it should be boring as shit. Instead, he thrilled to the chase, the knowledge he would obtain the verification required to destroy an international terrorist and his cohort.

Before Makepeace could move again, a woman came into view. Dressed in a high-collared off-white tunic and gauzy navy blue pants, her head was shaded by a matching blue scarf. Zane could see her face and a little of her honey brown hair. When she turned from profile to full on, everything outside and within him seemed to stand still.

His breath hitched in his throat and his body took instant notice.

Jesus.

Golden brown eyes looked right in his direction, and for a second he panicked. Could she see him? No, he'd placed himself far enough away that even a camera pointed in their direction shouldn't cause suspicion.

Zane surveyed her like a starving man. Spaced in proportion to a slim, small nose and lush mouth, her eyes held a strange sadness he felt down deep where he didn't want to feel. Long, beautiful dark eyelashes fanned to her cheeks as she blinked. Her face held strong angles, her jaw a little square. It gave her face instant strength and matched with the vulnerability he sensed within her. Arousal stirred in his groin and startled him. He didn't have time to become interested in a woman with questionable connections. Hell, he hadn't had time for any exciting female contact in the last several months. The job demanded everything he could give; everything else could wait.

Realizing that he'd been gawking at the woman without taking photos, he snapped a series of pictures sure to damn both Makepeace and his companions. The woman shook hands with the big blond, and when Makepeace put his arm around the woman, Zane captured the image. Did Makepeace have a woman on the side? The old bastard had been married fifty years, but maybe that didn't mean anything to him.

Again, as if she sensed something wrong, the woman glanced his way. Another flash of those intriguing eyes and the air in his lungs sluiced in and out with difficulty. She reminded him of a jungle creature peeking out behind lush flora, watching and waiting. For what?

As Makepeace and the woman talked with Hollister, Zane wished he could read lips. Makepeace reached in his burnoose and brought out a small envelope. He handed it to Hollister and then stepped back. Rapidly snapping off the pictures, Zane took satisfaction in collecting the damning evidence.

He moved closer, inch by inch. Not long after, he realized the conversation between Makepeace, the woman and Hollister seemed to be ending. Maybe, if he worked this right, he could also pick up some of their conversation. He reached into his shirt pocket and extracted a cigarette packet. He left the camera hanging around his neck while he tapped the packet so the end of a cigarette popped out.

Not that he'd ever smoked in his life, nor did he plan to start. He shoved the cigarette pack back in his pocket, as if he'd gone for a smoke and then decided against it. He smiled with satisfaction. The packet would record everything Makepeace and his cohorts said; the microphone should be powerful enough to record their voices.

Zane neared the small group and propped against a wall, making sure he looked everywhere but the group so they wouldn't suspect him.

As the camera whirred with shot after shot, Zane felt unusual stirrings of worry for the woman. She looked innocent, unprotected. As his gut clenched, he realized he'd allowed his sympathy to get out of hand. She couldn't be trusted.

"This isn't good enough. Haan will not be happy," Hollister said, his American accent coming through loud and clear.

"You have to tell him this is impossible. I need more time to deliver the item," Makepeace said, his Queen's English upper-crust accent soft but firm. A thin line of desperation tinged the old man's voice.

"You don't have a choice, old man." The blond bruiser nodded toward the woman. "What happened to your wife could happen to her."

Alarm slid through Zane's blood. Something ugly lingered in the air like a bad stench. His instincts told him to be ready for anything.

"Damn you to hell, sir. You are not a gentleman," Makepeace said, a growl in his voice that almost altered his polite veneer.

"Grandfather." The woman's voice came to Zane's ears, as distinguished as her grandfather's but with an American accent. "Please."

He should have known. He hadn't seen a picture of Makepeace's granddaughter before, but Mac Tudor, his Section Chief at SIA, had told him about her. Keira Marie Jessop, an archaeologist and criminal. Intriguing combination, and probably damned deadly. It disgusted him when a woman this talented and beautiful threw her life away by consorting with vermin like Hollister.

Zane took the chance and glanced at the group. The woman held her grandfather's arm. Hollister's expression held clear contempt for Makepeace and the woman.

Come on, Blondie. Say something nice and incriminating. Open that big mouth of yours and just say what I wanna hear.

"Remember, old man," Hollister said, putting his hands on his hips. "You give Haan what he wants, or it's hell to pay."

The blond started to stalk away and left the old man talking with the woman. They moved a little father away.

"Shit," Zane murmured when he realized he couldn't hear what they said anymore.

Zane almost took the chance and walked into the middle of the square and toward a cart where he knew he could fake looking at merchandise. He stowed his camera in the small over-the-shoulder camera case nestled at his left hip.

Shifting away from Makepeace's sheltering arm, the woman gestured with her hand. Anger crossed her smooth features, her eyes flashing. Makepeace held up his hands and frowned, his gaze intense with warning. She shook her head. The old man appeared to plead with her. Seconds later he stalked away, major displeasure written in every line on his face.

So the old bastard would leave his granddaughter standing out here alone? Zane's protective instincts fired to life. His gaze snagged on Hollister returning to the square and heading straight for Keira. *What the fuck – ?*

In his peripheral vision Zane saw movement, swift and deadly. Around a corner, the long nose of an M-16 appeared and pointed right toward Keira and Hollister.

Zane hurdled into action and ran toward Keira. "Get down!"

She whirled, her eyes wide with shock as he dashed toward her. Zane grabbed the woman and yanked her into an alcove. Her gasp of outrage stifled against him as he flattened her against unforgiving wall just as gunfire erupted in the plaza.

People scattered, women and children screaming, and men shouting. Display carts tipped over as chaos erupted.

He reached for the small weapon strapped to his ankle. One swift movement and he gathered the gun in his right hand.

More automatic gunfire made Zane edge her deeper into the niche until they couldn't go any further. He pressed her head against his shoulder to shelter her face, making sure not to smother her.

"Let me go!" Keira struggled against him, her voice muffled against his shirt.

"Stop it." She started to bring up her knee and he pressed her harder against the wall. "Don't even think about it."

Another spate of bullets peppered the wall near the recess and he stiffened, hoping to hell the bullets didn't ricochet. Her entire body shivered against him, as if fear made its way into her mind. Daring to peer around the alcove wall, he kept his weapon at the ready. If someone intended to kill her, he needed to find a safe way out of here. Screaming and shouting echoed against the walls and in the distance a siren wailed. At first he didn't see anyone hit by the spate of bullets. No bodies or blood. Then he saw Hollister lying face down not far from the entrance to an alley. Bullet wound damage to the back of his head assured no medical assistance would help him. An eerie silence, punctuated by a woman's weeping, settled over the market.

Another scan of the area showed no sign of the assassin.

Taking a clarifying breath, he glared down into her amber eyes and drank in her female scent with one deep breath.

Her eyes betrayed anger and confusion. "Get off me."

"Damn it, stop squirming." Leaning down a little so he could align his gaze with hers, he conveyed the truth. "Those bullets may have been meant for you. If you want to live, stop fighting me."

Warm and curved, Keira's body felt vulnerable under his weight, but the alcove didn't afford enough room for him to move back without making his back a target. For the first time he saw fear in her eyes. She shivered and the little movement made him too aware of soft, full breasts and slim body concealed by layers of cloth. Primal male inside him reared up and took notice in a big way.

His cock didn't care that he'd just survived a dangerous situation that might not be over yet. All it cared about was the woman glued to every inch of him. Her eyes widened as she realized that he sported a growing erection. *Damn it all to hell.* She probably thought he was a rapist. Self-preservation said something must give.

He eased up on her a little and cupped her face with his left hand. He didn't see any blood on her, but concern still made him ask, "Were you hit?"

"What?" she asked a bit breathlessly.

"Are you hurt?"

"No. No. Who *are* you?"

Nope. He couldn't tell her. Not now, if ever. "We need to get you to safety."

She pressed her hands against his chest and the feeling of warm, small hands against his pecs made his cock grow harder. Her mouth opened as if she couldn't decide to tell him to go screw himself or if she wanted a kiss. God, those lips looked soft and like they might taste so fucking delicious. He stared down at her like an idiot, a man who had the stupidity to think about sex after getting shot at.

On the other hand, he knew that reaction often came with the territory. Many of the male agents he knew maintained they felt horny as hell after danger passed.

"Don't," she said, her voice quavering the slightest bit.

"Don't what?"

She didn't answer, her gaze locked with his in a moment that seemed to hang on to eternity.

He couldn't help but drink in those big, gorgeous eyes and that made-for-sex mouth. A wild-assed vision of her sucking him with that mouth made him want to groan. She overwhelmed his senses, his body going into riot. He'd always been a sitting duck for a damsel in distress and it didn't seem to matter right now if she was the criminal he'd been tracking since she entered Cairo. She appeared young and innocent, but he knew she couldn't be.

She shook her head. "Please."

Please what? Please kiss you, honey?

"Release her immediately," a stern English male voice said.

Her eyes widened as she looked past him, and Zane whirled. Using his body to shelter her, he pointed his weapon right at the man.

Makepeace put his hands up. Zane saw strength holding back the man's alarm.

Keira gasped and grabbed Zane's left biceps with both hands. "Don't hurt him!"

Zane lowered his gun and Keira darted out from behind him and into her grandfather's arms.

"Just what the blazes did you think you were doing?" Makepeace asked.

Anger destroyed the wild arousal he'd felt for Keira. "Keeping her pretty little ass from being shot off."

Makepeace cuddled his granddaughter closer. "That's not what it looked like to me."

Zane wanted to keep his gun in hand, not one hundred percent certain all danger had passed. Instead he quickly slipped it back into the ankle holster. "I don't care what it looked like to you."

"Why you insolent—"

"Grandfather, please. He did save my life. He's—" She swallowed hard. "He's telling the truth."

Makepeace assessed him with wise, untrusting eyes. "Very well. In that case I owe you a wealth of gratitude. Whoever you are."

The mild contempt in the old man's tone assured Zane he didn't have the Brit's trust. Not that he needed it. His cover, in a sense, was shot all to hell the minute he'd sprinted into the square to prevent Keira from being murdered.

"A tourist," Zane said. "I'm just a tourist."

Makepeace snorted. "Right. A tourist with a weapon."

Zane crossed his arms. "Let's just say I like to stay safe."

"In case of unexpected gunfire," she said with the smallest hint of humor in her tone.

Zane nodded. "Exactly." Tired of dicking around, he continued. "If I was you, sir, I'd keep a close watch on her from now on while you're in Egypt." He nodded toward Hollister's lifeless form in the square, now half surrounded by curious people. "I don't think he was the only they wanted to hit."

Dawning realization and renewed suspicion crossed the man's lined face. "What are you saying?"

Keira looked up at her grandfather. "Someone may have wanted me dead, too."

The fright in her voice, mixed with a strength he couldn't help but admire, made Zane want to offer shelter. He could escort them to their hotel, to the airport and see them off.

No. That would be pushing too far.

"I heard weapon fire and came back right away." Makepeace looked down at her with love written on his face. "I thought…"

Tears welled up in her eyes and Zane felt another emotional punch to his gut. He brushed it off with a brisk suggestion. "Both of you had better get the hell out of here before the cops come and start asking questions."

She peeled herself out of her grandfather's grip and walked toward Zane. "Is there anyway I can repay you for saving my life?"

If her grandfather hadn't been standing there, and he felt just grouchy and horny enough to do it, he would have tugged her into his arms and kissed her.

"Not a damn thing," Zane said, aware he sounded rude as hell.

Then he walked away without looking back.

Chapter One
One Month Later
Place: Special Investigations Agency
Section Chief's Office
Location: Colorado, Top Secret Facility

Dr. Keira Jessop thought maybe her hearing had gone bad.

She looked across the large desk at Section Chief Mac Tudor and asked, "You want me to go where?"

"San Cristobal in Puerto Azul."

Excitement stirred in her stomach, a tingling akin to sexual arousal that startled her. She'd never been there and the archaeology of the area had always intrigued her. At the same time, she didn't like tropical areas much and she'd experienced all the danger she needed for a long time.

"You want me to go to Central America?"

"Puerto Azul is one of the most stable countries in the region. It's proximity to Costa Rica and the stable economy makes it a desirable vacation spot."

She'd planned on staying in London with her grandfather for awhile until his grief mended. Until *her* grief mended.

She took a deep breath and pushed away the anger that threatened to rupture civility and reasonableness. "I don't know if I can. I really wish someone had told me what this was all about before I left England. My grandfather needs me. Besides, you probably have offices in England somewhere, don't you? Why couldn't I have gone there to discus this?"

Her tone held accusation. Lately she found her temper getting the best of her. She'd been ushered to this place, secured deep within the mountains of Colorado, well aware through rumors that this agency worked worldwide and not just within the United States. Why they'd wanted to talk to her, though, did scare her. She didn't like intrigue. After Egypt she didn't want adventure ever again.

Mac frowned and leaned on his desk. "I apologize for the inconvenience. That's why we sent the tickets. We don't want this trip to be a hardship on you."

"If my grandfather hadn't encouraged me to come here, I wouldn't have."

"I'm very glad he did."

His sincere smile lit up the room. Despite irritation, feminine interest flitted through her. The man was insanely handsome in a rugged, totally kick-ass-and-take-names way that appealed to her. She liked men of action, and she guessed this tall, muscular man had been a field agent for the SIA at one time. Sitting behind a desk took nothing away from his appeal. When her gaze noted his wedding photograph sitting on the desk behind him, and the plain gold wedding ring on his hand, she allowed her intrigue with him to fade.

"Even if you'd refused to come, we would have tracked you down," Mac said, his voice edged with steel. "It wouldn't have stopped us."

"I see. Well, whatever it is you want me to do, I don't think I've got the time. I need to return to London immediately. My grandfather is in poor health."

"I heard about what happened. Please accept my deepest sympathy."

She hated sympathy; it did nothing to shove aside the sorrow eating at her gut while she watched her grandfather waste away from a broken heart. If she went home to San Francisco she would be with her mother and father, and her mother seemed to be taking her grandmother's death reasonably well.

Her lips felt wooden as she said, "Thank you for your concern. Now, when can I leave and go back to England?"

"You haven't heard why I called you here."

"I don't need to hear anything about it. I already know that the SIA is an international agency designed to thwart terrorist and other similar threats around the world. This summons to Colorado probably means you want me as some sort of consultant. Why, though, I can't imagine. There are plenty of archaeologists around you could ask for help."

Mac leaned back. He picked up a pen from his desk blotter, then clicked it open and shut a few times. "I was about to tell you."

She rubbed her eyes, jet lag making her sluggish and beyond tired. She didn't care if she sounded rude anymore. "All right. What is it you want?"

"We want you to work for us in Puerto Azul to find an artifact."

Now she did want to slap him. She sat up straighter. "Why you would need to me to go to Central America when you've got plenty of agents with archaeological experience junketing around the world? Couldn't you send one of them?"

"We already have a man on the ground. He's going to meet you at the airport in San Cristobal to ensure the mission is completed."

All the hair on the back of her neck prickled. She glanced down at her hands, clenched in her lap, and realized she no doubt looked as nervous as she felt. She'd recovered stolen artifacts before, but only after a police agency obtained the artifact from the one who'd stolen the piece. This assignment sounded less sterile and far more dangerous...like her experience in Egypt. When she looked up at him, he paused with a patient expression that said he could wait for hours.

"Why me?" Something didn't add up and an alarm went off in her psyche. "I've specialized in Egyptian and British archaeological sites all my life. My specialty doesn't cover Central American archaeology."

"It does now." Mac turned his swivel chair toward the credenza behind him and reached for a small remote. With one click the serene landscape portrait behind him slid almost soundlessly upward into the ceiling and revealed a plasma widescreen.

She smiled without humor. "I don't have time to watch home movies, Mr. Tudor."

He chuckled, the sound deep and appreciative. Instead of answering her sarcasm, he watched as the screen lit up with a large picture of a jungle-covered high plateau. A breathtaking green, the flora-covered photo intrigued her at the same time it repelled.

"This is San Cristobal Plateau located deep in the *Selva Negra* Jungle. Although the city is nearby, no one ventures into the jungle. It's one of the few places in Puerto Azul that hasn't been explored in great depth. The only man who dared penetrate the area in recent years is Ludwig Haan."

"The Ludwig Haan? The fashion designer?" she asked in disbelief.

"Believe it or not, yes. He led a little-known expedition into the jungle last year and when he came back, he claimed to have discovered a fountain of youth. But we think he discovered something else."

She almost sneered. "The last photograph I saw of him, he looked older than ever."

Mac nodded. "The SIA has watched him closely over the years and we're certain he's into smuggling artifacts out of countries and into his own personal collection." Mac clicked the remote and another picture came into view. "This structure is *Rancho La Paz* owned by Haan. It sits just within the outside boundaries of *Selva Negra*. His area is little traveled and then only by his special guests or rebels who like to attack unsuspecting tourists. Other than a select few people, almost no one is allowed to enter Haan's complex. The last agent we sent in to investigate turned up dead in San Cristobal a few days later. We couldn't prove Haan had the agent killed, but we suspect it."

The three-story wood and glass structure stood in a small clearing surrounded by jungle. Designed to look like a glamorous hut nestled in a serene rainforest, it conveyed decadence.

"It's a ranch?" she asked in disbelief.

"No. That's just what he named it. Haan entertains an international cache of select guests at *Rancho La Paz* when he's not jetting around to fashion shows in the United States and Europe." Mac turned his chair back to her. "We want you to infiltrate his lodge and discover whether a particular artifact is hidden there."

Her mouth popped open in incredulity. "What?"

He didn't blink an eye. "You'll leave in two days."

"At the risk of being rude, Mr. Tudor, not only no, but *hell* no." She stood slowly. "This is one of the stupidest things I've ever heard. Why would I want to go into a dangerous situation like that just to tell you whether Haan has a stolen artifact?"

This time Mac's smile didn't materialize. Maybe she'd pushed him too far. Good. She didn't have time for this.

"Because your grandfather helped him steal it."

Keira felt the world tilt, just as it had a month ago in Egypt. She couldn't take two wallops so close together. Pain sliced through her as she battled with an urge to cry. Her eyes stung with tears but she held them back. She'd suffered a blow learning what her grandfather had done to try and save her grandmother. Now this.

"No," she whispered.

Mac's eyes didn't hold a trace of sympathy. "Unfortunately, yes. We've been tracking Aloysius Makepeace's movements in the archaeology world for some time, Dr. Jessop. He's done more than work for the Chesterham Museum; he's been stealing from them for years."

Anger roared up inside her. "My grandfather's position as an assistant curator ended when he retired ten years ago. How dare you—"

"It's true."

"Then why, in God's name, didn't you have him arrested a long time ago?"

He looked up at her. "We needed definite proof."

A lump rose in her throat and she swallowed hard, ire destroying the tears threatening moments ago. "So you say my grandfather has been stealing from the museum and selling to numerous clients, or just Haan?"

"Several clients over about a ten-year span."

Keira closed her eyes as resentment stung her like a whip. No. She couldn't believe it. She *wouldn't*. "You're lying."

"I don't lie, Dr. Jessop." His voiced deepened along with his frown. "I know this is hard to hear." Mac turned back to the plasma screen. "And I think this will convince you."

The picture on the screen changed to a photograph of her grandfather, clothed in a robe and talking with Darren Hollister, the man who'd destroyed their lives last month in Egypt. Mac clicked the remote again and a snapshot of her with Hollister and her grandfather in the market place come up on the screen. One photo after another appeared on the screen, including one of her staring in the direction of the camera. She'd been looking right at the damned camera without knowing it.

Someone took these pictures right before an assassin had murdered Hollister. Her mind flashed back to that horrifying moment and the man who'd saved her life. She'd often wondered about her rescuer and his identity. More than that, she'd replayed those intense moments in the alcove over and over again when she lay awake at night.

"Dr. Jessop?"

"If you believe all these things about Grandfather, why ask me to help you? Why *would* I help you?"

She saw something flicker of his expression, an acknowledgment that he didn't care much for this assignment or what he asked her to do. "Because if you want to clear his name and yours, you'll take this assignment. It's the only way to clean the slate."

More hot anger swelled up. "Blackmail?"

He nodded. "The SIA wouldn't do this if we didn't have a good reason."

She shook her head and glared. "I don't see how any of this can be legal."

"It is. And we want to give you a chance to prove your innocence before the law decides this is a matter for prosecution. The photograph shows you and your grandfather with one of Haan's associates, Darren Hollister."

Her mouth dry and her heart aching, she said, "I didn't know there was a connection between Hollister and Haan."

Mac nodded and turned off the plasma screen. It slid back up into the ceiling as if it had never been there at all. "He's more than connected; he was a part of his cartel."

Her thoughts went into chaos and her stomach clenched with nervous nausea. "Someone from Haan's cartel killed Hollister?"

"It's possible, but we're not certain. It's a tangled web. Your grandfather sold artifacts to Haan in the past, and we have the evidence you and your grandfather spoke with Hollister before he was killed. For all we know, your grandfather arranged to have Hollister killed."

A gasp slipped from her throat and she sat forward in her chair. Her fingers gripped the armrests. "How dare you? My grandfather is a good man. He would never do anything like that."

Mac's expression eased from hard-nosed to sympathetic. "You're right, I don't know your grandfather or his motivations. Just as I don't know you. Help us trap Haan at his game and perhaps the courts will go easy on your grandfather."

She closed her eyes and sighed, a sense of inevitability sweeping her. "In other words, do this assignment and our so-called transgressions just go away?"

"You could say that."

Never in a million years could Keira have imagined this happening even one week ago. Her life had been cleaved by the trip to Egypt. She'd tried to keep perspective, but with this much stress she knew it would be difficult. Now her life started a new pace towards hell.

"What happens next?" she asked, her throat tight.

He slipped a file across the desk. "Your tickets and travel information."

She lifted the folder, placed it in her lap, and flipped through the papers inside. When she looked up she sighed. "This artifact you're looking for. Why is it so important to the SIA?"

Mac sat back in his chair. "This is the part that's difficult to believe."

She sniffed. "Hah. This whole setup is hard to accept. I want to know why I'm putting my neck on the line."

"You'll have to suspend a lot of belief. I know I did, and I've seen and heard some very strange things in my career."

"Such as?"

"Nothing I can talk about. I can tell you this case is tricky. Many things are not what they seem. You'll need to be on alert." This time he didn't appear so casual, his expression more concerned and less business-like. "That's why an agent is going to be with you at all times."

He stood and walked to the window, one of the few she'd seen in this huge complex. Bright summer sun and cerulean high-altitude sky reminded her that the world outside existed.

He leaned back against the windowsill. "The artifact you're seeking is extraordinary. It's actually two statues that interlock together with an octagon-shaped base. It's about seven hundred years old. It's often been called The Octagon, but in reality that doesn't describe it very well. The museum had both pieces of the statue, but they disappeared last year not long before Haan's fateful expedition into the jungle. The statue is also called *La Pasion* and when matched together both pieces weld tremendous power. When both statues are sealed together, the result is often catastrophic."

"Power?" she asked doubtfully.

"A terrible force."

More doubt poured into her. "How does anyone know this force is so terrible? Have they put the statues together?"

Mac's lack of answer, the way his lips went grim and tight—well, that gave her the answer.

"What happened?" she asked when the silence went on too long for her comfort.

He walked back to his desk, but he stood rather than sink back into the high-backed executive chair. "Back in forty-five, after *La Pasion* was transported to the Chesterham Museum, the curator of Egyptian antiquities put them away. He had the help of a young assistant who went with him into the bowels of the building."

"They didn't display it to the public?"

He shrugged. "No. You know how museums can be. They store a lot of things that never get shown to the public. It's probably a good thing considering what happened next." Although his voice stayed steady and calm, her insides twisted with tension. "The curator took the assistant into the basement and even though the curator had been given strict instructions not to open the crate, he did. The assistant watched as his boss place the octagons together on the crate."

She realized she sat on the edge of her chair.

He moved back behind his desk and sank into his chair. "The assistant said there was a blinding flash of light, then he passed out. When he came to he was lying on the floor next to the curator's smoldering body."

Her stomach did a flip. "The curator was burned?"

"To a crisp."

She swallowed hard to stem the nausea the image created. "Why wasn't the assistant burned?"

"No one knows. The rest of the room was singed and smoking. From that day forward the items were put into the deepest bowels of the museum. That's where they remained, separated from each other, until a year ago."

She couldn't suspend her disbelief, even though something told her she should. "This is ridiculous. It sounds like the curse of the mummy story that was fabricated and circulated about King Tut's tomb. Are you sure it isn't a story made up to keep people from stealing it?"

The Section Chief gave her a sardonic smile. "I wish it was fiction."

Pieces of the puzzled started to come clear. She drew her twinset sweater across her breasts and buttoned it against the air conditioning and the cold settling in her heart. "And you think my grandfather sold both pieces to Haan last year sometime."

She didn't want to believe it—couldn't believe it.

"The United States government does," Mac said.

"But we weren't in Egypt a year ago."

"Your grandfather didn't deliver the device to the thugs personally."

Renewed irritation rose inside her. "So just because you say you have proof my grandfather has been stealing from the museum, you think he sold the octagon statues, too?"

He put his arms on the desk and folded his hands, a picture of sincerity and seriousness. "Correct."

She felt like a guinea pig ready for the slaughter. "If I refuse this assignment, what happens?"

"My agent goes in and gets the statues anyway, and when legal action is taken by the museum, my guess is that your grandfather, and perhaps you, will be prosecuted."

Prosecuted. A sharp, unforgiving word that fit the deed. Simple days and simple times faded away into deceit and jeopardy.

"What will it be, Dr. Jessop?"

What choice did she have? "What's the plan of action? How am I supposed to get near this Haan character?"

Mac reached for his thermal coffee mug, something she hadn't seen him do since she walked into the large office. He took a sip of liquid. "The agent you'll be with at the complex has lived in Puerto Azul for six months establishing a reputation. Haan believes he's a wealthy dealer who wants to purchase rare and unusual artifacts. Haan invited the agent to stay at *Rancho La Paz.*"

"If your agent is a dealer, where do I fit in?"

"As the archaeologist, of course. The agent will give you other details when you get there about your cover."

She couldn't speak, astonished that so much happened in so little time. How could she do this? Did she have enough strength to pull it off?

"What do I tell my family, Mr. Tudor, when they realize I've run off to Puerto Azul?"

"That you're taking relaxing on the fabulous beaches in San Cristobal and don't plan on coming back until you're feeling more recovered from your grandmother's death."

Those horrible words rang in her head like a dirge. Grandmother's death haunted her, a fading echo not one hundred percent accepted.

When she tried to formulate another angle that would keep her from agreeing to this scheme, Keira couldn't think of anything that might sway the SIA and the other authorities involved.

As she let out a long slow, breath, she gave him the answer. "I'll do it."

He smiled and she could feel the satisfaction radiating from him. "Good."

"Isn't this the part where you say I won't regret it?"

Again a mask of seriousness wrapped his face and narrowed his eyes. "I'd like to say that, but I can't. There's no way to tell the outcome."

She tossed him a half-sarcastic smile. "What about this agent I'm supposed to meet in San Cristobal?"

"Ah, yes." Something in his voice sounded cautious. "His photo is in the file folder at the bottom."

The man in question didn't look anything like she expected. No, she expected middle-aged and pudgy or maybe bald. Nothing could be further from the truth. A visceral punch landed in her stomach as she viewed the agent in the eight-by-ten headshot.

Her gaze snapped up to Mac's. "This is the man who saved my life in Egypt."

"That's right." Mac didn't sound the least surprised that she recognized the man.

"So *that* explains how he was so close and why he had a gun." Then she remembered the small camera case strapped to the man's side and renewed anger made her sit up straighter. "He's the one who took these pictures."

"Very astute. Good thing he was in the right place at the right time. If he hadn't seen the assassin's weapon aimed your way…" Mac shrugged. "As it is, he broke his cover that day by helping you."

Mac's phone rang and he answered. "Yes. Of course. Be right there." He put down the receiver and stood. "Excuse me, I'll be right back."

He left her to stew for a moment in her doubt. She frowned at the photograph in her lap. As she looked at the guy, whose name she still didn't know, Keira remembered what she'd felt plastered up against his unabashed masculinity. More than once she'd seen desire in his eyes and his erection had pressed against her in a way that spelled S-E-X in big letters. At one point she thought he intended to kiss her right before Grandfather interrupted.

One night Keira dreamed the whole horrific scene in blazing color, including a hot, sexy kiss from the handsome stranger. She'd woken up ashamed. Mortified for craving a man she didn't know and would never see again.

At least that's what she thought until now.

Exhilaration stirred in her belly at the thought of seeing him. Apprehension tried to smother the inappropriate excitement.

In the photograph he didn't smile, and his black eyes held an edge packed with equal parts fire and ice. Thick lashes outlined those haunting eyes. Wavy but not curly, glossy black hair curled just over the collar of his white Oxford shirt. His nose looked patrician, but not large, and his mouth held an insolent touch mixed in with a straight, humorless line. His upper lip and jaw line, covered with a day or two worth of stubble, supplied him with a bad-boy nuance she couldn't miss. She wondered how hard he worked to cultivate that rock-hard, hell-bent-and-knowing-it expression.

Oh yeah. The man defined rugged. His astonishing looks screamed arrogance and assurance. The face of a man formed by his experiences, a slate ready to be written on by all he saw and did. With the hint of squint lines around his eyes, she guessed him somewhere between thirty and forty years old. Past his first blush of youth, but not out to pasture.

When he'd crowded her into the alcove and shoved his big, muscular body against hers, Keira had been astonished she could feel anything other than terror. When it became apparent that he'd saved her life and meant her no harm, common sense left the building. She'd reacted, as adrenaline had continued to surge into her limbs, like a woman who wanted and needed him. Chaotic arousal had raced through her, demanding fulfillment. His gaze had assessed her as a woman. A desirable woman he wanted to touch and kiss.

But no. This man worked for the SIA and took the incriminating pictures that put her right in the perilous position she occupied today. She had no business being interested in him.

She groaned. *Could things get any more screwed up?*

Mac came back into the office and sat behind his desk. "Sorry about that. So, now that you know he's the agent who'll accompany you in Puerto Azul, what do you think?"

She quickly shut the folder and returned her gaze to the man behind the desk.

"What's his name?" she asked.

"Zane Spinella."

Words came out before she could stop them. "He looks a little…rough."

Mac's eyebrows tilted up. "And?"

She shook her head, not sure what she meant.

"You expected someone who looked like an accountant?" he asked with a smile. "Don't worry. He doesn't bite. You're safe with him."

Right. Even in a photograph the man had the power to make her insides tremble. She didn't like what he made her feel. "Why him?"

"Because he's the inside man for Puerto Azul and he requested this mission after I told him about it."

Requested? That's interesting.

"You'll take the assignment?" he asked when she didn't reply.

She said the one word she hoped she wouldn't regret. "Yes."

Chapter Two
San Cristobal International Airport
The Republic of Puerto Azul

I really hate the tropics.

This entered Keira's head the minute she stepped off the plane. From the outside, through the small windows on the aircraft, the airport looked modern and sleek. But as she walked through the air conditioned tube connecting the plane to the terminal, she remembered a hot, humid blast of air would feel like a wet, smothering blanket. She'd spent time in enough out-of-the-way and not so out-of-the-way tropical locales to regret it.

As she rolled the small carryon behind her, she wished she'd worn shorts. The heavyweight green sweater over the tank top would have to go. Her good luck charm, a square pewter Celtic design necklace, stuck to her flesh where it lay against her skin. Long khaki pants would work for the jungle, but they clung to her body in uncomfortable places. Her fanny pack felt too tight around her waist and she couldn't wait to loosen it.

Her head throbbed and she rubbed her left temple. She knew part of the problem. Flying left her dehydrated. She could never get enough water rushing from place to place while traveling.

She'd flown into Mexico and stayed there overnight at the hotel connected to the airport. Unfamiliar with the country and exhausted, she'd fallen into bed to sleep. She knew meeting Zane Spinella in Puerto Azul wouldn't be a good idea if she was jet-lagged to the nines. After managing ten hours of sleep, she'd made the rest of the flight to San Cristobal this afternoon.

Now she could face Agent Spinella. At least she hoped she could.

First impressions bombarded her weary body as she trailed behind an elderly couple walking feebly toward the welcoming arms of two young women. Keira glanced to the left into the open terminal, which bustled with noise and what seemed like hundreds of people greeting disembarking passengers. The terminal, built with bright chrome and glass motif, hummed like a beehive without the organization. Advertisements for car rental companies, hotels, and the usual tourist information plastered the walls in several different languages. Wildly colored posters across the room proclaimed Puerto Azul the new adventure capital of the world. Laughter and the ringing of a cell phone reached her ears. She winced as the noise made her head pound that much harder. Her gaze cornered at least two men along the perimeter of the crowd wearing dark navy-blue uniforms and patches that declared them military. Both of them held automatic weapons.

She glanced at faces around her and noted that most of them appeared of Spanish decent. Many natives mixed with the crowd of bustling tourists eager to get to their hotels and enjoy a drink next to the pool.

Then she saw a tall man standing above many of the smaller people in the crowd, his stance bristling with anticipation, as if he expected the need for action any second.

Zane.

She'd never been good at remembering faces but after her encounter with him in Egypt and the photograph in her folder, she couldn't forget him. This man relayed hard-edged danger no one could forget. His eyes lit up with acknowledgement but he didn't smile. In fact, his gaze looked downright hostile for a few seconds.

Oh goody. A guy with an attitude. Just what I need.

The crowd surged forward and blocked any chance for her to head his direction immediately. She gave him a hint of smile, her mouth feeling like stiff cardboard. Struggling through the maze of humanity, she finally made it to his location near a pillar. He grinned as he stepped forward, a self-assured, striking smile that took some of the darkness from his eyes and surprised the hell out of her.

His photograph, as they say, didn't come close to doing the agent justice. A mere picture couldn't send an untamed, inappropriate shiver straight into her tummy and down to her loins. A photo couldn't express the high-test masculinity that permeated him. A male animal like this didn't come along often, and every female within fifty yards would have difficulty keeping their eyes off him.

Ruggedly handsome described him in a superficial way, but up close she saw he possessed enough imperfection to make him that much more delicious. His nose looked a bit crooked at the tip, and a new scar formed over his left eyebrow. She hadn't noticed these things trapped in the alcove that day in Egypt. No, she'd been too busy trying not to notice how his body felt pressed up against hers.

She couldn't remember ever feeling small next to a man, but Zane must be at least six-four. *And what a gorgeous body.* Not noticing his wide shoulders encased in a muscle-hugging navy T-shirt with Puerto Azul splashed in tropical fruit colors on the front and not noticing the well-developed biceps and forearms would be damned difficult.

"Welcome to Puerto Azul, Dr. Jessop." His voice, deep and sinfully husky, rolled across her body with a tingle of electricity both thrilling and soothing.

She reached out to shake hands and his big fingers felt callused and strong, his palm warm and firm. He shook her hand without smashing her fingers together, his strength tempered by caution.

"Agent Spinella. Pleased to meet you. Again."

"Call me Zane, please."

She nodded, encouraged by the warmth in his handshake. "I'd prefer Keira. Dr. Jessop makes me sound like I'm ready to perform surgery."

One of his dark eyebrows spiked upward. "Are you?"

She sniffed. "I have a doctorate in Anthropology and Archaeology."

"Ah, just as your dossier said."

Dossier. A word that sounded so important. So...criminal.

Someone bumped into her and he reached out as Keira stumbled forward. His fingers clamped her waist to steady her.

Zane's fingers slid from her waist around to her mid back and her breasts brushed a chest as hard as it looked. She inhaled as her nipples beaded into tight points. His gaze captured hers as he kept his touch on her mid back. Those black eyes heated, his nostrils flaring the slightest bit as he looked down on her.

Man, he smells...yep, like all man. Earthy and blended with a delicious musk, his scent stimulated a primitive stirring low in her stomach.

She'd wondered if her attraction to him in Egypt had been false, a reaction to danger rather than genuine interest in the man. Now she knew her pull toward him wasn't happenstance.

She didn't often run into, literally or figuratively, men who carried high-test sex appeal on their chest like a medal. Sex, strength, and another primitive emotion gathered in his midnight eyes. Her palms landed on his chest and his sculpted pectorals made her fingers itch to explore. Male interest and distrust mingled in his gaze, as if he couldn't decide to eat her for a snack or to hate her.

As one of her British cousins would say, *Bloody fuckin' possession.*

Startled, she drew away from his hold. "Sorry."

"No problem," he said, as if they hadn't shared intimate space. "Let's get your bags."

Before she could object, he reached for her carryon and snapped it up in one hand so it no longer rolled on the wheels.

"I can carry that." She walked fast to keep up with his long stride.

He threw her a glance, his lips tipped in a mocking way. "I'm sure you can."

He continued to the escalator. Deciding his macho decision to carry her bag didn't rate an argument, she stepped onto the escalator behind him.

Damn, but he was big. His Herculean shoulders stretched the T-shirt and she wondered if he wore all his shirts nice and snug to impress women. New jeans displayed long, muscular legs and what her friends called a bitable ass. Keira was sure there was no such thing as the word bitable, but it described his butt to the maximum.

Okay, girl, you must be losing it. Now is not the time to go gaga over a man you don't know.

When they arrived at the luggage carousel, a crowd had already formed and once there he didn't seem inclined to talk. Her head continued to throb with relentless fury and she realized if she didn't get some water soon the headache would become worse. After they collected her second piece of luggage, they moved through the crushing crowd.

They continued out the automatic doors into the pickup area. As that hot, wet blanket atmosphere hit her, Keira sucked in a breath. Sticky, heavy air seemed too thick with oxygen for her lungs. She'd get used to it after a few days, but in the meantime it added to the exhaustion threatening to dull her senses. Apparently ten hours of sleep on this trip didn't qualify as enough to get rid of her jet lag.

She needed to keep her wits about her, despite the SIA agent beside her. It didn't matter that being near him gave her a strange sense of security; the feeling didn't mean squat. Bad things happened in the world even with big, strong men nearby. So what if he'd saved her life once. He couldn't guarantee her safety. Shrugging off her crawling sense of vulnerability, she took in her surroundings.

The air smelled good despite the humidity, brushed clean by a steady wind that caressed her hair and cooled her perspiring skin. She pulled her sweater over her head and tied it around her waist. She caught Zane looking at her and his glance landed right on her full breasts cupped by the tank top and sport bra.

His gaze snapped up to hers. Hot appreciation flickered, then extinguished as he turned to hail a cab.

Okay, so the man ogled her breasts. An SIA agent probably didn't have it written into his little manual of rules that he couldn't look at a woman's chest. So far as she knew, it wasn't against the law.

Female satisfaction warred with a feminist need to be offended. Then she remembered the type of feminist she was—a woman who believed in equal rights and treatment, but not someone who thought men could or should stop all their caveman reactions. She didn't believe in denying that men had primitive needs, or that women shouldn't express their own cravings.

Somehow she was certain Mr. Macho Agent would agree with her.

As Zane and the short cab driver loaded the luggage, she noticed the natives drove on the left side in Puerto Azul, and the cars were right-hand drive as well. Since she'd lived off and on in England for a variety of years this didn't seem unusual to her.

Zane opened the cab door for her and spoke a rapid spate of Spanish to the driver. They all climbed into the vehicle.

The driver turned in his seat and smiled. His round face and mustache spoke of friendliness. His grin came across genuine, and his voice rusty as an old pipe. "I'm Eduardo La Vega. Welcome to Puerto Azul. You'll be in our country long?"

Zane nodded. "*Sí*. My fiancée and I are the guests of Ludwig Haan."

Eduardo's wide mouth opened, a startled expression widening his eyes. "Ludwig Haan."

Keira's bit back a retort at his fiancé designation.

Zane smiled as he glanced at her first, then Eduardo. "*Sí*. He's an important business associate."

Eduardo turned in his seat and started the engine. "Right away. We're off."

Zane settled onto the seat and said to her, "We're going to *Hosteria El Sosiego* for the night."

Faster than she expected, they pulled away from the curb and the cab driver screeched into traffic. She searched around for seatbelts and found none.

"*Por favor, ve mas despacio,*" Zane said to the driver a little sharply.

"*Sí.*"

"What did you say to him?" she asked, distrustful.

"I asked him to please slow down."

She grabbed onto the headrest in front of her when the cab careened out of the airport. The vehicle went around a corner too fast and she slid across the bench seat and smack into Zane's right side.

"Sorry," she said a little breathlessly.

Before she could move, he slipped his muscular arm around her shoulder and kept her close.

"Let me go," she said with a calm tone.

"I think I heard you say that once before. I don't think so."

Irritation welled inside her. What kind of stupid game was he playing? "Look—"

"Shhh."

Her mouth opened on a protest, but he interrupted when he spoke in Spanish to the driver. Eduardo gave a bark of laughter.

"What did you say?" she asked, feeling like a broken record and filled with resentment.

"That you're on the rag and a bit testy."

His gall made her want to kick him in the teeth. "You bastard."

He grinned and looked way too delighted. "I've been called worse."

Furious with his pig-like manners, she strained back against his enveloping arm. "I can imagine."

He leaned down and nuzzled her ear, whispering low. "Play along, damn it." His hot breath puffed into her ear and made her shiver in warm delight. "We're staying at a hotel tonight, then a limo is coming to take us to *Rancho La Paz* in the morning. During this trip we're posing as a couple."

Right. She believed that as if she believed the moon was made of cheese. Did this guy think that because he surpassed Adonis in the looks department that she would believe his waist-high excrement?

She pulled back from the intoxicating touch of his mouth against her ear. Then she gave him a seductive, placating smile and leaned as close as she could to murmur in his ear. His musky exotic scent and the heat of his body felt too arousing for comfort.

"Bullshit," she said.

He frowned, all amusement dissolved. He slipped his hand into her hair and tilted her head so his lips grazed her earlobe and the husky purr in his voice sent new curls of sensation into her belly. "I guess Section Chief Tudor was afraid you wouldn't do it if he told you. *I am not bullshitting you.*"

She whispered into his ear. "I don't believe you."

"Start believing it. The characters we're dealing with don't fight fair and they don't give a shit we're Americans. They will kill us if they realize what's really going on. I'll tell you more about our cover when we get to the hotel. If you want to get dead quickly, then don't listen to me. You're in my territory now and I know Puerto Azul well. Do what I say and survive."

Emotion seemed scarcely harnessed inside this man. A volcano of seething desires and complications hovered right on the edge. He cupped her face with his other hand, brushing his fingers over her jaw in a comforting, sweet caress. The touch of a man in love with his woman.

Enforced into intimacy within less than an hour of meeting him again, she had difficulty understanding her physical response. Other than tiredness, dehydration, and pure lust, she had no excuse for feeling this way. She doubted the first two factors could make her that susceptible. She settled for lust.

Bare inches separated their lips; she half expected him to kiss her. Keira sensed a feral intensity that broke all rules and remained leashed for the present. Any kiss he bestowed would be ravenous and earth-shattering. She shivered and wished he'd abandon his game. Beneath the thin cotton stretch of her tank top, her nipples pushed against the sport bra in reaction to continual physical contact. She closed her eyes, not wanting to see the untamed light in his eyes or experience a primordial reaction. She tried to relax under his touch but the tension humming between them made her want to scream in frustration and confusion.

She made the mistake of glancing at his mouth.

When her gaze darted back to his eyes, she saw molten emotions boiling inside the dark depths, including desire. If she didn't speak right now, she knew this man would kiss her.

"Maybe you're telling the truth about the couple cover," she said softly into his ear, "but I won't believe it until I hear it from Mac Tudor myself."

He looked like he wanted to argue, but thought the better of it. She turned away from the fascinating likelihood that Zane Spinella wanted to kiss her, and endured his arm around her shoulders as she absorbed the landscape out the window and tried to relax.

"Music, *señor*?" Eduardo asked.

"*Sí*. Something hard. I need to stay awake."

"Eh…you like country or heavy metal?" Eduardo asked.

"I like both, but I think heavy metal would be great."

Eduardo's radio blared static until he adjusted the tuner and came up with, to her complete surprise, a station featuring good ol' rock. A heavy rock song by an American group spilled from the radio.

Unable to help it, Keira released a laugh.

She looked at Zane and he said, "Not exactly heavy metal, but I like it."

Sounding as eager as a puppy, Eduardo asked, "You do like it?"

"It's fine, Eduardo."

She loved the sexy tune, and having a muscular body pressed against her while she listened served to ratchet up her libido. Soon the lyrics repeated in her head and she wanted to sing them, caught up in the rhythm. *Heat in your veins so high, you will go insane.*

Suddenly Zane's voice uttered the words in a dynamic, sexy singing voice. "*Your desire is burning hot and you want to do it again.*"

She stared at him a second in amazement. "You sing very well."

He winked, his expression saying the song was for her, to her. "Thanks."

"Most definitely," Eduardo said from the front seat.

She couldn't help chuckling.

Zane didn't sing again for awhile, and she wondered if her observation had made him shy. Nope. Not much chance of Zane having a reticent bone in his body. Confidence came from him in tangible vibrations, a man with strength both physically and mentally.

"*Take me quick, do it now.*" Zane's voice flowed over her in a hot, velvet wave. He paused, then continued. "*How hot can our love be…*"

Eduardo started singing along with Zane, his voice crackling and heavily accented. When Eduardo hit a discordant note, she winced and Zane grinned. Nope, Ricky Martin, the sexy Latin singer, didn't have anything to worry about.

Well, okay…Zane might give Ricky a run for his money.

"You go, Eduardo." Zane added another phrase in Spanish.

"Stop that," she said.

Zane glared. "What?"

"Slipping in little segues in Spanish."

"Don't worry, Miss," Eduardo said, gesturing elaborately with his right hand. "He didn't say anything bad about you this time. In fact, he said—"

Zane clamped a hand on the driver's shoulder and squeezed. "Can it while you're ahead, Eduardo."

"Can it?" The man asked in confusion.

"Stop trying to help," Zane said.

"Oh, *sí*."

The driver went silent and Zane sang increasingly suggestive lyrics.

She tried in vain to concentrate on the city outside, but as the tune continued, all she could hear was Zane's incredible voice making love to the lyrics. Her pulse fluttered and quickened, then her heart took up an excited new cadence. Sex and sin seemed to fill the cab, and her body responded to the torrid words and the liquid fever in his voice. Heat filled her face as his fingers trailed over her shoulder and then down in a repetitive caress both casual and designed to inflame.

Damn him. He knows just what he's doing.

When the next song came along, something unfamiliar, he stopped singing. And not any too soon. If he'd kept performing in that stunning voice she might have caught on fire. He also stopped stroking her shoulder and arm.

Despite her heightened awareness of Zane and Eduardo's unsafe driving, she managed to take in the scenery with some pleasure.

She'd picked up a travel guide on Puerto Azul that outlined most everything she wanted to know. San Cristobal, the capital of Puerto Azul, had developed into a hub of tourism, agriculture, electronics exports, textiles and clothing, fertilizer and plastic. She knew this from the small fact sheet tucked into the folder in her carryon baggage.

She supposed she should be grateful Zane knew the lay of the land. She couldn't recall the last time she felt more out of her element and vulnerable. She tried to turn her mind away from chaos and concentrate on the world outside the cab.

A dazzling array of life flourished in the countryside, a place of contrasts where nature fascinated and challenged humans. Impressions bombarded her as the lush landscape formed outside the cab window. In the far distance, toward the south, she saw the large San Cristobal Plateau and knew somewhere near the rocky outcropping *Rancho La Paz* resided and so did its owner, Ludwig Haan. San Cristobal's population was around two hundred and seventy-five thousand people and the city bustled like a much larger enterprise.

Tall skyscrapers reached for the intense blue sky, their glass and metal bodies a tribute to this county's modernization. As they sped along an amazingly modern four-lane highway, she saw a graveyard full of crypts nearby. Warehouses rose toward the center of the city not far away, their redbrick structures forlorn. Stucco office designs spoke of heavy Spanish influence.

They left the highway and dipped deeper into the city, toward the center of a busy metropolis almost as modern as anything she knew in the United States.

Moments later they turned down a palm-lined four-lane avenue. She realized she'd become so distracted by Zane she didn't know whether they went north, south, east or west.

Eduardo pointed toward a ten-story modern building not far ahead on the right. "*Hosteria El Sosiego.*"

They turned into the circular drive under the hotel awning with an audible screech of tires. Eduardo helped them unload her luggage, and sputtered happily when Zane handed him a healthy tip.

Zane gestured toward the cab. "Get seatbelts in that deathtrap before we call on you again."

The short man's eyebrows shot up. He dug a card out from his shirt pocket and handed it to Zane. "You call on me again?"

"Tonight. For dinner. I made reservations at The Imperial."

"*Sí.*" Eduardo's grin went wide. "Of course. Right away."

He jumped back into the cab and took off with more noisy tires and billowing exhaust.

Keira waved her hand in front of her face and coughed. "Lovely."

A bellhop wheeled her luggage into the hotel, and as they entered the lobby, she took in the interior. Traditional accoutrements appealed to her more than glossy coldness, but she admired the bold décor.

Ultramodern and sleek, the lobby screamed sophistication. Huge windows showed the tropical garden landscape toward the back of the hotel past the huge lounge area. The dynamic foyer featured a gigantic silver and crystal chandelier. Toward the middle near the lounge large palms and other tropical vegetation she couldn't identify graced the area. She half expected to see birds fluttering around, or maybe monkeys swinging from the giant plants in the center. Well-heeled guests strode about clad in clothes that spelled money. She allowed herself four seconds to feel dowdy.

Then she saw something that made her pause. At least three men positioned around the lobby wore S.W.A.T.-like dark navy gear. They held serious automatic weapons.

Out of instinct she stopped. "Who are those men?"

"Hotel security." He didn't look the least fazed. "Tourists are easy marks, even in Puerto Azul. If you're ever in this lobby without me, one of those armed guards will be by your side the whole time."

Hair on the back of her neck prickled at the implication. "Even among all the posh surroundings it isn't totally safe?"

One of his dark, thick brows twitched. "Have you ever been anywhere on earth that is totally safe?"

"No. I guess not."

She started toward the check-in desk when he clasped her upper arm gently. "Where are you going?"

"To check in."

He glanced at the bellhop and smiled, then back at her. "I already have our room, darling. This way."

Brimming with agitation, but not wanting to blow their cover, she smiled weakly. "Oh, of course."

Zane insisted on lugging her bags to the elevator without the bellhop's assistance. Perhaps he wanted to show her how strong and macho he could be, and the idea amused her.

As they waited for the elevator, she glared at her partner in crime. "One room?"

His expression didn't even change. "We're a couple, remember?"

An elevator opened and they slipped inside. After pushing the button for the eighth floor, he leaned one shoulder against an elevator wall and stared at her, his gaze admiring. He hooked his thumbs in his belt loops, his fingers nonchalantly curved toward his zipper. Keira drew in a breath, her face going hot as she noted the generous bulge again. Her gaze snapped up to his and his eyes showed a knowing fire. Damn the man. He knew what she was thinking as surely as if she'd screamed the words.

Careful. This guy isn't someone to play with and give the wrong idea. Staring at his crotch must cease and desist this moment.

Besides, SIA agent or not, Zane Spinella might be dangerous and unscrupulous.

Zane started to sing again, the words caressing her ears. *"My blood is in flames, my fever raging, I'm so hot for you."*

Incredible. She tried to remember if she'd ever met a man with more cheek in her life and couldn't come up with anyone in recent memory.

Again the suggestive lyrics followed. *"Come on darling, you don't have to read my mind to know how I feel."*

Against her will her skin started to heat once more. Her body had become a traitor to her since she stepped off the airplane and saw this rascal. He sauntered away from his station against the wall and came toward her.

"I can show you serious lovin' like you've never known."

In any case, she had to get him off track and make him think of something besides serenading her. "So does the SIA —"

"Keira." His voice came out strong and sharp. Before she could blink, he came so close she bumped into the elevator wall. He planted his hands on either side of the wall next to her head.

Gee, this feels familiar.

He whispered in her ear. "Don't say anything about SIA while we're in the elevator."

"But —"

He pressed closer, until his body almost touched hers. "God, I've missed you so much, my love."

Stunned by his quick movement and the husky passion in his voice, she couldn't speak. *Oooookay.* Did he think the elevator had bugs planted or had he decided to have a little fun at her expense?

Heat from his body made her nerve endings sizzle with sensory overload. She opened her mouth to fake her delight in seeing him, to try out her college acting classes from about a bazillion years ago. The unbelievable temperature flaring in those shadowy eyes short-circuited everything she planned to say. Then she didn't get a chance to speak at all.

His mouth came down on hers. A quick, hot enveloping of her lips that couldn't have lasted more than a few moments, but felt like eternity. Enough time for her to feel the expert devouring as he caressed and challenged. His kiss went deep without being too intimate, a dominating touch that held back an essential ingredient. Stirring sexuality, a brazen desire to taste her more deeply hovered in his intentions but didn't form. She knew it, in some weird way, that he wanted more from her than this cursory meeting of lips. Then, to her amazement, her mind went blank with pleasure.

Her nipples prickled, turning hard. Every one of her senses came on line, her skin heightening with sensitivity, her body yearning towards his a little. A tingling coasted over her and she couldn't help responding the tiniest bit to his kiss. A breathy moan left her throat.

He moved back suddenly, his eyes scorching her. God, when had a man ever looked at her like that before? As if he wanted to possess, to take, to fuck her blind?

Never.

Frozen to the spot, she didn't move when the elevator door pinged and opened.

He moved out of the elevator first. She jerked out of her daze and followed him. She'd allowed Zane to "fake her out of her jock" as one of her old boyfriends used to say. Embarrassment flooded her face for what seemed like the umpteenth time that day. He acted like nothing extraordinary occurred in the elevator, while her body continued to hum with unable-to-deny arousal.

"Something wrong?" he asked. "Don't like my singing voice?"

Surprise him. Go ahead and give him something to contemplate. "You know I like it, sweetie pie. But don't you think it's a little brazen for you to sing suggestive lyrics to me out in public?"

He flashed a satisfied grin. "You know I'm a brazen kind of guy."

He stopped in front of room 888 and slipped the key card into the lock. With an audible snick and flashing green light, the door opened.

He rolled the bags into the room and left them next to the queen-sized bed near the large window looking out at San Cristobal Plateau.

One bed.

Oh hell.

She glanced at the long, comfortable-looking sofa sleeper on the other side of the room. Good. *He* could sleep there.

When she opened her mouth to speak, he put up one hand and shook his head. He reached into his pocket and drew out his wallet. A strange-looking device, slim like a credit card, emerged. He held it up and started walking around the room with the card held out in front of him. A bug tracking device, perhaps?

"Darling, do you think you'd like a hot bath before we go to dinner? We have reservations at seven-thirty," he said.

Okay, she could do this. "That would be wonderful. I'm just absorbing this wonderful room. It's so beautiful."

She wasn't fibbing.

The luxurious suite, decorated in a blend of navy, gold, silver, and green, had an old-world flavor. Everything a couple could want, with a mini-bar, microwave, and gas fireplace. She strode toward the bathroom and flicked on the light. Double sinks, a large-enough-for-two whirlpool tub, a vanity, and a tiled shower big enough for a football team filled the bathroom. A shaving kit sat by the sink nearest the doorway, a clear sign of his masculine presence. At one end of the enormous bathroom she saw a walk-in closet.

She turned around and surveyed the opulent room. "Very expensive."

She winced. Would a rich-bitch say something like that?

He winked and continued searching the room. "Only the best for you, honey."

She almost snorted at the sickening little endearments uttered in his deep, compelling voice. No, this man would whisper sexual things in woman's ear, and his endearments would be impassioned and sincere. She tried not to assume much about a person until she'd gotten to know them, but Zane possessed a banked energy she couldn't quite understand. An agent for SIA would be the best, she figured, that the government could offer. Somehow she knew, with gut-wrenching certainty, that he would make love with the same fire and aptitude.

"It's clear." He slipped the credit card-sized device back into his wallet. "You can talk freely now."

Keira said, "You could have warned me before we got on the elevator. I suppose that kiss was a way of shutting me up?"

"Exactly."

He said it so dispassionately that she decided not to let that cursory, but blinding kiss mean anything to her. "There are other ways of letting me know things. Kissing wasn't necessary."

He shoved his wallet into a back pocket of his jeans. A quick, wicked smile passed over his lips. "Yeah, but it was a lot of fun."

Exasperated beyond words, she tossed her weatherproof fanny pack on the bed. "Have you ever found bugs in here?"

"Other than the crawling, multi-legged kind, no. But it's a precaution I have to take every time I come back to the suite."

Zane crossed the room until he reached the open closet. On the top shelf, next to extra pillows, a medium-sized safe was tucked in the corner. He whirled the combination dial. "We're a wealthy couple, so our rich tastes have to be in line with what Ludwig Haan expects. There's something else we need to complete the picture."

Ludwig Haan. Her stomach went a bit queasy, adding to the insidious pounding in her head. She didn't like the reminder of what she faced.

"You think he has spies in the hotel and bugs in the room paying attention to whether we seem appropriately well-off?" she asked.

Another clicking noise assured Zane's success with the combination lock. He opened the door and retrieved a red velvet ring box. He offered it to her in the palm of his hand. "I know he has spies, but I'm not sure who they are. That's why we need to play it safe at all times."

She stared at the box in his hand like it contained all the secrets of Pandora. When she didn't take the small container, he moved closer.

As if he proposed to a woman he loved, he opened the box and held it open so she could see the contents. "Will you marry me?"

Snuggled in white velvet, the two rings in the box defined lavish wealth. A wide platinum band held a radiant-cut emerald-shaped diamond. Nestled on the shank on each side of the diamond were two princess-cut diamonds. A matching wedding band featured three radiant-cut emerald-shaped diamonds, a little smaller but no less beautiful.

Unable to resist, she reached in the box and took them out. "How many carats is this?"

"The engagement ring is six carats. The wedding band is four carats. Put on the engagement ring."

She slipped the engagement ring on her left hand, her heart picking up the pace as she wriggled her finger and smiled. She expected such a big ring to look funny on her long, elegant fingers, but it didn't. The diamonds sparkled with unparallel brilliance.

"It's a perfect fit." She frowned at him. "How did you know my ring size?"

"Come on, think about it."

She didn't have to think about it for long. The SIA had done its homework. She couldn't have expected anything less.

"Don't worry." He closed his hand around the small container and it disappeared in his big palm. "The diamonds are highest grade rough cubic zirconia. The ring is platinum-clad white gold. Even the SIA wouldn't put out that kind of cash for a real diamond ring. You'll wear the engagement ring when we go out tonight."

Tired and becoming more impatient, she rubbed her forehead. "Why is there a wedding band to go with it?"

His mouth curved in one of those sinfully rich grins, intoxicating and sensual. "Because we're getting married on Ludwig Haan's estate."

Chapter Three

Zane watched Keira's eyes go wide and her mouth form a circle of total surprise.

"You can't be serious," she said, her voice hushed, almost strained with disbelief.

"It's part of the plan." He brushed a stray hair back from her face. "We'll be married at his estate the day after tomorrow."

He loved catching her off guard and seeing her fight for a way out of this complicated situation. Maybe he should feel guilty for putting her through the wringer, but he didn't. One thing he knew for certain, he didn't like the way her innocent act ate away at his resolve to remain cool and detached. He completed dangerous missions twelve months out of the year because he could do it with skill no questions asked. This woman threatened his equilibrium in ways he didn't understand one hundred percent.

He flashed back to his first sight of her amber eyes in Egypt and the close body contact they'd shared during a life-threatening moment. His reaction had been fierce, and when he'd seen her in the airport her subtle beauty had arrested him again.

Unfortunately he'd spent way too much time daydreaming about her flashing eyes and stubborn, full lips. He'd read a lot about her since he'd left Egypt and returned to Puerto Azul. Few women of his acquaintance captured his attention like her. Sure, he knew her vital statistics; hair the warm color between brown and blonde, a shade he'd call honey, her height about five feet six inches, her eyes gut-wrenchingly beautiful amber brown.

He'd even read details in her dossier most wouldn't consider important. She knitted. The irritating woman knitted, for God's sake. He'd never pictured her sitting in a chair like a granny, smiling and designing booties or a sweater. She made candles, loved to read romance and science fiction novels. He could picture the sci-fi novels but not the romance. She seemed hard-edged in a way, too aloof to read romance.

But he only needed to know one thing to understand this mission.

Keira conspired with her grandfather to steal from the Chesterham Museum, plain and simple.

He moved toward her until he stood way too close, drawn by that intoxicating, light scent that surrounded her. He couldn't keep away.

Irritation made her eyes turn golden with fire. She paced away across the room, then swung on him like a tigress. "This is ridiculous. So we play a little kissy-face for the sake of the cover. How can we go through with a real marriage?"

He shrugged. "Easy. We fake it. Haan will have a priest there to perform the marriage."

"Priest?"

"Most of the country is Catholic. Haan was brought up Protestant, but when he asked me what denomination we needed, I said Catholic. Made things easier and—" he shrugged, "—I'm Catholic."

She sighed but didn't speak, clearly disturbed.

"We'll have to sign a real marriage certificate, but it's not valid in the United States."

Her frown went deeper and she put up one finger to make a point. "Don't get any ideas about playing house, Zane. Besides, I'm not Catholic."

"And?"

"Well, if this priest asks—"

"He won't. Believe me, if Haan requests him to be there for the ceremony, he'll do it, regardless of whether he believes in the sanctity of the event or not. When Haan asks a person to do something, there are no questions asked."

"Including you?"

"Within reason," he said and then switched gears. "There are a few things we need to make sure of before we meet Haan for the first time."

She rubbed her eyes. "Such as?"

"Details a couple would know about each other."

"Like favorite color and zodiac sign?" Her mouth twisted into a sarcastic smile.

"Along those lines." He walked to the big window and peered down at the bustle below in the street. "We'll need an intimate working knowledge of each other."

Disbelief clouded her gaze. "In two days?"

"In two days."

She went silent. When she didn't say anything more, he turned back to her. Worry darkened those pretty eyes. "I don't know if…"

He saw her distress, so the first sign of tears filling her eyes and pain clutched at his gut. Damn, he couldn't stand to see a woman cry. It always hit his soft spot, something he could never admit to having in the first place.

"What's wrong?" he asked.

She inhaled deeply, as if aware she'd let her guard down. "Nothing." Fire returned to her eyes. She put her hands on her hips. "Why do we have to get married in the first place?"

"Because it gives us more credibility. The fact we will go along with a Puerto Azul wedding ceremony shows we're serious."

She covered her eyes with one hand for a moment, shielding him from the tigress inside. Then she glowered. "All this just to convince a thug we're his good buddies? How did you get so snugly with a grade-A jerk like Ludwig Haan? How do I know you're not a double agent?"

Admiration and amusement hit him at the same time and he laughed. "If you don't trust me, then call Mac Tudor. He'll vouch for me. I was even a groomsman in his wedding. We're good friends from way back."

She seemed to consider the idea. "That doesn't answer my question. So you've spent six months here and all of a sudden Haan trusts you?"

He shook his head. "He doesn't trust a soul on earth and that's probably what has kept him alive so long. A man like him doesn't have true friends, only enemies."

One of her well-shaped brows, honey-brown like the rest of her hair, tweaked up. Skepticism continued to cloud her eyes. He decided not to give her too long to think.

"Trust my judgment where this is concerned, Keira. I've been an SIA agent for ten years."

Instead of answering she went pale and put her hand to her temple. "Is there any bottled water around here?"

Concern spiked through him and he came toward her. "You all right?"

"I'm dehydrated. I should have been drinking water from the moment I got off the plane but—never mind. My skull is pounding."

Immediately he went for the small fridge and brought out a tall bottle of water. Then he took her by the arm and led her toward the bed. "Come on. Sit down."

After uncapping the water, he handed it to her. Clear pain in her eyes and the moisture beading on her forehead worried him. She gulped the water.

"Hey, drink that slowly." He reached out and touched her forehead. She was warm and moist. "You'd better lie down and take it easy. The last thing we need is for you to get heat exhaustion or heat stroke. How long have you been feeling like this?"

"Since before the plane landed. This always happens to me when I travel. I'll be fine after I take an aspirin and drink an entire bottle of water." She reached for her purse on the nightstand and extracted a bottle of painkillers. After taking one, she sighed.

"You're an archaeologist. How do you manage to participate in digs if this sort of thing happens?"

She quirked that disapproving eyebrow one more time. "Most of the digs I've been on have been in cooler climates like Britain or Ireland. Besides, it doesn't happen when I'm on digs, only air travel. Don't worry, I'm not going to become a liability."

He saw it in her eyes, a desire to say something sarcastic. He hardened his reaction to her and went into command mode. "Lie down and rest. I'll be out of the room for awhile. You'll probably want a shower before we go to dinner anyway."

She took another slow sip of water. "What's the dress code for the restaurant?"

"Tropical but well-dressed."

A tiny panic flared in her eyes. "No one informed me I'd need a fancy wardrobe. I didn't bring anything like that with me."

Fighting a sudden urge to reassure her, he strolled toward the front door and said, "Don't worry. Look in the walk-in closet in the bathroom. You'll find everything you need there."

As he left, he closed the door with a sigh. This wouldn't be the easiest assignment he'd ever completed.

* * * * *

Keira crept along the jungle near the base of a high plateau, the sounds of rainforest life all around her. In the high canopy the insistent chirp of birds echoed. A monkey chattered and she thought she heard the distant rumble of a big cat's growl. A profusion of colors exploded all around her, from the brilliant reds, whites, and yellows of orchids, to the deep jade of ferns and lianas. Greenery enfolded her with suffocating intensity until she felt as if the jungle pressed against her in a deliberate attempt to intimidate. Sweat beaded her forehead and her whole body ached from exhaustion. Her arms and legs felt like rubber, her mouth rusty from thirst and her stomach hollow from hunger. They couldn't stop and eat. The werejaguar threatened close behind, his endless pursuit guaranteeing their death.

Wait. Zane wasn't behind her. She whirled in fright. The jungle came closer, the leaves animating in a weird caricature. Oh God. Oh God. Fear sizzled up and down her body, chasing away the high temperature and replacing it with cold dread.

Keira jerked awake, the dream fresh in her mind. She blinked and shivered as her body adjusted to reality. She thought she heard someone moving around in the bathroom.

She'd pulled the thick curtains before she lay down, and murkiness covered the room. Elemental fear started a slow, thick assent into her bloodstream. She knew, deep down, that stress could cause bizarre reactions to mundane situations. At the same time, she couldn't seem to stop her reaction. She lay frozen until she heard cheerful whistling. Would a person intent on mayhem whistle?

"'Hi-ho, hi-ho, it's off to work I go...'" She heard the lyrics in the whistling, even though the male voice didn't sing the words.

Unsure whether to laugh or be terrified, she eased off the bed and turned on the bedside lamp. She held her breath for a second. No one leapt out of the shadows, and she took a deep breath to clear away fuzzy thinking. She could hear the shower running and the bathroom fan. A pair of big black lace-up boots sat on the floor by the dresser, as well as the shirt and jeans Zane wore earlier. Relief eased into her, but with a slowness that proved tension still held her prisoner. She rubbed the back of her neck. Damn it, she needed something to chase away the stress.

At least her headache had disappeared and other than high-strung tension across her shoulders, she felt healthy. She could use a good stiff jolt of caffeine right about now and headed for the coffeemaker. After she started the java, she took in the intoxicating scent and hoped the mere smell would awaken her.

The shower shut off. He escalated the singing, this time a song in Spanish she couldn't understand. A tingling darted into her belly at the melting, sexy quality of his voice. She floated in a dream world, lured by the melody and the passion she heard in each word. When the bathroom door came open with a click, she started. Steam exited the doorway and he stepped out right behind it. Masculine aftershave or cologne, musk, and a touch of leather, touched her nose. She'd smelled the warm, enticing scent on him earlier. Not too intrusive, but enough to drive her bananas and make her want to get closer.

With a big white towel knotted around his waist, Zane looked more delicious than any half-naked man she'd seen before. Even semi-wet the man managed to ooze danger. She'd never been in the presence of a man so flawlessly proportioned. With his hair slicked back his features seemed a little sharper. He'd shaved off the encroaching five o'clock shadow. Water beaded on his broad shoulders and down over the bulging contours of biceps and forearms, the highly conditioned muscles of a man who takes care of himself and works out. His chest…well, his chest made her mouth go dry. This man was, as they say, cut.

Dark hair fanned over his pecs, then narrowed down over a defined six-pack stomach and into the towel hovering low on his hips. Her glance darted over the towel and she realized either he'd been thinking of sex while in the shower, or her mere perusal of his assets caused him to get excited. The towel tented right over his groin.

He combed his wet hair, and mischief flickered in his eyes. "Hi, Sleeping Beauty. You look like you feel a lot better."

"I do, thanks. The headache is gone."

"I figured I'd crash around the room enough to wake you, but you slept like the dead."

She dragged her fingers through her mussed hair. "I felt like the dead."

"That coffee I smell?"

"Would you like some?"

"Yeah, sounds good."

She couldn't even be annoyed at him for calling her Sleeping Beauty. Her red blood cells continued to react to the sight of obviously aroused delectable male flesh. If he loitered any longer in that towel she would forget her own first name. For distraction, she turned and started pouring the dark brew into a ceramic coffee cup. The low light gave the whole encounter an intimacy she didn't want.

Zane came up behind her and stood so close she found her brain short-circuiting. If he would back away, maybe she could get some air into her lungs. No such luck, the damned man moved in until he almost touched her.

He grasped the mug and looked down on her. His heat enveloped her, just like the jungle in the nightmare. She frowned as she thought about the clarity and force of the dream.

"Something wrong?" he asked.

For self-preservation she grasped her mug and walked away. After taking a tentative sip of the liquid, she set it on a coaster on the coffee table. "I had a horrible dream that we were in the jungle around the plateau. A werejaguar was following us. I turned around and realized you weren't there."

His brows creased as he sipped coffee. "I can analyze that for you."

She didn't expect him to say that. "Oh?"

"You want guidance and you also fear your own aggression. Or you fear *my* aggression."

His quick explanation for the dream kept her quiet for a moment while she absorbed the possibility. She said the only thing she could think of. "Very interesting."

"You don't sound convinced."

"I don't think dreams are that easily dissected. What qualifies you to analyze them anyway? Do you have a degree in psychology?"

His grin went broad and challenging. "Actually, yes. I have a Bachelor's in Criminology and a Master's in Psychology from Georgetown University."

Primordial

Okay, she could be impressed now. Feeling out of sorts because she'd underestimated him, she said, "How did you manage it if you were gallivanting around the world playing secret agent man?"

"I did it all before I became an agent. I always knew I wanted work like this, so I jumped right into the degree programs straight out of high school. When I finished the bachelor's I kept going. Took me about five years in an accelerated format to get both degrees."

"You must have been a young agent."

He nodded and took another gulp of coffee. "I was twenty-four when the agency recruited me. I'm thirty-three now."

She didn't expect plain chitchat with him to be interesting, but at the same time, she discovered she liked learning more about him. Talking about everyday things served to distract her some from his looming masculinity.

He put the coffee cup down and headed back into the bathroom. "I need to get dressed so you can get a shower."

As he walked away she realized his erection had calmed down; the damned man didn't seem the least embarrassed about walking around the room with a serious hard-on.

She lay back on the bed with a sigh and closed her eyes as the bathroom door shut. Was she destined to be in a permanent state of arousal around him? God, she hoped not.

When he came out of the bathroom a short time later, she'd opened her suitcase and started removing items. She turned when he came into the room and her jaw dropped before she could stop it.

The man had looked like sin on two legs when half naked. Wearing a pewter gray silk polo shirt and dark slate slacks, Zane looked delicious. Either his clothing allowance at the SIA was generous or he had enough money to buy the best.

A quirk of his eyebrow said he could tell she liked what she saw. Disconcerted, she grabbed her makeup kit and started toward the bathroom.

61

"Did you look in the walk-in closet and dressing area earlier?" he asked.

"No. I collapsed and went to sleep."

He hitched a thumb that direction. "Check it out."

Curious, she walked into the expansive marble and tiled rose-colored room and trekked into the huge closet. When she flipped on the light, she gasped. He'd said the agency provided appropriate attire. Appropriate must mean designer. She investigated the labels on his clothes and found Armani and Murano with some Ralph Lauren thrown in for good measure. Her clothes featured three or four designers as well as workhorse garments designed for the jungle. Six dazzling evening ensembles caught her eye. They looked too fancy, based on what he wore, to be right for this evening.

"Having trouble deciding?" he asked from the doorway.

She threw him a cautionary glance. "Go away. You're disturbing my concentration."

He laughed and the deep tone made new shivers run over her body. Her stomach heated. After he closed the door she put her makeup kit on the large double sink area. Oh yes, this closet full of clothes looked like most women's fantasies. In some ways this entire situation presented itself like a dream. What woman wouldn't want a tall, dark, handsome man, a swanky hotel, and a closet bursting with expensive clothes?

She made a decision right then. She could play a role, a part in this strange and complicated setup. It might be the only way to survive.

When Keira left the bathroom a while later, cleansed of travel grime, she did so with attitude. She walked with a confidence she didn't feel and an expression she hoped showed indifference to what anyone thought.

The royal emerald green dress, a sleeveless silky number that clung to her curves without remorse and flowed down to her calves with a sweep, felt wonderful against her skin. It didn't matter that the neckline plunged or the push-up bra she'd chosen from the selection in the closet gave her a rack to die for. It didn't matter that she hadn't worn a garter belt, stockings and high heels in ages. She'd totter along on the strappy green sandals if it killed her.

Zane watched a Spanish newscast, attention glued to the television until she sauntered out. His eyes widened as his gaze roamed over her body with an intensity she found disconcerting.

"My God," he said his voice husky and low. "You're beautiful."

Pleasure sluiced through her, even though she'd tried not to care. How could she help it when he looked at her like that? "Thank you."

His admiration stirred something deeper and more primitive inside Keira. Warm, liquid satisfaction stirred, an ancient tribute to sexual awareness. He walked toward her, a ravenous adoration sliding over his handsome features. Before she could move he reached up and touched a strand of her hair, rubbing it between his fingers a second before releasing it. She'd styled her hair in record time, deciding the unruly mane curling about her shoulders disliked the humidity. She'd tried taming the brown strands into her usual flipped-up-in-back style and succeeded somewhat but not enough for her satisfaction.

No time to be vain. Again, she reminded herself she didn't care if he liked what he saw.

Yeah. Right.

Again he stood close, his body heat warming her through. "I'm afraid to take you out to dinner."

"Why?"

His gaze dropped to her cleavage, then skipped to her face. "Because the men around here appreciate a beautiful woman. I'll make sure I stay close." He turned away quickly, as if searching for restraint, and headed for the coat closet. "That engagement ring on your finger is dazzling as is, but you need more jewelry."

She glanced at the sparkling ring. The pinpoints of light dancing off the spectacular ring could stop traffic. "The ring and this dress should be enough."

He unlocked the safe and brought out a jewelry box, this one a lot bigger than the ring box. He opened it.

Her eyes widened in surprise. "Please tell me this stuff isn't real either."

He winked and drew out a two carat emerald and matching emerald earrings nestled in a metal that looked like platinum. "It isn't real."

"Good. The tourist books I read said we shouldn't flaunt our wealth."

"We're not typical tourists," he said softly. "Think of us as spoiled and hedonistic. Haan expects it so we'll act the part. Remember, we don't want him to think we're particularly intelligent, just filthy rich and ready to buy whatever he has to sell."

Act the part again. Well, she could do that. Maybe.

"Like I said, when we go out, stick close to me. The restaurant we're going to caters to affluent clientele and it has security, but it's always better to be careful." He handed her the earrings. "Here put these on while I fasten the necklace."

Before she could tell him she'd do it herself, he went behind her and slipped the necklace around her throat. His fingers brushed the back of her neck, and she had difficulty concentrating as she took off her plain gold ball earrings and put on the emeralds. When his warm palms eased over her shoulders and squeezed, she twitched in surprise.

"Easy. I don't bite." Amusement slipped into the velvet quality of his voice. Despite what he said, the seduction in his tone made it hard to think straight. "At least not until I'm asked."

As he returned to stand in front of her, she shook her head. "Why don't I believe you?"

"Because you seem afraid of me. Are you?"

How did she answer and sound confident? She took a deep breath and made sure to look right into the depths of his dark eyes. "See this situation from my perspective. I've been thrust into this international intrigue with a moment's notice and into strange surroundings. I'm supposed to play fiancée to a man I don't know. Most women would be apprehensive."

She saw struggle in his eyes, as if he wanted to reassure her but held back. His gaze cooled, the banked heat she'd seen sizzling around the edges diminished. She didn't know whether to be grateful or disappointed.

"Whatever you do, take this assignment very seriously." Looking invincible, he put his hands on his hips. "The men we'll be dealing with are nasty characters in every sense of the word. Haan has thugs posted all around this city. It's one of the reasons we can't let our guard down anywhere. We don't act the part, don't keep on watch every moment, we get dead real fast."

Hard-edged, his words held the nuance of anger, as if she'd done something to piss him off. His ire served to remind her she didn't like him or the circumstances. Good. She needed a reality check.

"Before we leave we have to make sure we know more about each other, remember?" he asked. "Have a seat and relax. There's a little time before Eduardo shows up."

She settled into the chair near the living area and waited, unsure where to start. He followed by sitting in the chair across from her.

"I'll tell you everything I know about you, and you can fill in the blanks," he said.

A tiny alarm went off in her head. Not that it surprised her he might know a lot about her, but she feared what he'd discovered through the SIA. "Fair enough."

He relaxed into the chair, and she envied the easy way he seemed to chill out no matter what. How did a man who bristled with such forceful energy calm down?

"Your full name is Keira Marie Jessop. You're thirty years old." He leaned forward, as if the next piece of information was juicy. "Your eyes are brown, but they're golden enough to be called amber."

She stiffened a little, surprised he'd called her eyes amber. Friends and family described her eye color that way, but she didn't expect a stranger to comment on it.

"You've lived in London off and on for four years. During the time you live in England you reside in a posh old home in Kensington with your grandfather. You're a native of San Francisco. Your mother, Diana Makepeace Jessop had a rocky relationship with her parents. Diana rarely speaks to Aloysius Makepeace, and she didn't go to your grandmother's funeral last month."

At his words resentment and hurt she'd been trying to forget reared and took charge. "It's complicated. I don't want to go into it."

He put his hands up in a placating gesture. "No problem. I'm just telling you what I know.

"Your mother was a homemaker her whole life and your father was a cop until he retired a few years back. Your relationship with them is also uneasy. You have three younger siblings, Catrina, Anita, and Albert, all adopted." He leaned back once again, those long legs spread in a gesture both casual and almost sexual. "You rarely drink, but when you do, you prefer a good Burgundy or Chianti. Your hobbies include knitting, reading, and scented candles. You played soccer in college and like to watch it on TV. You love harpsichord and organ music."

When he stopped she waited a bit before speaking. Her emotions flittered in disarray. Part of her wanted to be angry he knew this much, but when it came down to it, he didn't know everything. Not the important bits, anyway.

"That's very personal information."

"You're surprised I know this much?"

"No. Just a little annoyed that a person's life can't be private anymore." She shrugged. "You know more, but you're not telling."

"True. But the list of what I know about you could go on a long time."

"Does the SIA investigate all their agents to this length?"

"Of course. We also receive extensive psychological evaluations before we're hired." He smiled. "You were an exception since they didn't have time for it."

Still jet-lagged and growing crabbier by the second, she said, "You're lying, Zane. If you didn't think I could lead you to this octagon artifact because I'm in league with Haan, they would have evaluated me, too. As it is, the SIA didn't care."

Zane leaned forward again, his obsidian gaze locking with hers. "Whether you like what the SIA has done or not, now is not the time to hold resentments. We need each other to survive. I need you to trust me every step of the way."

She scrubbed her fingers through her hair in frustration, aware the motion had mucked up her hairstyle. "If you were me, would you trust an SIA agent you ran into in Egypt a month ago during a shootout? Would you trust the man who spied on you and took photographs with the intention of incriminating you to the authorities?"

He drew in a hefty breath, his stern air but unwavering. "I was doing my job then, and I'm doing my job now." For a second a flicker of uncertainty seemed to gather in his eyes. "What do I have to do to gain your trust?"

Good question. "Get me through this alive maybe? That would be great for starters." She sighed. "Haan already must know who I am. Isn't he going to be suspicious of me? I'm Aloysius Makepeace's granddaughter."

"Yes, he knows who you are, but he probably doesn't know about your love life. Did Hollister ever come to your grandfather's home in London?"

"No."

"Did your grandfather ever talk to Hollister at length about you?"

"I doubt it, but I don't know. My grandfather doesn't even know I'm doing this."

"We want to keep it that way. What was your excuse for leaving England?"

She stood up and headed to the refrigerator, her mouth feeling dry again. Once she'd retrieved a new bottle of water, she took a large swig. "I told him I'd be on a dig in Montana. A very inaccessible part of Montana for two weeks with no way to reach me. Even cell phones don't work there. That's what I told my parents, too. You don't understand how hard it was to lie to them. Especially Grandfather. He's fragile right now."

Concern crossed his face. She didn't expect for him to care about her feelings one way or the other. So when he stood and came toward her, she waited to see what he would do. She leaned one hip against the small refrigerator, the bottle of water clutched in her right hand.

He stopped in front of her and looked her over with the worry of a man for his woman. "You know if there's anything you want to tell me at any time, you can."

Aha. The man was damned perceptive. He might know, just as the SIA might know, that her grandmother's death was related to Hollister. And now that she knew about Hollister's connection to Haan, she realized Grandmother's death might have been ordered by Haan alone.

She must protect Grandfather somehow, and if that meant getting Haan off his back, she would. What if she confessed all to Zane and he turned out not to be trustworthy? What if he did not only his duty to his country, but sacrificed her and her family in the process? She couldn't trust him.

The phone rang, breaking the heavy silence. He moved to the bedside table and picked up the telephone on the second ring. "Eduardo. Excellent. We'll be right down." When he hung up the phone, he said, "I called him when you were in the shower. He's waiting for us."

She rushed back into the closet and transferred some items to the small matching green, silver-beaded silk clutch she'd found to accompany the dress.

Zane entered the bathroom behind her and adjusted the collar on his polo shirt. "Remember one thing. Play the part. Whatever you do, if I touch you don't flinch away."

She left the closet and shut the door. "I see how this is. You want to be able to play footsy without me objecting. Haven't you ever heard of couples that don't get along?"

He turned back to her, his eyes concentrated with determination. "No. I don't want Haan thinking he can come between us. This man is dirtier and far more sinister than you could imagine. He wouldn't hesitate to manipulate you if he thought it would get him something."

She sniffed. Secret agent man would try about anything to keep her in a neat, tight little box following his directions to the letter. "Who says he can manipulate me?"

"This isn't a game, Keira. He's powerful, ruthless, and very canny." He rubbed the back of his neck and winced. "He's unpredictable, but he'd probably try and seduce you. Be friendly but let him know you're in love with me. Do everything to assure him through your actions and deeds that I'm the only man for you."

Hearing Zane say *you're in love with me* sent a wild thrill through her stomach. All she could do, she decided, was to protect her interests and her grandfather's wellbeing. If that meant pretending to be sickening-in-love with this man, she'd do it.

"All right. I'll play it to the hilt."

He smiled and the gentle grin lit up his face and removed darkness from his eyes. "Thank you."

She didn't expect the earnest statement, and it melted a little of the armor residing around her heart. She smiled. "You're welcome. I think."

He left the bathroom and she looked down at the engagement ring again. It felt substantial and way too real. It glittered and sparkled under the artificial light. This ring gave her a chance to glimpse what it might feel like to have a real engagement ring on her finger with the right man next to her.

As they left the hotel room, renewed nerves knotted her stomach. When they reached the lobby she glanced out the glass entranceway and saw Eduardo parked in the circular drive. He wore chauffeur's attire and leaned against the back door of a long, white stretch limo. Keira glanced at Zane, but he didn't seem the least surprised by the setup.

"A limo?" she asked.

He clasped her upper arm and leaned down. His warm breath touched her ear and made her quiver. "Eduardo has two jobs."

Suspicion made her curious but she said nothing else. Zane slipped his arm around her waist and squeezed.

Eduardo, far less scruffy than he had been earlier, bowed when they stepped into the bright sun. "*Señor y Señorita.*"

Once ensconced in the limo, Eduardo put up the partition between them. With the darkened windows and the rich interior of the limo, she felt like a million bucks. Cream leather interior with wooden trim screamed wealth. She'd been in a limo a couple of times, but this one had deluxe everything. Bar cabinet, television, extra-long bench seats, you name it.

She glanced outside as Eduardo turned the vehicle toward the restaurant. Images bombarded her from all sides as they drove into downtown *San Cristobal*. Vendors along the streets hawked wares and other stands promised a taste of local fare.

To her surprise, Zane remained silent during their trip. She kept her attention on sightseeing as a way to calm her nerves. Sometimes when she traveled she went on overload, unable to appreciate beauty around her. Now she felt she needed that distraction or she'd go insane. Thinking too much about what she faced on this adventure could turn her into a bundle of shivering nerves.

"There is *La Bestia Salvaje*." Zane gestured to sleek modern building about ten stories high. "The restaurant is on the top floor."

"What does the name mean?"

"The Savage Beast."

Less than fifteen minutes later they pulled into an underground parking garage and came to a halt at an elevator leading up to the restaurant. When they stepped out, Zane put his arm around her waist and pulled her close.

He handed Eduardo a wad of bills. "Wait for us."

Eduardo nodded and smiled. "As you wish, *Señor*."

After Eduardo drove away to find a parking place, Zane snuggled her against his chest and whispered in her ear again. "The entire building, including the restaurant, is owned by Ludwig Haan. Keep your eyes and ears peeled. Haan might be there. Remember, we're on stage from here on out."

Feeling hot and a little flushed, she melted into his embrace, determined she wouldn't show any outward sign of discomfort. She looked up into his eyes and smiled, then decided she'd do the one thing he wouldn't expect. This man had thrown her off guard ever since she'd arrived in Central America. He deserved a little of his own medicine.

Sliding her hands over his hard chest and up around his neck, she buried her fingers in his hair and pulled his head down. Then she kissed him.

Chapter Four

As Keira's lips brushed against Zane's in a gentle caress, a sweet, quick taste of mouth against mouth, she got more than she bargained for.

His arms drew her flush against him, her breasts pressed to strong muscles, her thighs against his powerful legs. Before she could take another breath, his mouth molded to hers with warm, passionate intensity. As a heated tingle filled her stomach, she allowed him to search her mouth with a deep, unrelenting passion. Fire laced her veins as he devoured with persistence. Hot and drugging, his lips shaped and cajoled, dining on her like a delicacy. The kiss in the elevator seemed tame in comparison to this possession, this unequaled bonfire.

As her lips parted, his tongue sought hers, caressing with skillful thrusts that teased and then demanded. Every deep stroke brought erotic jolts darting straight into her belly, then flowing deep between her legs. She imagined his cock, hard and thick, making the same motion inside her body and she ached for it.

She moaned softly as his relentless embrace brought her skin to life, her body to wild awareness of Zane and all that made him devastatingly male.

Penetrating, plunging, he delved into her in ways she'd never experienced. Her heart pounded, breath coming faster. Everything pinpointed to that moment, an uncontrolled adventure promising a lifetime.

Lifetime? What am I doing?

She drew back with a gasp, then remembered eyes could be watching. Her pulse raced, her body hot and face flushed.

His eyes blazed down into hers. "I can't get enough of you."

The husky words made her stomach tingle. "Mmm. Save some for later."

The soft grin that formed on those carved, masculine lips turned her inside out. "That was delicious, babe. I can't wait to do it again."

With total lack of subtlety, he allowed his palm to slide down her waist and cover one ass cheek with a quick, affectionate brush of hot skin. A shiver raced over her and started a chain reaction. She reached up and slipped her fingers across his cheek, a caress designed to prove she wouldn't shy from his blatant sexual gesture. She saw uncertainty, a bewilderment that went through his eyes and made him look like a little boy.

He pressed another soft, quick kiss to her lips before shifting gears. "Come on, let's go inside."

The elevator opened on the top floor, and as they stepped into the foyer, her gaze caught the brilliant dazzle of crystal chandeliers and opulent Victorian decoration. She schooled her face and made sure she looked blasé about the blatant wealth she encountered. While her grandfather was well-off, the money she saw in the hotel and in this restaurant surpassed him by quite a bit. She hadn't grown up surrounded by riches and moving in this world took some adjusting.

The hostess, a young Hispanic woman with glorious long coffee-colored hair and beautiful green eyes, seated them immediately. When they slipped into the cozy booth way in the back, Keira sighed in relief. She'd felt curious eyes upon them as they'd walked by. She'd also noticed quite a few women's gazes tracking Zane. A weird and unwanted tickle of jealousy needled Keira.

Watch it. Just because you're playing a part with him doesn't give you privileges.

"Your waiter will be with you momentarily," the hostess said in clear English and departed.

To Keira's surprise, Zane's attention didn't linger on the gorgeous hostess. Instead he concentrated on Keira. When those incredible dark eyes turned her way and held her gaze, it felt like all the oxygen left her lungs. Why couldn't she control her body's reactions to this guy? All he had to do was look at her in a way that held possession, desire, and incredible heat and everything inside her went off the Richter scale.

She glanced around to regain equilibrium. The high sides of the booth, rich red velvet, made it so they couldn't see or hear the patrons on either side of them. The booth across from them remained unoccupied. Embraced by intimacy, she wished they'd been seated somewhere less confined. Despite the cozy comfort and the fact no one could bother them, she felt vulnerable in a whole new way.

"Interesting booth," she said.

"Very interesting. Makes things easier for what I had in mind tonight, darling."

God, when he says an endearment like that it sounds so damned real. Like he really means it.

A scrawny, tall waiter with salt and pepper hair came up to their table. A skinny mustache rode his lip and matched his small mouth. He spoke with a smooth, thick accent. "Welcome. I'm Salazar. I'll be your waiter this evening."

Zane looked over the extensive wine list and ordered a bottle of champagne. The waiter grinned widely as he walked away.

Zane slid closer to her in the booth, his arm slipping about her shoulder as he leaned in to whisper in her ear. His hot breath made her shiver. "We made him happy. He thinks a big tip is coming if he plays this right."

A thrill rippled into her stomach and a dangerous need to play the game made her ask quietly, "Is that what you think, Zane? You're going to get a big payoff if you play this right?"

"Of course." Husky and deep, his voice sent vibrations quivering through her. "When we get back to the hotel tonight, I'll show you exactly what kind of payoff I expect."

She dared turn her head to look at him and almost bumped noses. "Is it okay to speak frankly? I mean, do you think this booth is rigged with a listening device?"

He grinned. "It might be. But there's enough noise in this restaurant and you're sitting so near, I don't think anyone could hear. Just keep close and when you need to say something personal, whisper it in my ear."

She'd never been one to take relationships with men lightly. Resisting this man's pull, his attraction seemed to suck away all her resistance. A daring buzz raced through her midsection and drew the breath from her.

"How convenient," she said.

"If you keep looking at me like that, I'll have to do something desperate, sweetheart," he said.

She reached for her water glass and took a long, slow sip before responding. "Such as?"

With one smooth movement he removed his arm from around her shoulders, then his left hand rested on her thigh. She flinched in surprise, a small gasp leaving her lips. He didn't look at her. His hand felt big and possessive, but he didn't stroke and he didn't squeeze flesh. No, he kept his long fingers and big palm there and tantalized with possibilities, with the mere presence of his flesh. One small shift and his thigh bumped hers. When she started to move her leg away in response, his fingers cupped and then inched up until his whole hand lay over her upper thigh, so near her crotch she could almost feel his touch there. Her nipples tightened, pressing against her bra. She imagined, with a flight of fancy deep and intense, his fingers tracing over her panties. Heat blossomed between her legs, a warm aching tingle starting in her clit.

I can't believe this.

She could hardly breathe. In defense she clamped her hand over his. He didn't remove his hand.

"What are you doing?" she asked in desperation.

He turned his hot, passionate gaze onto her. "Touching my fiancée."

She withdrew her hand from on top of his. Before she could speak the waiter came back with the champagne and poured a glass for Zane to test. After Zane approved, the waiter poured them both a glass. All the while, Zane kept his hand on her leg.

Salazar's gaze landed on her chest and hovered way too long for her comfort. When he asked them if they wished to order, she tilted her nose up and said no. She figured giving this guy the haughty treatment might work wonders at keeping the ogling to a minimum.

Once the waiter left them to look over the menus, she relaxed a little, but not much. How could she when Zane kept his hand on her thigh? Granted he hadn't put his hand up her dress, but she wouldn't be surprised if he tried.

Going for distraction, she held up her champagne flute and said, "I propose a toast. To us."

With a broad smile, he winked and picked up his glass. "To us."

They clinked together the champagne flutes. As she took a slow sip of the pricey drink, she savored the delicate, fruity taste. It might be the last time she imbibed in bubbly this expensive. "This is delicious."

"Just as you are."

She laughed softly. "You're relentless."

"Always."

She believed it. She'd never run into a man this ruthless with his attentions, so determined to put on affection, desire and love. She must be mad for allowing him to touch her like this.

When he removed his hand he made sure to caress her thigh all the way from top to knee, and another shudder of reaction touched her. Then, as casual as if he'd never touched her, Zane helped her select a dish from the menu. Before long the waiter returned and took their order. Again Salazar blatantly ogled her chest.

Zane cleared his throat and stared at the waiter with a clear message. Then with a crisp voice he said something to the man in Spanish. Salazar paled, nodded, and slipped away.

She smiled in appreciation. "What did you say to him?"

Zane brushed her hair away from her ear and whispered into the sensitive shell. "I told him your pussy was mine and if he looked at you like that again, he would lose his job and maybe his nuts, too."

When Zane drew back he didn't look amused. His eyes took on a smoldering quality rife with possession and anger.

Heat burned her face. "Zane."

"Yes?"

"You are... You are..."

He pressed a kiss to her nose, then to her chin and she forgot everything she meant to say.

His mouth hovered over hers. "What?"

"Irredeemable."

"It's my specialty, thank you."

For a wild moment she thought he might kiss her, but instead he picked up his champagne. A long silence passed while they savored their drinks and listened to soft Spanish guitar music in the background.

"I'll be right back," she said, needing some space from his intoxicating presence.

When she started to slide across the bench seat, his hand covered hers. "Where are you going?"

She frowned. "To the ladies' room."

He nodded and she yanked her hand out from under his. Walking a little unsteadily on her high heels, she didn't feel in control. After attending hundreds of functions at art galleries, museums, and political events over the years, she couldn't remember any of them being as nerve-racking as a simple dinner with Zane.

She located the ladies' room at the front of the restaurant. The opulent table and chairs in the small area at the front of the ladies' room beckoned to her. Maybe if she sat down for a while she'd be in command of her reactions. She sank onto a small, not exactly comfortable chair and stared into the large mirror. Touching up her makeup and hair didn't take long; getting up the courage to leave the bathroom did.

Threats from the law notwithstanding, she must follow through. Her grandmother couldn't be saved, but perhaps her grandfather could. Fortified with renewed courage, she left the room.

Standing in the cubbyhole leading to the ladies' room was a man she recognized immediately.

"Good evening," he said with a slight German accent.

Keira remembered him from television appearances and magazine shoots. Elegant and almost effeminate, the high-powered fashion executive looked every inch his fifty years. Thin and wiry, his body seemed poised for action and strength. He might look weak, but she felt a power emitting from him that seemed almost supernatural. When his pale, almost silvery blue eyes snagged hers, she shivered.

His thin, straight hair receded at the temples and brushed back from his high forehead. With sharp cheekbones and a razor-sharp nose, his face looked cadaverous, his lips reddish. Lined and pale, his skin appeared delicate, as if touching him might break blood vessels. He wore a polo shirt in a bright peach color and his Bermuda shorts looked gauche in the elegant setting. She imagined this man didn't care because whatever he wanted, he got. A man this rich, this powerful could have dressed in a burlap sack and everyone would tell him he looked fabulous *darling*.

"I'm sorry," the man said. "I've startled you. I'm Ludwig Haan." Haan extended a pale, thin hand to her. "And you must be Dr. Keira Jessop."

"Mr. Haan." She gripped his hand with confidence as his cold fingers wrapped around hers. She restrained a shudder of revulsion as she smiled and nodded. He squeezed her hand and hidden strength made her wince as he pushed her fingers together against the huge engagement ring. "Pleased to meet you. Zane has spoken of you often."

Mischief entered the man's eyes, as if he might be ready to play a game with her. The man kept a grip on her hand, then released it with a slow slide of his fingers over hers.

"What has Zane told you?"

Her heart thudded in a slow, rising dread. "He said you're preparing a fabulous wedding for us. Thank you so much."

"Why of course. Even though you're eloping, I can't let you have a wedding without all the accoutrements, now can I?"

"It's so kind of you." She modulated her voice, aware she sounded uptight. "I can't wait to see your estate."

"There is much to see there that you'll enjoy. The exotic. The untamed. Do you like new and unusual experiences, Dr. Jessop?"

Unsure if his statement extended to sexual innuendos but somehow imagining it did, she gave him a broad smile. "But of course."

He chuckled, the sound a low, breathy quality. "Then you are in for a treat beyond your imaginings. By the way, Salazar just told me that you and your fiancée had arrived. I'm so sorry I couldn't greet you at the door."

"Not at all," she said, trying to keep her voice steady. "We've enjoyed the fine champagne and the music."

"Ah, yes. Quinto plays the guitar wonderfully. You must dance later on." His gaze traveled to her bodice and lingered there a moment.

Irritation rose inside her. First Zane, then Salazar, now this creep. All the men in the world seemed to be attracted to her breasts today.

"My dear, may I say that is the most amazing dress." He touched her shoulder, fingering the silky, shimmery fabric. "It fits you wonderfully. Most of my runway models are so thin." He laughed softly. "But you, my dear. You have a wonderful shape. Curved in all the right places."

Slimy bastard. He's coming on to me already.

Instead of cutting Ludwig with a sharp comment, she headed him in another conversational direction. "Thank you. I don't think I'd enjoy modeling. I like my current career too much."

"Archaeology, isn't it?"

She nodded. "Yes."

"Then you will love seeing all the delightful artifacts at *Rancho La Paz*, my dear."

His fingers hadn't left her shoulder, and it took everything inside her not to flinch back. "I can't wait."

Again the pale man's attention cruised over her, a thorough assessment she felt all the way to her toes. "I'm so sorry, Dr. Jessop, but I must be off. I may not have the opportunity to stop by your table this evening and pay my respects to Zane. Please say hello for me. We'll see you tomorrow?"

"Absolutely."

"*Ciao*, then." With a wave, Ludwig walked off.

Keira's heart started to beat again, her breath sluicing out in a deep sigh.

Control, Keira. Get control or you'll never make it through this charade. She drew on a river of strength inside her.

After taking another cleansing breath, she strode back to her table and slid into the booth. She avoided Zane's gaze as she nestled close to him.

When she picked up her water glass, her hand shook. Water slopped over the edge as she almost lost her grip. "Damn it."

"Hey." His eyebrows drew together as he frowned. He kept his voice low. "What's wrong?"

She took a sip and sat the glass down slowly. She edged nearer to him and then leaned in to whisper in his ear. "I had an interesting encounter with Mr. Haan."

"What?" he asked a little sharply. "Where?"

"Outside the restroom. It was if…as if he was waiting for me to come out."

He slipped his arm around her shoulder, his gaze hardening. A dangerous light filled his eyes. "What happened?"

"Nothing really."

"Tell me." His big palm rubbed up and down her arm. "You're shivering. Are you cold?"

She gave a shaky laugh, ashamed. "No. He took me off guard. It was so unexpected."

After she explained in detail what happened, Zane's expression turned cool and uncompromising. She thought he might burst out with profanities, but instead he said, "When we're around him at *Rancho La Paz*, I don't want you to ever be alone with him. Understand me?"

Keira could have objected to the stern demand in his voice, but his expression made her change her mind. Another shiver rippled through her, but this time it was related to the way he looked at her. Fierce tenderness and a protective light made his eyes seem deeper, more intense.

"I can handle this," she said in defense. She didn't know if she spoke about the way unnerving ownership in his eyes, or the bizarre encounter with Haan.

The waiter brought their food, delaying any comment from Zane. After he'd placed their dishes in front of them, the waiter left.

Zane picked up the champagne and topped off her glass. He didn't fill his glass, and she glanced at him as he started to cut his steak. "Are you trying to get me drunk?"

Throwing a cocky smile at her, he said, "Yeah. Drink up."

She laughed softly.

They ate in relative silence. Hungrier than she could recall being in some time, she ate her salmon with lusty enjoyment. She dabbed her mouth with the snowy white napkin and savored the last taste in her mouth.

"Hear that?" he asked as a sultry Spanish tune floated on the air.

"Yes."

He pushed away his plate and threw her one of his trademark glances filled with possibilities and seduction. "Let's dance."

"I can't dance. I'm not coordinated enough."

"Right."

"No, really. I'm all feet."

"I'll teach you."

He took her hand and tugged gently until she left the booth with him.

"Zane," she said with a warning tone.

"Come on, sweetheart, humor me."

Sweetheart again. The word, meaningful in his velvety seductive voice, about melted her into a puddle.

Without hesitation he drew her toward the dance floor where two other couples swayed to the music. "I don't do fast dances."

As his arms slipped around her waist, he brought her against him. "This isn't fast."

"Zane—"

"Shhh. Just enjoy it."

Fuming a little, she clamped her mouth shut and allowed him to lead her around the floor. Then she saw why Zane apparently decided dancing would be a good idea. Haan was making the rounds of the tables, talking with his patrons. Haan's gaze fell on them with concentration.

"He's watching us," she said.

"Exactly," he whispered into her ear. "Relax now. You're so tense."

His fingers eased up her back in a slow caressing, massaging motion. He cupped her shoulder blades, then moved downward until he fondled her lower back above her buttocks. Quivers of delight raced across her skin and headed straight for erogenous zones. God, the man didn't have to do much to set her afire. Her body responded, nipples tightening. Her pussy pulsed and clenched and she felt a warm trickle of moisture.

Searching and reassuring, his touch cruised everywhere. They swayed, moving with the liquid, heady rhythm.

"That's it." His voice stayed husky, the sound arousing her. "Just let the music take you."

As they circled the dance floor she forgot everything but his embrace. The entire room disappeared, and the people dancing near them didn't matter. The guitarist strummed the instrument with loving attention, his eyes closed as he gave the dancers a beautiful melody. Though she couldn't understand the Spanish lyrics readily, they seemed to whisper of sultry days and even hotter nights under a blanket of stars.

A couple could make love to this song.

The way Zane touched her, his hands so gentle, his body leading her around the dance floor, *was* lovemaking. She couldn't escape the pleasure and the craving heating every inch of her body.

When the song shifted to a somewhat faster beat, he drew her expertly into step. Every movement flowed, all senses pinpointed on how his touch felt against her. She wanted, with an aching passion, to feel his big hands on her naked skin. She wanted his fingers exploring, caressing, and bringing her to the top.

"Oh yeah." His low, almost moaning words brushed against her already fired libido. She ached with desire.

Plunging her fingers into his hair, she pulled back far enough to check his eyes and evaluate what she saw. Fire. Pure sexual need.

When his hard, fully erect cock brushed against her stomach, she gasped. Muscles between her legs tightened in reaction. She palmed down his neck to his wide shoulders and allowed her breasts to press tighter against his chest. "Zane, maybe we should return to the table."

"Honey, you can't stop dancing now. Let me get back some control."

She saw hunger in his eyes and wanted to take away his starvation. Feeling more wanton than ever in her life, she enjoyed her female power to arouse him. She allowed her hips to brush against his again.

"We'd better ease up." His voice sounded strained as he burrowed his face into her neck, then traced tender kisses up the long column of flesh. He licked her ear. "Or we're going to have to find somewhere in this restaurant where I can fuck you."

Stunned by his explicit suggestion, she couldn't think of a coherent reply. She wanted, down deep in her aching core, to take him up on the suggestion.

Oh, my God. She shivered as delight raced up and down her spine. She couldn't remember the last time she'd been this turned on. This man held a potent sway over her emotions and her body. Crazy emotions darted inside her, threatening to take over. Feeling feminine and protected had never done this to her before. This man wanted her and she couldn't deny her body reacted to him in the strongest way.

For the rest of the song she held him at arm's length, their dance so proper they could have been two strangers. She avoided his gaze and concentrated on cooling down.

As the song eased away, so did Keira. He followed her to the table and when the waiter came to their table to ask if they wanted desert and coffee, they declined. Salazar gave them the check and Zane extracted a titanium card out of his wallet. Not a gold card or a platinum credit card. Titanium.

Silence reigned at the table while they waited for Salazar to return. She felt Zane's stare and his gaze glided over her with a look that said everything. He hadn't forgotten that their dance made him harder than a railroad spike.

After the waiter brought the credit slip and Zane signed it, he said, "Come on, let's get out of here."

Urgency in his voice surprised her; she didn't know what to think. He took her hand and they left the restaurant in a rush. When she started for the elevator, he pulled her down the hall, his face cool and harsh.

"Is something wrong?" she asked.

His gaze flickered to her for a moment, then away. "Not a damned thing."

He sounded angry. Well, hell. Let him remain pissed off, she didn't care.

When she saw he was headed for the stairwell, she said, "We're taking the stairs? Ten flights?"

"I can use the exercise."

Right. The man was made of steel and obviously took care of his body.

"Then I'm taking off my shoes." She took off the high heels and then they started downward.

After they'd accomplished one flight, he stopped on the landing and turned toward her so fast she almost ran into him.

"What are you doing?" she asked.

He backed her toward the wall until she bumped into it. His hands came up on either side of her head like a cage. "What I wanted to do after we danced."

Peril danced in his eyes, their burnished depths asking surrender. His earlier words raced into her head. *We'd better ease up or I'll have to find somewhere in this restaurant to fuck you.*

Recalling the heat in the way he'd spoken the words sent forbidden tingles through her loins.

Oh, my God. Maybe he wants to make love to me right here.

In the stairwell.

All the masculine attention, focused on her alone, held powerful influence. If she gave in and allowed him to manipulate her emotions, she would lose a piece of herself inside him. At the same time, she couldn't ignore her physical response to the man, the essence of his sexuality that drew her closer and closer to him with every minute.

She glanced upward and saw a security camera on the landing, way up in the corner near the ceiling. Maybe Zane staged this to keep Haan entertained, or his security amused at the least.

"Are we playing a game here?" she asked quietly as his gaze followed hers to the camera.

"That's what I was going to ask you." He smiled, turned slightly and gave the camera the bird.

She didn't know whether to smirk right along with him or be alarmed. "Zane!"

"Don't sweat it." His grin vanished, encompassed by the unparallel desire she saw brimming in the silky darkness of his eyes. "I'm sure the security cameras have seen a lot in here."

"They won't be seeing anything unusual with us."

"You sure?" His gaze flamed and she knew she'd pushed him too far. "What have you got on under this, honey?"

Indignation and excitement warred inside her. "You should know. You had your hand on my leg earlier."

Reality and fantasy blurred. Did he talk like this to her to cement the fantasy for their cover, or did the words reflect this man's real desires?

Without apparent hesitation, he used one hand to pull up the long length of her dress and the silky slide of fabric rasped against her leg with stomach-melting sensuality. When his fingers touched one slim strap of the garter belt along the back of her thigh, she quivered in reaction.

He chuckled, the low, deep sound rolling in his throat. "I love garter belts and stockings. Shit, honey, why did you have to wear a garter belt?"

She couldn't react fast enough to object as his lips came down on hers.

Her shoes clunked against the landing as she dropped them in surprise.

A sound slipped from his throat like a growl. Plundering her depths, his tongue took instant possession. She clutched at his collar and allowed the invasion. She couldn't get close enough, pressing against his muscles, gripping his clothing and body with vengeance. Any woman with sense would fight him off. Instead she wanted to bring him closer, to imprint his body tighter against hers.

He didn't feel like a stranger, but a man whom she'd been intimate with for some time. A man she'd loved long and well and hard. Inflamed by hunger she took his kiss, accepted it.

His hands slipped into her hair, then eased her closer. Hard and forged of iron, his amazing body made her feel protected at the same time he took her mouth with relentless thrusts of his tongue.

He pinned her against the wall again, his body a blanket. Flames licked at her clit and her pussy clenched and released, needing something hard and hot inside. Her mind couldn't catch up with the response in her body as it cried out for his touch. His cock felt hard and ready for action as he pressed against her stomach. Keira palmed his shoulders and felt as if she had to claw her way into him, unmercifully inherit all his thoughts, emotions and lust. She swayed in his grip as he locked her in his arms with no hope of dignified escape and no desire to leave.

Denise A. Agnew

Licking deep, his tongue learned every inch of her mouth. She responded, tangling her tongue with his. Dazed, stupefied by her appetite for him, she allowed his touch to slip over her rib cage and to cup her left breast in his palm.

He broke from their kiss, his breathing hard and quick. A slight red flush covered his cheekbones and his pupils dilated. The heat of his hand encompassing her breast left her aching for more. More attention, more love. His eyes held desire beyond anything she'd seen in a man, and she hardly believed all that passion belonged to her in this crazy encounter.

As his eyes blazed down into hers, he said, "You could come right now. Right here. All I'd need to do is clasp this sweet nipple, then thrust hard and deep between your legs. You'd go off like a rocket."

Arrogance dripped from him, but he didn't smile or mock her. He believed what he said. Such confidence spoke to her soul, to the very depths of Keira. A slow, savory smile slipped over his lips as he brought his fingers closer to her nipple. Her flesh tingled and she realized he taunted her. He wanted to see her fly to pieces under his touch, beyond control, giving in to his compelling desire and making it hers.

Without mercy his mouth covered hers. A relentless onslaught began. Keira stroked her tongue against his, learning and enjoying the way he gave as much pleasure as he took. She arched into his touch and his hand tightened on her breast and started a sweet, slow stroking all around her nipple. With each brush of his fingers, she muffled a soft groan against his lips. One hard thigh slipped between her legs and pressed upward against her mons. She shivered as the pressure against her clit felt so exciting. He moved that thigh and the friction against her clit and folds sizzled through her body. It felt so good she arched against his unyielding muscle with pleasure.

Yes, yes.

Then he took it to the next level.

With slow intension Zane flicked his thumb over her nipple and she gasped into his mouth. Out of her mind and wanting more, she clutched at his shirt and moaned softly. With a rhythm that could be nothing else but heady arousal, she moved against his rock-hard muscular thigh.

She needed more. More.

She went for broke, to savor this strange, wild interlude in time. She may never be here again, in this same way, with this same pleasure flowing in her blood. Raw need overwhelmed her, reckless want and power not far behind.

Sweet bursts of excitement tingled in her breasts, her nipple ravaged by the insistent brush of his fingers. She wanted naked skin against naked skin. How much more wonderful would it feel if he could take her bare nipple between his finger and thumb and pinch it? Lick it? The idea sent fresh arousal straight to her feminine depths and she arched against his thigh in ravenous need. Pressing and rubbing against him, she wanted desperately to come. Her body ached for it, needed it, wanted it. She could almost feel it deep down in her pussy where an ache built with each passing moment.

She knew, down deep, if he could have reached her naked breasts without ripping her dress off, his tongue and lips and fingers would be working her nipples into screaming hard points right now.

The idea inflamed her and she writhed on his leg, wanting an orgasm with a fierceness that ripped her down to the core.

He broke from their kiss and pressed his forehead to hers, his breathing harsh and rapid. "Keira, you're burning me up. Let's finish this in the limo."

Finish this.

Right here, where anyone could find them, they'd writhed like two horny teenagers on the loose. She froze in his arms and pushed against his chest.

He let her go. She leaned over and retrieved her shoes. He took her other hand and continued down the rest of the stairs. It would be a long walk, and as she had time to think, she realized she couldn't do this.

She couldn't allow this man she barely knew to tie her up in sexual knots. She didn't sleep with men she didn't know well and couldn't trust. When they reached the garage level and stepped out to find Eduardo parked nearby, she didn't speak. Eduardo hopped out of the limo and opened the door for them, taking them in with a knowing look. Her lipstick was smeared and her hair mucked up, not to mention the dazed look no doubt lingering on her face. Even Zane's hair looked a bit disheveled and his shirt askew. If Eduardo didn't know they'd been making out, he couldn't be too smart.

Without hesitation Eduardo enclosed them in the deluxe comfort of the limo and before long they moved out. She almost wished Zane would enclose her in his arms immediately, but instead he kept some space between them. Maybe he'd reconsidered this ill thought out sexual adventure. His gaze, though, held the passion of a man ready to complete what he'd started.

"This is crazy." His voice went to a soft rumble. "I just realized something, after all this time. I can't believe it's taken me this long. Whether you know it or not, you like the unexpected. It turns you on."

She scoffed. "Don't be ridiculous. I don't like to be in danger."

He shook his head and leaned in so his breath feathered over her ear. "I felt it back in Egypt while we were in the alcove and just now in the stairwell. We both get off on doing things that have an element of the unknown. You like to discover things. To search out the mysteries under the dirt. And right now, you're playing with my head."

"What?" she asked, half in anger.

With gentle fingers he brushed back her hair. Warm and affectionate, his touch shimmered like a gold thread connecting her heart and emotions to wanton physical sensation. Yearning for more, she leaned into his hand. His thumb brushed her cheek like a lover intent on giving her pleasure.

"We were on fire, Keira. You can't deny it." His gaze glittered with intent, a man ready for serious action. "You don't know how badly I wanted you on the dance floor. And how much I wanted you in that stairwell." His mouth touched her forehead in a soothing kiss. "But we have a job to do and I can't afford the distraction."

So he wanted her. For real. The idea was oddly gratifying and almost overwhelmed the sharp disappointment racing through her upon hearing his rebuff.

While his rejection could be considered nice as far as dismissals went, the common sense of his statement didn't keep the burn from hurting. He wouldn't take this physical entanglement a step farther, despite what he'd said in the stairwell.

"Who are you trying to convince? Me or yourself? I have never met a more self-confident man than you, Zane. Except, maybe, my grandfather. Both of you have this disgusting pride that is sure to get you killed one day." When he didn't say anything she continued. "You like playing with women? Turning them on and then tossing them away? Well that isn't a game I'm willing to play."

His mouth popped open, a little astonishment registering in his eyes. "What we're doing here is treacherous. Relationships like ours—hell any relationship like this between two agents is not condoned by the SIA."

"So you're saying we're breaking the rules."

"In an unwritten sense, yes."

Good. Let the rules decide. If regulations said hands off, she'd be less likely to feel the sting of his dismissal.

She sighed and glared at him. "Like you said, let's just keep this to business from now on, okay?" Crossing her arms, she frowned deeply. "We can be public, but when it comes to private I'm strictly hands off from now on." On a roll, she decided to set some ground rules. "And one of us can sleep on the sleeper sofa, too."

She scooted farther away from him, her pride a little wounded. No matter. She knew when to cut her losses. So they owned a hot attraction that went out of control and they lost their heads. It didn't mean she couldn't handle it.

Yet even as he settled back in his seat with perturbation on his face, she knew she lied to herself once again.

Chapter Five

Morning sunlight brightened the limo windows but didn't intrude on the intimate and comfortable enclosure. As Zane sat across from Keira—way across—he wondered if last night's royal fuck-up would come back to haunt him. Whatever he'd expected to happen when he danced with her at the restaurant, he hadn't anticipated sprouting a major hard-on from holding her in his arms.

Then again, he hadn't expected to suffer a raging, overwhelming protectiveness and a need to claim her as his own as soon as he heard she'd encountered Haan. While he liked sex as much as the next man, he'd never before experienced the wildly out-of-control need like this one. With that desire to shelter evolved a need to put his stamp on her. To somehow get so far inside her any man within a hundred miles would know she was his and so would she.

As an agent, he'd received plenty of instruction in how to circumvent unsuitable and useless emotions while on a mission. With her, every rule went straight down a rat hole. When he pulled away from her last night and realized that if he continued he would probably be fucking her in the backseat of the limo, he regretted having to stop. God, how he regretted it.

Everything about her inflamed him last night. Her body in that dress, the realization she wore a garter belt and stockings, her kiss when she'd responded wholeheartedly. The feeling of tight, aroused little nipples between his fingers.

Shit, shit, shit. He'd been within seconds of shoving her dress up, ripping her panties off and taking her there in a public place. Not very classy, Zane. Not classy at all. But shit, she would have been sweet, hot, wet. Damn it.

He gritted his teeth and tried to rein in the hard-on threatening to break through his pants. He took several deep breaths and tried to remember last night in a less sexual manner.

Her reaction surprised him a little. Hell, everything about this stubborn, feisty, pretty woman staggered him. While she said no to physical involvement, he knew she'd wanted him as much as he'd wanted her. She'd been so hot, so ready to be fucked.

Good thing I pulled the plug.

He'd worked with a couple of female agents before but he never once felt so damned horny around them the way he felt when he came near Keira. They'd never crossed the line with him and he'd kept his paws off. Why the hell couldn't he do that with her? Again he rubbed his neck and willed away conjecture. He couldn't waste valuable time wondering why his hormones had jammed into overdrive. Professionalism aside, he couldn't trust her.

Last night after they'd arrived back at the hotel, she'd stayed quiet. She'd slipped into bed early and he retreated to the foldout sofa. To his surprise he'd fallen asleep right away. Tormented by dreams of her warm, beautiful body encasing his cock in silky, wet heat, he'd woken up in the morning with a boner the size of Mount Olympus. He'd retreated to the bathroom before she woke up. In the shower he'd relieved the tension by jacking off. Better to release the pent-up need than have his hormones testing him for the rest of the day.

While traitorous thoughts dominated Zane, Eduardo drove them closer to *Rancho La Paz*. They left the highway and headed south, the road growing into a twisting, meandering snake. Here the houses looked middle-class, then deteriorated into a jumble of shanty areas proclaiming a steady decline into a poor neighborhood. Children played in their yards, their bright summer clothing flashing like rainbows as they ran, jumped, and laughed. Solemn-faced housewives watched the limo pass by. He'd been in those poor areas before and it always twisted his heart in a way he couldn't explain. Extremes fascinated him, compelled him to explore. Maybe that's what made him a good agent, but it also put him on the edge of destruction. He watched for the danger signs, just like last night when thinking with his cock almost drew him into major trouble.

The road made yet another twist and the limo headed south again. Soon the houses came few and far between and the lush rainforest grew closer to the road. Another thirty minutes and they'd arrive at the gate to Ludwig Haan's estate. Anticipation stirred in Zane's gut as it did the ten other times he'd been to Haan's lair.

Zane groaned and rubbed the back of his aching neck. Never again would he try to be the gentleman and sleep on a hard fuckin' sleeper sofa. So much for high-class accommodations at *Hosteria El Sosiego*. He needed an aspirin but hesitated to ask Keira. Ever since last night, through this morning and their room service breakfast, she'd been cool and remote. She'd gone mannequin on him, and he didn't know how to remedy it.

Today she wore a peach cotton top that hugged her round breasts in a way that kept drawing his gaze back repeatedly. Her cargo pants screamed Ralph Lauren rather than jungle explorer and looked similar to the pair he wore. Her selection of shoes, a sturdy pair of hiking boots, was practical. He'd give her points for common sense.

When he glanced at her a second later her coolness seemed to dissolve a little.

"Are you all right?" Soft concern in her voice, she leaned forward the slightest bit.

He grinned and explained about the sofa sleeper. "Thing was hard as cement."

One of her shapely brows tilted up. "Sorry. I didn't realize or I never would have..."

As she realized what she almost said, her face went pink. He liked it when she blushed. The last time had been when he'd told her they had to cool it or he'd find a place in the restaurant to fuck her. Her cheeks had turned bright red at the suggestion.

"We don't have to worry about it for awhile," he said. "Haan's accommodations are first-class. I doubt he'll have a sleeper sofa in our room since he expects us to sleep together."

Discomfort crossed her face, the kind that said she didn't want to think about it. "What are we going to do about that?"

Unsure, he swallowed hard and pushed forward with a proposal. "We'll sleep in the same bed. I can restrain myself if you can."

"Oh no." She twisted her fingers in her lap and her bottom lip went between her teeth. "Um, I meant that we'll have to think of some other way to deal with the sleeping accommodations."

Though he felt like he might be lying between his teeth, he said with a smile, "We'll put pillows between us so we don't accidentally touch."

Seriousness in her eyes said she didn't like the joke. Then she started digging around in her fanny pack. "That's not good enough."

He couldn't resist. "Why? You think you'll be so turned on that you won't be able to keep your hands off me?"

She stopped her search and glared at him. *Ah, damn. Here it comes. I should have kept my mouth shut.*

"Has anyone ever told you that you're full of crap, Agent Spinella?"

"More than once. Frequently, as a matter of fact." He didn't take offense, waving a hand in dismissal. "We'll wait and see what our room is like when we get there. Maybe if he gives us one of those California king-sized beds we can build a fort between us."

She pulled a bottle of aspirin from her fanny pack and tossed it at him. "Here."

He caught it easily and opened the bottle. After retrieving a bottle of water from the small fridge, he took a pill. They went silent again and he found he liked the quiet to reflect. Taking Keira along on an assignment as dangerous as this bothered him, but what choice did he have? He wished Mac had given him a real agent, a woman with training and guts like Mac's wife Destiny. Then again, Keira seemed brave enough, a woman faced with challenges. She hadn't fallen to pieces in Egypt, even though someone shot at her. He would give her credit for that. She didn't whine but looked the problem square in the face.

Unless it came to sex. He guessed when it came to lovemaking she hadn't given in to her most feral side. Images of her lips parted, her head thrown back as he'd cupped her breast last night—oh, yeah. Some snapshots deserved remembrance, and Keira Jessop with her hair tangled, her lips plumped up from kissing, and her skin hot...yeah, that would be worth recollection forever.

Anger swelled inside him. What did it matter? He needed to keep his hands off her.

He glanced outside and noted the jungle grew closer on either side. He wished they didn't have to keep up this pretense of tremendous wealth, since he'd rather travel in a well-equipped, rugged SUV.

"Tell me more about Puerto Azul," she asked suddenly.

Surprised she wanted to talk after their war of words, he felt relief. They'd have to ease into a reasonable relationship at some point before they reached *Rancho La Paz* or the tension rolling off them in waves would show.

"There's a lot to know about this country," he said.

She nodded and kept her gaze pinned on the scenery outside. "I didn't have much notice from the SIA about coming here, so I didn't have time to read up on the country."

He shifted on the limo seat. "What you don't know about Puerto Azul can hurt you."

"Such as?" She brushed her hair away from her neck.

"This place is full of cataclysmic forces, and I don't mean the human kind."

"If you're talking about volcanoes, I read about them."

He took another sip of water. "Volcanoes, yes. But there's more. Like neighboring Costa Rica we have around a dozen climatic zones. *La Montaña de la Jaguar* in the far interior has ice and snow on it in the colder months."

Her eyebrows edged up in curiosity. "Interesting. I've always been fascinated with natural disasters like those that covered Pompeii and Herculaneum in Italy. I wish I'd worked on both sites."

Zane enjoyed the clear interest in her sparkling amber eyes. "*La Montaña de la Jaguar* did some damage to the small hamlet of St. Lucia about twenty years ago. It's been putting out some steam in the last year, but the experts say it isn't due to blow. Not everyone believes them. There's a volcano about forty miles away called *Rincon de Salvo*. Several other volcanoes in this country have been harnessed for geothermal energy."

"Fascinating."

She shifted on her seat as if uncomfortable and looped one ankle over her knee in a casual look saying she didn't care about looking feminine and prissy. Liking her attitude and the confidence it took, he smiled. To his surprise she returned the grin.

He liked the ease they'd created and wanted to keep it rolling. "There's a legend about *La Selva Negra* and the San Cristobal Plateau."

She laughed softly. "Of course there is."

"Countless numbers of people have been lost in the jungle over the years."

"That's not surprising, is it? I would think it fairly common."

He shook his head. "No, it shouldn't be. Natives to this country usually know better than to wander off into uncharted territory without a guide."

Keira shifted again, leaning forward and clasping her hands between her knees. "Mac Tudor said the jungle around *Rancho La Paz* isn't well explored and that Haan is one of the few people to venture there. How can that be? I mean, it isn't the Amazon."

Zane didn't know all the answers, but he knew enough rumors. "I've heard tales from the locals in my six months here that would curl your hair."

Her eyes widened a little. "Then tell me. I love a good hair-raising horror tale."

"You're sure?"

She gave a gentle, feminine snort. "Of course. I'm not a woman who flinches during a scary movie."

"I guessed that." He realized he still held the bottle of aspirin and he put it on the seat next to him. "The first story is about a werejaguar."

Understanding came over her face. "Like some of the tales told in Mesoamerica?"

"Same thing. This one says that a half-man, half-jaguar roams the jungles outside *Rancho La Paz* and watches out for the innocent." He gave his voice a dramatic tone and matched her by leaning forward in his seat. "People who aren't pure of heart, who have greed and avarice as a part of their personality are devoured by the beast. The innocent are protected against all harm."

He paused for effect, and she grinned. "Who is the man part of the jaguar supposed to be?"

"No one knows. They say he's been in the jungle since the beginning of time." He cleared his throat. "Then there's a story that Haan swears is true."

"Which probably means it isn't?"

He hesitated, unsure whether to proceed with this tale. "Hard to say. Haan's a man of weird contrasts. We know he's a ruthless bastard, number one. Yet he's also done everything he can to preserve the rainforest in this country. He's thrown thousands of dollars into conservation, especially in the immediate area. It seems to be working. He's paid companies in the United States to plant hardwoods as supply so nothing in the rainforest is cut down for furniture and farming—you name it, he's done it for preservation."

Surprise colored her eyes and lines formed between her delicate brows as she frowned. Reminded of how those eyes shimmered like gold during passion, he reined back on a desire to move to her side of the limo and absorb her female heat.

"Why do I get the feeling his good works around the local area aren't so good?" she asked.

He tapped his temple with his index finger. "Good thinking. My guess is that he preserves the rainforest around his ranch because of the tale he tells. It serves several purposes." He ticked the points off on his fingers. "One, he can keep the ranch isolated and somewhat protected. Two, he keeps his own mystique. By playing the Good Samaritan part of the time, he fools a lot of rich people into thinking he's an okay guy. Three, he holds back on information and keeps his powerbase."

"Mac Tudor told me that Haan claims to have found some fountain of youth in the jungle. Is that his legend?"

"You got it. He wandered into the jungle about a year ago with an expeditionary team. Several of them were locals. He used them as pack horses of sorts. A few others were rich benefactors who wanted to be seen as conservationists. Others were Haan's bodyguards and employees. They went on a trek that lasted four days. When they came out, only four of the original team out of ten was alive."

She blinked, then blinked again. "What did Haan say happened to the rest of them?"

"He didn't say much. Before the team left they each signed a statement saying no family members could hold Haan responsible if anything bad befell them on the trip." Zane rubbed his neck again. "That wasn't much of a problem for some of the staff lost on the trip. Haan goes through staff like liquid through a sieve. One of the celebrities was Patrice Allegheny, the actress."

Her mouth formed another one of those little ohhs he was starting to find too damned intriguing. "You're kidding? I remember hearing something about her disappearing in Puerto Azul but I didn't have any idea it was on Haan's little jaunt."

"That was the one. Supermodel Livie Graystone was also on the expedition and was lost."

She leaned back against the seat, a puzzled expression on her finely drawn features. "You'd think the authorities would have investigated."

"They did, but apparently they bought Haan's stories. First he said they discovered a strange city of labyrinths with exotic pictures on them similar to some of the carvings on temples in India."

Mischief danced in her incredible eyes, and he found his attraction to her stirring to life again. She threw him a clever grin. "Exotic as in erotic? Not fit for virginal eyes?"

"Yep, that's right."

"I've never heard of anything being found like that in this region."

"Neither has anyone else." His suspicious nature, honed by years on the job, rose to life and overpowered his growing interest in her as a woman. "I'm surprised you hadn't heard of this mysterious find."

Keira shrugged. "I'm not. I've been buried at least six months out of the year in digs and site surveys in England. We're supposed to keep up on our professional reading, and most of it doesn't extend to rumors and fairy tales. What do you think really happened to all those people?" she asked.

"Maybe they did find a fountain of youth there and the people who didn't come back decided they wanted to stay."

She sniffed. "Right."

"Watch out. You're starting to sound cynical."

"And you're not?"

"I never said that. I'm one of the most cynical people in the world."

She inhaled deeply and his gaze locked on the way her firm, plump breasts strained just right against her shirt. He echoed her breath, looking for control. He didn't need a monumental hard-on as a distraction.

As they rounded a sharp curve the aspirin bottle rolled and slid off the bench seat onto the floor. She unbuckled her seatbelt at the same time he did. They both reached for the bottle as it rolled toward the front of the limo.

A tremendous force slammed them forward at the same time, a crunching sound mixed with rending metal, and the scream of burning rubber added to the noise. He went flying against the bench seat to the north side of the car, jamming his ribs and drawing a curse from his lips. Keira's cry of surprise rang in his ears as she fell in a heap at his feet. The car titled slightly to the right.

"Damn it!" He groaned as pain rolled through his ribs. He reached down for her and grabbed her shoulders from behind as she sat up. "Are you all right?"

She turned to look at him, eyes startled and with her hair flopping over her face. She managed to say breathlessly, "Yes. My God, what—?"

The partition drew back and Eduardo's frantic expression filled the opening. Blood trickled from his forehead. "We've got big problems! The limo is surrounded by rebels!"

"Maintain your position. We can't afford to fight that many." Zane looked through the windshield, then toward one of the side windows. All of Zane's instincts went on high alert when he saw what awaited them. "Shit."

A deuce and a half military vehicle blocked the narrow road, and Eduardo had tried to swerve around them. Instead the soft shoulder crumbled and sent them straight into the jungle and face-first into a huge tree.

Zane quickly moved off the bench seat and pulled on the drawer below it. Out popped a drawer containing a nice selection of weapons, including a handgun. "The bastards deliberately ran us off the road."

"What? Why would they do that? They look like military," she said. "And why does this limo have a cache of weapons?"

"No time to explain. The guys in the camie gear aren't military."

"Who are they?"

"Rebels. Probably enemies of Haan or anyone associated with him. They patrol this countryside sometimes when they feel a juicy need to pick up money or weapons from Ludwig's cohorts."

"Then we'll explain we're not Haan's friends."

He snorted. "I'd like to be able to say that would work, but there's no guarantee. There are a couple of small factions running around in Puerto Azul that would like to destabilize the democracy here. There's one group that wants to take down Haan, but they aren't always gentle about their methods. From the looks of them, they could be any of those groups."

He saw the fear in her eyes, then her expression solidified into determination. "We'll keep the doors locked. They can't get in."

If he left the vehicle without a weapon, he would be sitting duck. On the other hand, he could still be in deep shit if he took a weapon. He made a command decision and yelled it to Eduardo. "We're going out slowly. No weapons drawn or we're dead."

He stuffed the weapon into the back waistband of his pants.

"What are we doing?" she asked.

The men piling out of the truck strolled down the small slope to the limo. "I think they're giving us two options. Surrender and surrender. This limo doesn't have bulletproof glass, and I'm not taking the chance one of those assholes is going to shoot through the door to get our attention. When we get out of this car, stay close to me. Keep quiet and let me do the talking."

"You're the expert, Cochise." She sounded cocky, yet he saw the underlying anxiety in her eyes.

Eduardo's driver's door flew open and someone yanked him out. One of the men outside tapped on the window and shouted a command in Spanish for them to get out of the car.

"This is it." Zane moved toward the car door. "Follow me and don't make any quick movements."

Zane opened the car door with the utmost caution and then someone jerked it the rest of the way open.

"¡*Vamomos, deprisa*!" the man gestured with his automatic weapon.

Zane exited the car and smiled. He switched to Spanish. "Gentlemen, we don't want any trouble. It looks like there's been a terrible accident."

The short, squatty man standing nearest the door moved back as another tall, bulky thug took over. His green camie gear had seen better days. None of the six men in front of them wore insignia or rank of any kind.

The man holding Eduardo by the back of his shirt collar possessed a hollow eye socket. Cyclops cuffed the driver in the back of the head when Eduardo mumbled something in Spanish. Zane wanted to leap forward and kick the shit out of Cyclops for hurting Eduardo, but he knew better than to start trouble.

"They have nothing you want. They are simple tourists," Eduardo said in Spanish, his gaze hazy with pain.

"Shut up," Cyclops said.

The tall creep said, "I am Paco Ortega. You were unfortunate enough to come into our path."

Ortega moved closer and Zane almost wrinkled up his nose. The stench alone assured Zane the man needed a bath at least two days ago.

"We didn't mean to cause a problem," Zane said in English to see if they could understand him.

Ortega's eyes, a glacial bottle green, shined fiercely out of his tanned, harsh features. His pockmarked skin gave him a tortured, used up look. "You have no business being on this road in this fancy car unless you are on the way to see Ludwig Haan. That is a problem."

Ortega's switch to English surprised Zane a little, although schools in Puerto Azul went to great pains to teach English along with Spanish.

"You are friends with this Haan?" the shorter, stubby man asked, putting his gun over his shoulder in a very nonchalant fashion.

Zane didn't know which direction this fuck-up would go, but he would keep it in his favor or die trying. "We were invited to Rancho La Pas, but we hardly know the man."

Stubby man shoved the automatic weapon barrel under Zane's chin. "You lie."

Behind Zane, Keira let out a gasp. "No."

Stubby turned his attention on Keira, exactly what Zane wanted to avoid. With a leer Stubby abandoned his assault on Zane and walked toward her. A burning need to cut off the man's balls almost overwhelmed Zane. *Damn it all to fuckin' hell. If the douche bag laid one hand on her —* He turned toward her and Stubby, even though he knew the gun in his waistband would be obvious.

One wannabe soldier grabbed his arm and pulled him back, then removed the gun from Zane's waistband. "He has a weapon, Manuel."

So, the stubby prick has a name.

"No shit," Manuel said. "So did the driver. Maybe we should frisk the woman."

Keira's eyes widened a little, then she schooled her features into contempt. She backed up against the limo. Zane couldn't run to her rescue without bringing death down on her and him. He would bide his time as long as they didn't hurt her.

Ortega spoke out as he strolled toward Keira and Manuel. "We have better things to do. Search the car."

While Manuel did what he was told, Ortega gestured toward Keira. "Give me that pack around your waist."

She complied.

"Your vehicle is destroyed, no? You cannot drive it," Cyclops said. "So we take it for parts."

Another man with a thick mustache and brown eyes strode up to the scene. He'd remained in the background and observed while his compatriots played this game. With his slightly lighter skin he looked a little different than the rest of these goons. Tall, with an air of command, the guy couldn't be much older them Zane.

"Welcome to *La Selva Negra*. This jungle is as it is named. Very dark and very dangerous." He lowered his automatic weapon. "Now that we are finished with the formalities, give me your wallet."

Hoping to keep the situation from boiling over, Zane did as told. When the man flipped through his wallet, he skipped over the money and went for the identification. "A California driver's license and a temporary license to drive in Puerto Azul. Mr. Zane Spinella. What is that? Italian?"

Zane thought the question strange, but he answered. "Yes."

"You are a rich man?"

Shit, shit, shit. Did this bastard think kidnapping is a good idea?

"I am," Zane said.

"An honest one, no?"

Zane managed a smile. "Sometimes. Sometimes not."

The man laughed as he shouldered his weapon. "Manuel, what did you find in the car?"

Manuel backed out of the limo. "Weapons, *El Jaguar*! Liquor. Food. Their luggage has nothing but clothes in it."

The man called *El Jaguar* took off his cap and thick, light brown hair sprang up as he raked his fingers through it. "Weapons, *Señor* Spinella? I think you are not an ordinary tourist."

Zane shrugged. "Eduardo keeps the weapons for emergencies."

El Jaguar didn't look convinced. "Very suspicious."

He turned his attention to Keira and Zane felt every muscle in his body tighten for battle. *El Jaguar* wandered up to her, his gaze assessing with clear male appreciation. Keira looked unruffled and Zane admired her composure. So far she'd displayed as much courage as any agent he'd worked with in SIA.

"Why are you here, *chica*?" *El Jaguar* asked.

She took a deep breath and eased back against the limo; maybe she wanted to get as far away from the man as she could without being too obvious. "Zane is my fiancé. We're here on vacation."

El Jaguar's gaze was hidden from Zane as the man watched her. At least the rebel hadn't made a step toward her since she'd retreated. He clasped her left hand and spied the huge ring. "I see. Very impressive."

Keira's expression didn't alter an iota. "If you want the ring, take it. Just let us go. All I care about is Zane."

The soft plea sounded authentic, a woman in love and concerned. Instead of taking her up on the offer, the man chuckled. The other men laughed with him, an edge of humorless cruelty in their tones.

"A woman who values her man over diamonds?" Cyclops asked. "Not possible. I say he's not her fiancé. His whore maybe, but not for marriage."

"Quiet!" hissed *El Jaguar*.

While he appreciated *El Jaguar* defending Keira, fire raced up Zane's spine at Cyclop's assertion. "She is *not* a whore. We're getting married tomorrow."

Manuel stood by the limo, his attention on the crushed front end. "Perhaps we take her ring to repair the front of this car, eh?"

El Jaguar cleared his throat. "We will take the ring from the lady since she does not want it." He drew the ring off her hand and held it up. "Exquisite." He turned back to Zane. "The man...we will take his money." He extracted money and credit cards from the wallet, including the bug tracking device. "You won't need these."

"Leave me one," Zane said quickly. "The Macon City Bank card. At least leave me that one."

For a moment *El Jaguar* looked defiant, then he smiled and slipped the card back into the wallet. He tossed the wallet back at Zane and pocketed the other items. "Leave the lady's money. As a gesture of my respect."

Manuel leered at Keira. "There's one thing I will take from the pretty *Señorita*."

He reached for her, jerking Keira into his arms with brutal force. His mouth slammed down on hers.

Everything male and protective inside Zane curled into rage and he lunged toward Manuel. "Get your fucking hands off her!"

Blinding pain shot through the back of his head and sent him down a black hole.

* * * * *

Keira thought she'd vomit as Manuel pressed his fat, stinking mouth against hers. She struggled and brought her knee up to jam him in the nuts. As her knee connected she heard and saw Zane rushing to help her. At the same time she cracked the asshole in the *cojones*, she saw Ortega bring the butt of his automatic weapon down on Zane's head.

Manuel went down with an agonized cry at the same time Zane hit the ground face-first. Eduardo shouted something in Spanish. Fear for Zane raced through her.

A shot rang out and everyone stilled. Perversely she expected to feel pain somewhere, but then realized *El Jaguar* had shot into the sky.

"Enough!" *El Jaguar* stomped toward Manuel and kicked the man in the ass while Manuel writhed and groaned. "I didn't authorize you to touch her! Nothing is done without my permission. Comply or die!" He turned on Ortega and pistol-whipped the man across the jaw. Ortega fell on his back, moaning as he clutched at his face. "I did not authorize disrespect toward these people."

Jolted out of her shock, she scampered toward Zane with Eduardo following close behind. When she dropped down on her knees next to Zane, she could see he'd gone out like a light. She quickly grabbed his wrist and tried for a pulse. A trickle of blood ran down the side of Zane's face, and she brushed his thick hair away to look for damage. Her heart pounded like mad, threatening to come up through her throat as fear cloaked her breathing.

When she felt an instant, strong pulse she sighed in relief. "Thank God."

Eduardo started to check Zane over, searching the agent's scalp. Eduardo's efficiency surprised her; his serious expression said he knew what he was doing.

Eduardo wiped Zane's blood off his fingers with a handkerchief. "*Señorita* Jessop, I don't feel a fracture. But we can't say for sure until he sees a doctor."

Worry sliced through her as hot and deep as razor blades. The thought of this vital, strong man seriously injured scared the hell out of her. Tears sprang into her eyes and she let everyone see how she felt. She didn't have to act. She leaned down and pressed a kiss to Zane's big shoulder.

El Jaguar hovered over them. "Your fiancé may be seriously injured, *Señorita*. I apologize for these undisciplined pups. They will be punished."

From the harsh tone in his voice, the penalty would be nasty indeed. She sniffed and tears ran down her cheeks. "We've got to take him for medical treatment."

"There is none for miles." *El Jaguar* gestured with one hand.

"You're just going to leave us here?" she asked, anger rising as more tears fell. "I swear, if he dies—" Just the thought made more tears come and she allowed them full power, dredging up the real pain as much as she could. "You can't leave us like this."

Eduardo shook his head. Something in his face, a kind glimmer in his eyes, gave her courage. "We will have to manage on our own. We have a medical kit in the limo." He glanced at the men surrounding them. "That is, if you don't take it from us."

El Jaguar nodded. "We will allow you to keep your supplies. All we require is your weapons."

With a glare she said, "Take the weapons."

Within a few short minutes *El Jaguar* and his thugs loaded back into the big truck, including a semiconscious Ortega and a grumbling Manuel.

El Jaguar remained longer, his gaze on Zane. "If I was you I would put this man into the limousine to keep the sun off him. *Señorita*, I wish we could have met under more pleasant circumstances. Perhaps another day."

He tipped his hat and returned to the truck.

She threw dagger looks at the vehicle as it retreated down the road. "Come on, Eduardo. At least that bastard had one good idea. Let's carry Zane into the limo."

"No one is carrying me anywhere," Zane said suddenly, his voice sounding a little weak. A groan parted his lips as he flopped onto his back and shaded his eyes in the crook of his arm. "Fuckin' A!"

She gasped in relief. "Zane! You're awake."

He kept his arm over his face. "I woke up a while ago. I heard a lot of the conversation."

Eduardo gasped. "You played...how do you say it in America? Possum?"

Zane laughed, then groaned. "Eduardo, don't make me laugh. You're killin' me."

She touched Zane's shoulder and squeezed gently. "Damn it, Zane. You scared the hell out of me."

Tears returned and she didn't understand why. She'd never been a weepy woman until now, never felt this vulnerable when she wanted to be strong.

Eduardo said something in Spanish that sounded prayerful and he chuckled. "Spinella, you are one tough son bitch."

When Eduardo said bitch it came out sounding like "beach."

Zane removed his arm from over his eyes and laid still, his face a little pale. He groaned as he sat up slowly. "Yeah, well I don't feel so tough right now. I feel like someone bashed me over the head with an automatic weapon."

A little surprised he would admit to any limitation, she pressed his shoulder and kept it there. "You might have a concussion."

He shook his head, then winced. "No, I don't think so. My vision is okay and I don't have any dizziness or nausea. I've got some medical training."

Doubtful, she watched him as he started to stand.

Eduardo got on one side and helped him. "I'll get the medical kit and we will check."

As Eduardo headed back to the limo, Zane reached for her. "Come here."

She didn't expect his sudden embrace and eager touch as his arms slipped around her and he drew her close against his chest. Keira felt so grateful to have his solid muscles around her that she made a contented sigh. His warm scent enveloped and gave her a sense of safety she didn't have around any other man.

Silent and grim, she absorbed power and undeniable protectiveness from him. God, it felt good. Right. His fingers brushed through her hair and then he released her. Caution and relief mixed on his handsome face. Almost as if he regretted drawing her into his arms but couldn't help it.

Niggling suspicion made her ask, "Why do I get the distinct impression Eduardo isn't everything he appears to be?"

The mischievous glint in the special agent's eyes turned into a full-blown grin. "He's a man of many talents."

She wiped her forearm over her forehead as sticky heat made her sweat. Her peach-colored T-shirt plastered to her back. "Uh-huh. I can see that."

He tilted her chin up with an index finger so she had to look into his eyes. "Are you okay?"

"I'm fine. Thank you for trying to come to come to my rescue."

He threw her a rueful grin, a little sheepish around the edges. "Yeah, trying is the operative word. It's a damn good thing that *El Jaguar* decided to stop the asshole." His eyes darkened, the humor lapsing. "I didn't think... I couldn't let them hurt you."

Amazement and warmth filled a new place in her heart, a tiny little spot that seemed to widen and expand as time moved forward. The more she saw him in action, the more he seemed to affect her. She wondered if she'd lost her mind allowing mushy emotion to intrude. Could she trust feelings generated during gut-wrenching danger? Could the affection she already felt for this rough-and-tumble agent possibly be real?

Zane brushed her hair back from her face, the tips of his fingers tracing over her skin and sending a sensual shiver through her. Then he wiped at the tears drying on her cheek. "There's something else wrong other than the fact you were in a car wreck and had the shit scared out of you."

She cleared her throat. "No, I—no that was it. When that creep grabbed me it was bad enough, but then when that guy hit you in the head and I saw all that blood—"

She gulped and stopped.

Oh no. No, I can't confess that. He'll believe I'm getting too attached if the words are out there hanging in the stratosphere.

Eduardo came up with the first aid kit and forestalled confession. An admission she couldn't, wouldn't make at this juncture, if ever.

"*Señor* Spinella." Eduardo gave the kit to her to hold, then extracted a penlight. "Let me see your eyes." Eduardo made some ums and ahs that sounded doctorial. "Your pupils are even. Everything looks good. You feel all right now?"

Zane rubbed the back of his neck. "Good news. The slam on the head has cured my neck ache."

She laughed, an almost hysterical yelp that made her slap her hand over her mouth in embarrassment. Zane's eyebrows went up and he chuckled at the same time Eduardo followed with a laugh.

"Sorry." She walked over to the limo and retrieved her fanny pack lying on the ground. "I think I'm losing my mind in this heat."

Eduardo used antiseptic to clean the cut on the back of Zane's neck, and while she watched the short guy working, she sighed. "What are we going to do next? We have no workable car and we're stranded miles from anywhere. Don't tell me we have to trek through the jungle to reach Haan's house?"

"We could," Zane said, "but we aren't going to." After Eduardo finished putting a bandage on the cut, Zane said, "Come on, I'll show you my secret weapon."

His weapon happened to be a satellite phone tucked into a hidden compartment below one set of bench seats in the back of the limo. He turned it on and within seconds he'd contacted Haan's base of operations. After going through a few hoops to speak to the man himself, he let Haan know what had happened and where they were.

He turned off the phone. "They're sending another limo for us."

Eduardo rolled his gaze skyward. "I will call my friends to help me out of this, *Señor* Spinella. I will stay with the car."

Zane nodded. "Absolutely."

Now that the drama had diminished, Keira realized the jungle surrounding them chattered with life. Colorful birds, none she could identify, anchored in the lowest branches of trees nearby. Their songs, some pleasant and some raucous, filled the air. Other unrecognizable animal sounds echoed through the jungle. They'd slid off into a small area where the jungle had been pushed back from the narrow two-lane paved road. Thick and mysterious, the green canopy above blocked light deeper into the jungle. Suddenly the rainforest seemed a hostile place rife with perils imagined and unimagined. Hazards closed in on all sides.

When Zane touched her shoulder she jumped. "Hey, what's wrong?"

"This jungle is giving me the creeps, that's what's wrong."

"It's a beautiful place," Zane said.

"Beautiful but often deadly," Eduardo said from the car as he put the first aid kit back into glove box.

"That's great, Eduardo. Give her even more confidence." His brows pinched together as he observed her. "Why don't you sit in the limo and get out of this sun?"

Once they settled inside the tilted car, she relaxed a little. Eduardo stayed outside.

"That feels better." She took a tissue out of her fanny pack and dabbed at her face and neck. "The sun was starting to feel like it was cutting through my skull straight into my brain."

Zane found bottled water in the fridge and handed her one. "Drink up."

As the cold water slid down her throat, she sighed in pleasure. "How long will take Haan to send rescue?"

He glanced at his watch. "No telling. The man's fickle. It could be less than an hour, it could be a few hours."

"A few hours?"

"Like I said, the man's fickle. He likes to keep people off guard. Figures if he stays unpredictable he's harder to kill."

She leaned back on the seat, sinking into the leather with a wince. With the door open, the humidity invaded. She glanced at him and took in his ragged exterior. His rich plum polo shirt and khaki pants had been stained with blood and dirt.

After a short silence, he leaned closer. "Hey, what's wrong?"

"Me? You're the one who got cloncked on the head."

"That's not what I meant." His eyes held empathy, a profound unease she found disconcerting. His gaze flickered to her arms and he reached out and clasped her wrist gently. "Tell me those bruises are from the wreck or whether that fucker put those marks on you."

She shivered under his gentle touch as his finger caressed the three bruises forming on her upper arm. "I don't know. It could be either one."

"Shit." His voice went soft and husky. "I'm sorry, Keira."

"About what?"

"That I let him assault you."

"What could you do? You couldn't have stopped it any more than I could. I'm just thankful it didn't go any further."

Zane brushed his fingers over her arm again and sweet, warm trickles of delight worked their way into her loins. She knew in her gut, from the flames in his eyes, that given the chance, Zane would have pulverized Manuel with one slam of his fist. A wholly female response rose inside her at the knowledge. Whether she wanted it or not, her body had gone cavewoman on her at the idea of this man fighting for her. A stirring started low in her belly. Her body responded to his on a needful level she wanted to deny but couldn't. Even hurt this man set her insides on fire with one action, one small look.

Zane nodded. "Yeah, if *El Jaguar* hadn't put a stop to it, it would have gone further."

She trembled a little, despite the heat. "Thank God for him, as weird as that sounds. Do you know who this Jaguar character is? Wasn't he a little harmless for a thug?"

"Harmless, my ass. My guess is that Manuel and Ortega might end up as predator food tonight. I've heard of *El Jaguar*. He's a mortal enemy of Haan, though no one knows why."

After she took another sip of water, she sighed. "Great. Haan and *El Jaguar*. With enemies like them, who needs friends, right?"

She watched his face transform from simmering anger to gentle understanding. Before she could even move, he leaned toward her and turned her face toward his.

"You did good out there, Keira."

Not believing his praise, but liking it all the same, she said, "Thank you. All I did was stand there like a geek."

He grinned and kissed her mouth softly. A quick, sweet touch that sent shivery warmth into her. "No, you were calm and cool. Besides, you layered it on thick and I appreciate that. I think it convinced them you were my fiancée because you acted like you really cared whether they shot my ass off. Your voice was trembling and you were crying. You're a wonderful actress."

The trauma of the last hour left her shaky and off guard. She whispered in a hoarse voice, "I wasn't acting. I did care whether they killed you."

She turned her face away, unwilling to let him see the additional tears threatening her eyes. She drew in a ragged breath.

"Keira." His voice took on a deep, gentle tone. "Thank you for caring."

Embarrassed she'd revealed too much, she didn't speak.

"Look at me." His gentle command made her turn toward him. His face, marred by smudges and a little blood, somehow managed to appear more rugged and handsome. "You're a brave woman. I admire that."

She didn't expect his praise. "Thanks."

This close she could see the fire in his dark eyes, the warmth banked for the moment but threatening something off the charts in the future. Deep inside, she trembled in a brand-new way. This man had her mixed up, her feelings a jumble of misfires and misunderstandings.

Deciding she needed a new approach to keep her sanity, she settled back and reached for her water. "I don't understand *El Jaguar.* He didn't try and hurt either of us. He seemed to be trying to protect us in a weird sort of way."

"Yeah, that has me puzzled, too. It doesn't make a lot of sense."

A few moments later, Haan's limo drove up and the tough-looking driver got out, weapon strapped to his huge chest. Tall, bald-headed and with a colossal handlebar mustache, the new driver looked ready for violence.

His American accent came out clearly. "Mr. Haan sent me. Get your things and supplies and we'll leave."

After they piled into the limo and left Eduardo, she whispered in Zane's ear, "Is Eduardo going to be all right?"

Zane grinned and cracked his knuckles. "Eduardo is always all right."

Something about Eduardo didn't add up and when it was safe to ask she planned to get the scoop. Zane took out the Macon card and scanned the limo. No listening devices registered.

Keira smiled. "*El Jaguar* didn't realize my ring is a fake. So much for financing his little army."

Zane chuckled. "Yeah, he's going to be pissed."

Chapter Six

When Keira awoke from her short little catnap, she felt as if she'd been underwater with no oxygen. She gasped and jerked in semi-fright.

"Whoa, take it easy," Zane's deep voice rumbled. "We're here."

His arm tightened around her and she realized her head was pillowed on Zane's shoulder and he cuddled her close against him. As warm and wonderful as his embrace felt, she pushed away and sat up. A woman could get way too used to being snuggled in his arms. The man ought to come with a warning label marked "Too Hot to Handle".

She didn't have time to blink or take a peek out the windows at their surroundings before the door next to her popped open. Bruiser, as she thought of the limo driver, stood outside waiting for her to exit. She slipped outside into the bright sun. Zane climbed out behind her.

They'd parked in a circular driveway in front of the sprawling two-story home of Ludwig Haan. The long driveway eased away into the jungle behind them. The photograph she'd seen of this house didn't capture the complete essence. The Ludwig compound resembled a luxury cabin gone mad, the mahogany-colored wood blending into the shadowy, fertile danger of the jungle surrounding them. Huge reflective glass windows on all sides seemed to watch them like dark eyes. Despite the modern exterior, the house screamed coldness and efficiency, not the welcoming home of a dear friend.

She followed the limo driver to the door as he dragged her bags up a ramp along the porch steps. Zane followed close behind; he didn't carry any luggage, playing the spoiled rich American to the highest degree.

The huge front door, a conglomeration of modern effectiveness and old-style Spanish Colonial design, swung open on whisper soft hinges.

"Good afternoon." Ludwig Haan smiled and gestured for them to come in. His grin immediately faded as they followed him inside the cool interior and the door slammed behind them. "I was distressed to hear what happened."

As they walked into the expansive two-story foyer, she noticed the jungle motif. Unfortunately the theme seemed faked, much like those overdone showhouses that lacked warmth to go with their manicured ambience. An overall impression of fake animal skins and paintings of animals native to the area ran across her senses before Ludwig turned back to her.

He reached for her hand and brought it to his lips. "My dearest lady, how fortunate you weren't hurt. And I see your beautiful engagement ring was stolen."

She pulled her hand from his slowly. "It's a small matter. Mr. Haan—"

"Ludwig. Please."

She didn't want to call him by his first name. Acknowledging him that way seemed to give him power. "Zane is hurt. Is there anyway to get medical attention at *Rancho La Paz*?"

Zane smiled down at her and pulled her close. He kissed her forehead. "I'm all right, sweetie."

Despite the warmth of his embrace and the riot of feelings dancing through her, she continued. "Please, Ludwig. I'm concerned about his head wound."

Nodding, Haan smiled. "Of course. It was selfish of me not to mention it first." He turned toward the stairs. The palatial center staircase went straight up, then branched into two wings. "I'll call my personal physician right away."

"Thank you," she said with genuine gratefulness.

Ludwig nodded toward the bruiser limo driver and the man started away from them with their luggage. "He's taking it by elevator. Even Douglas doesn't have the muscle to haul two sets of baggage. I'll show you to your room; then if you're hungry, I have a luncheon set for noon."

Food sounded beyond good at this point, but she wanted to make sure Zane hadn't suffered serious injury first. A little surprised that Ludwig would consider showing them their room and not asking a servant, she moved out from under Zane's arm and followed Ludwig. The wiry, tall man proceeded ahead of them.

As they wended down the long hallway to the left, she felt like she'd stepped into a shopping mall. Oddly designed, the area showed a room or two and then a gap which held a long, tall window. Jungle rioted beyond the open area in back. A huge pool, shaped like a kidney, sparkled in the intense sunlight. Lawn chairs sprawled in various areas, as well as a small bar-like vicinity that probably served during a party.

Ludwig opened a door to the right and entered. Her jaw about hit the floor. She'd seen plenty of high-priced hotel rooms on television and in magazines. Even the room at the hotel back in San Cristobal had been extravagant. This room surpassed their lavishness and then some. Zane entered the room last and Douglas brought in the baggage and dumped it near the bed. Ludwig dismissed Douglas and the man left without a word.

Unlike the hokey décor downstairs this room belonged to a harem dream. The huge king-sized bed, definitely the California king Zane referred to, was overlaid by a gauzy orchid purple canopy that halfway enclosed it in privacy. A satiny matching purple fabric covered the bed. Dozens of pillows stacked up against the dark wood, elaborately carved headboard.

"Wow," she said involuntarily. Her heart sped up when Zane threw her a cautionary glance. A rich woman wouldn't be surprised by this room. "I mean, this room is so wonderful. How generous of you, Ludwig."

She strolled toward the large sliding glass doors that opened onto a big balcony that featured two brown wicker lounge chairs and a table. Right now the doors stayed closed and she felt the cooling relief of air conditioning spreading through the room.

"It's wonderful, as always." Zane ambled toward the bed, looking as if he might like to sink down on it and sleep. "I think you've surpassed yourself this time."

Ludwig's smile broadened and he held his hands out. "But of course. For the bride- and groom-to-be I'd do anything." He clapped one hand on Zane's grubby shoulder. "Of course it would be better than a bachelor suite." His gaze traveled to Keira and when his cool eyes caressed her form in that lascivious way, she shuddered. "My dear, I never thought to ask something important. Forgive me. Perhaps you're an old-fashioned woman? Would you prefer your own room until the wedding night?"

Something about the way he looked at her made her skin crawl from head to toe. While earlier she would have jumped at the chance to have a separate room from Zane's, now she didn't. "No." The word came out with force, and she smiled and softened her voice. "No, I'd love to stay here with Zane."

Did she see a small flicker of disappointment in Ludwig's eyes? Before she could be sure he started for the door. "Very well. I'll leave you to rest and refresh while I call the doctor. He should get here in short order." He started to leave but then turned back, his gaze intent on them both. "You said you were attacked by *El Jaguar*?"

"That's what he called himself. You know him?"

Keira waited, breathing on hold, for Ludwig's answer. Ludwig shrugged. "The name is not familiar to me. He must be a petty criminal intent on harassing law-abiding citizens. No matter, he cannot harm you here. This place is as tough to get in as…what do you call it in America? Fort Knox. Anyway, there will be no problems while you are here." He smiled suddenly.

"You know, I think I have just the thing to replace your engagement ring until you are wed."

Startled, she started to speak. "Mr. Haan—I mean Ludwig, that isn't necessary—"

"Of course it is," he said in a clipped tone. "Both of you wait right here. I will be back in a few moments."

With that the man left, closing the door behind him. Zane immediately put his index finger up to his lips in a gesture that asked for quiet. She nodded and went to lock the door while Zane took out his Macon card to check for bugs. To her surprise Zane found no listening devices in the room.

He frowned. "I wonder what kind of ring he wants you to wear?"

She shrugged. "I'm sure it's no big deal."

Zane's frown deepened. "It's a big deal all right. Remember one thing about Haan. Everything he does is calculated. Everything. Never forget he's a dangerous man."

How could she forget when Haan was responsible for her grandfather's suffering? For her suffering? Each time she saw Haan a new fire for revenge built in her gut. It had taken everything inside her not to flinch away from him when he'd lifted her hand to his lips. *Ugh.* She couldn't stand the man.

Before she could speak a knock came on the door. "It's me. Ludwig."

Speak of the devil. She glanced at Zane and he nodded. After she unlocked the door and allowed Haan inside, the man immediately brought a small box out of his front pants pocket.

He handed her the box with a smile and assuming Zane would approve of her wearing the ring. "Here, my dear. I'm sure you'll like it."

With reluctance and a smile painted on her face, she took the box and opened it. She half expected the ring to be ugly to match Ludwig Haan's dank soul.

A huge, muddy stone, almost the color of smoky topaz, shouted from its white velvet prison. In a high setting, the oval, opaque stone seemed obscene. Thought it looked like white gold, it had the patina of something worn many, many years. An antique, perhaps. So what if she'd worn a fake diamond the size of a doorknocker. This ring looked cumbersome and uncomfortable. Down along the sides of the ring, intricate scrollwork formed an antique filigree pattern. She found it as intriguing and flattering as a gumball machine ring.

"It's amazing," she said, her voice coming out in a dry croak.

"I'll say," Zane said as he neared her. "Thank you."

"I thought you would approve." Haan looked small next to Zane's powerful build, but the toughness in his eyes made up for some of that. "It's six carats."

"Son of a bitch." Zane chuckled.

Haan laughed in return, his chortle sounding rusty with disuse. He nodded and then retreated out the door. "Wear it in good health until Zane can purchase another engagement ring."

Real feelings powered up and asked for recognition. She held the box out to Haan. "No, I really can't. I mean, it's only one more day until we're married. There's no reason for me to walk around with your valuable piece of jewelry. I have my wedding ring."

He pushed the box back toward her, a spark in his eyes warning her. "Not at all, my dear. You see, it is said the stone comes from deep in the jungle surrounding the San Cristobal plateau." He shrugged. "I can't vouch for that one hundred percent. In my journeys into the area I never saw anything like it. But who is to say?"

"Your family has been in Puerto Azul for generations?"

Zane's gaze narrowed on her, as if he wanted her to back off but couldn't come out and say it.

"No. We have visited over several decades with each generation, but until I built *Rancho La Paz* we have never lived here." Haan took a deep breath, as if the subject made him emotional. "No matter. I will leave you to rest a little while I contact the doctor."

After he left she locked the door and turned back to Zane. Afraid Haan could be listening at the door, she moved to the middle of the room. Zane followed, curiosity on his features.

She looked down at the open box. "This has got to be the most hideous ring I've ever seen."

He laughed softly, reached for the box and put it on the dresser. "So don't wear it until you go out and expect to meet Haan."

"Yuck," she said again as she gazed at the ring.

Zane's irreverent smile said he enjoyed her discomfort. "Get over it."

To her surprise he moved away a little, just far enough to stretch like a cat. He groaned and pulled the stained polo shirt over his head. "I don't know about you, but I've got to get a shower."

"Shouldn't you wait until the doctor examines you?"

He held the polo shirt and frowned. "Why?"

"What if you pass out in the shower? I mean, you could get dizzy and…"

She faded out as she saw his expression change to a stunning, gut-wrenchingly sexy grin. His expression went with that gorgeous chest. "I'm all right. I don't have a concussion or believe me, I'd know. And I wouldn't take any risks with it." He chucked her under the chin gently with his index finger. "Thanks for worrying, though. It makes me…"

As his statement floated unfinished, his gaze darkened and she saw the danger, and could do nothing to stop it. He edged nearer and she drew in his masculine musk. He dropped the polo on the floor and gripped her shoulders. Her hands landed on that expanse of hair-roughened, muscled flesh. He felt so good, so delicious and sinful she couldn't keep everything female within her responding to his maleness.

His eyes captured hers and she sank into an abyss of heat and need. He came closer, then nearer still, until his lips touched hers with tender reverence. She sighed as a sweet, gentle relief eased from his mouth to hers. He caressed, a gliding meeting that stirred down to her soul. He retreated and desperation raced through his eyes, then blinked out so quickly she couldn't be sure she'd seen it.

He walked away like he didn't have a care in the world, and she couldn't help but watch his back muscles ripple. Her gaze fixated on his wide shoulders and the way his back tapered down to a slim waist and incredible backside. She blinked, wondering if the not-so-fabulous escapade they'd suffered destroyed every last common sense brain cell she possessed. A deep, warm heat penetrated her loins, a pleasant awareness she understood too well.

Arousal with a big capital letter A.

He disappeared into the bathroom and she heard the shower start. He left the door open, like a real lover might, unashamed. As she sank into a chair by the huge sliding glass doors, her imagination kicked in with a vengeance. Why did he keep doing this to her? She resolved to give him a little surprise of his own, to show Zane Spinella he couldn't faze her any longer. She felt dirty and grubby, and at the very least she needed to use the facilities. She needed a hot shower, too, but she'd be damned if she'd step inside that steaming enclosure and join him.

She stripped off her espadrille sandals and walked across the sinfully thick carpet. When she reached the bathroom, she half expected him to be standing there naked and grinning at her in satisfaction over the shock value. She took a deep breath and entered the huge bathroom. The pink and white marbled extravaganza rivaled the bathroom at the hotel. Once she finished in the commode room, she stepped back into the main bathroom and observed the amenities. No expense had been spared in brushed pewter fixtures, a huge whirlpool tub, two sinks, and huge mirror. A vanity with another mirror and chair awaited a princess.

A deep voice issued from the shower. "Come to join me?"

A ripple of heat passed over her. "You wish."

Good, Keira. That sounds lame. Like something from grade school.

He laughed and started singing, this time a Spanish tune with sexual tones. While she didn't know the song, she recognized the intent. Sex simmered in the sultry words, brushed by generous love and devotion. For the first time she looked right at the large shower enclosure. Frosted glass covered her view, thank goodness, but it couldn't disguise the telltale shape of a big, hard-muscled man lathering soap over his body in a shower big enough for four people. Twin shower heads spewed water over his tall figure.

To her mortification, a jolt of unadulterated lust jolted through her, a desire to connect with him on the most physical level possible. Then she stamped down the urge. The wild ride to *Rancho La Paz* and the resulting trauma did weird things to the libido.

She could testify to that fact.

"Ouch!" His guttural curse made her flinch and she stepped up to the shower, reaching for the latch before he said. "Damned sore spot on my head."

Her hand hovered above the latch, then she snatched her fingers back before the damage could be done. "Are you all right?"

Wonderful. Your voice sounds like a strangling chicken. Get a hold of yourself.

"I'm great." His voice held confidence as he continued to sing.

As heat flushed her body, she turned away, her body defiant and needy. Pleading for her to take what she wanted for once without worrying about consequences. "Hurry up. Don't take all the hot water."

She left the bathroom started unpacking and hanging up clothes. She hadn't gotten far when the shower went off. She stiffened as she realized all his clothes lay in his suitcase. Warm, soapy delicious scents floated out of the bathroom along with remaining steam.

For some reason sex seemed forever printed on her mind today, no matter what the situation. Her fingers slipped over satin and she picked up a red, lace-trimmed teddy nestled in her suitcase. She jammed the slinky lingerie into a drawer with a resentful movement and wondered what twisted person at the SIA gave provocative underwear to agents on assignment. She tried to rein in ridiculous emotions. Not the kind that belonged strictly to sex, but those related to a desire for Zane to be well, to regain the strength she remembered when she first saw him. The thought of him anything but potent and capable frightened her on a deep, undefined level. She didn't want to think about it anymore.

Zane appeared wearing a purple towel around his waist. As before in the hotel, the water beaded on his chest and clung to his hair and face. He moved with confidence. Arrogance always pissed her off, but his attitude appeared drawn from pure self-confidence and not an overblown ego. At least he felt well enough he could project that cocky exterior. After retrieving his shaving kit, briefs, and a fresh polo shirt and jeans, he went back to the bathroom without taunting or smiling. Amazing.

Quicker than she expected he left the bathroom shaved and redressed except for shoes. A knock came on the door and Zane went to open it. Haan stood outside the door with a short, rotund Hispanic man with a cheerful smile.

"Zane, this is Dr. Ramirez from San Cristobal," Haan said. "He was in the area and was able to make it here fast."

Zane stepped back and allowed the men to enter. Both the doctor and Haan scanned the room, almost as if they looked for something. She thought it was damned odd response, but decided maybe she'd become paranoid after a trip like this. She brushed off apprehension, glad to see Zane would receive medical attention.

Haan gave that little formal bow. "I'll leave you in the capable hands of the doctor. Come down to lunch when you're ready. I'll be downstairs if you need me."

"That'll be great," Zane said his smile sincere.

Her stomach growled, not quite loud enough for anyone else to hear, but a signal to her that her American stomach on American time wanted lunch.

"*Señor* Spinella, would you please sit on the bed, and I'll do my examination," the man asked Zane.

Zane complied, but when the doctor stopped cold and gazed at her quizzically, she said, "Is there something wrong?"

The round man straightened to his full height, which couldn't be more than five foot three inches, and gave her an imperial look. "I prefer to do examinations with no one else interfering."

She started to object, but Zane spoke up. "It's okay, darling. Why don't you be a good girl and sit out on the balcony while he checks me over?"

Be a good girl? Annoyance turned to full-blown irritation. *Oh yeah, there will be hell to pay for that chauvinistic statement, Mr. Spinella.*

With a glare she turned on her heel. She unlocked and opened the balcony doors and they moved on smooth, well-oiled tracks. Sticky heat walloped her in the face, but she went outside anyway and closed the door. At first she couldn't decide if she liked being on the balcony. Part of her wanted to explore. The vast majesty within a fingertip's distance beckoned in a mysterious way she'd never encountered. While the jungle had given her the shivers earlier, she found a strange draw to it now as the tension eased from her body.

As she'd noted before, the balcony offered two dark wicker lounge chairs and a long table, and she sank onto one of the lounge chairs. She didn't bother to look at the scenery, weariness making her close her eyes. She yawned. Her adventure with *El Jaguar* proved exhausting. Zane's nonchalant attitude about what happened to him disturbed her on a fundamental level. How could any woman endure the thought of her man being in such danger all the time? Then again, how did a woman stop loving a man just because of danger?

Okay, Keira, what was that all about? You're attracted to him and concerned for him as a human being. That's all.

What seemed like eons passed before the balcony door slid open and Zane stepped outside to say, "I'm finished."

She jerked, eyes flying open at the disruption. She felt as if she'd slept for hours, but she knew it couldn't be more than a few minutes.

As she sat up straighter, she asked, "What's the verdict?"

He shrugged. "I'll live. The doctor doesn't think I have a concussion, just as I said. Everything is okay. I might have a bit of a headache for awhile today, but he told me to take some painkillers."

"And call him in the morning?" She stood and followed him into the room.

"That's right."

"I'm glad. I mean, that he says you're all right. You don't need any stitches?"

"Nope. In fact, it got a good washing when I took a shower. Stung like hell, but nixed the germs."

"What's our next move?" she asked as he closed the sliding door.

"Play things easy. Have lunch with Haan, then get married tomorrow afternoon. Should be interesting."

The plush carpet felt decadent under her bare feet, yet it couldn't make her feel secure about the wedding. "You said the wedding would be real."

He nodded. "It will be. I'm sure we'll hear more about it at lunch."

She shook her head and put her hands on her hips. "I don't know, Zane. I mean, we're mucking around with sacred vows here for a mission. Doesn't that seem a little...?"

She didn't know how to say what she meant.

He frowned. "It's a game you've got to be willing to play. We can't afford to lose momentum here." He lowered his voice. "Haan is a ruthless bastard and you know it. We've got to do whatever it takes to outwit him, get *La Pasion*, and get out of here alive."

Defensiveness arose inside her. "There's something about this mission you aren't telling me. Mac said this was the only way to clear my name and my grandfather's. But if I was in on Haan's little plan and if my grandfather was truly the awful man the SIA thinks he is, how could me being here help things? Wouldn't I thwart your plans at every turn? Make things difficult for you?"

He snorted. "Who says you aren't?"

She marched up to him, determined to play his brand of intimidation. She glared up at him. "I see. I'm being a bitch now because I won't agree with you?"

He heaved a sound of derision. "No, but you should know you can trust me by now. What have I done to break that trust?"

She didn't know and didn't want to admit it. Raging doubt continued. "And another thing, the little woman act you want me to play isn't going to wash—"

"Whoa." He put up one hand. "Now wait a minute. I don't know what the hell you're talking about."

A headache started in her temples. "When that doctor came in here and said I should leave the room while he was examining you, you called me a good girl. I'm not any man's good girl."

Exasperation and humor mixed in his expression. "I don't think it hurts anything if Haan and his cronies think you're subservient. Probably make things easier all the way around." He cupped her shoulders and the warmth of his hands on her arms felt protective and sensual. "Haan is a male chauvinist from the word go. He believes most women should be seen and not heard. He won't dictate to another man's wife what she should or shouldn't do, but for himself..." He shrugged. "The man is pretty ruthless with his women." When she didn't answer, he frowned. "Look, can't you let go of this affront for the good of the cause?"

"I'm not anyone's woman." Keira said it softly, but she meant every word. "Just because Haan thinks he can push a woman around, that doesn't mean I'm going to let you treat me like an imbecile."

"Whatever." He stalked toward the door. "I need some fresh air. Come down to lunch when you're ready."

The door slammed when he left the room. She rubbed a hand over her eyes and sighed. Immediate regret wormed into her. Okay, so maybe she overreacted a little, but she didn't trust his motivations one hundred percent. Few people in her life could be trusted, except for her grandfather.

Frustrated, she grabbed a gauzy fern green dress from the closet that would float around her ankles and a pair of flats. When she dug around in the chest of drawers for fresh underwear she looked at the skimpy red items. She would wear the push-up demi-bra and the tiny bikini panties. Wearing something sexy under the dress felt right. With the heat she didn't want to wear nylons, so it was easier to just slip into shoes.

She snatched her makeup bag and retreated to the bathroom. A half hour later she emerged from the bathroom refreshed. There was no sign of Zane. Her heart did a peculiar skip of fright and the room seemed excessively small for her. As her breath quickened she decided maybe a stroll would remove disconnected, free-floating fears.

The hell with staying in this room while Zane did whatever he pleased. What would it hurt to venture out to the pool for a few minutes before heading downstairs? On the way out her gaze caught on the velvet ring box. It wouldn't do for Haan to catch her without the ring, so she slipped it on her finger. The jewelry felt cold and heavy and the stone must weigh a ton because the gargantuan fake diamond she'd worn earlier hadn't felt this burdensome. She expected this ring to slide around on her hand, but it fit pretty well.

She left the room and paused at the doorway, expecting to hear signs of human habitation. Instead the wide hallways echoed with bizarre silence. Almost as if she'd been left alone in this cold place. A shiver coasted along her arms and suddenly she wanted out. Wanted into the sunshine and the relentless heat that baked her earlier.

Hurrying down the wide staircase, she reached the bottom and then wended her way to the left. She should be able to find a back door to this place. When she located a doorway leading into a large solarium, she smiled at her good luck. With a sense for adventure, she strolled into the room. The glass St. Paul's cathedral-like dome roof allowed hot sun to pour over the various lounge chairs and the steaming hot tub in the middle. Hot tub? Who in their right mind would want to hot tub in heat like this?

A vision of Zane, wet and naked, popped into her mind. She visualized him in this hot tub or the one in their room. Her mouth watered. God, thinking about Zane naked could drive any woman with hormones into a critical meltdown. It didn't concern her libido that she didn't like Zane that much.

That's right. I don't like him at all.

Closed French doors at the opposite end opened onto the patio where the huge pool resided. She strode outside and drew in a breath of thick, hot air. Pungent flower scents hit her, as well as an earthy odor she associated with damp soil.

She wandered toward the pool. Sea green tile surrounded the water, adding to the welcoming appeal of shimmering liquid. Maybe she'd take a dip later.

Lounge chairs dotted the perimeter close to the surrounding jungle. Huge fronds reached from the encroaching vegetation, banyan trees strained for the heavens and sunlight.

The canopy echoed with a million sounds, many familiar and some not so familiar. While the rainforest drew close in some areas of this vast building, a small fissure through the foliage gave a breathtaking view she didn't expect.

San Cristobal and surrounding mountains rose high in the distance, ringed by a strange fog. Dozens of huge waterfalls cascaded from the plateau, the rushing, pounding sound of their power almost discernable. Now she understood why Haan had chosen this spot for the pool. He enjoyed the lush beauty, perhaps, as much as the next human. Even if he was a poisonous snake upon this beautiful land.

She glanced at the plateau again and wondered what mysteries lay hidden there. What had Haan found in the jungle when he'd ventured to the plateau?

Again the ring felt heavy, dragging her down. As she brought her left hand up and gazed at the cloudy stone, she experienced a strange stirring inside, an odd desire to move forward, to walk toward the depths of the jungle and step within.

As if two people invaded her body, she felt duel sets of emotions. One part of her rebelled against the ridiculous idea of walking into the unknown and danger she couldn't predict. The other part of Keira demanded she go forth. One foot stepped ahead against her will and she gasped as a sick feeling entered her stomach.

Oh my God. What's happening?

Like a puppet she marched with slow deliberation toward the jungle.

Chapter Seven

Zane entered the bedroom after his quick recon of the house. He'd needed to walk to cool his jets. He couldn't stand to be in the same room with Keira without wanting to rip her clothes off and fuck her into the next century. Yes, he'd been angry, but he'd also wanted her spread out under him with his cock sinking hard and deep to her center. He wanted to feel her pussy clutching around him, milking him dry as she came and came and came.

Face it. The woman makes you hot.

Hornier than a bull elk and perhaps as rampant. When she'd stepped into the bathroom and watched him shower through the opaque glass, he'd almost grown a raging hard-on that begged for a finish. Next time she did that she might get more than she bargained for. He shook his head to clear it. He needed to concentrate on their true mission—getting *La Pasion* away from Haan.

Haan had bodyguards but they stayed out of Zane's way, nodding to him as he passed by and not acting the least concerned. Most of them looked like the limo driver, no-neck assholes with permanent scowls and watchful eyes. They didn't consider him an immediate threat, he knew. And he wasn't. At least not for the moment.

"I'm home, honey," Zane said in a cheerful, mocking voice as he closed the door to the bedroom.

Silence greeted him.

Surprised, he checked the bathroom. No sign of her.

She'd probably gone looking for him, and he didn't want her wandering this house alone. With Haan salivating over her, Zane didn't feel comfortable. He knew the strange ring Haan gave Keira amounted to a come-on. From the bizarre photographs of strange temple glyphs on Haan's den walls, Zane deduced that the man liked kinky sex. Not that Zane cared what Haan put on his walls, but he did care a hell of a lot about how the man looked at Keira.

Suspicion made Zane pause in the middle of the room. Could she be meeting with Haan now to conclude unfinished business? Did she have a relationship with the older man?

Relationship his ass. Haan didn't have relationships, he had dominations. Just ask the man's four—count 'em, four—ex-wives. The first two ended up in asylums for the mentally ill. The third got smart early and left Haan after a week of marriage. The fourth and final match disappeared into the jungle outside the house without a trace ever being found.

A strange apprehension rose up inside Zane. Something was not right.

He hurried downstairs and through the solarium area to the pool. When he stepped out of the house, he gazed into the rainforest with all senses alert. He took a deep breath and let it out, attuning to his surroundings and relaxing.

Huge dragonflies danced among an immense tree as it rose more than twenty stories in the air, the *drop, drop* of water as it fell from the leaves a loud plopping noise. Puffs of mist rose above the San Cristobal Plateau. At the water in the distance a gray tiger heron strode along the bank and a white-faced monkey screeched angrily in the distance. He watched leaf cutter ants scurry across a branch near the ground, intent on their business.

Fear started a slow, insidious ripple through him as he found no sign or sound indicating Keira's whereabouts. "Keira!"

No answer.

He tried several times, calling her name into the wilderness and incurring the wrathful wail of howler monkeys and cackles of birds. He returned to the house and checked all the lower floor rooms.

"Fuck," he said as he hurried to find Haan and get some equipment for search and rescue.

He ran through the lower floor of the house, meeting no one in the desolation of chrome and glass mixed with wood and wicker. When he reached the area outside Haan's den, he forced himself to stop and take a deep breath. He needed to remain calm, even though his heart banged in his chest and adrenaline streaked through him.

Despite his calm, he forgot to knock and walked right into the room. A hand flashed out and grabbed him by the neck, swung him around and slammed him against hard wood.

* * * * *

Keira came out of the fog in her mind astonished, dazed and confused. "Where am I?"

Only incessant jungle noises answered. All around the racket seemed louder, more fearsome than when she'd left the house. She stood not far from the edge of the shimmering lake she'd seen from a distance while at the pool.

Fear snapped inside her like a pistol shot, painful and sharp. She gazed at her surroundings as trepidation snaked through her, a menacing boa constrictor around her lungs.

I can't remember. How did I get here?

Instinct told her to stay silent when she felt like shouting for help. In wonder and fear she took in her surroundings, a perilous mixture of paradise and menace.

The mists she'd seen floating high along San Cristobal Plateau's ridges merged with approaching storm clouds. Sunlight dipped behind the clouds, removing the dazzling, diamond-point glint on the water. From the angle of the sun she could tell she'd been gone from the house for a few hours.

A few hours.

Fear trickled inside her, the insidious, creeping sensation accompanying a good horror flick. Only this time the situation was all too real.

The dark lake stretched in front of her like a mysterious beast, murky and harboring monsters. She'd heard somewhere that Puerto Azul boasted a creature similar to Loch Ness's famous Nessie in Scotland. Cold shivers cascaded over her skin despite the humid heat.

Dragonflies flew like blue and purple airplanes along the water edge. A huge, hairy spider half the size of a dinner plate raced across her path and she gasped and took a step back.

Lovely. A tarantula. The creature disappeared under a clump of gigantic ferns. She recalled reading that some people in South America ate tarantulas and her stomach flipped in revulsion.

New worries arose as she put her hands to her face and felt the big ring. Jumbled thoughts battled for supremacy in her head. Had she suffered a breakdown? How did she get this far from the house? Then she remembered standing at the pool and looking into the ring. Everything within her had demanded she walk away. She couldn't resist the pull. After that her memories stopped. She'd suffered amnesia, and the thought sent cold, hard terror racing through her normally steely calm exterior.

Rustling behind her made her whirl around. Seconds crawled to mind-numbing slowness as she searched the jungle rising up on either side of her on this lonely trail. It couldn't be natural for this trail to be here in the first place; jungle ate up land if the conditions became right. Places such as Angkor Watt in Cambodia had remained obscured by jungle for centuries for this very reason.

When she didn't see an animal ready to pounce, she took a deep, raspy breath of hot, humid air. Her entire body felt as heavy and exhausted as if she'd trekked miles.

God, did I walk miles? Come on, think. Get control. Slow your breathing and think clearly.

How?

How did a person lose a few hours? She turned in a circle, again trying to get her bearings. From this vantage point she figured she'd walked from east to west. The vast plateau rose in

front of her miles away. Turning back to the east, she noticed
something standing on the edge of the rainforest. As she walked
closer she saw a circle of six strange statues shaped like
phalluses. Despite the situation, humor wasn't lost on her. She
took tentative steps toward them, curiosity overrunning fear.

A snake slithered out of the bushes ahead of her. The
yellow and tan animal didn't pay her the least attention, but the
sight of the four-foot-long, thick-bodied creature stopped Keira
cold. She continued drawing in those cleansing breaths, her
heart pattering an erratic beat born from the unknown. She felt
trapped in a dream, a horror movie of her own making. Why
had she come here and how would she get out?

When the snake left, she crossed toward the standing stones
and looked them over. About four feet high, their weathered
faces held engravings she didn't recognize from any previous
archaeological experiences. The hash marks appeared similar to
Viking Runic markings, but she could see enough differences
that she knew they couldn't be related. From the texture and
wear on the stone she guessed this couldn't be a recent
undertaking.

Involving her archaeological mind took away some of the
relentless anxiety dogging her every step. She knelt in front of
the stones and studied the intricate carvings below the hash
marks. The first stone showed a clear sexual act. A woman on
her knees sucking a man's cock. The second stone featured a
woman with her legs around a man while he took her up against
a wall. The third stone showed a man taking a woman from
behind as she stood, hands flat against a wall. The remaining
three stones all showed wild sexual positions that looked almost
impossible.

Erotic carvings. Interesting. She wondered for a few
moments if this could be an elaborate setup by a man like Haan
to show his sexual proclivities. The more she thought about it,
the less likely it seemed. After studying the stones for several
moments, reality came back to bite.

She must find her way back to the house. Common sense kicked in, along with swift internal condemnation. If she left this spot she might wind her way deeper into the jungle. She couldn't be one hundred percent certain how far she'd wandered, and she didn't have a watch on to tell how much time had passed. Maybe, if she stayed put, there would be a chance for rescue.

* * * * *

Zane's air cut off as a hard forearm pressed against his windpipe and forced him back against the den's dark-paneled wall. Haan's bodyguard and limo driver, Douglas glared at Zane, teeth visible as the large man snarled. Zane would give the asshole about five seconds before he'd take him down.

One. Two. Three.

"Release him, Douglas!" Haan's voice held steel certainty.

Douglas immediately freed Zane. Zane couldn't help the involuntary gasp for air as the man's arm left his throat.

Rage boiled inside Zane as he stepped toward the slightly taller, beefier man. "What the fuck was that all about?"

Haan had been sitting behind his big desk, but he now stood, his smile placating as the other two men faced off. "Douglas is a bit impulsive and protective. You know you should knock before you enter my rooms."

Right now Zane didn't give a flyin' fuck. "And I'll tell you very politely that I don't give a shit." Haan and Douglas bristled, but Zane continued. "Keira is missing."

Puzzlement passed over Haan's face. "What?"

"She isn't in the house. I've looked all over."

Haan smiled and Zane wanted to wipe that supercilious expression right off his pansy face and feed it to him. "Calm down. We need to think this through. You're absolutely sure she's not in the house?"

Fuck yes, you moron. He wanted to scream the words but knew it wouldn't be wise.

"Yes. I need your help to find her. If she's wandered off in the jungle..."

He didn't need to finish his sentence; the implication said everything.

Haan didn't look the least concerned, the cold bastard. "I'm sure she's all right wherever she is. But I'll give you the supplies you need. Douglas here can help you look for her."

"No," Zane said with ice-hard determination. "I'll do it alone."

"Alone in the jungle?" Douglas laughed. "You're not too bright are you?"

Zane noted the Special Forces tattoo on one of Douglas's biceps. Internally he allowed a snarl of contempt to roar. Not because he had particular enmity for Special Forces, but he knew the ego this man must possess to have survived the training and to endure this life with Haan. The fact Douglas was in league with Haan proved the guy was an A-number one asshole.

Zane schooled his expression. "I'm experienced in extreme situations."

"I'll just bet you are," Douglas said with contempt.

"Boys." Haan waved his hands like a referee. "Let's not do this. Zane, you need to find your fiancée. I'd go with you, but...well, I have an aversion to going into the jungle nowadays."

Even though Zane didn't want Haan with him, he knew the man harbored knowledge about this jungle Zane couldn't hope to know. "You're familiar with this jungle."

Haan actually paled and shook his head. "Not anymore. I haven't been out there since the last expedition that took so many of my friends. Come. I'll show you the supplies you'll need."

All the way to the basement Zane wondered why the man didn't show at least fake concern about Keira. His inability to express real distress shouldn't have surprised Zane, but he figured a good show would be right up Zane's alley. *Yeah, something is definitely rotten here.*

Haan led Zane to a huge storage closet in the massive basement. The megalomaniac had supplied his downstairs with enough food to feed an army for months. The closet held supplies for a voyage of some size.

Zane rummaged through the assortment of provisions and jammed items into the large camie frame backpack Haan supplied. Soon his backpack was filled with food and water for a couple of days plus a first aid kit and a space-age set of thermal blankets and one large sleeping bag that could hold two people. After tacking on a small lean-to like tent, the pack weighed a ton. Zane didn't give a shit. He could handle it.

He needed one other thing, and he couldn't afford to be shy about asking.

"Do you have a weapon I can take with me?" Zane asked. "Preferably a semiautomatic or automatic weapon. Small. Light."

Haan's eyes widened and a small smile curved his thin mouth. "You guess correctly. I have just the thing." Haan retreated to another closet. He opened the big double doors. A blank wall greeted them. He pressed the single button on the door jamb and the blank wall slid up into the ceiling.

"Impressive," Zane said as an array of weapons came into view.

Haan stepped back and gestured toward the cache of firepower. "They're yours. Whatever you may require."

Zane immediately spotted an M-4 and decided it would do. He snatched it off the rack and then noted another drawer below. "Ammunition?"

"Take as much as you think you'll need."

Stepping away to another set of drawers, Haan produced a map and small GPS device. "You'll need this to know where you're going."

Haan's expression said he doubted Zane's abilities, but Zane didn't plan on enlightening the man just how capable he could be. Zane took the map and GPS. He strapped the weapon to the side of the pack with the compression holder.

Fueled by urgency, Zane hauled ass upstairs with the backpack, grim-faced and ready to face the great outdoors. He changed into a short-sleeved khaki camp shirt, sturdy jeans, thick socks, and hiking boots. After he jammed an old boonie hat on his head, he slathered on his SIA high-power sunscreen and bug repellant. To do anything less would be foolhardy in this country. He rolled up some old sweats and stuffed them into the pack. He charged down the stairs aware that although he left in daylight, they wouldn't be able to get back before the storm broke.

Haan waited for him outside by the pool. The man's cold eyes held little sympathy or concern, and it made Zane angry enough to chew through leather.

Ease off, Spinella. There isn't a damn thing more important right now than finding Keira fast.

Zane realized he didn't have a clue which direction to start looking. Worry sliced his gut. *If I don't get to her soon who knows what will happen to her.* His insides twisted thinking about the numerous ways she could die in the hostile environment.

"You're wondering which way to go," Haan said. "I can see it on your face. I'd take the west border. I don't have any fences there because the land is considered protected. So if she went that way, she'd be in the worst danger. At least my property line in front keeps out most of the more aggressive creatures."

Reluctant gratitude made Zane say, "Thank you."

"Storm clouds are coming," Haan said as he looked toward the horizon and the darkening shape of the plateau. "You must find her before nightfall."

Night would bring out the predators. The thought sat in the air between them, unspoken yet understood.

Zane nodded without a word and started into the rainforest.

* * * * *

Keira resisted two things as she sat on a rock near the water's edge. First, a desire to take a dip in the deep blue water. Second, a need to keep wandering, to lose herself in the majesty of this place and discover a new wonder around every corner. She stayed put, resisting the nagging pull that landed her in this hairy predicament in the first place. She must be ten times a fool to consider wandering away from the house.

"And on the first day I get to the place." She spat the words in self-recrimination, uttering a curse she almost never used. Who cared? The jungle didn't. So she said it again. "You are damned stupid, you know that?"

More than being an idiot, she must be unbalanced. It made no psychological sense that she couldn't remember how she'd arrived here. She looked down at the ring Haan had given her. When she glanced into the depths of the stone, she felt the world revolve on its axis. Tingling raced through her hand and she felt so lightheaded she had to grasp the side of the rock to keep from falling off. Panic threatened. Could she be physically ill and this is why she experienced these strange feelings?

Her world went mad, turning without allowing her to jump off the merry-go-round. Dizziness assaulted her senses, and she put her other hand over the ring in defense. Tears of angry frustration stung her eyes. She hated feeling helpless.

"Damn it, I'm not helpless."

She stood, staggered, then righted herself. She tried to take a step, then one, then two.

Thunder rumbled in the distance and she looked toward the mountains. Above the plateau clouds climbed high, their puffy heads reaching thousands of feet into the sky to form thunderheads. She moved back toward the lake slowly, wondering where she might find shelter. She didn't relish the idea of going into the jungle on either side of the clearing. Only

God knew what would fall out of the trees if the rain came. Not that the huge trees climbing stories into the sky would keep her dry. No, when the storm came she'd get drenched no matter what she did.

She walked back to the rock, convinced staying put would bring Zane to her aid. Despite the disagreement they'd had, she didn't believe he would leave her out here to die. But not knowing how far she'd wandered or how long it would take for him to locate her, relying on her own strength would have to do. Although nagging fear always rested in the back of her mind, she'd never been one to give up. No, surrendering was not an option and neither was dying.

Again the ring called, this time with a powerful pull that drew her eyes down to her hands. Down, down. Unmercifully, irrevocably. She would obey. Her gaze locked on the gloomy stone and her legs lost all power. She sagged, stumbled, tried to stay upright. She tripped on a stone, gasped, and cried out as she flailed her arms for balance. Instead she went straight into the water with a shriek of indignation. Water closed over her head.

A thousand images of what could be in the water threatened to undermine her calm. While she didn't know what parasites or insects or deadly water snakes existed in this water, the mere thought assured quick raging anger as she held her breath. No, damn it. She wouldn't, couldn't die like this. She would show Haan and people like Zane Spinella that she could survive. Kicking, she forced her way through the water, her eyes stinging, her lungs burning for air. As she broke the surface she gasped. She kicked again, bringing herself closer to the bank. She struggled, never a fantastic swimmer to begin with, to reach the edge of the lake. Finally she climbed out and crawled away from the edge.

As she sat there shivering, a new threat emerged, this one from the menacing clouds overhead. Lightning crackled. While she didn't fear storms extraordinarily, she knew standing near a large body of water while electricity flickered overhead didn't qualify as intelligent. She moved away from the lake, her body dripping with water and beginning to turn cold even with the heat. Standing under an individual tree would be foolish, too, so she took the plunge and moved into the jungle near the standing stones to wait. No sooner had she stepped into the thick greenery than the rain came down. Torrents pounded the canopy overhead. She braced her feet, unsure what would come next, but certain it wouldn't be pleasant.

Lightning struck overhead with a vicious reverberation as rain poured down. Like a bucket of water dumped over her head, the additional moisture flooded Keira with icicle intensity. Pinpricks hit her flesh and she shuddered. In the back of her mind primitive uncertainties arose. What would fall out of the sky next?

She heard a funny rustling sound behind her and whirled around in surprise and fright, a gasp leaving her throat.

A man stood near the clearing between the jungle and the path. He wore a torn, dirty khaki shirt. His pants, an olive drab green, were so filthy they looked as if they could walk on their own. His storm-dark eyes went cold. On his head sat a green hat with a wide brim. His thin, cadaverous face held a sneer, his eyes contemptuous. A wild thought ran through her head because of his sudden appearance. Maybe he was a corpse, a ghost from Haan's doomed expedition.

As he walked toward her, she flinched. What did he plan to do? Did he know the way out of here, and if he did, would he tell her? Primitive fear stiffened her muscles as she readied for any outcome.

When he came closer she put her hand out. "Stop right there. Who are you?"

She didn't dare edge into the thick brush any further. She spied a long, thick stick about two feet long near her feet. *I've got to take the chance. It may be the only one I have.* Squatting down and keeping her gaze pinned first on the man, she picked up the stick.

As the man continued to move closer, her mind spun frantically for a solution. "Stay back! Don't come any closer."

A moment later a snarl came from behind her and she stiffened in absolute horror. It sounded like a big cat. A very big feline with hungry intentions. All of today's challenges ran through her mind, and incredulously she wondered what she'd done in life to deserve one preposterous adventure after another. Did the gods inhabiting this archaic forest decide she should be punished for venturing into sanctified space? Whatever the reasons, she must take action now before it was too late. She couldn't run or the cat might attack. She could maybe outrun the man, but it was doubtful she could escape the animal.

Okay, Keira, how do you plan to get out of this one?

Chapter Eight

Adrenaline zipped up Keira's spine as she decided the cat posed a bigger threat than the man. Tightening her grip on the stick, she eased to the side, turning so she could see both problems at once. Any second she expected teeth and claws to slash into her body.

The animal stalked her, the long, lean body belonging to a jaguar. The animal's attention switched to the man. He'd stopped about twenty yards away. He no longer looked aggressive, his stance frozen and his eyes wide as he stared at the cat. The story of the werejaguar came to her mind.

"Step back," she said to the man, hoping her voice didn't incite the feline's attack. "It's the werejaguar."

A shot rang out.

She started, her heart jumping into her throat. *What now?*

The sleek cat leapt away, diving into the thick brush and disappearing. Her heart pounded as one threat left. When she glanced over at the man he, too, sprinted out of sight.

"Keira!"

Zane's voice, edged with desperate worry, filled her with relief. Body still poised for action, she held the stick out in front of her as a weapon. Maybe she'd imagined Zane's voice, maybe this whole damn thing was a dream and she'd wake up—

Oh please, please let me wake up.

"Keira!"

"Zane?" Her voice croaked. She cleared her throat and tried again, hoping against hope. "Zane!"

A crashing in the bushes ahead of her made her stiffen, ready for attack from the unknown. As Zane appeared, all the fight drained from her. A hat and poncho sheltered him from some of the rain. He pointed a vicious-looking automatic weapon at the ground. Three impressions hit her at once.

He looked pissed.

He looked worried as hell.

He looked so good she wanted to run to into his arms. Instead she couldn't move, her body frozen with shock.

Over the pounding rainfall and intermittent thunder, he said, "Keira, put down the stick. It's all right now."

Angry tears rose in her eyes and she threw down the stick. She didn't know what to say, what explanation to give for the stupidity that led her into the jungle in the first place. She hated that he had to rescue her, yet relief at seeing him made her knees quaver with sudden weakness. He walked toward her with deliberation, each quick step made as if he feared she would run.

When he reached her, he slung the automatic weapon over his shoulder and cupped her face with both hands. Eyes narrowed, he searched her face. "Are you hurt?"

His voice sounded hoarse and his dark eyes held deep concern, though the racket from the storm made it a little hard to hear.

"No-no, I..." Her legs trembled with adrenaline letdown. "Zane, I'm sorry—I don't know..."

"Shhh." He pressed a quick kiss to her forehead. She didn't expect what he did next. He slipped one arm around her and brought her up against his chest, his grip tight. "Damn it, Keira, you scared the hell out of me."

She drew warmth and comfort from his big body, a momentary respite as cold rivulets ran down her face. Burrowing her face into his shoulder, she wrapped her arms around his neck and held on for dear life. All too soon, he drew back and peered into her eyes. He slipped his weapon off his shoulder and laid it on the ground, then pulled off his hat and poncho.

"What are you doing?" she asked.

"Put these on."

"I'm already wet."

"You're shaking like crazy. This will help."

"But what about you?"

"I've been in worse, believe me."

Deciding now was not the time to argue, she slipped on the extra clothing and absorbed the wonderful body heat remaining within the hat and poncho. "God, that feels better."

He shouldered his weapon. "Come on. This storm doesn't look like the type that's going to give up soon and we need shelter. We're not going to make it back before nightfall."

"Where are we going to get shelter around here?"

"My backpack is on the trail. It has a makeshift tent we can put up and get out of this mess."

Disjointed words popped out of her mouth. "Something really strange is happening to me. I can't explain it."

"Explanations can wait. I'm just glad I found you before nightfall."

He started back toward the trail and located his backpack. When they reached the standing stones, he said, "What the hell are these?"

"Primitive standing stones. I've been studying them since I arrived here."

His quizzical gaze said he meant to ask serious questions about how she got here, but not before they put up shelter. "We'll put the tent between the standing stones."

They made quick work of erecting the tent. Heavy cloud cover kept the area gloomy and it wouldn't be long before night closed in.

"Hurry, get in," Zane said as they crawled inside the shelter and zipped up the opening.

Inside the interior they could barely stand and sitting or crawling made a more viable option. They had just enough room to put their arms out on either side, or to lie flat and stretch out. Another plus was the waterproof flooring protecting them against the damp earth and insects. Ignoring the cramped quarters, she enjoyed having Zane near and shelter against the rain. She quivered; the poncho couldn't stop uncontrollable shivering.

"I brought sweats." He rummaged through the big backpack, and she realized the weight of it must have been a significant burden on him. "You'd better get out of those clothes and into the sleeping bag to warm up."

"Undress?" She heard herself ask, but she felt detached from her body, as if she wasn't talking.

He snatched the cap off her head and tossed it aside. "I'll roll out the bag. You need to change clothing and then get inside." When she hesitated, he frowned. "I'm going outside while you undress, so you don't need to worry about your modesty."

She almost laughed, relief at her new situation making her giddy. She drew off the poncho and placed it near the hat. "No—I mean, you can just turn around. Don't go out in that weather again."

Reaching for the poncho, he drew it over his head. "I'm going outside to make sure that man isn't around."

"What about the jaguar?"

"I doubt it'll be back."

After smashing the hat onto his head, he unzipped the tent and went out. Her numbed mind didn't allow her to do a thing at first. Then she realized he'd be back soon and if she didn't hurry he'd catch her half dressed. Her underwear, damp and clammy, would have to go. Shuddering as her naked skin was exposed, she removed her flats, then slipped the dress over her head. After removing her bra, she wriggled into the huge sweat suit. The navy fleece-lined material felt wonderful. By the time she'd burrowed into the sleeping bag, the shock of adventure started to wear off. Humiliation returned. She sighed, closed her eyes and tried to relax. A difficult thing to do when the world outside remained a dangerous place. When the zipper opened on the tent, she instinctively reached for the heavy club-like flashlight resting next to her.

Zane appeared at the opening and she let out a pent-up breath. "You scared me."

Crouched in the opening, automatic weapon slung over his shoulder, he looked like a ready-to-kick-ass soldier. His gaze held hers, a blazing intensity burning inside them that suspended her breath. With water running down his neck and a grim expression tightening his lips, he represented hard, uncompromising male. The sight of him with lethal firepower gave her a feral, feminine thrill that pulsed through her stomach in an entirely sexual response. *You're losing it.* Yes, she must be ready for the loony bin if the sight of a man packing a weapon could turn her on in this situation.

"Sorry, I should have called out." He zipped the tent against the rain. He put the automatic weapon aside and started taking off the hat and poncho. "No sign of the man. I don't think he'll be back."

"How can you be sure?"

"I can't." Clipped, his response said anger coursed through him. He patted the weapon. "This will go a long way to keeping us safe."

When she didn't answer he leaned over her and cupped her face. "Shit, you're cold as ice." He looked deep into her eyes. "You're not getting hypothermia, are you?"

She shook her head. "I don't think so."

"What's your name and where are you?"

She smiled, understanding why he asked the questions. "My name is Keira Jessop and I'm in some godforsaken jungle in Puerto Azul."

"Good."

With a nonchalance she found disconcerting, he removed his boots and socks quickly, then stripped off his shirt. He situated the wet clothing in one corner of the tent so it might have a chance to dry. She should have been immune to the sight of his broad, muscular chest and powerful arms, but she wasn't. He'd unbuckled his belt and started working on the zipper before she could think of a thing to say.

Finally she found the words. "Um...what are you doing? There isn't another set of clothes, right?"

"Nope." When he caught her staring at him, a tentative smile slipped over his lips. "You've got two choices right now. You can either watch or close your eyes, but I'm getting naked and into that sleeping bag with you right now. I'm freezing my ass off."

"Naked?"

"Naked."

She closed her eyes as he started to work his way out of his jeans. This man was going to slip into the sleeping bag with her in the buff. Nude. Without apparel. Oh God. She could protest, but how could she deny him the same warmth she sought in the sleeping bag?

"There's another sleeping bag, isn't there?" She almost groaned at her own lame plea.

"No."

She felt the zipper go down on the sleeping bag and she tightened up. Within a heartbeat he slid into the bag and closed it. The sound of the zipper going up made her muscles constrict even more.

"Come on, I'm not going to bite. You can open your eyes now."

All the good bits would be covered. She'd just have to watch where her hands went. Of course, as soon as Keira shifted, her hand brushed against his long, hard, naked thigh. With a gasp, she jerked her hand back.

His laugh came out as a soft rumble, and he squeezed her arm gently. "Easy. You're as skittish as a horse."

Tears wetted her eyes. Her mind whirling with everything that had happened, she said, "Wouldn't you be if a naked man had just slipped into your sleeping bag?"

He laughed again, this time harder. "Uh, yeah. But you can be damned sure a naked man is never getting into a sleeping bag with me."

Cringing when she realized what she'd said, she sighed and opened her eyes. The flashlight offered a little illumination. She turned her head to look at him. Gentle amusement in his eyes and on his face removed the ire that started to bubble up inside her at his teasing. Luckily the sleeping bag was long enough to come up over his shoulders. He turned toward her and propped up on one elbow so he could look down at her.

He must have seen her struggle to hold back tears, for his face grew serious and he reached out to brush his fingers over her cheek in a comforting gesture. "Hey, it's okay. You're safe now. I'm even going to give you time before I ask you what the hell got into you wandering out here. And don't tell me you weren't lost."

She heard the edge in his voice and recognized the anger behind it. "No, I want to tell you now. I was lost, but I...I don't know how I got here."

Incredulousness narrowed his eyes as he frowned. "What?"

She shrugged. "I don't know." All her defenses seemed to waver under the weight of what happened, but she abhorred showing weakness. She sniffed and forced her tears to dry up. She expected him to look at her like she'd lost every marble. "I went out to the pool and happened to look into this ugly ring and all of a sudden I felt dizzy and then this incredible pull to walk toward the jungle. I couldn't stop myself. I don't remember a thing until I got here."

His brow creased in concentration. "You mean you had amnesia from the time you looked into the ring until you arrived in this spot?"

"Essentially, yes." She sighed. "Look, I know how crazy this sounds, but that's what happened. When I got here I wasn't sure how far I'd walked, but I could tell by the sun that it had been a long time."

He looked at the big watch on his wrist. "I'll say. Try four hours."

She swallowed hard as reality punched hard in the gut. "That's even longer than I thought. How far did I walk?"

"Not as far as you would think. About seven miles."

She gave a half-hearted laugh. "In sandals. No wonder my feet ache. But…but that still doesn't make sense. I could have walked more than seven miles in four hours."

He shook his head. "Not necessarily. Think about where you are. You're in a thick jungle and wearing unsuitable clothing and shoes. You didn't have a machete to clear the way and the path from the house doesn't go in a straight line. It's not like you had a straight shot and no impediments. By the way, I crossed a swollen creek across a log on the way here. Unless you waded into the water, you had to cross that log. And it's a few feet high above the water."

"A few feet?"

"Try six feet high. The creek is probably around four feet deep. More a river than a creek."

Trembling started in her stomach, a weird nervousness that she couldn't shake. What could she say? Tell him again she couldn't remember crossing any log over a stream?

Instead she asked, "Then the path at *Rancho La Paz* points to here eventually?"

"Yes and no. Some of the trail disappears into the undergrowth so no one could follow it directly to here without getting lost. *Unless* they already knew the way here."

Oh, so that's how it was. He thinks I must know the way.

She chuckled again, amazed at the incredible ridiculousness of her tale. Of course no sane person would believe her.

Grim and tight-lipped, he stared. She saw disbelief warring with another unknown emotion on his face. "Forgive me if I don't think this is funny, Keira. You left without saying a word to anyone where you were going—"

"What?" Anger erupted. "I just told you, I didn't leave because I wanted to. I was drawn here. I don't even remember the walk. It was like I was a zombie."

If she expected understanding, she didn't get it. His expression turned grimmer. "Excuse me if I have a difficult time believing you. It sounds like some ridiculous crap made up in desperation because you came out here for another reason you don't want known."

Simmering like a ready to boil over pot, she swallowed hard and tried to keep from yelling. She never screamed, but this man tempted her beyond reason. "Okay, why do you think I came out here? What person in their right mind would tramp out here in sandals and a dress and without supplies and protection? I don't know this jungle and from everything I've heard it's a dangerous place. I've already seen creatures I don't want to meet again in a million years. Including the jaguar and that weird man."

His frown eased a little. "I saw the jaguar. Damn it, Keira, you could have been killed."

The hoarse note in his deep voice sounded scared. She considered the possibility for a moment and then brushed it aside. This man would never worry about her; she was a liability, along for the window dressing and to play a part in a precarious game.

He sighed. "So you say you looked into this ring and it enticed you for no reason to go into the jungle. Why?"

"If I knew, don't you think I'd tell you?"

Skepticism drew tough lines into his face. His dark hair, still wet from the storm, curled and waved around his head in a tantalizing, sexy flow that short-circuited her anger with him for a moment. His eyes, dark and intense, held mysteries she couldn't phantom and yet wanted to know.

He shook his head. "None of this makes sense. You're saying something paranormal happened to you."

Well, there. He'd said it. The one thing she didn't want to think about and hadn't considered a possibility in her life until now. "Maybe. I don't know."

He scowled. "Come on, you can't believe that. You're a scientist."

What could she say? "You pegged that right. I shouldn't believe this. But I can't pretend it didn't happen to me."

"You're a damned lucky woman. Anything could have happened in those miles you walked. Spiders, deadly snakes, rebels."

She didn't know what to say. Yes, luck followed her in this case, but it still made no sense. "That doesn't explain how I got here or why this…" She didn't dare gaze at the ring. Instead she slipped it off her finger and laid it aside. "There. No chance of me looking into this thing again and disappearing into the wilderness. I don't want to wear it."

"You have to wear it. Think about it. A gift from a very wealthy, powerful, dangerous man."

His bossy tone ticked her off and she struggled with a desire to tell him where to go once and for all. Then she saw the logic behind his insistence. She shouldn't defy Haan, not knowing what she did about the man…the horror he could inflict. A shuddering breath went through her and she closed her eyes. Grandfather had found out the hard way.

"Still cold?" Gentleness laced his tone, a complete difference from a moment ago.

"No. I-I was just thinking about what Haan might do if I defy him."

"Let's do everything we can to keep on his good side until we find *La Pasion*. Keira, you know you can trust me. If something else is going on here you think you can't tell me, I need to know before this gets any worse."

Her eyes snapped open and met his probing gaze. God, the man had such deep eyes, so depthless and intriguing. Since she'd met him she wanted to know what really resided in his thoughts and his soul. His heart.

No, she couldn't invade his secrets. That would mean intimacy, desire, an understanding she could never have with this man.

Still, she couldn't look away, a woman caught in a snake's mesmerism. "How can I trust you? You think I'm up to something illegal and have made no compunction about telling me so. Explain to me how that's supposed to engender a desire to open up to you? Would you trust a woman you don't know well with your secrets?"

She had him there. Seeing the change, the semi-resignation on his face almost gave her relief.

"All right," he said. "What do you want to know about me? Ask me anything."

Blindsided by the request, she didn't speak. *What do I want to know about him? Do I even care?*

"Start from the beginning," she said after a long pause.

His silence stretched longer and Keira thought maybe he'd change his mind and keep clammed up. Instead he nodded. "We've got nothing else better to do. This rain isn't letting up soon. And we're not trekking back at night."

She hadn't thought about that for a few minutes; perhaps she'd denied that truth. She would have to lie in this tent, with Zane stark naked and only inches away.

"Go on," she said.

He rolled onto his back, sparing her the penetrating gaze. "You already know I'm thirty-three and a career agent with the SIA. Vital stats, I have black hair and black eyes. I'm six-feet-four inches. I work out, ski, play tennis, and I'm an excellent marksman."

"Okay, but that's not personal enough."

He gave his trademark male grunt. "Nope. Not until you tell me something about yourself."

Oh no. No. She didn't want to tell him a damned thing. But if she wanted to understand who she dealt with, she'd have to give a little. "I'm five-feet-six inches tall and have brown eyes and light brown hair. I'm a native of San Francisco and live there part of the year. The rest of the year I live in London."

"That's all stuff I know. Give me more."

"Your turn."

He scrubbed one hand over the growing five o'clock shadow on his chin. The shadow on his skin intrigued her. If she didn't watch it she would be studying his every movement instead of listening to what he said.

"I like fine gourmet food, country and heavy metal music. My favorite reading material is horror novels. I was born in the Napa Valley of California and currently live in Denver, Colorado."

When he paused for breath she took in his rundown and found some of the stats surprising. "That's all rather impressive. There aren't too many people I know that like country music *and* heavy metal."

He flashed her one grin before he looked at the tent ceiling again. "Gee, and here I thought you were talking about my degrees. Your turn."

She shifted in the sleeping bag, feeling a little less intimidated by his presence, but not much. "I love jeans, T-shirts, and sweaters. Dressing up makes me a little nervous."

He laughed softly. "Oh, yeah? Could have fooled me with the way you looked the other night at the restaurant."

Her breath hitched in her throat. "The way I looked?"

"Like a damned goddess sent to torment me." His voice went a little rough, a husky nuance he couldn't hold back.

What could she say to that? Somehow Keira found her voice as heat filled her face. "That wasn't my intention." She moved on before he could say more. "Tell me something more personal about you."

He turned his head and pinned her with those obsidian eyes. "Such as?"

"About your family."

"I've got a great set of parents. Dad and his two brothers own Spinella Wineries in Napa Valley. I have two younger siblings, Mira and Trevor, and they both work in family business."

"Now that's interesting. Didn't your father want you to work in the family business?"

"He did, but when I told him I wanted to go into some form of criminal justice instead, he gave me his full support. My mother supported my decision, too."

Sharp envy filled her. "I wish I could say the same about my parents."

Zane shifted again, turning onto his right side. *Oh great. Now his chest is staring me in the face again.* Despite everything she itched to touch him, learn the contours of his body the way she had in the stairwell at the restaurant last night. She could lose herself in his body and forget being in Puerto Azul in the middle of a perilous jungle.

"They didn't want you to be an archaeologist?" he asked.

She gave a soft snort. "Mom was...is a little old-fashioned. She thinks women should stay home and take care of babies."

One of his eyebrows twitched up. "What about your dad?"

"He's about the same, I'm afraid."

One corner of his sinful mouth turned up. "Why doesn't it surprise me that you did what you wanted?"

She tossed a critical glance his way. "At a young age I realized if I didn't follow my heart, I was doomed to failure."

"It's unusual that at a young age you realized that."

She smiled, pithy words coming to her lips easily. "I'm unusual."

His noncommittal grunt said everything. He agreed with her, all right. She didn't know whether to like or dislike his agreement.

"I had my grandfather's approval." She closed her eyes again, not wanting to get into her family's long history. "He encouraged me, no matter what."

"You have any other family?"

"My parents adopted three children after me when they discovered they couldn't have any more." She shrugged. "As a teen I was...I felt extreme jealousy that their attention transferred to the others. They sort of forgot me." For a strange reason she couldn't understand, tears welled in her eyes. "Catrina is twenty-eight, Anita twenty-five. They just adopted Albert ten years ago. He's fifteen."

"They wanted a big family," he said softly.

"Yes." She swallowed hard as the lump in her throat threatened to strangle her. "My relationship with my parents is complicated."

"I sense enough angst to fill a gymnasium."

"That's about the size of it."

She saw new understanding and sympathy enter his gaze as he looked at her. "If your parents were set against you being an archaeologist, how did you manage it?"

"I inherited my father's stubbornness I guess. I was always trying to prove them wrong. There was another influence in my life that helped. Mrs. Annie Bruswick."

She paused, the lump in her throat growing tighter by the minute. She didn't understand why talking about her family right now made her weepy, but the desire to burst out crying became almost overwhelming.

Zane reached out and brushed his finger over her arm, a small gesture that spoke volumes. Almost as if he wanted to give her comfort and yet didn't know how to say it. She absorbed that impression, drinking in the joy his touch brought.

"Who is Annie Bruswick?"

"An older black woman who was my second grade teacher. She got around my low self-esteem and helped me to see I could do anything I wanted." She tucked her hair behind her ears. "In some ways she was more a parent to me than my own mother. Annie loved children and it showed. All the kids in class responded to her. She was such a dignified but loving person. She died five years ago."

When she turned her head to glance at him again, genuine concern covered his face, a compassion she hadn't expected. "I'm sorry. You must miss her."

Keira nodded. "I do. She was a wonderful woman." His surprising openness and gentleness pushed her to ask, "Was there someone special that influenced you?"

"Yeah. My father and my uncles Frank and Joshua. They're great guys. I learned a ton from all three of them growing up." When he smiled she saw the warmth glowing deep in his eyes for his relatives. "My work has been demanding the last few years so I don't see them as much as I'd like. I have Christmas off this year, as long as you and I can crack this mission."

Deep in her heart she more than envied him that familial feeling, the genuine love Keira felt she missed with her mother, father and adopted siblings.

Silence came down over the tent, punctuated by the relentless rain. She wished for sleep to take her away from the continual hum of awareness she felt as he lay so close.

Her gaze caught on the swirling hairs on his chest and the taut curves of his pecs. God, no man could look this gorgeous and be real. Maybe she'd tramped into the jungle, been bitten by a snake or horrible insect and now she lay in a stupor daydreaming about being with Zane. Nothing else explained this wild situation.

She had to talk before the silence grew to epic proportions. "Enough of this maudlin family stuff. Tell me more about how we're going to get *La Pasion*."

"Very carefully."

"How are we going to search Haan's estate?"

"By slight of hand. We have free run of the place on our wedding night. Once we're married I plan to take full advantage of it. Haan said we could use any room in the house. So if we have to make out like we're fucking in every room as sort of a kinky lovefest, that's what we'll do." He snapped his fingers. "Damn, that's good. I like that idea."

His blunt description and enthusiasm for the plan caught her off guard. Zane cracked a cocky smile. Sexual interest burned in his eyes for a flash fire second. She saw it, felt it cascade through her breasts, her stomach, her feminine secrets.

"That's your plan?" she asked, her voice cracking a little.

His sinful grin faded slightly. "You got any better ideas?"

"No, but you think telling him you want to have sex in all his rooms is going to work?"

His grin widened, this time more self-assurance than sexual. "Oh yeah. In case you didn't know, Haan is into kink. He's into bondage and his basement has a bondage table. Haan isn't into consensual sexual adventures, but the type where one person in the partnership isn't willing."

She cringed inwardly, her suspicions about Haan roaring up and slapping her in the face. "You're not thinking we'd go into his basement to—" She cut herself off as Zane nodded and a wider smile curved his lips. "You are."

"Don't worry." Zane's grin appeared unapologetic. "You're a good actress, aren't you?"

Heat warmed her face as she remembered the kisses and the dancing she'd shared with him. "I'm not that confident about my acting abilities. What's that have to do with anything?"

"There are probably cameras in several places in the house. I checked our room for cameras, too, and didn't find any, but we have to assume I'll be able to find other devices in the house while we're searching."

She frowned, determined to clarify. "How much acting are we talking about here?"

"Enough to convince Haan we're going at it hot and heavy."

"But that's..." She could hardly get the words out as the implication hit her. "We'll have to..."

"Spit it out, honey," he said softly.

Damn him.

"If there are cameras we'd have to take off our clothes." Building momentum on her objections she said, "Mac Tudor and the SIA couldn't have authorized it."

She half expected him to say the SIA had sanctioned disrobing and getting down and dirty to find *La Pasion*

Instead, Zane laughed. "Of course not. All we have to do is fake some orgasms so they can hear and see what we're doing if we find a room that has these devices in them. The rooms that don't have the devices, we'll be able to check them without any worry about being detected."

She slanted a critical glance his way. "Right."

He heard her skepticism and reveled in the way he'd made her squirm. This minute she appeared ready to hit him over the head, so he'd better change the subject. Being in this sleeping bag, naked, warmed him in more ways than one. Whenever and wherever her gaze touched him, he believed he saw a need for more connection. Hurt tightened her voice earlier and made him long to remove those sorrowful feelings, no matter where they originated.

Damn it, Zane, don't get hooked. The woman could be an A-number one manipulator. Allowing her to bite your Johnson isn't going to finish this mission with full-fledged success. Keep cynical, keep cool.

Deciding to change the subject yet again, he said, "You still believe you were led here by that ring?"

"Yes." Rock-hard conviction in her voice said she did believe it. "I don't understand it any better than you do, and frankly it scares me to death."

Internal struggle flickered over her smooth features. He wanted to plunge his fingers into her hair and draw her close, hold her near to keep all the demons away. Her lower lip trembled a little and it about did him in. *Don't cry, Keira.*

"Look, I realize you don't believe me," she said when he didn't comment. "But think about this. How would you feel if you woke up someplace and didn't know how you got there?"

"I'm sure, if it really happened, I'd be confused."

Her eyes lightened, as if happy he now understood. He didn't.

"Then you do understand?" she asked.

"I don't believe what you said about the amnesia. You can't expect any reasonable person to believe that unless you've had a psychotic break or maybe a head injury." Worry spiraled into his gut, sudden and repentant. "Damn it, Keira, did you hit your head during the limo accident and not tell me?"

Her gaze widened a little. "No." She flapped one hand in dismissal. "This isn't a brain injury. It's something bizarre. Something I can't explain."

The scientist in her quavered, he could tell. "You encounter these bizarre incidents very often?"

This time she wrinkled her nose. "No. Not until today."

He digested everything that happened today. When he looked back at her, she yawned. "It's getting late. If you want to sleep, go ahead. We have a walk ahead of us tomorrow."

She stared into space for awhile. "What I really wish is that I had a camera so I could take pictures of the circle outside."

He grinned. "What do you make of the sexual symbols on the pillars?"

"I'm not sure what to think. They're not like the carvings I've seen in India or Italy or anywhere else there are significant drawings related to sexual activity."

Sexual activity. No, he shouldn't be thinking or talking about sex around this woman. Not with her so accessible, so damned pretty, and so crazy-making.

"Any idea how old they are?" he asked.

"They're probably a few hundred years old at the least, but beyond that, I can't say without doing some testing." Her pert nose twitched. "Besides, I'm supposed to be looking for *La Pasion*, not pillars representing human sexual activity."

She yawned again.

"Take a rest. Like I said, tomorrow is a long day."

He watched as she closed her eyes.

"Stop watching me," she said.

He laughed and closed his eyes. "That better?"

"Much."

Within moments he heard her soft breathing and not long after he felt the sandman take him down to slumber.

Chapter Nine

Warmth encompassed Keira in a gentle blanket as she lay on her right side in the tent. She drew in a deep breath and savored the delicious comfort and the undeniable, scrumptious scent of man. With dawning awareness she sensed Zane's muscular frame. She would know that taut, well-built body anywhere. Spooned against him, she felt the pressure of his chest against her back, the encompassing power as his arm draped over her midsection. His large hand splayed over her ribs as he drew her closer, tighter. Every inch of his incredible strength shifted in a languid way, like a tiger stretching. A heavy sigh eased from his chest. His breath tickled her ear, hot and arousing. She shivered delicately. *Oh yes. God, he feels so good.*

She opened her eyes long enough to see that night fell over them and the tent had darkened. Somewhere along the way, he'd turned the flashlight out.

Then his hips nudged hers and she let out a tiny gasp of surprise at Zane's tremendous hard-on.

She didn't know whether to feel embarrassed for herself or him or both. He shifted again, his cock so hard he wedged it with assurance between her cloth-clad thighs. A woman couldn't ignore the huge, solid strength of his cock if she tried. His hand slipped upward and covered her right breast, encompassing her flesh in heat and gentle pressure.

Oh my. Her nipple prickled with a sweet burn and went hard.

Zane's touch sent lightning quivers over her frame. The hair on his naked forearm tantalized and she brushed over it without thinking. Such power resided in his muscles, such capability.

Again, like a cat, he stretched against her. His cock edged deeper between her thighs. He felt spike stiff as his thickness rubbed against her clit and labia through the sweats. A tight jolt of pleasure coiled in her stomach.

"Mmm." His soft sigh against her ear said he might or might not be awake.

His lips moved over her earlobe in a gentle foray and she gasped at the piercingly arousing feeling. Her stomach muscles clenched and a throbbing feeling heightened deep in her pussy. She wanted...she wanted...

Restless yearning spread deep inside her body and created a firestorm of desire she couldn't remember feeling with any man before Zane. Again his mouth explored her ear, the shifting, feather soft feeling of his tongue and lips a torment that made her writhe in his arms.

He cupped her cloth-clad breast with rhythmic, gentle squeezes. His fingers drew up over her breast until he brushed over the tip with a flick. Fire darted into her nipple and she barely stifled a gasp.

Oh yes. He's awake.

"So sweet and hot," he said against her ear.

Husky and deep, the low, sexy sound of his voice untied her one thread at a time. She shivered against his big, hard body and felt every inch of her feminine vulnerability. This man could hurt her emotionally. Physically.

Relentless, he licked her earlobe and breathed into her ear an earthy groan as he tasted her. Just the sound of that masculine moan drove a spike of hot, liquid desire into her deepest regions.

With full and total freedom she allowed abandon to take over. Whatever happened between her and Zane from now on, she wanted to grasp onto what they had this second.

His hand moved again, not content to torture one part of her body. With cupping, caressing motions he explored down over her hip, then back up in a silken, seductive slide up over her waist and arm. He kneaded her left shoulder, then licked at the back of her neck. She shivered as her enflamed senses shouted for fulfillment. All her inhibitions crumbled as his magic plied and plucked and stroked her into a blazing firestorm of female needs that refused to stay buried.

Molding her to his will, he plumped her breast, drawing his hand from the base to the tip, always teasing her nipple in the process. She tried holding back soft moans as his caresses continued, but they slipped from her. Her breasts felt weighty, nipples aroused into hard points that ached for each brush of his fingers, each plucking motion that drove her to within inches of begging for fulfillment. Unable to resist, she squirmed back against him.

Incredible feelings spiked deep inside her as she grew hot and moist. Her breathing quickened, her heart picked up speed. He slid one hand down over her stomach and inched the sweatshirt up so he could trace his fingers over naked flesh.

Upward. Upward. Up over her stomach until he captured her naked breast. His hot flesh against her skin made her moan with delight. He clasped her nipple and tugged gently. She moved against him with steadily building craving. Creamy and slick between her legs, she pulsed and ached high up in the deepest regions of her core. Needing him, wanting him to put the fire out that built with each passing moment.

He moved back and forth between her aching breasts, drawing his fingers from root to tip with agonizing precision. All regrets, all desire to stop the continual sexual need rushing through her came to an abrupt halt. She couldn't think, only experience and feel.

As a low groan issued from his lips, he licked her ear with tiny, brushing touches that sent shivers of delight coasting over her skin.

"Zane," she gasped.

She reached back and clasped her hand over his thigh, enjoying the rough hair and the skin encased over steely muscles. Without hesitation he plunged one hand into the waistband of her sweats. Quivers of excitement danced over her skin as he palmed her belly. *Yes, oh yes.* He worked his way slowly across her stomach to her hip, then back enough he could cup her ass. Anticipation made her ache.

She trembled with need, realizing she played with fire. Instinct parted her legs and he allowed his hand to travel up over her hip again and then down between her thighs.

When he touched wet, swollen folds, a low, soft growl of male appreciation left his throat. "Oh yeah."

Searching with tender, patient fingers, he rubbed over and around, touching Keira in ways she'd never been stroked before. Probing moist secrets and being exquisitely gentle, he drew one finger around her folds. Nothing could stop her excitement as it drew tighter and tighter in deep in her pussy.

She couldn't remember the last time she'd been this excited. Her body reacted to his tenderness, the liquid arousal evidence of how much she needed him. When he drew his finger over her swollen clit, the blaze of pleasure made her shiver.

"Oh God, Zane."

He licked her ear again, then plunged his tongue inside. He thrust one finger through parted slick flesh. She panted, her breath coming in bursts as he withdrew, then slid back inside, then allowed his fingers to trace circles over her folds, brushing and provoking.

As he kissed her neck and shoulder, his touch drove her to within an inch of total meltdown. His hips moved against her as he eased two fingers deep into her.

Shaking with longing, she couldn't think. All senses focused on the way his touch enflamed vulnerable tissue. Her heart raced as excitement escalated. No man ever made her feel this way until now; out of control and not caring if the sun rose in the morning as long as he didn't stop. As his fingers moved inside her, she released control. Nothing mattered but executing the dance. When he returned to ply her clit with repeated strokes she thought she'd die with ecstasy.

He pressed, plucked, manipulated until all her muscles tensed and fire took over her veins. She writhed as his continual touch threatened to blow her apart.

"Feel it," he said hot and guttural into her ear. "Let it come."

Easing two fingers deep into her, he slid back and forth against sensitive, slick walls. It felt so good, but she needed more.

"I can't stand it," she moaned, her yearning expanding to mind-blowing proportions. "Please."

As he wedged three big fingers deep inside her, the full, spreading feeling blew her away. She imagined his cock would feel like this. Tight, buried deep, he would pump in and out with precise strokes designed to ignite her.

Panting, reaching for the stars, she headed for the rapture. As lights seemed to go off with a flash bang inside her, she climaxed with a scream. Pulsing pleasure jolted her center as he continued to slide his fingers in and out. Sheer ecstasy shuddered along her muscles and nerves in rippling waves, her whimpers of happiness attesting to amazing pleasure.

When the earth shuddered under them, and a growl penetrated the air, she jerked in surprise.

"Jesus, honey," Zane said, his voice sounding breathless. "The fuckin' earth moved."

Still breathing hard, she shivered as her body came down from bliss. "Was that real?"

He kissed her ear and laughed huskily. "Which event?"

She smiled. "The ground moving. That rumbling noise."

"It was an earthquake."

"Uh-huh." She sighed, contented. "For a minute I thought it was…you know."

His soft, rumbling chuckle against her ear threatened to set her off again. That and the fact his fingers still rested against her mound. She could come again. Now. But she wanted him inside her first. Wanted him pounding out his lust between her thighs.

The afterglow surrounded her, lulling Keira into a daze. She wriggled her hips against him and his cock remained hard against her.

He moaned softly. "Don't."

Defiant, she slipped from his arms and turned to face him. Tentatively she reached for his erection, wanting to give him whatever he needed to find the same explosion she'd experienced moments ago. She found his length. His gasp of pleasure spurred her on as she encased his width in her grip. Hot, extremely hard, and big. Very big. She'd never had a cock this large inside her before, but the idea of experiencing every long, thick inch excited her beyond words.

"Keira." His voice sounded strangled.

He couldn't mask the hungry growl in his voice. Zane wanted relief and she intended to give it to him. With a firm stroke she measured him from base to tip and back again.

"No." He put his hand over hers and stilled her movements. "I want like hell to fuck you, but I didn't bring protection with me. I don't have any diseases, but I won't risk getting you pregnant."

His statement gave her pause. She didn't need protection from pregnancy; she had a birth control implant.

Before she could speak he jerked upright. Through the thin nylon encircling them, the stone pillars started to glow.

"Holy shit," he said as he jumped out of the sleeping bag and jammed his legs into his cargo pants.

He reached for his weapon.

Another small glow, this one emanating from inside the tent, caught her attention. "Oh my God! The ring. Zane wait. Look at the ring."

With the tent halfway unzipped, he turned to glance at the ring lying on the tent floor. "What the—?"

One quick motion opened the tent the rest of the way. She wouldn't be left behind with the ring, so she jumped to her feet, ready to follow him out.

"No." Zane turned back to her. "Stay here until I know it's safe."

She snorted. "It's not safe in here with the ring glowing. I'm going with you."

Rebellion flashed in his eyes and he grasped her by the arms. "Bullshit. Stay here."

As soon as he stepped outside and zipped up the tent, she did a little rebelling of her own. She'd be damned if she'd stay in this tent with this freaky ring. It couldn't be that bad outside. She unzipped the tent and stepped outside.

The rain had stopped, and moonlight spilled over the area, mixing with the ethereal glow from the pillars.

Zane stood stock-still and watched the eerie spectacle in front of him. She expected him to turn on her and snarl and order. Instead he kept his gaze pinned on the pillars.

"Holy shit," he said again.

Indeed. Glowing pillars was bad enough. Pillars with moving figures were another thing all together. Total disbelief smacked her between the eyes. *I must be hallucinating.*

Animated, the carvings performed specific sexual acts. She put her hand out toward one of them and the heat made her move back.

"Are you seeing what I'm seeing? Or have I lost my mind?" she asked.

"Looks like we've both lost our minds."

She glanced over at him and something strange happened. Even though her heart already palpitated like crazy because of what she witnessed, her belly fluttered with renewed excitement when she looked at him. Sure, she'd seen this man without a shirt before, but in the golden glow thrown off from the pillars, he looked like a god.

An aroused, incredible god.

His five o'clock shadow now stood out starkly against his skin and gave him the rough-and-tumble look of a bandit. His dark eyes captured hers, daring her to say anything. One word that would set him off. The way he looked at her, hungry and hot, said it wouldn't take much to change his mind. To convince him he could have her right here and right now, regardless of the peculiar, carnal things they witnessed.

His erection pressed against the zipped front of his pants. His chest heaved up and down with his accelerated breathing. She ached to touch the hair-rough planes of his chest, to smooth her touch over firm muscles. Keira longed to search Zane's secrets, to demand his vulnerability so that she could drive him as insane as he did her.

Walking toward her, he kept her gaze firmly pinned with his. "You're the archaeologist. What the hell do you make of this?"

She almost smiled. As if he asked her about the sexual feelings pouring back and forth between them and not the pillars. "I've never seen anything like it. I don't know what's happening."

When he stopped close, she breathed deeply of his heady, masculine scent. Her senses whirled, attraction doubling as an ache started deep inside her, begging for another completion, a finish to the inexorable craving.

As she looked up into his gorgeous face, she reached up and touched his jaw, felt the roughness stubble over the softer skin of her fingers. "Do you suppose the earthquake started this…uh…encounter?"

His hands slipped over her shoulders and he brought her closer. "Maybe. Beats the hell out of me. I've never been this confused in my life."

She suspected he wasn't talking about the earthquake but the need for sex boiling inside him. The idea gave her power. Like one of the little figures enjoying sexual abandon, she felt wanton, uninhibited. Losing control once more.

He drew her nearer, his hands sliding down to grip her waist. He leaned his forehead against hers and closed his eyes. "Tell me this isn't happening."

"It is. It *is* happening."

He groaned softly, then pulled back far enough to gaze into her eyes. She allowed her hands to slide over his pecs and when she brushed his nipples with her palms, he made a small indrawn breath. She explored, her hands tracing over the ridged, defined muscles in his stomach, the narrowness of his waist and hips.

"Maybe, just maybe, there is something to my story about the ring," she said.

This time, when he looked at her, understanding lit his eyes. "Maybe."

His nostrils flared the slightest bit, his grip on her hips moving back to her butt. He slipped his hands in the waist band and cupped her naked ass. Her breath caught. Her body opened and softened. A sexual haze settled down over her.

Keira couldn't take her eyes of the tableaus that played out in front of her and Zane.

"I wonder if these pillars are going to keep fucking all night," Zane said with a raspy quality to his voice. Then he let out a hoarse chuckle. "I wonder if this was the primitives own version of a porno show."

She couldn't help the giggle that slipped from her. "Unbelievable. No one back in London or San Francisco would ever believe this."

"Will you tell them?"

She grinned widely. "Are you kidding?"

Before she could say another word, he covered her mouth with his. He tightened his grip on her butt and jerked her against his hips, grinding his cock against her belly. She gasped against his lips at his raw display of need, his passion for her still startling and fresh and new.

Awash in the rush of heat, she grasped at his naked shoulders and held on, eager to experience, to feel, to know more. With an expert twist of his lips he parted her mouth and his tongue moved inside. Stroking, pumping his tongue over hers, he set her on fire. Gliding and slick, his deep possession owned her, made her understand for this space in time she belonged to him. His hands caressed as they traversed her back, their insistence gathering momentum. She shivered in his grip, transported by the tenderness underlined with a fierce sentient need. As if she might break, he fingered her rib cage with tender exploration. His gentleness made tears come to her eyes. Nothing inside her prepared for this crazy need, this resolute sexual pleasure.

She tensed a second under his touch and he hesitated he gentled the kiss, returning to a slow, methodical caress of her lips that didn't insist on completion but only offered it.

When he drew back, raging desire burned in the dark warmth of his eyes. "Tell me you don't want this and I'll stop."

But she did want it. She sought more of his sizzling touch, his aggressive drive to set her on fire. Unable to speak the words, she slid her fingers into the hair at the back of his neck and pulled him down to her. When their lips meshed, a groan left the back of his throat.

Sharp need struck her in the belly like a punch.

Lust gripped her, dragged from the center of her being. She must have him regardless of consequences. Regardless of place and time.

He tore his mouth from hers, his breathing ragged. "Tent. Now."

As he released her his gaze flamed with a force she couldn't recall seeing in his eyes before. Animal need etched his features.

All around them the pillars seemed to glow brighter. Deep in the back of her mind, in the rational sense, she knew they had something to do with how Zane acted right now. How she reacted.

She couldn't stop it and didn't want to.

When she followed him inside the tent, she knew they'd crossed the line for good. No going back. No pretending.

He zipped the closure.

An ethereal glow from the pillars and the ring gave the tent a strange atmosphere, unreal and exciting. Before he could say a word, she dropped to her knees in front of him and reached for his waistband. He'd left the button at the top undone, and she grasped the zipper tab. He'd given her pleasure earlier, now she needed with a building lust to give it back to him. She needed to touch him so badly. With a slow, gentle caress, she allowed her hands to trace upwards over his six-pack belly.

God, oh God. He is so gorgeous. So hard and masculine.

She watched his expression as she touched him, and Zane's penetrating gaze fired her into life, increasing her cravings by the second.

His fingers slipped through her hair and stopped her movement. He looked down, eyes hot with longing. "When we get back to civilization, we're going to fuck in every one of those positions on those pillars outside. I promise you."

His declaration heated her more than anything else he could have said. "We *can* do it all. Now."

"What?"

As she slid down the zipper and grasped his cock firmly, she whispered, "I have a birth control implant."

His fingers tightened in her hair, and she saw the untamed passion build in his face. "Are you sure about this?"

She didn't hesitate to gaze deep into those liquid dark eyes, pleading with him to finish a wild fantasy. "Yes. Yes."

His cock jerked in her grip as he grew longer, harder, thicker. Her mouth encompassed him, sliding down, down over his strong length. She encircled the base of his cock in her grip. She loved the heat that pulsed from his hardness, the strength and testimony of masculinity that caused her body to react. To want and need with a piercing desire. Her breathing quickened, her heart renewing a frantic pace as she tasted the strength beneath her lips.

He moaned as she tasted him and his whole body shuddered. She closed her eyes and felt, touched, caressed. Steely and thick, his cock represented power, the assuagement of every desire with the relentless push and pull of cock within wet, aching flesh. She imagined him within her, removing that ache and yet building it, giving her all his passion and holding nothing in reserve. She would know him inside and out, his needs and wants, before this night finished.

As she worked his cock with her hand, she followed with her mouth. From tip to wide base, she pumped and licked and savored until he grew thicker and so hard his cock felt steely. Encompassing his flesh she moistened him, covering him as far as she could go.

Stroking slow and sure, she made certain to clasp him just hard enough to increase the friction with each movement of her hand downward and upward. In the few lovers she'd taken, the very few, she never wanted to give them head as much as she wanted to give this man. The concept startled her, yet at the same time it set her free.

She teased by licking from the base to the tip, then back down, using Zane like a huge lollypop she couldn't stop tasting. Ah, she knew how to tantalize him to within an inch of meltdown, knowing instinctively what would drive him crazy. She covered him again, a gentle twisting motion of her hand to add stimulation. With each movement of mouth and hand, she felt the trickle of hot cream building in her center, aching for a hard, hot and fast completion.

Moving into the rhythm, she listened to his breathing, his moans that told Keira he loved what she did. Zane expressed his pleasure in more vocal ways.

"Oh yeah. That's it. Suck it."

She did as told, wanting nothing more than to taste him in her mouth and throat. Slick, hot and feverish, her tempo quickened. When she allowed that pace to slow, she reached down and rubbed the area between his anus and his balls.

He jerked in her grip. "Oh, fuck."

His head dropped back as he abandoned restraint to her hands. Then she did something she knew he didn't expect, that she didn't know she would do until it happened. She touched his tight back entrance, teasing his anus with the steady stroke of her index finger.

"Yes, yes," he said, his corded thighs tensing and his body shuddering as he panted for breath.

She kept one hand wrapped tight around his cock as she sucked him and pressed her finger against forbidden territory.

His fingers clenched and released her hair as his moans escalated. He began to move his hips, fucking her mouth. Excitement coursed hot and substantial in her veins, and she wanted him inside her with a burst of heat.

"Shit, oh God yes!" He growled as he tensed, his entire body quivering as thrust one last time and his semen jetted with heavy blasts into her willing mouth.

She drank his elixir, taste and scent an aphrodisiac to her already overstimulated body. She waited until a last pulse of his excitement spilled in her mouth. As she licked her lips and glanced up at him, he kept his fingers entwined in her hair. What she saw in his eyes astonished her. True caring, a melting heat in his eyes that owned more to admiration and worship.

He released her long enough to yank his pants off the rest of the way, then dropped to his knees in front of her. His chest moved up and down with his breathing, his muscled body provoking need inside her to touch and explore. Zane moved like a god, a man hand-carved by nature's desire for perfection. As she touched his shoulders and embraced their broad strength, she enjoyed the silk over steel quality, the golden hue of his skin. As she placed her hands on his chest and savored the texture of hard pecs, he cupped her face between his hands and gazed deeply into her eyes.

He placed tender kisses to her forehead and her mouth. Feral intent blazed in his eyes, a renewed desire that wouldn't quit. "That was indescribable."

She smiled. "Tell me what you want to do next."

"I'm going to slip inside you and stay there for a long time. I'm not going to move and your hot, wet pussy is going to get tighter and tighter around me. And while I'm lying inside you, I'll kiss and lick your breasts until you beg me to finish it."

She'd thought her excitement couldn't get any higher, but it did. His hungry words stirred her passion to slick, moist eagerness. Allowing her hands to wander down to his waist, she wrapped her arms around him. Her breasts ached against the press of his chest.

"Then what?" she asked, shivering with want.

He kissed his way to her ear, then whispered, "You'll be so ready you will come with one stroke."

Hell, she felt like she could come now with the first stroke, the first thrust through burning hot need.

"Mmm." His lips traveled down her neck, licking and pressing with tender kisses that belied the out-of-control look in his eyes. "Then I'll fuck you hard until you come again."

Before she could respond he covered her mouth with his and took her down to the sleeping bag. There would be no turning back.

As his lips explored hers with a gentle reverence, their bodies moved with a silky flow, a cadence of skin against skin and lingering touches that explored softly. She felt his building passion and knew this time he wouldn't hold back. Slowly Zane stripped her until he tossed aside the sweat suit. Naked at last, she savored his tender care and the eagerness of his caresses. His touch lingered everywhere on her breasts, her throat, her inner thighs, a teasing counterpoint to what she needed so urgently.

Already primed by his earlier lovemaking, the ache inside her grew so hot, so tight, she couldn't stand it.

She moved against him, enjoying strong sinewy muscles against her softness. "Zane, please. I...I need you now. Please."

A husky groan, filled with male animal satisfaction, burst from his throat. He rolled with her until she lay under him, his hair-roughened legs parting her thighs.

In those sweet seconds between hesitation and completion, time seemed to slow. Her breasts flattened against the unyielding hardness of his chest, his stomach muscles taut with tension brushing against her belly.

His sinewy thighs pressed her legs wider apart, his breath hot against her ear as he whispered. "I'm going to fuck you now."

His carnal statement, husky with passion, made her tremble. She quivered on the verge of knowing Zane as she'd never experienced him before, of combining her body with his in a way so intimate and forceful, and the thought momentarily terrified her.

But then his hard cock pressed against her sensitive, passion-swollen tissues and she moaned softly, caught up in the pleasure of one simple touch. He kissed her, his tongue plunging deep as he edged the broad tip of his cock into her folds and thrust. Easing inside her with steady pressure, he caressed supersensitive tissues screaming with need to come and come hard. When he finally seated completely to her womb, his cock spread her wide and deep.

She'd never felt anything so incredible or been so turned on in her life. Her pussy literally shivered, muscles trembling with a savage need to climax.

It wouldn't take much to bring her to a peak. One stroke. Maybe two.

So hot. So big. So incredible.

His tongue stroked hers, beginning a rhythm she wanted deep inside her pussy as well. She moaned against his lips, unable to contain the trembling pleasure rocking her body. Whimpers of stunned ecstasy issued from her throat as he followed through with his earlier threat. He stopped kissing her and leaned down to lick one nipple, fluttering over the tip.

She clutched at his shoulders, holding onto him as the storm inside her threatened to rage. "Oh, yes. Oh, God, Zane."

With a relentless cadence he worked her nipples with lips and tongue, sucking deep, then licking gently. Every rasp of his tongue drew her nipples tighter until the tingling pleasure added to the overwhelming arousal burning deep inside her core. He nibbled on her like the finest delicacy, the most mouthwatering flavor he'd ever encountered. All the while he stayed buried deep.

She lifted her hips, eager to start a motion, anything to ease the tormenting arousal as she teetering on the edge. Instead he pinned her down with his hips, keeping his cock tucked up high and hard inside her, his balls pressed against her ass. All she could do was caress him from within, her pussy clenching and releasing frantically on the cock inside her.

With relentless fervor he licked her nipples, drawing his tongue over the aroused tips, then drawing on them with deep pulls of his mouth. She moaned steadily now, mindless with need for completion. She'd never imagined a sensual torture could be so heavenly, but as he plied her with steady caresses, she thought the world would explode into a million fragments and she would never come together again. An eternity later he stirred his hips, the barely there motion caressing her walls. Another lick and deep suckling on her nipples and she'd had enough.

The man meant to torture her into screaming.

Clutching at his shoulders, Keira panted and quivered. The muscles in his shoulders and arms bunched under her grip, a testimony to his strength. Feeling that power under her fingers melted her with fresh desire. Incoherent with lust and pleasure, she released control. All ladylike tendencies, all hesitations disappeared in searing hot desire.

She gasped. "Shit! Oh, please, please if you don't—oh please!"

With a rough sound of male satisfaction, a man delighted with the sexual inferno he'd created, he drew his hips back until he pulled almost all of the way out. His exit felt almost as excruciatingly wonderful as his first thrust.

With a guttural sound in his throat, he thrust hard.

A climax burst in her pussy.

Keira screamed, the eruption boiling up and overflowing. Panting and quaking, she shook in his arms. All the while he kept his cock deep inside her, buried to the hilt, pressing all the way to her cervix. The orgasm seemed to go on forever, racking her body with pulse after pulse of mind-melting pleasure so staggering she could hardly catch her breath.

As she came down from the pinnacle, she realized he remained hard inside her.

As he kissed her, he moved again, drawing back and thrusting solidly. Again. Again. Each deep stab into her center made her groan with renewed excitement. In every way she became an animal, allowing lust and searing emotions too long held inside to bring them into a frenzy.

Just as he'd promised, he was fucking her hard and relentlessly.

And, oh, how she loved it.

Hammering into her pussy, he pressed hard against her clit. She spurred him on, gasps and half-formed pleadings falling from her lips.

"Please don't stop," she whimpered. "Please don't."

It didn't take long for her body to answer his call. As he reared up on his palms and powered into her, his grunts and groans of male enjoyment sent her over the top again. She screamed aloud as soul-shaking orgasm sent her skyward. Splintering deep inside, she rocked against his hips, accepting each thrust as deep as she could take. Working her throbbing channel over his cock, she gloried in the raw, primal sensation of being totally out of her head with bliss.

Only her body, her nerves, her muscles could feel.

He stiffened, roaring in masculine pleasure as he shivered against her. Hot, thick pulses of cum filled her pussy and she felt each pulsation as his orgasm seemed to go on and on.

When he eased down from the climax and rested upon her, waves of emotion stunned her to the quick. Tears sprang to her eyes at the beauty of what she'd experienced, the passion and tenderness. For when he left her body and looked down upon her, she could see the remnants of his own feral emotions. Heat still burned in his eyes, as if he could go another round right this minute without pause. Instead, he kissed her gently and rolled off her. Then he took her into his arms, nestled her against his side and enveloped her in his powerful arms. The tender way he held her made Keira feel like spun glass. When she'd first met him she'd imagined his sexual drive would be strong and heady. But this giving lover, a man intent on her absolute pleasure, surprised her in a while new way.

"God, that was..." he said and his breathing started to slow.

"Yeah," she managed to say.

Rustling sounds, almost imperceptible, broke the silence. The glow from outside the tent and from the ring disappeared.

"What the hell is that noise?" Zane asked.

"Another rescue party?" she asked, trying to see him in the renewed darkness.

"Get dressed." His voice snapped, a sharp, un-lover-like tone that wiped her desire slate clean.

Chapter Ten

"What's going on?"

He started putting on his clothes. "It could be anyone, friend or foe. Most likely it's foe. We don't have long before they get here."

As they dressed frantically in the dark, she said, "What are we going to do?"

He grabbed his automatic weapon. "Make a stand. They'll see our tent and we don't have time to pack up the supplies."

Fear renewed inside her. "This is crazy."

"Welcome to the life of an agent." Sarcasm entered his tone, along with humor. "The excitement never ends."

"But if whoever it is finds us, aren't we taking a risk they might want to harm or kill us?"

"Everything is a risk. If we lose this stuff to some rebels we'll be wishing real soon we hadn't. If we don't provoke a fight, they might let us keep our supplies so we can make it out of here in the morning." He unzipped the tent and looked out. "Come on. Stay close to me."

Clouds obscured most of the starlight, and a new well of fear pumped into her heart. She heard him doing something with his weapon, a clicking noise.

A strange glow came from high above the trees to the northeast.

"What is that?" she asked.

"There's another trail just north that leads from Haan's house to the plateau that's separate from the one you took to get here. My guess is that glow up ahead is a campsite or someone is coming this way very quickly."

"I thought this area was totally isolated from human traffic."

"Not totally."

As the trampling noise continued, she said, "They're not much for stealth, are they?"

"Maybe they want us to know they're coming."

Suddenly a loud cracking noise came from the northeast and they both twitched with surprise.

He slipped an arm around her shoulder. "Shhh."

She tensed even under the comfort of his arm. The night, no longer pounded by rain, renewed with squeaks, squawks, and the incessant din of billions of insects and other creatures traveling the night. What seemed like hours later, the glow of flashlights pierced through small holes in the jungle and came straight toward them.

Zane's entire body went rigid and he released her. He held his automatic weapon at the ready, in case whoever approached had ideas about starting a fight. His body still hummed from his sexual escapades with Keira and a definitive thought ran through his mind. He'd protect her with his life, but if the enemy took him down, he wanted more than anything in his life for her survive one way or the other.

"If this gets ugly," he said as adrenaline streaked through his veins, "duck and run at least until the firefight is over. If something happens to me, submit. At least you have some chance of surviving if you're taken captive. In the jungle without your supplies, you have almost no chance." When she didn't say anything, he added, "Give me your word, Keira. You submit and survive."

"Yes."

Her voice sounded out-of-breath, and he imagined the fear she must feel right now, the same dread curling within his stomach. At the same time he wouldn't concede defeat until the party was over and it sure as hell wasn't over yet. He heard machetes slashing into the foliage as people came toward them.

He thought it might be ten or twenty men; he couldn't be certain.

"*Señor* Spinella, is that you? We come in peace."

The voice sounded familiar, but he didn't relax as the lights bobbing among the trees and the human shapes moved nearer. He kept his mouth shut.

"*Señorita* Jessop? Dr. Jessop, are you there?"

He prayed she wouldn't speak. When she didn't say a word, the sounds of people coming nearer accompanied faces they could see.

The voice spoke in Spanish to his cohorts. "Do not do anything without my permission."

Zane suddenly knew who the voice belonged to, but it didn't give him an inch of peace. "*El Jaguar!*"

"*Sí, Señor* Spinella." Finally the group came close enough they could see each other. The tall man moved away from the trees, advancing without displaying his weapon. "You may put down the gun. We mean you no harm."

Zane didn't comply right away as ten more men came out of the bushes. He didn't see Ortega, Cyclops, or Manuel with *El Jaguar*, but that didn't mean the new entourage couldn't be as brutal. "I'll keep my weapon like this, thank you."

El Jaguar carried a flashlight and pointed it near the ground, obscuring his face in the semi-darkness. "Very well."

Surprised by the rebel leader's compliance, Zane almost let the tip of the weapon drop. Trust never came easy to him, and it wouldn't start now, especially not with *El Jaguar*'s motivations unclear. At least a new group of problems hadn't walked out of the trees. Dealing with a known entity should be easier.

"What do you want?" Zane asked.

"We heard from a friend that you needed assistance. Our camp is a short distance away. Come with us and we will provide shelter for the night and your safe return in the morning."

Zane kept his weapon trained on the rebel and asked, "What friend?"

El Jaguar smiled. "You wouldn't believe me if I told you." He waved with one hand back toward his group of men. "It's taken us all night to find you. Now that we're here, you would not insult our hospitality."

Fuck'in A. Yes, he would. He'd been perfectly happy tucked in the tent, delirious from the hard, deep fuck between a woman's thighs. Not any woman, but one that set his blood on fire and made him feel things he'd never experienced for a woman before. He glanced at Keira. She might be putting on a good face, but he could sense her fatigue and worry. She stood with her feet braced slightly apart, hands on hips. He almost smiled. *That's it, honey, look strong.* Hell, she didn't only look strong, she was. He'd felt it inside her from the moment he'd met her. It didn't make having her here now, danger all around, any easier for Zane to swallow.

"Why are you being all kissy-face with us now?" Zane asked. "Earlier you allowed your men to club me and brutalize Eduardo and Keira."

El Jaguar laid his weapon on the ground and approached slowly. "*Señor* Spinella, you misunderstood our intentions. We never intended to run you off the road. Your chauffeur, Eduardo, is a clumsy driver, no? He takes the road with great speed." The tall man stopped near Zane and Keira. "And the men who attacked you and Miss Jessop have been punished. Harshly."

"Where is this shelter you're talking about?" Keira asked out of the blue.

"We are on the edge of Haan's reach. He no longer ventures into the jungle this far, as you know. It gives us more freedom to roam."

"Then you're Haan's enemy?" Keira asked.

El Jaguar nodded. "Most certainly."

This news flash altered Zane's game plan. While he couldn't trust the rebel in front of him until he knew more, he wondered if *El Jaguar* might be able to help him and Keira in their quest for the octagon statues. Maybe this meeting could be advantageous after all.

El Jaguar centered his attention on Keira, reaching for her hand and lifting it to mouth to press a kiss there. "Anything to make such a lovely woman comfortable."

Jealousy ran hot and sudden in Zane's blood. He didn't like the childish feeling, but possessiveness hit him in the gut hard. The hunger in *El Jaguar's* eyes for Keira didn't hide much. Zane knew this man admired her, probably wanted to take her as his own.

Not acceptable.

When *El Jaguar* kept Keira's pale, slim hand in his, Zane said, "Keira is off-limits."

Keira's gaze snapped to his and held, irritation glowing in her eyes. *El Jaguar* released her fingers and erupted into laughter. Some of his men laughed, too. He walked with slow deliberation around Zane. Zane's muscles tightened, readying for possible battle.

"*Señor* Spinella, as much as I admire your woman, I would never presume to take her. It is clear she is yours." His gaze darted back to Keira for a second. "And the way she defended you when you were knocked unconscious, it is plain she has deep feelings for you."

Zane tried not to let the words mean anything to him. "You can assure me no man in your camp will try and touch her?"

"Of course, you have my word."

Somewhat placated, Zane said, "I'll hold you to that."

The rebel smiled again, his teeth straight and white. "As I said before, we offer you shelter and comfort. We have dry clothes and food if you wish it. Come, the night is wasting. Gather your things."

Calm but looking exhausted, Keira asked, "How did you know where to look for us?"

The rebel leader's eyes glinted, a fire that equaled the searing look from a jungle cat. "As I said, we had a tip from a friend. No other explanation is needed for now." *El Jaguar* paced away a couple of steps, nearer now to Zane than Keira. "Would it make you more comfortable to know there are women and children at this camp? We are not complete barbarians."

Caution stayed in Keira's eyes. To reassure her, Zane nodded and lowered his automatic weapon. "All right. Take us to your camp."

Zane hoped he hadn't made the biggest mistake of his life.

* * * * *

Dawn broke over *El Jaguar's* camp, daylight struggling to penetrate the thick, towering canopy above. Zane stepped out of the tent into fresh air. He left Keira sleeping like the dead. They'd fallen asleep in their borrowed attire last night, but he'd redressed in his own clothes this morning. When they went back to Haan's estate they couldn't afford to walk in wearing garments that belonged to rebels.

He stretched and yawned, his weapon dangling over his shoulder. He didn't intend to go anywhere without this very big, very effective piece. He was comfortable with the vibes here for the moment, but as an SIA agent he couldn't become lazy with security.

Right. What the hell was I doing last night? Playing fuckin' tiddlywinks, that's what. Getting deep inside Keira had been his priority right before the rebels showed up. Not exactly cautious of an SIA agent. He figured Mac Tudor would be chewing his hide big-time right now if he knew what he'd done. Emotional entanglements didn't belong on a dangerous assignment like this.

What emotions?

Other than wanting to protect and fuck her, he couldn't afford anything else.

He'd wanted to stay up through the night and watch over her, fear lingering in the back of his mind that she might be harmed. Possessiveness had never harnessed him before when it came to a woman, and this new development bugged the crap out of him. Perhaps the jungle broke a man down to his basic elements and showed his true substance. But he didn't have time to analyze the chaotic feelings bouncing inside him. He needed to learn what *El Jaguar* really wanted from them and if the rebel could be an ally.

After they'd traveled by foot the additional three miles through harsh jungle last night to *El Jaguar's* camp, Zane felt a total lack of danger. Few people had wandered the area. Men had circled the locale at intervals on watch, a couple of women walked with small children, their eyes curious and cautious about the newcomers.

This place and these people still gave him the willies. Nothing in his time in Puerto Azul had prepared him for supposedly peace-loving rebels. What about this so-called friend who alerted *El Jaguar* to their presence? Who could it be?

What about the glowing pillars with animated sexual positions carved into them, and the ring Keira claimed had lured her away from Haan's estate? He hadn't believed a word Keira said about the ring until those damned pillars started glowing and he saw the ring light up, too. Something fucking strange was going on in the jungle. On the way to *El Jaguar's* camp Keira asked Zane to keep the ring in his pants pocket.

Shrugging off unease, he turned his attention to the camp. He admired the village-like settlement around him now that he could see it in daylight. Zane watched the camp stir to life. Several women walked into the jungle escorted by men, bundles of clothes in their hands. Maybe they planned to wash garments at a nearby water source. He smelled food cooking and his stomach protested. He hadn't broken out the MREs, meals-ready-to-eat, that Haan had given him.

As a little relaxation returned to his muscles, he started across the encampment toward *El Jaguar's* tent.

The two guards packing rifles and knives standing outside one tent attested to *El Jaguar's* presence inside. Zane relayed his wish to see the leader.

One man ducked into the tent and emerged a few seconds later. "You may go in."

A little surprised the guards hadn't tried to relinquish him of his weapon, Zane entered the tent. *El Jaguar* sat on a fold-up chair behind a small collapsible desk. His tent wasn't bigger than anyone else's, and he'd covered most of the floor space with maps. He wore a clean khaki camp shirt and dark pants, his hair clean and combed.

One thing he would give the man, he managed to be one of the most civilized rebels Zane had ever known.

"Welcome, *Señor* Spinella. I trust you slept well?"

Zane wanted to cut right to the chase, but decided he could produce a couple of socially acceptable responses. "Like a rock."

"Excellent. And your woman, she slept well?"

"She's still sleeping."

"Good. She looked very tired last night. You'll want breakfast soon, of course."

Enough with the small talk. "Yes, thank you. I appreciate your hospitality, but there are some things I need to know."

"Of course." *El Jaguar* leaned back a little in the fold-up chair, resting his clasped hands on the little desk like a corporate executive. "Ask me anything."

Zane snorted in disbelief. "I asked you last night who this friend was that told you about Keira and I being in the jungle. You didn't answer that question."

El Jaguar smiled. "You're right. That is the one question I can't answer."

"Then tell me this. Why are you Haan's enemy?"

"Why are you his friend?"

Busted. How could he probe *El Jaguar's* motivations if he didn't reveal his own? The SIA book of rules said an agent never revealed his agent status to a stranger. A cardinal rule. At the same time, he couldn't discover this man's relationship to Haan without a bargaining tool.

"I'm not his friend," Zane said, hitching his weapon higher over his shoulder.

El Jaguar nodded. "Then we are at an impasse. I cannot tell you why I am his enemy and you choose not to tell me why you are his friend."

"I just told you I'm *not* his friend."

"You are staying at his estate."

"A business deal only. Nothing else."

Again the man nodded. He reached down for a small thermos, then popped off the top. The scent of hot coffee teased Zane's nose. He could use a caffeine injection right about now. *El Jaguar* reached into a bag and produced two milky-white, chipped coffee mugs. Man, this guy was equipped with everything. Living on a shoestring, yes, but still...

"Coffee?" *El Jaguar* asked as he poured the steaming brew into one mug and held it out to Zane. "We do not have accoutrements here in the jungle. Black coffee is all we have."

Accoutrements? El Jaguar rated as the most articulate rebel Zane had encountered in Puerto Azul.

Zane took the mug and sniffed it, savoring the comforting scent. "Thank you." He waited until the other man had taken a few sips of his coffee before drinking. The taste burst on Zane's tongue, a delicious blend that surprised him. He'd expected bitter. "Why would you care, if you think I'm Haan's friend, whether I'm stuck out in the jungle?"

Shifting, *El Jaguar* turned his small chair around so it more directly faced Zane. "I will admit something, *Señor.* You and the *Señorita* seem very capable people. I think you are more than simply a rich engaged couple."

Shit. Zane shrugged. "You don't think rich people can be capable?"

"Many of them are not. They are waited on hand and foot and are spoiled. They barely know how to boil water much less trek through the jungle unmolested. Your woman is obviously very strong."

Zane smiled. "I know a lot of capable rich people. You're hanging out with the wrong ones."

El Jaguar shrugged. "Perhaps. But as I said, she is an extraordinary woman."

Zane's grin grew wider. "I didn't know men in Puerto Azul believed women could work outside the home."

El Jaguar's dark eyes crinkled at the corners as he maintained a friendly face. "We are modern in many ways. Not as modern as the United States, perhaps. But we have progressed far past many countries in this region. Give us our due."

"Machismo never dies." Zane almost snorted at his own statement. *He* sounded like a feminist.

El Jaguar chuckled, then shrugged. "No nation is perfect."

The rebel's penetrating gaze held Zane's for solid seconds, as if he might read his mind. Niggling disquiet grew moment by moment as Zane felt the man continue to stare.

"I felt an energy connecting you and the woman that says she is also not who she says she is," *El Jaguar* said.

Hell. When he'd first met him at the limo crash, Zane hadn't given the man this much credit for intelligence. Deciding what to say now would take extreme care.

"What does this have to do with you coming to our rescue? If you think we're capable, I don't see why you bothered coming out to us last night."

"Did *Señorita* Jessop become lost earlier in the day?"

"Yeah. How did you know?"

"The friend who told us where to find her."

Screw the friend, Zane wanted to growl.

Suspicions, ugly and penetrating, reared their heads. He remembered the man who'd been stalking Keira when he'd found her yesterday and described him to *El Jaguar*.

El Jaguar's eyes narrowed, misgiving lighting his eyes as well. "I do not know a man like you've described." He gulped his coffee, then wiped his mouth. A pause lingered between them until the rebel came to a conclusion. He smiled and laughed, which Zane didn't expect. "The ring we took from your fiancée is a fake. Does she know?"

Zane's muscles tightened across his shoulders, but he tried to keep his breathing even. Interesting. "You had an appraisal done since yesterday?"

El Jaguar nodded. "Of course. Your fake ring is glorious."

"Keira didn't want to travel with her real ring, so I had a duplicate made."

That knowing grin never left *El Jaguar's* mouth. "I see. With good reason, it appears."

"You don't seem angry at being cheated out of the money."

El Jaguar shrugged. "The money will come from somewhere else, if not from a beautiful woman's jewelry."

Zane allowed his fingers to clench the cup when he wanted to grip the other man's neck. "She's off-limits, like I said."

Instead of getting pissed, the other man's gaze turned thoughtful. He crossed his legs and put his mug down on the small table. He hooked his thumbs in his pants' belt loops. An almost fatherly expression resided in his eyes, although he couldn't be much older than Zane.

"Does she know what a possessive man you are?" *El Jaguar* asked. "Or maybe you are not certain of her loyalty."

Zane shouldn't have been amazed by the man's outspokenness, but his concise and truthful perceptions cut to the quick. "She understands me and knows I demand fidelity."

He chose the word fidelity to make sure the rebel understood what type of loyalty he meant. *Lie through your teeth well, man. You don't know if she's trustworthy to anything but her grandfather, and maybe not even him.* A twinge of self-disgust hit. Last night he'd betrayed his own ethics by succumbing to her charms. He'd fucked her without benefit of knowing whether she represented the enemy or not. Who was he kidding? She remained guilty until otherwise proven innocent, as far as he could tell. When he thought back to the almost animal intensity of their reactions to the pillars and the ancient porn show, he wondered if they'd been seduced. Never one to believe in the mystical, he didn't like to think a force beyond their control had sent them into mating frenzy.

No, *damn it. That is too fucking impossible for words.*

Yet he'd lost his mind over her, wanting nothing more than to take Keira in every way possible.

"*Señor* Spinella, I noted last night you pitched your tent within the breeding circle."

"The what?"

"The breeding circle."

"It has a name?"

"Of course. It's been in the area for as long as anyone can remember. And you must know why it was given the name."

Zane drank the rest of his coffee. "No, why don't you tell me?"

"It is said that anyone who stays within the circle for long will have insatiable sexual needs."

Zane didn't speak, unwilling to confirm that maybe this is what happened to him and Keira. *El Jaguar* shifted back on the small chair, his hands clasped at his waist. Almost as if he told an old friend a ghost story around a campfire, he looked at ease with the world. "When my people came to this land they discovered many artifacts, great statues and buildings erected before them, including the breeding circle. They revered the artifacts because they believed the builders were gods. The

Indians didn't build structures like these, especially not those with sex depicted in so many ways. They spoke about the buildings in whispers, as if the ghosts of these gods would come down and burn them."

Zane sat up straighter. "There are other buildings in the jungle?"

The rebel nodded. "Yes. Rumor says Haan discovered them once and all—how would you say it?—all hell broke loose."

Zane thought about that statement. "Hard to separate rumor from fact. The San Cristobal and Puerto Azul authorities tried to determine what happened on his expedition and nothing came of it."

El Jaguar shrugged. "He is a very powerful man."

"What about you? Are you a powerful man?"

The rebel chuckled. "More than you know."

Knowing better than to ask again why the man in front of him was Haan's enemy, Zane tried to enter the back door. "How did you get the name *El Jaguar*?"

Standing up and pacing over to one of the many maps strewn on the floor, the man stared down at it with narrowed eyes. "Only my people know that answer."

"I take it the individuals in this camp are your people?"

"I am their leader."

"And what are you leading them to?"

The rebel's turned his dark gaze on Zane, a fire inside those eyes that spoke of long struggle and determination. "To return to them what is rightfully theirs."

Instinct reared inside Zane. "Did Haan take your land when he built his property in the jungle?"

El Jaguar made a careless shrug. "He encroached on what is sacred to my people and with many around here who are not in my tribe."

"It's an old story fought in many places around the world. There is always someone bigger trying to subdue the weak."

El Jaguar bristled, the same intensity coming off this man in waves that Zane had seen at the limo wreck. "We are not weak. We are subtle and relentless. We do not rely upon firepower to gain every objective."

Zane nodded, realizing he'd stepped on this guy's pride. "I didn't mean to imply your people are weak. I meant this situation has played itself out all over the world at different times."

"You mean history repeats itself."

"Yeah."

"I can deal with my piece of history, *Señor*. Nothing more. I can't change what happens anywhere else but here in Puerto Azul."

Cynical to the core in some ways, Zane didn't know if he could agree even that much. "Do you think being subtle is the way to win?"

"Sometimes, it is the only *right* way to win."

Reluctant admiration eased into Zane, even though he still didn't know if he could trust *El Jaguar*. He sensed the rebel's integrity and it confused Zane on a fundamental level. Haan was the enemy, but could *El Jaguar* be a friend?

Zane did the one thing he could; he questioned motives. "You have guns and you're willing to rob the rich to get what you need."

Striding back to his small desk and chair, *El Jaguar* sank down and smiled, all upset gone. "I never said I was a saint, *Señor* Spinella. But then, I think, neither are you."

Smiling, Zane looked into his coffee. "You got that right. What do you think you can do against a man like Haan? Get him to abandon his property?"

"Perhaps."

"You think if you terrorize him enough, he'll relent?"

"Every man has a breaking point."

Zane chuckled, the sound lacking mirth. "Don't be so sure about that." When *El Jaguar* simply stared at him with cool, unflinching nonchalance, he continued. "What have you done so far and what do you plan?"

El Jaguar's expression hardened, and Zane wondered if he'd pushed too far. "You seek my plans? I do not think so."

Trust, eh? One thing he wouldn't obtain from *El Jaguar* anytime soon. Zane took another tack and switched the topic. "About my situation. I want some guarantees."

Twitching one thick eyebrow, *El Jaguar* asked, "You think you are in a position to make ultimatums?"

"I think I'm in a position to compromise. Give me what I want, and maybe I can give you what you want."

Outside a rustling and commotion startled Zane. Jumbled Spanish, guttural and heated, split the morning air. *El Jaguar* retrieved his weapon and pointed it at the door, his eyes now icy hard. Taking his cue, Zane did the same thing.

"I must see this *El Jaguar* immediately," came Keira's uncompromising tone. "What has he done with Zane Spinella?"

* * * * *

Keira glared at the two guards who trained their weapons on her with stern intent. Her harsh words a moment ago had been tantamount to "take me to your leader." She didn't care. When she'd awakened to an empty tent and no sign of Zane anywhere, a rare panic engulfed her. Heart beating fast with alarm, she'd charged across the camp toward the tent with the biggest guards. Fear that they'd hurt Zane made her reckless.

A demanding flow of Spanish came from the tent, and she recognized *El Jaguar's* voice. Yes, she'd come to the right place. When the tent opened and out stepped the rebel leader and Zane, she scanned the SIA agent for signs of torture or injury and saw his scowl instead.

"*Señorita*, I hope you slept well?" *El Jaguar* asked. "Your accommodations were satisfactory?"

Taken aback by his friendly manner after she'd created havoc, she sputtered her reply. "I was... Yes, it was fine, thank you."

"Did you want something else, *Señorita*?"

Before she could say a word, Zane latched onto her upper arm and started away with her. "We'll check back with you after breakfast, *El Jaguar*."

"But—" she started as he pulled her along with him back to the tent.

"Be quiet until we get inside our tent."

When they reached the tent, he unzipped it, then said softly, "Get in."

Throwing him a dirty look, she ducked inside the tent, then turned back to him. She stood straight and tall. "What was that all about? Did you have to haul me across the camp like a disobedient child?"

He put his automatic weapon near the tent flap, then took the few steps required to get right in her face. She decided not to move and give him the supreme satisfaction of intimidating her. For a full thirty seconds his mysterious eyes cataloged her like he'd never seen her before, a man trying to discover the meaning behind the universe.

"Damn it," he said between his teeth, "what possessed you to charge across the camp and confront two heavily armed men? You could have been seriously hurt."

His words hit her over the head like a sledgehammer. She didn't do outrageous things without a plan, and yet she'd been foolhardy this morning in a way that defied common sense.

He is right. Damn it, he's right. Embarrassment and residual anger threatened to shoot her contrition in the foot.

She swallowed hard and tried not to snap at him. "I'm sorry. I..." *Okay, girl, just admit it to him. It might ease his ire.* "When I woke up and you weren't anywhere around, I was afraid they'd done something to you."

To her surprise his expression went from tough-as-shoe-leather to amused and a bit gratified. "You were worried about me?"

"Well…yes."

His mouth softened a little and his eyes held a rare tenderness that made her belly fill with heat. When he edged nearer until their bodies almost touched, she looked up and up into those gorgeous eyes. "I can take care of myself."

"I know that, but I just reacted."

He smiled, but it didn't remove the sheer force in his gaze that compelled her to melt right then and there into useless putty. All he had to do was look at her a certain way and her heart galloped, her pussy moistened, and her brain seemed to transform to mush. Damn. *I hate that.*

"You're pretty brave, you know?" he asked.

Words came from her without thought, refusing to be screened by protection mechanisms. "Do you like that in a woman?"

"Yeah, I do." His voice dropped lower, a husky, compelling sound as he moved even closer. "But do me a favor. Next time you charge to my rescue, use a little less vinegar and more honey. You can't be certain what these people will do."

She knew he didn't want anyone to hear them. "What were you doing in *El Jaguar's* tent?"

"Trying to figure out who and what he is."

He cupped her shoulder with one hand, then her face with the other so he could whisper into her ear. Hot breath tingled over her ear and sent a shudder of excitement through her.

With quiet deliberation, his voice a murmur of heat in her ear, he explained what he'd learned. Emotions, jumbled and uncertain, made her pause. She felt a little fuzzy from what happened all yesterday and last night. A rush of heat filled her at the memory of Zane's touch, his lips, his cock. She'd made love with Zane, a man who scared her with his level of passion, his rough edges and dangerous life.

It had been the most glorious, wild, uninhibited sex she'd ever experienced.

What was I thinking? Obviously she hadn't been thinking at all. A wild fling with a man who didn't trust her—whom she couldn't be certain she trusted—made no sense whatsoever. Hormones and the peculiar circumstances had pickled her brain.

"Then maybe *El Jaguar* isn't our enemy, but just Haan's," she said around her confusion.

"Until we know for certain, keep your eyes peeled and don't let your guard down for a minute."

Huh. She could say the same thing about him. Her body still hummed from a low-level sexual overload that seemed to happen whenever he came near her. Hell, all she had to do was see him and it happened.

Maybe the wild episode in the jungle last night hadn't worn away one hundred percent. She wished it would. Getting all hot and bothered and acting like a teenager around him would create problems for her in a heartbeat.

He chucked her under the chin with his index finger. "Thanks."

"For what?"

"For being worried about me."

Grudgingly she said, "I suppose it's good for your male ego."

He laughed. "Come on. Let's find some breakfast."

They checked the main supply tent and a woman there gave them a dish of fruits and breads. After they returned to their tent and consumed the food in record time, Zane headed out to ask *El Jaguar* about obtaining more supplies for the trip back to Haan's estate.

Keira felt stronger now that she'd taken sustenance. She also wanted a bath in the worst way.

As if on cue, a young woman's voice came from outside the tent. "*Señorita* Jessop. *El Jaguar* sent me."

Keira opened the tent and a pretty, dark-haired woman stood outside the tent. She cradled towels, a bar of soap, and a pile of clothes in her arms.

"My name is Christina. *El Jaguar* said if you wished to bathe, I should take you to the small waterfall nearby. It is very tiny, but clean and safe there. It is not far." Crystal clear and beautiful, the girl's voice held genuine kindness.

Still, Keira had her doubts about leaving the camp. "I don't know if we should."

Christina reached for her hand and tugged her out of the tent. She started for a clearing not far from the tent. "Your man doesn't like you to be clean?"

Keira smothered a grin. "Yes, he does, but is it really safe to go out here?"

"It is around the corner. Very safe. We've bathed here before." Christina's patrician nose wrinkled. "Besides, you stink."

Instead of being offended, Keira chuckled.

Seconds later they popped through the small jumble of trees and a ridge of rock with a small pond and a trickling waterfall nestled in an oasis of close jungle and clear skies. Birds chattered and the high jungle canopy rose around them in a blanket of security. A little paradise, the area held surprises wherever she looked. Along the rock face of the small outcropping near the water, she saw an iguana. The lizard quickly disappeared from sight. Orchids danced in a wild breeze. Trees dripped heavy amounts of dew from their leaves as the waterfall sent up spray. The profusion of nature added to her fascination. Philodendrons, mosses, and lichens occupied the nearby area.

Christina placed their towels and soap on a rock and started to strip. "Come on. Get undressed."

Keira glanced back at the camp, not so far away. "Won't someone see us?"

Christina shrugged and the camp shirt fell off her shoulders. Young, firm, plump breasts, unbound by a bra, came into view. She then slipped off her pants. Disgustingly beautiful, the girl's cocoa skin seemed unblemished by anything, including time.

Christina looked almost confused by the question, then she nodded and smiled. "Oh, *sí*. I understand. You're American."

Keira frowned. "What does that have to do with anything?"

"You are shy about nakedness."

"Well, sometimes, yes."

"Our people are not. While in Puerto Azul you should...how do they say it?...when in Rome, do as the Romans do?"

Keira laughed. "You're right."

Reassured and eager to remove grime and sweat, Keira decided she would take the plunge. After looking around for critters and half afraid she might step on something, Keira took off her sandals then the sweats. She dumped her sweats by the rock, slipped out of her underwear and bra, and walked shamelessly into the water. The water wasn't deep enough to cover her breasts from the sun or a peeping Tom should one appear.

The young woman tossed Keira the soap. The soap smelled of lilac, and Keira took great glee and scrubbing her hair and her body. She sighed and moaned her delight. After scrubbing and rinsing her hair, she closed her eyes and lay back to float.

"Your man is very handsome," Christina said.

Keira kept her eyes closed. "He's okay."

"Okay? He is *mucho* sexy. You don't seem to like him. Maybe you try too hard."

"Try too hard? I don't know what you mean."

"You try to act as if you don't like him. It must mean that you do."

For such youth the girl owned too much wisdom. She didn't want to get into a discussion about Zane either way. "You're mistaken. How could you know what I think of Zane? You were in the tent a few moments with us."

"Sometimes that is all it takes in this world."

What world? The earthly one or the place these people seemed to inhabit far beyond civilization and wrought with mystery?

"You're wise for someone so young," Keira said.

"I have lived in this jungle all my life except for the four years *El Jaguar* sent me to college."

Keira's eyes snapped open and she put her feet down into the water, no longer content to float. She watched the other woman swimming with steady laps around the pond. "*El Jaguar* had enough money to send you to college? Where?"

"In the United States where my mother lives."

"Why don't you live there with her now?"

"Because I like the jungle and *El Jaguar*. He is most kind." When the woman saw Keira's expression change, she said, "It is not like you think. *El Jaguar* is my father's friend. He thinks of me as a niece, nothing more."

Pondering this new and startling knowledge, she almost asked Christina where *El Jaguar* got the money to send her to college, then thought the better of it. Perhaps *El Jaguar* saw himself as Robin Hood. Besides, he'd taken the fake engagement ring with every intention of using it to finance his cause. Despite the startling consideration the rebel leader had shown them, Keira felt something remained missing from the picture. She couldn't admire a man who operated outside the law, even if he was Haan's enemy. In his own way, *El Jaguar* might be no better than Haan.

"Why did *El Jaguar* really want to bring us to this camp, Christina?"

"Because he knows you are true of heart. He is very good at seeing into a man or woman's heart and understanding their true purpose."

"He reads minds?"

"Some would call it that," Christina said, her voice clear and melodic. "When I was a child he always knew when I was lying. We look into your eyes and into *Señor* Spinella's soul and we know who and what you are."

"We?"

"My people. We are capable of extraordinary things."

A shiver cascaded up and down Keira's spine. The woman's imagination must be working overtime. "Such as?"

"I cannot tell you. It is forbidden."

"Why?"

"Our secrets must remain isolated with us. Anything else would bring death and disaster to us."

Doubt entered Keira, but she didn't want to be rude to her hostess. "Thank you for bringing me here. I feel much better."

"You are more than welcome."

Weary of the questions running full speed through her mind, Keira closed her eyes and floated again. Drifting in and out of a meditation state, she allowed the water to caress her body with a lover's touch. As the liquid lapped at her body, she wondered what it would be like to grow up in this jungle, surrounded by nothing but nature. The peace would be profound, but loneliness more difficult. Would the isolation make a woman like Christina imagine the supernatural lurked in the rainforest and her people possessing unusual power?

She went back to floating and drifted on the water for a long time before she noticed the stunning quiet. She couldn't hear the birds and the wind whispering through the huge trees. With a start she opened her eyes. The pile of towels and clothes lay on the rock, but Christina was nowhere in sight.

"Christina?"

Birds broke away from the trees with a shriek that made Keira jump. She swam to the edge of the pond. When she looked up, two big, booted feet stood near her clothes.

Chapter Eleven

With a gasp of surprise, Keira jerked away. With hands on his hips and cap on his head, Zane towered over her. His unshaven cheeks and chin gave him an almost piratical look.

"Come on, we need to get out of here. I passed Christina on the path and she said you wanted to stay out here for awhile. I didn't think it was a good thing for you to be here alone, no matter what she says." Zane's words snapped at her rapid fire, his gaze burning like fire.

When she realized he could see her breasts, she sank into the water as far as she could. "God, you scared the crap out of me." She looked around the banks of the pond. "I can't believe I didn't hear Christina leave."

Clipped and precise, he said, "Get dressed."

She wanted to be pissed at him, but something more primitive called to her. She would teach the hard-nosed agent a thing or two. "Not until you wash up. If I'm going to all the effort, so can you."

He glared. "We don't have time for this."

With a sense of womanly clout, she stood up straight. She strode toward him, as uncaring and cool, at least on the outside.

Oh yes. She felt the power grow in her; control that said she could influence him body and soul. He's seen her naked. He'd brought her to screaming climax and she'd given him head. They'd made love. Modesty shouldn't come into their relationship at this point.

She half expected him to growl at her, but instead his eyes sparked with renewed interest in her as a woman.

"Like I said," he said huskily, "we don't have time for this."

As her entire body exited the water, she savored the liquid flowing down her body, caressing her skin in private and not-so-private places. His jaw tightened as she walked toward him. She saw his Adam's apple bob as he swallowed hard. *Yes, I'm getting to him all right.*

"What's wrong, Zane? Feeling a little heat?"

He drew his cap off and tossed it on the big rock. "Fine, I'll get washed up. Then we're going."

She tried not to blush or acknowledge in any way that his hungry perusal of her nakedness turned her on. His gaze raked her from head to toe and drank Keira in like a starving man would do with water. He then tore his attention away from her and removed his boots and socks. As he yanked off his shirt, pants and briefs, it was her turn to swallow hard. Seeing him naked in the light of day defied coherent description.

Powerful arms, wide chest sprinkled with that dark hair, narrow waist, hard stomach and a cock to...oh, my God. He stood with feet a little apart. His cock, surrounded by dark, curly pubic hair, was thick and more than ready to make love. The head was bigger than the rest, and a drop of pre-cum slicked the tip. She wanted to lean over and lick it, grasp him in her hand and suck him like a delicious hard candy. She wanted to hold that hard, thick length in her pussy and feel in moving back and forth, caressing her walls and driving her insane.

His cock looked so hard and tight he might be ready to burst. She almost offered to put him out of his misery. At the same time she liked that she'd done this to him and that she could bring Zane to a point of screaming need. Excitement, forbidden and hot, surged through her in great waves as she devoured his glorious body. Without a word she tossed the soap to him.

He came toward her and instinct made her take a step back. "You're playing with fire, honey." His voice held that rusted, husky quality of a man who desired with burning intensity and could barely hold back. "If you want a fuck right now, one that doesn't mean anything but takes the edge off, I can accommodate you immediately. Otherwise, stop looking at me like that."

Her mouth fell open in surprise, then a flash of heat coasted over her entire body. In that moment she knew that despite the pleasure making love with him this minute would give her, she needed something more than a quick fumble and the few hard thrusts that would probably get him off and leave her cold.

"That's what I thought," he said as he turned and walked to the water.

When he sank into the water he plunged his entire body under for a moment.

Disturbed at her own actions and ashamed at the way she'd tried to manipulate him, she dried off in a rush. She slipped into the sweats. After she dressed, she left Zane washing in the pond, and returned to camp without a word.

* * * * *

"The jungle is beautiful, you know." Keira said as they neared Haan's house. "Very dangerous, but interesting."

Zane gave her one of those male grunts and kept walking. His broad back became her anchor point as they'd hiked through the dense foliage. Three hours passed since they'd left *El Jaguar's* camp. Zane made her stay close to him as they hiked, not that she would have done anything else.

Maybe he was angry with her, and she couldn't blame him. Tantalizing him like that at the pond had been foolhardy. She'd let a little pleasure in his arms—okay, earth-shattering pleasure—dictate her actions. From now on she'd keep her sexual desires in check.

Despite the surly silence Zane maintained along the trip, she enjoyed seeing the jungle she'd trekked through the other day without noticing. Moments later she saw another iguana about four feet away sunning on a rock.

"Zane, look. An iguana."

He turned around for a second as she pointed at the miniature dinosaur. "Yeah, that's a tree chicken all right."

"Tree chicken?"

"The locals eat iguanas sometimes. The ctenosaur is more edible, though."

She swallowed and licked her lips. "Yuck."

"Don't knock it until you've tried it."

She wrinkled her nose. "You've eaten iguana?"

"Yeah."

"Let me guess. It tastes like chicken and that's why they call it a tree chicken?"

He just laughed and kept going.

Happy that she'd gotten a chuckle out of him, she took one last glance at the reptile and continued onward.

Shortly after she spied some tiny tree frogs which Zane promised packed a big noise at night. At intervals she identified a woodpecker and a heron. When a salamander scrambled across her path, she jolted in surprise and barely kept back a girly scream. She realized the creature was harmless, but with the initial movement she thought it was a snake. The entire jungle seemed out to either impress her or scare the shit out of her.

A white-faced monkey screamed at them from a tree branch as she trailed behind Zane.

She grabbed his arm in reaction to the noise, and as her fingers dug into his arm, he glanced down at her. "What's wrong?"

She immediately released her grip on is arm. "Nothing. It just startled me. I can't believe I made it all the way through this jungle yesterday without getting killed."

His eyes narrowed and she saw long-held suspicion in them. "Neither can I. You were wearing a skimpy dress, sandals, you had no hat, no food or water."

She nodded. "I know."

"Tarzan wouldn't have liked this jungle, you know." He gestured upward. "He wouldn't have liked the wasps, ants, and saw-toothed edges of the canopy vegetation. He would have been bitten, stung, and cut into ribbons. And yet you made it through all this the other day on your own. You're either the toughest damned woman I've ever met or you sprouted wings and flew."

For a moment she thought he might say more, then he shook his head and moved out.

"Women have done things like this before on their own, you know," she said.

"Yeah, but they were trained for these type of situations. You're not."

She left it at that, unwilling to argue with him. Fatigue threatened as the heat increased. Sweat trickled down her neck into the bandana she'd soaked with water and tied around her neck. Despite being in damned good shape, the heat made this trek never-ending. A wide-brimmed hat borrowed from Christina helped prevent sunburn.

Tired, Keira blinked away the desire to collapse right here. As the sun beat down relentlessly, she drank enough water to avoid dehydration. Then they remembered that her hat would be a dead giveaway that she'd encountered someone else in the jungle, and they pitched it under some vegetation where it wouldn't be found.

When Haan's house came into view, she let out a little exclamation of joy. "I never thought I'd say that about this place. All I want now is a hot bath. I'm so sticky I feel like flypaper."

When they ventured toward the back door, Haan appeared in the conservatory as if he'd been watching for them. "Thank the heavens." Although the man's eyes lit up with a smile, she didn't feel as if he meant one word of his relief. "If you hadn't made it back soon, I was going to call the authorities."

Just like you called the authorities the last time someone disappeared?

Haan hugged her and she smiled and acted glad to see him. "Thank you, Ludwig."

He held her at arm's length, his hands gripping her forearms as he looked her over. She saw the pretense of concern in his eyes. "You've had an adventure getting back, I see. Why did you venture out on your own yesterday? Don't tell me you were getting pre-wedding jitters and decided it best to run away?"

She smiled weakly. "Believe me, Ludwig, if I'd wanted to run away, I wouldn't have gone into the jungle. Something strange happened—"

Zane stepped up. "Can we talk about that part later? She needs to rest and we both need showers."

Ludwig's gaze sharpened, but his voice went conciliatory. "Of course. I'm just happy to see you both alive." As they trailed Haan back into the main house, he said, "I trust this will delay the wedding one more day?"

"Yes," she said.

"No," Zane said.

Zane forestalled comment by slipping his arm around her and drawing her tight to his chest. The man was a fine actor; she could almost believe the desire she saw running wild and deep in his eyes. "Darling, I'm so happy to have you back, I want to marry you right away."

She didn't expect what he did next. He leaned down and kissed her, exploratory but gentle. The kiss couldn't have lasted long, but it sent feverish tingles deep into her belly and lower into her pussy.

Ludwig laughed. "If you wish, then it will be done. The priest, Father Trujillo is here already. He's waiting to meet you both. You can be married tonight."

"Splendid," she said, but didn't mean it. "I'm so tired, though. I need to get some more sleep. What time do we want the wedding?"

"Whatever time you designate," Ludwig said.

Zane's arm tightened around her. "How about seven o'clock?"

He looked down at her for confirmation, a warning light in his eyes that begged her to cooperate.

Thinking she must be insane for agreeing, she said, "Sounds wonderful."

She managed to trudge through the jungle twice and encountered rebels on this little adventure. Now all she needed to do was survive a wedding and a wedding night. *Wedding night.* That one didn't bear thinking about too much.

Every muscle ached as they trudged upstairs, her in the lead and Zane following. Ludwig puttered along behind them like a benevolent father, ordering a maid to bring them meat, cheese, and breads on a tray.

When they reached their room and went inside, Zane locked the door and came toward her. He dumped his pack and weapon on the floor by a chair, then shrugged his shoulders as if they hurt. Over forty pounds of junk lugged around for several hours could do that to a person. She wanted nothing more than to ease his muscles with a massage, but knew she couldn't and shouldn't offer.

"Why do we still have this stuff?" she asked with a sigh.

"We might need it for when we leave with *La Pasion*."

"When we find it how are we going to skip out of here without him knowing what's going on?"

"It won't be easy. We'll need a major distraction. I'm working on that one."

Tired and a little cranky, she rubbed the back of her neck. "You're just now thinking about it?"

"Yeah." His rough tone said he wouldn't argue the point. "Why don't you take the first shower, okay? I'm going downstairs to talk to Haan for a few moments."

"About what?"

"To explain what happened when you went into the jungle."

Disbelief arched through her. "You're going to tell him the ring gave me amnesia?"

He shook his head. "No. I'm telling him that we had a fight and that you just wandered off and got lost."

"Great, now he's going to think I'm a total dingbat."

He frowned. "What the hell do you care what he thinks of you?"

She rubbed her forehead, weariness coming on strong. "You're right. It doesn't matter. I can play the part."

"From now on, whenever you put that ring on, I'm going to be with you. No more amnesia episodes, okay?"

"Believe me, I don't want anything to do with that ring as it is."

"Good. I'm also telling Haan that you and I want to spend our wedding night fucking in all the rooms in his house. He offered, so I'm taking him up on it."

Alarm ran through her. During her sojourn in the jungle she'd forgotten the plan to search Haan's house with the pretense of making love in every room. More than fearing they'd get caught scouring the rooms, she feared the play acting required to accomplish it. "The kinky angle, eh?"

A smile flickered over his lips, then left as he headed for the door. "That's right. The kinkier the better."

Without another word, he left the room.

After she stripped off her filthy clothes, she decided a quick rinse in the shower to remove basic grime would be in order, then a soak in the tub would do her good. Her bones even felt like they throbbed. How could she get through a wedding tonight? After taking the shower, she eased into the bathtub with a groan and laid her head back. Sleep overcame her and she drifted into a warm sea.

* * * * *

Zane returned to the bedroom after his talk with Haan, his nerves strung tight. Telling the man about his eccentric fiancée's foolish junket into the rainforest and the honeymoon plans didn't ruffle Zane's feathers. Hell, no. Pretending to be in love with this woman at the wedding…that alone gave him the jitters. Haan seemed thrilled that Zane wanted to visit all his rooms in the estate, and then he explained why. He told Zane that he and his last wife put sex toys in every room in case they needed them. Haan said he'd bought new items in anticipation of their visit. Then he told Zane where to find them for each room they planned to explore. Zane decided he wouldn't tell Keira in advance. She'd freak out; he could tell she found the idea of faking lovemaking in the rooms to be distasteful.

Since they had a late night ahead of them, he hoped to sleep off the effects of their jungle walk for a few hours.

When he walked into the bedroom, he half expected to see her asleep on the bed. When there was no sign of her, a mild flashback panic set in. What if she wandered off again? She wouldn't, would she? He'd wring her neck if—

He saw the closed bathroom door and sighed in relief. The sun must have baked his brains. Of course she wouldn't wander off after what she'd just experienced. He checked his watch. He'd been gone thirty minutes and she'd decided to take a shower or a bath. With another sigh, he peeled off his dirty clothes. He smelled like hell. He tossed his shirt onto a chair, then worked on his pants.

He didn't want a repeat of earlier in the morning when they'd bathed in the pond. The little vixen had wanted him to suffer. She'd shown him the full view of her smooth, silky body and he couldn't help the reaction. His cock had come to attention like a flagpole after one glance of her flesh. He'd been so damned tempted to draw her into the water with him and slide deep inside her heat again. Thinking about those soft, beautiful breasts, that small waist, rounded hips, and long legs made his cock rear. When they'd lain together in the tent and he'd been unable to resist touching her, Zane thought he'd go mad. Plumping those breasts in his palms, tugging on her little nipples—Jesus, God, they'd been delicious—had almost made him come. Touching the slick flesh between her thighs had sealed his fate. From that moment forward he knew he had to sink his cock inside her. Having her mouth wrapped around his cock had been paradise, but her pussy…yeah, that *was* the ultimate.

"Get a grip on yourself," he muttered to the empty room.

Gritting his teeth against the vision of her nakedness, he went to the door. He knocked gently. "Keira? It's too quiet in there. You all right?" When he got no response he knocked a little louder. "Keira, answer me."

Seconds eased by and not a sound came from the bathroom. Unreasoning panic punched him in the gut. He tried the doorknob and breathed a sigh of relief.

As the door opened without a squeak, he saw why she hadn't answered. Sprawled out in gentle relaxation, Keira lay in the tub with her head tilted back on the porcelain. Sound asleep. She'd propped one smooth leg on the rim of the tub, and her delicate-looking arm hung over the side. Her small, fragile fingers, those same fingers that had caressed his cock into screaming madness, also dangled and brushed the bath rug. He knew if he stepped closer he would see that stunning beauty again, and he couldn't stop himself as he walked toward her.

Zane sat on the edge of the tub and indulged his need to watch her. Admiration for her strength came to him once more, whether he wanted it to or not. His desperate need to remain detached emotionally and physically eroded every second. Try as he might to restrain his emotions, whenever it came to Keira, they ran high and deep. Half the time he wanted to throttle her, the other half he wanted to fuck her.

Before she woke up, he wanted to drink in the essence that belonged to her alone. As his gaze glided over her face, he saw vulnerability there. Her small nose and mouth and the subtle arch of her brows. Her hair, wispy and fine, kicked up around her face in a wet mess that made her adorable. The long column of her neck begged to be kissed, the high, plump breasts dared him to lean forward and suckle. Beyond that, her small rib cage and flat belly needed to be caressed.

Under the water, with her leg tilted up on the rim of the bathtub, her female mysteries were open to him. Dark pubic hair curled over her mound, then down around the pink folds of her sex. *Her pussy...God, yes, her pussy.*

He didn't think she trimmed her pubic hair or shaved it, and he didn't mind. Nothing he liked more than a woman in her natural state, lush and delicious. His gaze feasted on the sight of her tender flesh and he licked his lips. More than anything he wanted to feel those folds closing around his fingers again, and watch her face this time as he brought her to screaming climax. Licking her sweet moisture and capturing her clit in his mouth would be the nearest thing to heaven. He wanted to slide his cock into her heat and feel the wetness, the tightness as it cradled him.

He wiped a dot of sweat off his upper lip. Too late to pretend the sight of her didn't turn him on. His cock stood at rigid attention.

Somehow he must ignore those divergent feelings and get to business.

His cock didn't care. It stayed at full erection.

"Keira," he said quietly, not wanting to frighten her.

She opened her eyes slowly, looking sleepy and uncertain. When she realized he sat on the edge of the tub drinking in her nakedness, she jerked like a startled fawn.

He laughed. "Easy."

Eyes wide, she gripped the edge of the tub, then drew her leg back down into the water, splashing him in the process. "What are you doing?"

"You didn't answer my knock on the door."

A smile curved his mouth as he allowed his right hand to drift under the water, passing within inches of her mons. Her gaze followed his movements with a look akin to alarm.

"I didn't hear you. I was taking a bath."

"I see that. You look exhausted. Why don't you dry off and take a nap? You'll feel much better for the wedding."

She shrugged and water pearled on her small shoulders. "So much for a romantic wedding, eh?"

Her lack of enthusiasm for the wedding made him feel a little strange. *It's a farce, Zane? Why do care if she wants to go through with it or not. It's part of the mission. You aren't going to be jilted at the altar.* "Like I said before, we'll get it annulled."

Sadness made her tawny eyes shimmer, and he wanted to do everything it took to remove that unhappy look. It made him crazy, but he couldn't stop a protective streak that erupted inside him the moment he'd saved her life in Egypt.

Why can't I keep my fucking mind on the mission?

He'd worked with other women agents before and not once did these crazy feelings overwhelm him. Most of them had been attractive, competent, strong women like Keira. So what made her different?

He had to touch her. He simply had to. After dipping his fingers into the bathtub and trailing his fingers over her arm, he felt her shiver.

She inhaled sharply. "Zane."

"Yeah?" he asked hoarsely.

"What are you doing?"

"What does it feel like?"

"You're staring at me like a man ready to devour a bowl of ice cream." Her gaze flicked down to his sizable erection. Her face went pink as she stared.

Her breathy voice, a little startled and maybe scared, made him laugh. "Sorry, but it's a little hard...difficult to keep my mind on business when you're lying there naked and wet."

Her eyes widened a little as she caught the triple entendre. Like a man without willpower, he touched between her breasts, then over the flat plane of that delicious belly. With slow precision he tested the waters as he tested her. Down, down, he moved until he touched her mons with the tip of his fingers.

She ran her tongue ran first over her bottom lip, then her upper. "Please."

"If I don't touch you now I'm going to die."

He couldn't help the confession, and he didn't care if she saw it as weak. His fingers smoothed between her slightly parted thighs and discovered the warm slickness between soft folds. Hot and wet, and not from the water, her entire body shivered as he strummed the sensitive area with continual strokes.

"Zane." Her pupils dilated and her hips tilted upward slightly, and he understood she wanted more.

With slow precision he plied her warmth. He could almost feel it, taste it. Whatever she wanted, he wished to give to her. Attuned to her body, he played with her, flicking her clit with soft touches until her breathing came hard, her eyes closed, and her hips moved continually. Her beautiful breasts rose in time with her panting breaths, those rounded hips twitching a little as her arousal heightened. Beautiful and open to experience, she allowed him the pleasure of showing her how he could make her feel yet again. With slow intent he slipped two fingers deep into her pussy and she gasped and shivered. Moving his fingers into position, he located her G-spot and rubbed with insistent pressure.

"Zane, oh God. That's... Oh God."

"That's it," he said. "Show me everything."

Her hands clutched the sides of the tub as she spiraled higher and hotter. As she tipped back her head, a flush rose on her cheeks heralding an imminent explosion. His drive to push her over the edge quickened as he stroked faster. By now her panting breath and soft sounds heralded her excitement, and he concentrated on working that spot inside to shove her over the edge. When she couldn't take it anymore her muscles went rigid and a loud moan left her throat. As she shuddered he enjoyed how her tight femininity contracted over his fingers. Finally she subsided back into the water and sighed.

When her eyes opened he saw the pleasure lingering there. Flushed, she looked ready and willing for anything else he might have in mind. Shit, he wished she wasn't so fucking tempting. Touching her had been too easy, and fucking her would be even easier if he didn't keep his mind on the mission.

Keira turned and spied him as he strode away. She swallowed hard and stared. Oh yes, she looked. She probably owned the same damned expression on her face as she'd seen on his a moment ago. Zane's beautiful back rippled with power, and those tight, incredible buns bunched with muscle as he ambled to the shower. Instead of glancing away, she kept her blatant stare on his strength as he stepped into the shower and turned it on.

How did a woman keep her sanity around him? Wearing a blindfold whenever he walked into the room?

When she'd awakened from her nap, he'd been staring at her like he'd excavated a treasure from a tomb and her heart had about jumped from her chest. She'd become wet inside all right, watching him watching her with a primitive look that branded her straight down to her toes. Then she'd allowed him to stroke her into the most maddening G-spot orgasm she'd ever experienced.

She stepped out of the tub; the water went cold long ago. As she toweled off he started to sing, this time with a melody that caught her by surprise. When he'd sung before the lyrics expressed sexual hunger. These words held tenderness, fraught with love and longing, a desire a woman could hope for from a man, but may never find.

As he continued to sing, she recognized it as a love tune from long ago. She'd heard the song several times and had always loved it.

"This time you've made me see, I've been lonely and deep in misery. I feel an emptiness that makes me realize, I can't live forever like this."

As he sang she stopped toweling off, listening to the words pouring from him in that beautiful, deep silk and velvet voice. Every word sounded sincere, feelings straight from his heart. She could hear the song revolving in her head, adding the music to his lyrics.

"I once met a woman who told me to believe in my heart, but I never believed it until there was you. Long ago I pretended I didn't care, but now I've tasted your hidden fire, I know I must have more of your hidden desire. I know my heart's in danger of falling so hard for you."

As she glanced in the mirror at her body, she saw a flush creep up her neck and into her face. His words turned her on as heat flashed through her body. More than that, the lyrics fed her soul, her heart in a way she'd never experienced before. She ached so badly she wanted to tear open that shower door and join him. Beg him to make love to her.

"Now I've got to decide whether to trust what I feel. God, how much of my soul can I truly reveal?"

Like a fool she started to sing with him as she fluffed her hair with the towel and continued to stare into the mirror. He had the order of the lyrics a bit mixed up, and it made her smile. No matter. His voice was so heartrending, so smooth and gorgeous, she about melted into a puddle right there on the cool tile.

"Your world has opened my heart, I never realized until I met you how often I cried…"

As the words flowed over her she realized her heart thumped harder and tears welled. She felt the pathos, the longing in this song and the way his voice made it sound added to the feelings.

"I once met a woman who told me to believe in my heart, but I never believed it until there was you. Long ago I pretended I didn't

care, but now we've joined passion for passion, I must have more of your hidden desire. I know my heart's in danger of falling so hard for you."

Her heart thumped with an erratic beat. As his singing faded, she realized exhaustion must be making her vulnerable to a seductive voice. Not just any voice, but the man who'd saved her life twice. For one clarifying moment she wondered what it would be like to be loved that way by Zane Spinella. Loved and cherished in the deepest part of his heart.

As she left the bathroom and closed the door behind her, she realized with a heavy sadness that she would never know.

Chapter Twelve

"Wake up," a husky male voice said close to Keira's ear.

She jerked awake as she had when she'd fallen asleep in the bathtub, her senses on high alert. She rolled over and scarcely kept the white terrycloth robe from slipping off her body. "What?"

Zane looked down at her. Her gaze coasted over the Italian designer black suit, and electric blue shirt and tie. Athletic cut, the suit fit him like a dream, emphasizing his broad shoulders and lean waist and hips. With his hair dry, his face shaved and a white smile that put every movie star she'd seen to shame, he made her heart turn over. She wished he would smile like that more often. Then she thought about it. He *did* smile more often than when she'd first met him.

No man has a right to look so good. Ever.

She gawked at him, then frowned. "What time is it?" She bolted upright and looked at the digital clock. "Damn. I've only got two hours to get ready."

Another male grunt confirmed his contempt. "You don't need two hours. You just had a shower—"

"I have to fix my hair. I slept in it wet and now it looks terrible." She rushed for the bathroom. She stopped dead at the door. "Wait. I don't know what I'm even wearing for this sham of a wedding."

"The white dress in the closet."

At the hotel she'd glanced at the garment without much thought. She hurried into the bathroom and the walk-in closet. She flipped garments aside until she found a gorgeous two-piece silvery white ensemble. Extracting the items, she held up and admired the simple, elegant design. Thin straps held up the demi-cut seed bodice that was designed almost like a corset with boning along the ribs. The waist tapered into a Basque waist. Seed pearls decorated the entire bodice.

The long, slim skirt skimmed over her hips and widened slightly at the knees. Beaded pumps with high heels went with the elaborate decoration on the bodice and hem of the dress. Plainly put, the outfit was beautiful. She hoped it fit her. Everything in the wardrobe did so far, but that didn't guarantee this dress would.

She looked toward the bathroom door, half expecting to see her groom-to-be to watching. Marching back into main room, she found him sitting in a chair near the bed reading a Spanish language magazine.

As she rushed by him and dug into the chest of drawers, she found a suitable half slip that would be long enough. She remembered the white long-line strapless bra and retrieved it, then grabbed white thigh-high stockings. When she saw the stockings didn't have elastic at the top, she hoped to hell the SIA had provided her with a white garter belt. The one she'd worn the other night was black. Her fingers found the lacy white scrap of seduction and smiled. *Yes.* She located a whisper-soft, lacy white g-string bikini and grabbed that, too.

Retreating to the bathroom, half afraid she'd run out of time, she rushed through the dressing process. She stopped after she'd wiggled into the bra and realized the push-up element would assure every male, taller than her or not, would be able to see her cleavage. She grimaced. *Damn it.* Then she shrugged. What could she do? These were the only undergarments that would work with this dress.

Finally she stood in the ensemble, ready for action. She cleared her throat. She hadn't worn anything this beautiful in years. Not even with her last boyfriend two years ago. Now, here she stood, ready to participate in a fake marriage and she gave a damn about the "fuck me" quotient in her underwear? She must be losing it. After she put on the long dress and struggled to zip it up, she slipped into the pumps. Not only did the dress fit like a dream, so did the shoes. Amazing.

She managed to wrestle her hair into a semblance of order and anchored one side of it back with a sparkling rhinestone butterfly barrette. After taking a cleansing breath to steady her nerves, she looked around the side of the door. He still read the magazine.

She stepped into the room. "What do you think? Will it do?"

As he lowered the magazine and took in her apparel, his gaze immediately went hot and appreciative. He liked the affect, all right. He tossed the magazine on the bed and stood. With a purposeful stroll, he walked toward her. She felt every minute of that walk as he perused her from head to toe, his gaze touching with intimate attention.

When he stood in front of her, she saw Zane take in the way her breasts curved in the bodice. "Beautiful." The one word came out rough with unexpected emotion. A frown marred his brow. "Haan is going to eat this up."

Haan. She didn't want to know how Haan would react to this dress. "Why should we care about that?"

"Because he's a lech of the first degree." He turned away and went to the dresser. He retrieved the strange ring Haan had given her. "Here, slip this on. I've got the wedding ring in my pocket."

When he clasped her left hand and started Haan's ring on her finger, she snatched her hand back. "No. I can't."

"Why not?"

"I told you what this ring does. This is what caused me to wander off into the jungle. You do remember the way it was glowing when it was in the tent last night, don't you?"

He stared at the ring in his palm for a second. "I remember. It was probably light from the pillars outside the tent."

"Right." She put her hands on her hips. "That sounds like the theory people use on other people who've seen UFOs. Light reflecting off Venus and all that."

She thought he'd demand that she put it on. Instead he shook his head and put it back on the dresser. "Fine. Maybe Haan won't notice." His gaze flamed, a little anger mixed in with defiance. "He'll be too busy looking down your dress to notice."

She flinched at his harsh tone. "You make it sound the design of the bodice is my fault. The SIA picked this out for me, remember? This isn't even a style I'd normally wear."

His eyes widened. "You've worn a wedding dress before?"

Heat touched her cheeks. "When I was younger, yes. You know, young women get together and try on dresses like this once in awhile and fantasize about what their wedding dress will look like."

He unbuttoned his suit jacket and hooked his thumbs in his waistband. "I remember my sister doing that."

"And I suppose you thought it was idiotic."

One corner of his mouth turned up, a crooked smile that looked way too endearing for her heart. "Of course. All boys think things like that is stupid girl stuff." Thunder rumbled close by and he looked out the window. "Great. Looks like our wedding day is going to be interrupted by rain. We'll get a bird's-eye view from the conservatory."

"That's where we're getting married?"

"Yup."

She snorted softly and fussed with the back of her hair a moment. She reached for a comb lying on the dresser and peered into the mirror with disgust. "Some wedding day."

She glanced out the window and flinched when lightning split the sky and thunder crashed close behind.

He walked toward her and held out his arm for her to take. "Come on, let's get downstairs. Remember, act like you're in love with me."

As she took his arm and left the room, a lump formed in her throat. With a shock she realized it wouldn't be all that difficult to pretend she'd fallen hopelessly in love with Zane Spinella.

* * * * *

Haan watched Keira with a strange light in his eyes that made her so nervous her stomach felt queasy. He hadn't asked once about his ring as they stood outside the conservatory waiting for the small string quartet to start playing *The Wedding March.* His eyes watched her like a hawk readying to swoop down on prey. Haan's expensive gray suit, green shirt and red tie looked odd and discordant, a complete mismatch with Zane's sleek, Italian design. She wondered who had advised him on apparel, then decided she didn't give a crap.

As she glanced through the French doors leading into the conservatory, she observed the elaborate production. A long red carpet weaved through the twists and turns on the path. At the end of that path Zane waited for her, and even though this wedding would be annulled, an unbearable excitement hummed inside her like electricity.

At the same time, she felt trapped, strung so tight she might snap. Although there would be no guests other than Haan at the wedding, she felt like a china doll on display, a figurine or artifact he'd stolen and planned to give away.

"You are nervous," Haan said as he stood far too close to her.

She looked up at his tall frame, situated to her left, and plastered on her most charming smile. "Of course. Isn't every bride?"

His thick brows arched. "Perhaps you don't like me giving you away?"

No, she didn't, but she couldn't say that. "I'm not old-fashioned. Why do you think I wanted a wedding like this? How many other women do you know who would wed in the house of a man they don't even know? In a jungle, no less."

Haan chuckled, his laughter a harsh, hard sound. "My dear, what your groom has in store for you tonight is even less conventional. Has he told you his plans?"

She batted her eyes for a second. "Of course. We're to go room to room tonight rather than hiding away in our suite. I'll admit it's a bit strange, but Zane and I like to mix things up."

Haan touched her shoulder, his fingers cupping her naked skin with a possessiveness that made her stomach tilt with revulsion. "The basement is for last. I have special...things in there I hope you will both enjoy."

Things. Her stomach did another strange flip. She didn't want to think too much about what *things* might mean. Other than what Zane told her earlier about Haan's penchant for bondage and submission, she couldn't imagine what paraphernalia Haan owned in the basement. She guessed she'd find out sooner rather than later.

Tonight.

Oh man. Can I handle this?

His gaze lingered on her breasts too long. The nasty grin spreading over his face gave her the willies. "If you find your groom isn't quite up to the challenge and you decide you want something more, I can provide for you."

"I don't think we'll need any help, thank you."

You filthy, horrible pig.

"Shall we begin?" His voice sound dispassionate, as if she hadn't given him the brush-off.

He opened the French doors and the string quartet of four men started playing. As beautiful music poured into the area, her heartbeat quickened with expectancy. She clutched the simple nosegay of tropical blue and red flowers in her hand. She took the arm Haan provided and started her walk down the red carpet.

If anyone told her a few weeks ago she'd be getting married, she wouldn't have believed them.

As the beautiful music rose to the heavens, she felt a strange new anticipation welling inside. At the other end of this carpet a gorgeous man awaited her. Tonight they'd discover if *La Pasion* resided in this house, and tonight she'd skirt the edge of sanity. Not knowing what would happen in the next few hours frightened her at the same time it excited.

As they rounded a corner she saw Zane at the end of the carpet, standing under a beautiful white arched trellis adorned with pink and red roses. Beyond the trellis the huge windows showed the jungle, the pool, and the driving rain.

Yet the look in Zane's eyes thrilled her far more than pretty flowers ever could. He stood with feet slightly apart, hands at his sides. Laser intense, his attention drifted over her; his expression filled with awe and love. Her heart seemed to skip a beat, then restart with a heavy thud. Tears welled in her eyes. Serious and intense, his attention said he wanted her with a need that couldn't be hidden.

As thunder rumbled outside, they reached the trellis and Haan released her. She turned toward Zane and his hands clasped hers. He brought her fingers up to his mouth and kissed them gently. The apprehension she'd felt eased into calm and she noticed the priest for the first time. The music halted.

She recalled that Haan said earlier the priest's name was Farther Trujillo. Dressed in his purple vestments, the short, plump Hispanic man nodded and smiled. His balding head beaded with sweat, and he looked somewhat frightened, a strange thing to see in a priest's eyes during a wedding. Considering who hired the man, she understood why the holy man would be scared.

As the ceremony started, she listened to the priest extol the virtues of marriage and love. All the while Zane kept her gaze trapped with his, a devouring, pure fire in his eyes. My God. This man deserved an award for acting. Her heart, her body, everything inside reacted with the fervor of a woman in love.

Other than when they'd made love, she'd never felt so feverish, so eager to be in his arms and show him how much she longed for him.

No, no. What I'm feeling right now can't be real. It can't be.

The ceremony passed in something of a blur as she recited her vows. When Zane retrieved the wedding ring from his pocket and slipped it on her left finger, reality sank in.

"I thee wed," he said softy.

After he passed her the groom's ring she swallowed hard, her throat dry as she repeated after the priest. Before she knew it she slid the ring on his finger.

Finally the ending words came from the priest in his heavily accented voice. "You may kiss the bride."

Realization screamed down into her bones, her sinew, her very soul until it stabbed her in the heart like a knife. True. Sharp. Terrifying and bittersweet.

We're really married.

Stunned down to her shoes, her heart raced.

Keira half expected Zane to press a sweet kiss on her cheek or maybe a chaste peck on the lips, but instead he took his sweet time. Her breath suspended as the tension expanded. She wanted this kiss with a craving that anchored in her body and wouldn't let go.

He cupped her face in his hands like a man cradling precious gold. With deliberate ease, as if he meant draw out the ceremony, he leaned in and brought her mouth up to his. His lips brushed against hers in the gentlest kiss, then he retreated. Disappointment hit her for a second, but then he came back at another angle. Hungry and unrestrained, his lips took hers. One skillful movement of his lips and his tongue plunged inside. He tasted mint fresh and delicious; the continual brush of his tongue against hers startling and creating a flashover. Quivering deep inside, melting warmth started in her stomach and headed downward. With a hedonistic kiss he ignited new firestorms she couldn't resist. She responded, meeting his tongue with equal fervor until taste blended into taste, and she thought in a wild moment Zane's heartbeat matched hers with a frantic cadence.

Screw the priest and Hann standing there.

Nothing existed but Zane and the way his mouth took hers.

When Zane pulled back, the overwhelming message came through loud and clear in his gaze. Their next kiss would be hotter, deeper, filled with all the desire they now held in check.

Haan clapped and so did Father Trujillo.

"Congratulations." Haan hugged Keira and then shook Zane's hand.

"Many salutations," the Father said. "I'm happy to see a young couple so in love brought together. Come. Sign the papers and all will be official."

The priest took them to a side table where they signed the documents locking them into marriage in Puerto Azul.

"This way," Haan said, his silvery eyes shining like a wolf's. "We have a spread laid out for us all in the dining room."

The string quartet played as they left the conservatory. Zane held her hand tightly, as if she might escape any second. She felt unsteady on her feet, energy sapped by too many ventures in too short a time. She couldn't believe this morning she'd been swimming naked in a pond in the jungle. Now she walked down the aisle in a white dress, a married woman. Zane slipped a possessive arm around her waist. All his movements portrayed a man deeply in love. A lingering touch along the back of her neck, a light kiss on her cheek. By the time they left the conservatory she felt so cherished, Keira almost believed he loved her. Returning his melting looks and possessive touches became easier and easier the longer she stayed with this man. Though she'd known him a short time, she'd shared so much, and the connection wound deep within her.

Not far from the conservatory, the large dining room boosted a table with twelve chairs. Gilded to the hilt, the room held an aura of nauseating Baroque excess rather than true elegance. Purple, gold, and red wallpaper, friezes of gods and goddess, dark wood and glittering crystal added to the opulent display.

Place settings decorated the table, glittering gold on white bone china and gold-plated utensils. A sideboard featured a repast fit for king and queen. The priest helped himself first, digging into the platters of bread, meat, cheese and fruit like a starving man as he heaped items onto his plate.

Zane offered to fill her plate, and she eased into a chair across from the priest. After Zane brought her food and sat next to her, Haan opened a bottle of champagne, then poured them all a flute of bubbly. He sat down at the head of the table, leaving a gap between him and the plump priest.

"I'm so glad you can dine with me before your honeymoon starts. I meant to talk to you at lunch yesterday, of course." Haan waved one hand dismissively. "Until you decided you'd rather have adventures."

The hot glance Zane slanted her way made her temperature rise. "Oh, I don't think she'll be having more adventures in the jungle for the rest of her honeymoon."

Keira tasted the champagne and found it fruity and delicious. Parched and hoping water would chase the heat from her face, she then took a large gulp of water. Her nerves threatened to get the better of her; Zane rattled her cage with his lingering looks and tender attention.

"Tell Farther Trujillo what you encountered on your trip," Haan said, looking at Keira.

At first she couldn't think of a thing to say. She stalled with another taste of champagne. "You mean my trip into the jungle, or out of it?"

Shrugging Haan waved his hand in one of those expressive gestures she noticed he liked to make. "Both times, my dear. I amazed how well you fared. In case you didn't notice, this area is risky. There is much to fear in the virgin jungle. Insects, snakes like the fer-de-lance and the bushmaster. Giant earthworms, flesh-eating fleas, you name it, we have it."

She nodded. "I'm lucky I didn't see all those things. Flesh-eating fleas?"

Zane broke in before Haan could answer. He wiggled his eyebrows at her. "They burrow into your skin, drink your blood, and lay their eggs in your body."

A shiver raced over her skin and she gave him a dirty look. "That's horrible."

Father Trujillo paused in stuffing his face long enough to speak. He wiped his mouth with a napkin. "I praise God you did not encounter any of those things while you were in the jungle. Angels must have been with you."

She sighed. "That's for certain."

Haan's penetrating, cool gaze took in her dress and landed on her cleavage for what seemed the hundredth time. She shivered this time from revulsion.

"Did you feel an earthquake last night?" Father Trujillo asked them all. "We haven't had one in quite some time. My parishioners worry more quakes will come."

Haan frowned. "Earthquakes are random. Nothing can protect against them."

Father Trujillo didn't look convinced. "Perhaps it is a pox on the land because sin and evil lurk about."

"I don't believe that," Haan said. "This region is always a little shaky."

A secret smile parted her lips until she saw Zane looking at her, a shrewd expression in his eyes. He must be thinking the same thing, and the realization sent a jolt of heat through her. He, too, remembered their heated lovemaking.

After Zane ate a cracker and made appropriate comments about the delightful food, he wiped his hands on his napkin and cleared his throat. "I've seen interesting items in your house that I meant to ask you about." He nodded toward a table near a china cabinet. "Take that incense burner. It's unique."

Keira noted the item and unease tumbled in her belly. The puma-shaped burner appeared comparable to one she saw in the Chesterham Museum a few months back.

Haan took a healthy swig of his champagne. "Ah, that item is from Tiahuanaco on the Bolivian border. A true masterpiece."

"How long ago was it made?" Zane asked.

Haan shrugged. "Honestly I don't recall. Perhaps Mrs. Spinella has an idea?"

Mrs. Spinella.

The words whirled around in her head like a mantra, and she almost didn't answer to her new title. "My specialty in archaeology is British and Irish archaeology. I'm not very familiar with artifacts from Bolivia."

Haan put his fork on his plate and nodded. "Of course not."

"What about the artifact right next to it?" Zane asked.

Haan paused as if he didn't want to say. Then he cleared his throat and directed his silver, big eyes on them both. "It is a Cibcha mask from Peru."

A lump grew in her throat about a mile wide. She remembered the red mask as one she'd seen in Chesterham Museum many times and it had been reported stolen two years ago. Shock reverberated through her, not because she thought her grandfather assisted Haan to steal the artifacts, but because someone else must have assisted Haan or his associates.

Someone framed her grandfather. But how to prove it?

Thunder rumbled in the distance, a low growl that sounded like a warning.

Haan turned his ice-cold eyes upon her. She met his gaze with calm endurance. To her surprise, the man shifted in his chair and turned his attention to his fingernails.

"You didn't see anything or meet anyone unusual in the jungle, I hope?" he asked.

The question halted the breath in her lungs. Zane reached over and clasped her left hand that lay on the table. The warmth and gentle pressure gave her extra strength.

"No," she said. "Did you see something strange on your expedition, Ludwig? The one that went wrong?"

"We saw odd things there." Haan reached for his champagne and drained the flute in one gulp. "We lost much trying to find the glory of the jungle."

"Some say the jungle is haunted by an ancient people," Father Trujillo said suddenly. "People who guard it from harm."

Haan snorted and poured another glass of champagne for himself, then held the bottle out to offer more to all. Everyone declined.

Haan fingered the stem of the delicate crystal glass and stared into the bubbling depths. "That legend has been around since before this region became a viable country. Back to the colonial periods and before that."

"What legend?" Zane asked.

She wondered if maybe Zane knew the answer but acted ignorant on the subject for a purpose. She played along. "Please tell us."

Haan kept his gaze glued to the champagne flute, his persistent fiddling with the stem making her nervous.

"Apparently hundreds of years ago, before the Spaniards came to this land," he said, "there were people who carved out a great city in the *La Selva Negra*. When we were on the expedition we saw some of the statues of rather explicit..." He trailed off and looked at her, as if he feared offending. "Scenes like you might find on some Hindu structures in India."

She nodded. "Of course. I know what you mean."

Haan's smile chilled her in a way nothing else could. "Once touched by these statues, you are forever altered. There is no escape."

Zane squeezed her hand, then released it. "Sounds ominous."

Haan shook his head and gave a brittle laugh. "I never want to see what I saw again."

Part of her believed Haan's act, but the other part couldn't be sure. A ruthless man like this wouldn't be afraid of anything but failure, would he?

Haan made another soft, sarcastic laugh. "That's why I wouldn't go into the jungle to help find you, my dear. I'm afraid I have a bit of a phobia about it now."

"I'm so sorry," she said, injecting as much womanly softness into the tone as she could.

For a while the conversation turned to more mundane and less threatening items as Haan told them more about his fashion designing.

Before she thought she'd go nuts from hearing about bone-thin models, Haan said to Zane, "I have a few pieces in my basement that I think you might wish to see."

Zane slipped his hand behind her neck and caressed, a steady, gentle pressure, which caused tingles to run over her skin. "Pieces for sale, I hope?"

Haan laughed. "Exactly. Perhaps you'll make it to the basement yet tonight. I am going out for a time this evening and won't be back until late or maybe even early morning, so of course you have the entire run of the house, as promised. Perhaps your lady will find something she likes there as well."

Father Trujillo's dark eyes snapped with annoyance, as if he found the innuendos disturbing.

"Then we'd better get it on," Zane said, his touch drifting from her neck down her arm all the way to her hand. "Come on darling. Let's start with the library."

She felt the other men watching them as they left, and while she was relieved to get away from Haan and the playacting, she knew what came next would change her world in more ways than one.

* * * * *

Zane locked the library door, and the click signaled a moment of truth for Keira. Deep in her bones she knew what happened in this room tonight would change her life forever. Uncertainty and anticipation made her blood heat with illicit excitement and steady trepidation. Her fingers tightened on the small bouquet of tropical red and blue flowers. She glanced around the room and breathed in the scent of leather. The entire room spelled masculinity with its moody burgundy and green colors. Dark brown, supple-looking leather couches and chairs dominated the room. Floor to ceiling bookshelves covered the walls. A sliding ladder gave access to the highest shelves. A huge fireplace commandeered one side of the room, while at the opposite large French doors led out onto a patio with chairs and tables fenced off from the jungle. Zane flipped one light switch and three lamps came on at once, giving the area a soft glow. He moved across the room and closed the heavy curtains to remaining daylight and the storm.

Plied with a glass of champagne and the heady day she'd experienced, she should have been past excitement, beyond desire. Instead, when Zane turned away from the curtains and looked at her, her breath seized up. Suddenly her legs weren't so steady. With his head tilted to his left a little and his arms crossed, his pose resembled a man curious about what she thought and determined to discover what she hid under those layers one by one.

God, he's too sexy. Too masculine.

She had to say something before she went nuts. "What now?"

He put his finger to his lips and shook his head. He reached into his back pocket and took out his wallet. He produced the listening device card and traveled from corner to corner.

A few minutes later he put the card back in his wallet. "No listening devices."

"What about cameras?"

He grinned. "I'll just have a look around and see if I can find any."

Uncertain, she stood there like a stork while he cruised over the room once again. Several moments later he said, "I don't see any cameras."

Puzzled, she frowned. "But can't they make cameras look like just about anything?"

He smiled again. "Yeah, but I'm trained to know what every type of camera can and does look like. There's nothing in here. Take my word for it."

Some of the tension eased off. "Good news. Where do we start looking for *La Pasion*?"

"Anywhere and everywhere. The museum didn't have any pictures of it, if you can believe that."

"How long do we have to search before Haan becomes suspicious? He expects us to...uh...try several rooms tonight, right?"

Zane smiled a little. "Yeah, that's right. But who knows. We might find this room has interesting possibilities on its own."

Her face heated and she took a deep breath. "We'll have to look behind each book, won't we?"

"Yep. I'll pop the champagne." He went for the bottle nestled in a champagne bucket on the coffee table in front of the fireplace. "We'll be thirsty by the time we're finished exploring."

Why does everything that comes out of his mouth tonight sound seductive and laced with double entendres? Is he doing it on purpose?

"How big are these statues supposed to be? How do we know what we're looking for?"

"I was told we'd know it when we see it."

"Oh, that's great. Nice and vague."

"Let's put it this way. It's bigger than a breadbox."

"How could it be behind a book then?"

"It might not be. On the other hand, if the shelves are deep and the books are only sitting at the front of the shelf…" He trailed off and shrugged. "Don't climb up on that ladder, especially not in those shoes."

The champagne popped without throwing fizz all over him.

She drew out one book and looked behind it. "I'll let you do the top shelves, Mr. Macho."

He grunted. She heard him pouring the champagne, but ignored the temptation to stop and further celebrate their marriage with a toast. After a short interlude he started working on the top shelves, going through them with steady and unremitting pace. After more than an hour of searching they'd looked behind most of the books and found nothing.

"Shit," he muttered under his breath as he climbed back down the ladder.

"This calls for a break." She headed for the crystal flutes he'd already filled with bubbly. She picked up one flute and handed him the other. "It would be pretty unusual if we found it right away, don't you think? Wouldn't Haan be a little cleverer?"

"Maybe." Over the rim of the glass, his gaze met hers. A question resided there and he asked it. "There's something that's bugging me. I've got to know the truth."

She took another sip of champagne, then put the glass down on a side table near the leather couch. "Such as?"

"Actually there are several somethings bothering me."

She smiled. "Okay, then start with the first one."

"When you put on that ring yesterday and wandered into the jungle, did you really not remember anything until you arrived at that clearing?"

A little stunned by the unexpected topic, she strolled away from him to lean against the one wall that didn't have anything against it. She felt safer with her back to the wall.

"Yes. Why are you asking that now?"

"You still say you didn't know Haan before you came to Puerto Azul and your grandfather had nothing to do with *La Pasion* or any other artifacts being stolen?"

She leaned her head back against the wall. "That's right."

When he headed her way she almost left her position. She could run away now, away from the interrogation he seemed intent on inflicting. Instead she stayed, eager to explore whatever might occur next.

"I don't believe you," he said.

She wanted to growl as her temper flared. "Well, what if I told you I don't give a crap anymore about whether you believe me?" A trembling started in her stomach as he walked toward her. "I have nothing to confess."

"Oh, I think you've got plenty to confess, and you're going to tell me everything before the night is over."

She could escape, run from the room. Her feet stayed rooted to the floor. "Damn it, Zane, we should be looking for *La Pasion*, not bickering again."

As the wall held her up, he moved in. She saw darkness in his eyes, and a determination to excavate the truth. This agent went after life with both barrels blazing and damn anything venturing into his way.

Butterflies danced and dipped in her stomach and heat flushed her body. Whether she liked it or not, this man turned her on. As his big body moved toward her, she stared in stunned fascination at his male beauty. She wanted to meet him halfway across the room, but she couldn't move. She craved his touch, the continuing closeness they'd feigned in the ceremony. Playacting wore at her defenses, a pickax chipping down the outer layer.

Less than six inches separated them. His hot gaze flamed and sparks of desire filled her lower stomach.

"You will tell me," he said. "Or there will be drastic consequences."

"Such as?"

"When I get you down in that basement I'll use a little bondage."

Her breath sucked in. "You would never."

"Wanna bet? Try me."

She almost sneered at him for his insolence, for the blatant challenge. Instead she continued. "Are you this way with all the women you know?"

"I've never been like this with another woman." His voice dropped. "You do things to me I've never felt before and it's driving me nuts. It's making me question everything, every move I make. I haven't been acting like a professional since I met you, and I know it. What I feel between us is overpowering, Keira."

His voice, warm and gentle, rough and masculine, made her name sound like a mantra. She wanted to hear more. Her heart started to pound and her breathing accelerated.

"I could get in the shower twice a day and jack off to relieve the tension," he said.

A tiny thrill of female power coiled tight in her lower belly like electricity. She'd never thought in a million years that arguing with a man would arouse her, but apparently with this man, it did. His stunning confessions fueled the pressure inside her, daring her to move nearer the border, to step over the line he'd drawn.

"Have you? I mean, jacked off since we've met?" She couldn't believe she asked it, but the words tumbled from her mouth.

Instead of laughing, his eyes burned. "Yeah. And all the time I was wishing your mouth was around my cock just like it was in the jungle." He allowed his gaze to coast down to her waist, to brush with total and complete brazenness over the front of her dress until his attention riveted on her pussy. "I want to be wrapped in your sweet grip again."

Sweet grip. He could mean her hands, he could mean her mouth, but she knew deep inside he meant the folds between her legs.

Half crazed from his intoxicating nearness, she said in last defense from the onrush of desire, "I'm here to help you find *La Pasion*, that's all."

His beautifully carved mouth caught her attention. A tight hard line held his lips immobile. His arms came down on either side of her, his body almost touching hers...almost.

"Tell me what you were doing in Egypt," he asked.

Energized in a strange way she couldn't understand, she defied him. "Nothing that is any of your business."

The temperature in his eyes said either she'd pissed him off, or his passions grew higher. "All right. What about those two items mentioned during the dinner? The puma-shaped burner?"

"It was similar to one I saw at the museum in London, but I can't be certain. I'm not the curator or the registrar."

"The Cibcha mask. What about that one?"

She nodded. "Yes. I recognize it. Unless it's a forgery or a copy—"

"Both of those items were stolen from the museum. I've got a list a mile long in my head of all the things that Haan pinched from Chesterham Museum."

She signed. "So why didn't you or Mac Tudor tell me this? Clue me in?" When he didn't say anything, staring at her with that inscrutable intensity, she understood. "Oh, I see. You wanted to see my reaction to the artifacts. See if I gave away my grandfather's guilt or my guilt."

He nodded. "Something like that."

"Well, other than thinking I recognized the items, I don't know diddly beyond that."

While trust didn't grow in his eyes, she did see his interest in her as a woman refusing to diminish. She'd had enough teasing. Enough waiting. Giving praise where praise was due had always been her motto, and she had a lot to thank this man for, despite wanting to tell him to turn down the high-pressure sexual vibes.

She reached up and laid her palm over his lapel, smoothing a nonexistent wrinkle. "Thank you."

Looking puzzled at her change in topic, he asked, "For what?"

"For saving my life in Egypt and in the jungle."

He nodded but said nothing, his gaze caressing her face.

She continued, leaving her hand on his lapel. "Give me the benefit of the doubt, Zane."

"No."

Bitter disappointment welled inside her.

An unexpected grin broke through his grimness. "Even though I know you're hiding something from me, I think I could trust you with my life, too. If it came to that."

A smidgen of her perturbation eroded. Her heart pinched with unpleasant fear at the thought of him in more danger. "Let's just hope it doesn't come to that." His nearness drove her to within an inch of meltdown, and she shifted against his body. Words came from her she hadn't planned to say. "Ever since I met you, I've been in this situation. You pursue me like an animal, pressing against me, moving closer."

He didn't bat an eye, his tough-and-tender mouth quirking in a new smile. This time the smile held male cunning. "Because since I met you, you've been on my mind day and night. Because you're making me crazy. When I saw you walking down that aisle today, I'd never seen anything so beautiful in my life." He took one hand away from the wall and skimmed his index finger down along the bodice of her low-cut top. "Or more deadly."

Tired of playing around, she grabbed the hand caressing her skin and held him still. "Me deadly? How?"

Rough with confusion and desire, his voice went deeper. "Because I told you and I told myself we couldn't do this...whatever *this* is between us. But my body doesn't seem to give a fuck. Every time you're near me I can't stop wanting to touch you."

Gratification flowed into her at his declaration. Surprised he'd admit his desire, she released her grip on his fingers. His hand returned to the wall beside her, caging Keira where he wanted. He shifted until they touched, and trapped between the wall and his body, she found no escape from the wild need assaulting her.

Uncertain but compelled, she touched his cheek, sliding her fingers over the strong cut of his jaw. "When you sang those songs in the elevator to me, what were you trying to do? Seduce me?"

A small smile flirted with his perfect mouth. "I was trying to throw you a curve ball. I was so damned attracted to you that I couldn't help flirting. Did it work?"

She pushed her fingers into his hair and enjoyed the thick, silken strands as they brushed against her palm. "Yes. And that last song in the shower today before the wedding?"

He frowned and dipped his head a little. He closed his eyes and a muscle in his jaw worked hard. Maybe she could ply another truth out of this hard-as-nails agent.

"Zane?" She moved her fingers through the hair at the back of his neck. "It wasn't the same type of song. It meant more."

His nostrils flared and he swallowed hard.

She must say it because she couldn't stand it any longer. The torture act, the not knowing how he felt drove her bananas.

"Okay, I tell you what I think it meant. You were singing about the way you want me. I think you care about me, Zane

Spinella, whether you want to admit it or not. Your feelings are confusing you, just the way my feelings are confusing me."

"You're right damn." His voice came out a bit guttural. "I do care about you. A hell of a lot more than I should."

Nowhere to go and nothing to hide any longer, she touched his powerful chest again. Her voice, when it came, trembled a little. "What do you want from me?"

Smoldering with turbulent emotion, his gaze told her she'd pushed him as far as she could. "This. Just this."

His mouth covered hers.

Chapter Thirteen

Exquisitely gentle, Zane's kiss coaxed her yearning in a way Keira didn't expect. God, this man must be determined to draw her on the rack, screaming for mercy, begging for a vanquishing touch, a hard thrust to put her out of perpetual misery.

She wanted that hard, sexual frenzy they'd experienced the other night in the tent. She wanted him hard and deep and fast. Fucking her into the next century.

Then she didn't have to imagine any longer.

His arms slipped around her back and waist, drawing her tight against his solid body and the undeniable erection pressed to her belly. *Oh yes.* He was hard all right—harder than before and ready for action.

Pounding desire hit Keira, and she didn't wait for him to ease her into a kiss. She devoured his mouth, her tongue gliding over his lips. Hungry and powerful, his response molded and shaped, taking with voracious appetite. Who needed to be eased into the ecstasy when it demanded, on both sides, to explode? They'd danced for too long, held out for too much. Their night in the jungle barely took the edge off. All they needed was here, now, and the dance their bodies wanted more than anything on earth.

His tongue met hers, allowing her to plunge into his mouth and explore, a bold invader. He caressed, lingering over her back with searching touches, then coasting down to cup her ass, then back up again. His hot skin against her bare shoulders and back corkscrewed her out of control. Zane broke away and looked deep into her eyes, then his hips pressed solid granite cock against her belly.

"Keira," he rasped, a worshipful expression in his gaze that sent rocket fuel straight to her belly. "You are so hot."

Stunned, because no man had called her hot before, she stuttered. "No...I..."

His intense gaze softened as he pressed a kiss to her nose, then her lips. "God, yes. All hot and ready to make love."

Make love.

Every time the man said he wanted to fuck her, her libido went into Roger Ramjet speed, and now that he said those magic words, that he wanted to make love, the burning desire deep in her belly turned molten. She must have satisfaction, the throbbing building between her legs so unrelenting she thought she might scream.

She thought she'd been turned on in the tent the other night, but that couldn't compare to the burning eruption of heady craving, of unmitigated lust that grabbed her by the short hairs and shrieked for fulfillment. As his tongue flicked over her ear, she shivered. *Oh no. Not that again.* He'd have her turned into a small puddle any moment.

He dipped and tasted the junction between her neck and shoulder, nibbling the sensitive flesh, then licking and kissing. Her body shivered as exquisite desire flooded through her. She couldn't stand it, the pleasure heightened to a razor-sharp point.

She floundered with one last resistance, with one inhibition that threatened to blow this liaison apart. "You don't trust me and I don't trust you. You don't believe me about the ring and how I got through the jungle."

Without pause he continued tender examination along her neck and ear. "I don't care if you flew across the jungle on a fuckin' U.F.O. All I know is I want to get inside you again so badly I can taste it."

With a wildness she never expected, she told him what he wanted to hear. "Then do it."

With a low growl he crushed her in his arms, his mouth coming down on hers. Sweeping emotions gathered her up and mixed with the demanding thrust of his tongue taking her mouth with quick, deep strokes. On and on the kiss persisted, a soul-searching greed that understood no boundaries.

Before she knew it, he'd unzipped the back of her ensemble. The top hung by the shoulder straps until he moved back long enough to slide the corset-inspired design off her arms. His gaze consumed as he inspected the low demi-cut long line bra. Without hesitation, he slipped the long garment downward until it pooled around her ankles. She stepped out of the garment and kicked it aside.

He edged back from her long enough to take in the long line bra, the garter belt, G-string panties and stockings. His gaze flared. "Holy shit."

She smiled and eased back into his arms. "Like it?"

"Do I like it? Mother of God, yes."

His husky declaration, filled with awe, made unexpected tears come to her eyes. Tears of happiness couldn't be defined or entrapped. She felt as if she'd wanted this man her whole life. Animal stirrings built inside her stomach, a crying out for a rapid breeding. Her breathing quickened as her heart thundered to his beat. An insistent tempo beat between her legs, tightening like a spring, threatening.

He reached behind her and undid the hook and eye bra one step at a time. When he finished with it he tossed it into the corner too, leaving her white and pink flesh naked for his view. "Look at you. Beautiful. When we were in the tent I couldn't get enough of these. I wanted to kiss and suck them all night."

She watched his expression, his hungry gaze as he reached out and traced with the gentlest touch each breast. He left her nipples alone, and as the areolas went tight and hard, she squirmed a little against his touch. Without warning he dipped down and pressed a soft, quick kiss on each nipple, and she gasped in surprise as shivering pleasure seared her.

With a swift, unexpected movement his hands slipped down her back and into the back of her panties. She expected him to cup her ass, maybe caress her cheeks. Instead he allowed one finger to dip between her legs and touch the wetness steadily moistening her pussy.

"Oh yeah," he said when he felt her wetness.

She jerked and gasped at his touch, at the pleasure his fingers gave her as he stroked once, twice, then drew the moisture back between her ass cheeks until he touched her anus.

In total surprise she jerked. "Oh."

"Like that?" he asked huskily.

"Yes. Yes."

She did, though she'd never had a man touch her there, in the most forbidden of places.

A feral grin touched his mouth. "We'll do more in that area later."

They'd do more later? Her breath caught in her throat at the possibilities and it made her heart beat erratic and fast.

"Right now," he said, "I don't think I can take this nice and slow." He pressed kisses to her forehead, to her cheeks, to her chin. His eyes, dark and fiery with passion, added to her excitement. "I'm not going to let you hide from me any more."

Oh shit. Yes.

She wanted that and so much more. She grasped his shoulders as with one heaving movement he lifted her off her feet and her legs came up around his waist. Zane wedged his pants-covered cock against her sensitive pussy. With the first brush of his hardness against her softness, she drew in a sharp breath.

His eyes locked with hers. "Tell me you want it."

She arched against him, gripping Zane between her legs as she closed her eyes and writhed against the hard, straining, enormous pillar of male sexuality. "I want it. Now."

Up and down, up and down she undulated, rubbing against his flesh as brand-new heat flamed up inside her clit.

Powerful and pounding, the excitement swept her up and took total control. At this rate who needed foreplay?

No doubt about it now. He *would* have her. Haan could pound on the door and scream fire and it wouldn't matter. All she cared about was burning up in Zane's arms and discovering again the sensation of his big, thick cock buried inside her.

"Please. Do it now," she said in desperation.

His chest heaved against hers with each fast breath. "Easy, honey."

Husky and unsteady, his voice sent rumbles of pleasure into her loins like the earthquake they experienced the other night.

Her throat dry and words aching to be free, she said, "Just...please...I need you so much."

As she opened her eyes to look at him, she saw him go over the edge. Virile heat, ravenous desire dictated from here forward. He reached between them, grabbed the front of her panties and yanked. She gasped as the delicate nylon and cotton ripped off her. He tossed the destroyed panties in the corner. Now she stood in his arms, almost naked in only garter belt, stockings and shoes. She'd never made love partially clothed, and the idea turned her on.

"That better?" he asked, his voice sultry.

Her breath caught in her throat, her tension, her need drawn tight. "Oh yes."

He reached between them and with a few swift movements undid his belt, his zipper and, oh—yes, yes, yes. Strong, hot cock nudged between her wet folds, searing her with the realization the moment had come. Along with her outrageous need for his body, her emotions ran high, blistering with a tenderness deep inside for him.

She cupped his face and stared deep into the onyx darkness in his eyes. She saw his craving burning there as it ate him alive with a need to complete their union and draw their bodies into the most primordial dance of all. He rubbed his naked cock against her, and she ached, her pussy begging with hot throbbing for him to thrust.

As he inserted the head of his cock into her hot opening, she shuddered with undeniable pleasure. So hot, so hard, he dipped inside just a little, then pulled back, then dipped. She squirmed, wanting that solid bar of heat as far inside her as she could take. Pleasure surged and ebbed, surged and ebbed as he entered just enough to tease her.

Unable to take the ravenous look in his gaze any longer, she tilted her head back and closed her eyes.

"No." His voice went rough, hoarse with desire. "Open your eyes and look at me. I want to see your eyes when I fuck you."

Fuck you.

The brutal honesty of those words aroused her so much, she wondered if she'd make it through his first thrust, or if she'd explode on impact.

"Come on, honey. Open your eyes."

She heard the plea in Zane's voice. He needed this from her, desired to see her true feelings. If he watched her eyes, if he looked at her while he thrust inside her she couldn't take it. Vulnerability spiked high, made her eyes moisten with tears. But for him, she realized, she just might do anything.

She opened her eyes and saw the carnal longing in his, his own defenselessness open to inspection. Trepidation left her.

"Yes," he whispered.

With one solid, straight push, his bare cock spread her walls and burrowed through wet, tender folds with steady pressure. A satisfied, relieved growl left his throat as he pushed deep, deeper, to the very end.

So hot. So thick and long and hard.

She trembled on the razor's edge, a whimper of excitement and wild fear on her lips. Fear that he would leave her, fear when this was over she'd never feel like this again.

His cock filled every wet, starving inch of her pussy. She gasped, her heart pounding as the pleasure rocketed outward from where he touched her. No man before Zane made her emotions rise and fall, surge and plummet the way he did.

Zane drew back until half his cock remained within her, then he thrust hard and deep. A little cry of pleasure left her throat as she received his final inches.

His mouth touched hers, a gentle tribute. He pressed kisses along her neck, down to her collarbone, lingering with light caresses that cherished and fed her desire. Shivers coasted over the sensitive skin as he tongued the hollow of her throat. With his tremendous strength he held her against the wall, and that power drove her desire higher and hotter. He remained motionless for so long she twitched her hips.

"Please," she whimpered as she tightened and released muscles over his rigid cock.

"Slow and easy," he said.

Slow and easy? Was he insane? She knew he wanted to plow into her, she felt it in the rigid alignment in his muscles and the effort exerted to hold her up. She burned inside. She gripped his shoulders, her fingernails scraping along the fabric.

He refused to move, so she clenched and released, clenched and released, gripping his cock inside her with ravenous grasps. She would climax this way, with him speared deep, captured by her heat, gripped in her firm walls. He shifted her in his arms, hefted her higher, and his cock stroked tender places.

Then, as he promised, he leaned in and took one hard, aching nipple into his mouth. She gasped again as he compressed her flesh in one strong, sucking motion, then his tongue eased over the hard nub.

A sharp moan left her throat. "Oh Zane. Oh yes."

Another pass of his tongue over heated flesh and she moaned as her nipple tightened and beaded, prickling with heat. He traveled between her breasts, his mouth an instrument of supreme pleasure. Warmth spiked into her stomach and clenched her pussy over his cock as he kept it high and hard inside her. The alternate pleasures of his tongue rasping and licking, and his mouth sucking drove her insane. So sensitive and tight, her nipples tingled and burned, tormented inch by inch as his tongue kept up a steady rhythm, broken only by his pauses to suck long and hard.

"Oh please," she whispered, the pleasure snaking along her body incompatible with coherence.

She moved her hips enough to stir him inside her, the subtle brush of his cock against sensitive tissues a wonderful friction. Back and forth, with smallest movement, her hips twitched and enticed and begged. His breath hissed out and when she opened her eyes she saw the concentration etched into his handsome face, his eyes ablaze with heat, his mouth a tight line.

Again he worked her nipples, licking and sucking until she thought she'd scream. He still didn't thrust; she moved her hips as best she could. Oh God, he meant to keep her hanging on a high wire, strung tight with desire until she came just from the pleasure of his tongue and mouth on her breasts.

"Please, please." She couldn't keep the begging out of her voice, the shameless desire racking her with power so profound, she didn't care what she sounded like. She couldn't say what she really wanted. Had never asked a man with rough, feral expressions to take her. All that mattered was here, now and the rapture she saw etched in his eyes.

"No," he said, his voice a husky growl.

"Yes."

She saw when he lost control, lost the battle to keep her hanging on the precipice of no return. With a single, guttural declaration, he said it all. "Fuck!"

He drew back and slammed inside her, a rough, low sound erupting from him.

She gasped, her eyes widening as the single, hot stab touched something deep within her that set her off. Starting as a tingle the pressure built in her core, her pussy rippling as waves of release soared through her, roaring upward. He leaned into her, his pelvis pressing hard on her clit and grinding his cock inside her. She held his gaze, forced herself to look at him, to meet his unrelenting wish. He wanted surrender and she knew it.

She surrendered.

Blooming heat splintered in her pussy, rushing in the most mind-blowing climax she'd felt in her life. Searing and hot the orgasm rode her hard, making her hips twitch, her entire body shake as she panted and gasped. Her fingers dug into his shoulders, crumpling the material of his jacket as she reached for an anchor in the storm.

As her climax started to ebb, though, a new beat began. He moved, rotating, grinding, a steady push and pull that urged supersensitive muscles in her pussy to vibrate to life again. She wanted to scream, to urge him faster. He kept the pace excruciating, an initiation into heaven as he thrust, rubbing with relentless fervor.

"Oh shit," he whispered.

She felt a quiver go through his body and groaned as the orgasm she thought had left fired into life. Deep inside another screaming release threatened.

She shivered. Shook. "Please."

Her beseeching did no good. He wouldn't quicken the pace, wouldn't put her out of her misery. Suddenly the thunder outside revived as it rolled around the house in a heavy rumble.

She jammed her hands into his hair as he looked down at her, his eyes blazing, his lips now parted in a grimace of untamed male. Her fingers tightened in his hair, a growl parting her lips.

Frontiers opened, her body a receptacle for the most knee-melting sex on earth, she urged him forward with new confidence, with the intensity of a woman determined to get what she wanted and needed.

"Harder." Then, oh then, what she'd never been able to say before. "Fuck me harder!"

He obeyed, jamming into her, hips pumping, every thrust hammering inside her pussy with a fury that set her on fire. A shriek erupted from her throat as the climax hit her like a tornado. With ruthless precision he fucked her, ripping apart her inhibitions and shattering them on the floor. She barely realized when she tugged at his hair, searched his shoulders, gripped his biceps and held on for dear life.

As climax rocketed in her body she absorbed each pounding thrust. Seconds later he stiffened and pushed unbelievably deep.

Another orgasm ripped through her, this one threatening to make her incoherent. She moaned and dizziness swept through her head, her breathing suspended as indescribable pleasure racked her core. Wrenching. Tightening and releasing as her pussy rippled around his cock with great waves of stunning climax.

Oh, *my God.*

He drew back and rammed her with another thrust.

A throaty roar ripped from him as she felt scorching blasts of cum fill her. He shuddered and a groan slipped from his throat with each steady pulse of his cock.

She couldn't believe it. She'd fucked this man into oblivion without even undressing him, and with her shoes on. It was the most erotic event in her life.

Zane couldn't believe it. As he stared into Keira's eyes and watched the pleasure remaining in the soft ocean of her eyes, he knew he could never go back to a comfortable relationship. What they had started in the jungle finished here and now. He'd broken the rules getting involved with her, but a warm, protective feeling rose inside him he couldn't squash. A primitive sensation, like a man of the cave taking possession of his woman. He'd loved sending her into the heavens; fucking her hard like an animal hadn't been his plan, but she'd driven him nuts.

Nestled inside her, still hard as hell and not finished wanting her, he kissed her deeply. His breath hissed inward as he enjoyed her tight clasp caressing his swollen cock. Breathing in deeply, he caught the scent of sex lingering on the air.

"You're incredible." He kissed her nose.

She looked a little shell-shocked, but then the astonishment eased from her face and she tossed him a sultry grin. "That was…it was the most amazing thing. That's never happened to me before."

"What's never happened?"

A blush tinged her cheeks. "I've never made love standing up before."

Teasing, he pushed gently back and forth, feeling her pussy grip him without remorse. *Jesus, that felt too damned good.* Her eyes widened and she shivered in his arms. If he didn't stop now, he'd start fucking her again.

With a groan he inched back into her, pressing deep, his pace gentle as her breath hitched in her throat. A flush rolled up her chest, then in to her throat and face. Again, he pulled back, then thrust, his pace slow and measured.

"You want to come again?" His throat felt tight and dry and he swallowed.

"Yes." This time her head fell back and she closed her eyes, her face showing the ecstasy they shared. Her mouth opened on a soft intact of breath. "More."

"Oh yeah. More." Gently, with a back and forth movement that caressed, he moved inside her taut, soaked heat with ease.

Down to his muscles and bones he felt her, more than her sopping pussy encompassing him, and more than the way her breath sucked in each time he thrust. He felt her in his heart, a forging of trust and deeper feelings he stopped fighting as soon as she enclosed his body with hers.

She clutched at his arms and he felt the press of her nails through his suit jacket, and as her breathing accelerated and little whimpers left her throat, her body contracted over his with rippling pulses. She shivered in his arms, the little climax shuddering through her body and into his. Zane held her until she stopped quivering, tenderness threatening to make him think and do things he had no time for.

As he reluctantly eased his body from her tightness, he helped her lower her feet to her floor. He cupped her face for a moment, loving the softness of her skin and the sparkle in her eyes. "Anything else you haven't done, honey?"

She licked her red, swollen lips. She looked like what she was—a thoroughly fucked woman. "Lots of things."

He nuzzled her nose, her forehead, and then her ear. "Damn it, I'd love to stay here, but we've got to move out."

As he moved away, she looked at his still fully erect cock. "You're still…"

"Hard?" He hitched his pants back over his ass. "I'm holding back until later."

She gawked at him in surprise, and he almost laughed. From the time he left his teens he'd retained high sexual energy. He prided himself on being able to fuck a woman long and hard before he climaxed.

"Why don't we move to the next room and search the place. If we don't find the statues in the living or dining rooms, we'll find something else to do," he said.

He turned away to locate the tissue box residing on the desk not that far away, then handed her a few.

His cock twitched and stirred as he watched her find her bra and cover those delicious pink nipples from his sight. Right now she looked frazzled, a little unsure of herself. Unused to Keira exhibiting anything but confidence, it worried him.

She stared at the floor, her clothes discarded all around her.

"Oh dear," she said, her voice vulnerable.

Concerned, he frowned. "What's wrong?"

She moved to the corner where he'd tossed her garments and picked up her panties. She dangled them from her index finger. "These are shredded."

"Sorry I ripped them?"

Her mouth opened, then closed, then a grin replaced her frown. "No. It was very...uh...arousing."

Male satisfaction coursed through his blood. "Toss 'em in the trash."

"Haan might find them."

He laughed. "Yeah, but it's what he expects to find, right? He figured we'd be in here fucking like bunnies."

She nodded and swallowed hard. "Yes." When she looked at the front of his pants, which he'd barely managed to zip over his erection, she smiled. "Looks like your suit has a little evidence on it, too."

He glanced down. Sure enough, his crotch showed evidence of their recent activities. "No kidding."

He knew she hadn't recovered from what they'd done, but he hoped she didn't regret it, either. "Come on. Let's find *La Pasion.*"

After securing their clothes, they unlocked the door and made their way down to the next room. He nodded toward the door as he gripped the doorknob. "This is the workout room."

As they walked in, she let out a soft breath of surprise. No less than ten workout machines graced the room. From the looks of Haan, he didn't use many of them.

After taking out the Macon card he searched the place and found no sign of listening devices or cameras.

"There's nowhere to hide anything," she said.

With the exception of artwork on the walls, the place was pretty bare.

As she moved toward a small refrigerator and sink area at the far side of the room, he speculated that Haan had hidden sex toys in this room, too.

"You think *La Pasion* might be stashed in a refrigerator?" she asked.

"Anything is possible."

He grinned as she opened the short fridge. "Nothing in here but bottled water." Unwilling to give up one hundred percent, she opened the cabinet door above the sink and checked it.

When she gasped and pulled a bag out of the cabinet and held it up, he couldn't help laughing. She held the bag almost as if it contained body parts and not the sex toys he could see through the clear plastic. "Please tell me the statues aren't some ancient sex toy."

"For all I know, they might be." He strode toward her and took the bag out of her hand. "This, though, is interesting."

He felt her curiosity and maybe a little of her embarrassment as he opened the bag and found two brand-new wrapped sex toys, a vibrating dildo and a butt plug, plus a container of lube. His cock twitched in anticipation. *Oh yeah.* This could get real interesting before the night finished.

An idea popped into his head that couldn't be stopped. "Take off your clothes."

Her mouth popped open. "What?"

"We're christening this room."

He saw the minute a fire ignited in her eyes when the anticipation of discovering untried sexual horizons appealed to her.

"Take your clothes off slowly," he said.

With a confidence that turned him inside out with desire, she strode toward him. Just like the moment he'd seen her walking down the aisle toward him at the wedding, his heart pounded. As she moved her hips swayed and made the delicate material around her ankles swish and swirl. The sound of material brushing against slim, sexy ankles dried his mouth. His cock took immediate notice, drawing up hard.

Shit, he had to get out of these pants before the pain of his trapped erection crippled him.

While he couldn't see her nipples through the top of her dress, he could damn well imagine them. He remembered their silky texture when soft, then the nubbins that hardened into points when aroused. His gaze slid down, caressing her lithe, yet rounded form. All her angles, all her soft curves, everything that made Keira Jessop unique stirred his blood. He wanted to explore those differences, the individuality that called to him stronger and harder than any woman before her.

Tonight he would lick and taste and travel the length of her body without remorse. No more playing, no more teasing.

All bets were off.

Chapter Fourteen

Keira turned around and presented her back to Zane, and as she did so, she wondered if she would ever catch her breath again. She'd seen the desire in his eyes, and although the room held nothing but exercise equipment, she thrilled at the idea of discovering what he planned.

"Unzip me and unhook the bra," she said.

"Yes, ma'am."

His big, warm fingers landed on her bare shoulders and she shivered as he caressed her upper arms before reaching for the zip and doing as she asked.

After he complied, she walked across to where she'd been before. Without turning toward him, she shimmied and the skirt fell to her ankles. Bit by bit she slid the top off her shoulders. Then she dispensed with the bra. This time she felt more naked, more exposed. She wore nothing but her pride, a garter belt, stockings and her shoes.

As she stood mostly naked and vulnerable, he shed his clothes. A stirring bloomed in her belly, a call to renewed need. She thought, with the explosive orgasm she'd experienced not long ago, that she couldn't become this aroused so fast. As he tossed his expensive jacket on the arm of an exercise bike, undid his tie, then unbuttoned his shirt with relaxed ease, she discovered how wrong she could be. She watched with rapt attention as he removed the shirt and it landed on the jacket.

Drinking in the sight of warm, male flesh made her lick her lips. Oh yes, she remembered the solidness of his chest, the muscled planes and glorious six-pack stomach. Her gaze followed the arrow of hair as it disappeared into his waistband.

As he yanked off his shoes, socks and then shucked his pants and underwear, she held her breath.

His masculinity, a brawny testament to how much he wanted her, turned her on so much she didn't think she could stand the long ride toward ecstasy. She needed him now.

His cock sprung out of lush, dark hair, thick and long. Her mouth watered as she drank in his astounding male perfection. The way he'd disrobed made her excruciatingly aware of her feminine needs and stark possessiveness. She desired to stake a claim on him no other woman could touch. While she knew their lovemaking wouldn't last beyond this journey through Puerto Azul, she knew this time couldn't be erased from her mind. All they experienced drew a pattern on her soul and engraved his name in her heart.

His gaze watched her with pure admiration, gliding with unabashed male interest over her breasts. Her nipples ached with a desire for his touch. Then his attention drifted down to her belly and the hair beneath. Her stomach fluttered as arousal dipped between her legs like a touch and made her throb with liquid yearning. He hardly paused before perusing her legs encased in the stockings.

His fascination with her legs gave her an idea.

Maybe remnants of champagne gave her courage, perhaps the devouring look on his face made the difference. Whatever the case, she decided to break all rules, taboos, and self-imposed uptight restraints. Before she moved toward him she reached up and slipped her hands through her hair and allowed strands of the messy tumble to tickle her fingers. Zane watched her keenly, and she saw the power she held to entice him beyond bearing.

She took a deep breath and ambled toward a big machine with two benches and counterweights between them. For the first time, with her body on display, she didn't feel as self-conscious as before. Here she became a queen, a goddess with a body that ruled.

Zane made her feel that way.

She took a risk. She placed one hand on the metal frame of the weight lifting machine. The other hand she put on her hip. Lifting her leg, she propped her foot on the bench. Cool air brushed her labia and tickled her clit. She inhaled and her mouth popped open as the sensation brushed her tummy and pooled between her legs.

As if she didn't have a care in the world, she turned her gaze to Zane. "What do you think? Would you like to work out?"

His eyes widened, his expression a little stunned at this newfound boldness. Instant gratification made her smile. Excellent.

"Yeah," he said, his voice hoarse.

Muscles rippling, he walked toward her, toys in hand. He stopped in front of her and placed the toys on the opposite bench. When he opened the bag and ripped into a smaller bag containing a butt plug, warmth splintered inside her. She'd never indulged in anal play before. Forbidden excitement warred with horrified fascination. He put the red, flexible jelly butt plug down on the bench, then he dropped to his knees.

His dark gaze simmered with an unchecked sensuality. "I'm hungry. I think I'll eat first."

Keira's muscles quivered at the rough need and innuendo in his voice. She held on tight to the machine as he edged between her legs. He clasped her propped-up thigh, and pushed it a little wider.

As she held her breath in anticipation, he looked up at her and held her gaze. When he smiled the warmth, caring, and hot need in that one glance made her heart melt. Her mind whirled with the realization that her feelings for him grew deeper by the hour.

Then he clasped her left butt cheek and settled in to feed upon her.

"Oh, look at this. Sweet and wet." His tongue slipped over her labia with a slow, luscious lick. "Delicious. Mmmm."

She gasped as he tasted her, his tongue an invader with no mercy. Tender folds, ripe with arousal, ached for his touch. She moaned as he investigated her silky juices. He worked the opening to her pussy, drawing his tongue around the outer and inner lips with the precision of a man determined to drive her insane. Each pass of his tongue over swollen tissues made her groan with the sweetest desire she'd experienced in a lifetime.

The more he licked the faster her breathing became, the more her slick, excited labia pulsed and tingled. He didn't touch her clit, and she wondered with the exhilaration of a woman on the edge when he would. Zane fed on her forever, his relentless pursuit warming her heart and searing her body.

When he moved back slightly she groaned in protest. "Don't stop."

"Easy, now. I'm not done. Close your eyes. I have a surprise for you. Something I think you'll like."

She did as told and she heard the bag being shuffled about, the crinkling noise of wrappers being opened. She ached to see what he planned for her, but kept her eyes shut. She felt him behind her, and his warm palm passed over her ass cheeks with a gentle caress.

"Bend over for a minute," he said.

Wondering what he had in mind, her senses screaming for a completion, she bent at the waist. He pressed open her butt cheeks. As something cool and wet probed at her back hole, she clenched up in surprise.

"Relax," he said with a smile in his voice.

His quiet request eased her into the idea. Then she felt the butt plug enter a slight bit and she deliberately relaxed her muscles. With one steady but slow stroke, he slid the plug home until it wedged deep and tight between her ass cheeks. Startled by the pleasure and the ease in which she took the plug, she drew in a deep breath.

"Hold it inside you." he asked. "How does that feel?"

As she straightened, he drew his hand over her waist and returned to kneel in front of her. "It's incredible. I never thought..."

She didn't know what to say.

"There's more to come. Close your eyes again." He got down on his knees in front of her again.

Within moments she felt something large, hard and wet probing her vagina and realized it was a dildo. She grabbed at his shoulders and he stopped. When she opened her eyes, she saw the intensity in his face, his eyes as he worked the thick dildo into her inch by inch. As the intruder parted Keira's flesh, she drew in a sharp breath.

It was good. Not as good as his cock and not even as big, but the relief it gave her sent spirals of taut, incredible pleasure through her she couldn't deny. She arched against the pressure, drawn into the battle between wanting to come and wanting it to last.

"That's it. Take it deep," he said as he withdrew the dildo almost all the way, then pushed forward.

He turned the dildo on and the vibration hit her as pleasure rocked in waves, causing her to clench over the objects inside her pussy and in her ass.

She drew in a swift breath, then moaned. "Zane. Oh, that's wonderful."

He reached around and took hold of the flared base of her butt plug and drew it out a little way, then pushed back in. Nasty enjoyment jumped up and bit her. She wanted to writhe around the double penetration, her senses taking in this new experience with eagerness. All thoughts drifted away as she permitted feeling to take over.

As Zane worked the butt plug in her ass, moving in and out with steady but tender strokes, she felt her orgasm rising quickly.

God, I didn't know what I was missing.

His tongue lashed at her clit and she groaned with happiness. *Yes, oh yes.* That's what she needed. A three-way torment started, designed to drive her out of her mind. As his tongue flicked her clit and ecstasy stung her, he manipulated the butt plug and dildo, fucking both holes with a rhythm gentle and stimulating. She gripped his head as she pushed her hands through his hair. Caressing the silky, thick strands, she hung on as the orgasm rose and spiked high and hard. She shrieked, the unexpected force taking her by surprise and throwing her into the heavens. Breathing heavily, she absorbed the continued thrusts into her vagina and anus as he continued to lick her clit. It was too much, the stimulation too fine. Her hips jerked in his grasp.

She wanted him deep inside her and said through panting breaths, "You. Now."

Without hesitation he drew the toy from her pussy but not the plug in her ass. He brought her against his big body, and his cock, long and hard, pressed her stomach with demand. His mouth captured hers and his tongue plunged inside. She accepted his searching like a starving woman. She explored without remorse as she traced the contours of muscles so strong and fierce. Body strength told a part of his story; his sharp mind and potent personality drew her more than any hunky exterior could.

When he parted from her, Keira saw the hint of mischief in those mysterious eyes. He sat onto the exercise bench, his back propped against the seat, cock straight up, begging for her attention. The drop of pre-cum from the slit challenged her. She could suck him, lick him until he exploded down her throat. Or she could give him the ride of his life.

She chose to ride.

Without hesitation she straddled him, and he caught her by the waist. Slowly, exquisitely, she slid down, down. As his cock entered, separating her folds, she murmured a sweet sound of enjoyment.

"So hot, so hard," she said, daring to stare into his smoldering eyes.

He leaned in and licked one nipple, a tantalizing combination of laving and nipping that made her gasp. Each time he drew a tender, aching nipple into his hot mouth, each time he sucked and licked and laved, the ecstasy building in her pussy went up another degree. He ate her with ravenous efficiency, voracious male and tender lover. Seated tight on his solid cock, she savored the mind-melting drag and push of his cock rubbing against her G-spot with gentle thrusts.

The few men she'd made love with in the past faded from recollection, muted shadows to Zane's commanding force. His sexuality didn't ease Keira into love and ecstasy; it propelled, aimed at her heart and removed all doubt. He owned her in a way no one had before, and no one would again. Happiness touched her soul, ripped away the fears she'd suffered.

She cupped his face as he gripped her waist. She no longer feared looking into his eyes, for all she saw there was ardor, acceptance and unrelenting desire. As the cadence caught her, she soared on the sensation of steely, broad cock pushing high and deep and the plug in her ass adding to staggering pleasure. He pumped his hips and brought more rapture to the dance. She felt the motion in her bones as she bounced on his cock with faster and harder strokes. Sanity hung in the balance, a here and now need that cared nothing about tomorrow.

Hammering into her pussy with steadily building thrusts, he growled out a command, "Fuck me, honey."

His guttural request sent her into frenzy. She rode him faster, driving downward onto his cock until her breathing went frantic, her body shaking with feral need and unstoppable desire. His hands gripped her waist, his fingers tightening almost painfully. Everything became their motion. Everything coalesced inside her, a screaming need to burst free. Breath coming hard and fast, she tilted her head back and gathered the commotion inside her until she became one with it, inseparable, unstoppable.

Her nails scraped over his shoulders as she anchored against this storm, ripped from her moorings by shattering desire. With a hard, soul-ripping burst, her pussy tightened over his cock. She groaned as the orgasm splintered and throbbed, shaking her from the inside out. Her soft, whimpering cry echoed in the room.

Zane's grip tightened on her waist as he drew her up and down, assisting her ride with fiery strokes deep between her legs. With a last plowing thrust, he slammed her down on his cock and burst.

His head went back. "God, yes!"

His cock poured jets of hot cum. His body shivered, his moans throaty.

When he finished coming he kept her seated on his cock, his arms looped around her waist, his face buried in her throat while he caught his breath. "Shit. That was fucking fantastic."

Satisfaction rang in his voice and she smiled as she pressed a kiss to his forehead. "You can say that again."

"That was fucking fantastic."

She laughed. A light buzzing and pleasant dizziness filled her head. Who needed the future with uncertainties and dangers when right now felt so wonderful? "What now?"

He looked at his watch, then nuzzled her neck. "I hate to say it, but we better move out to the other rooms. We're running out of time. Haan could be back any second."

"I'm surprised his cronies aren't around to keep an eye on us."

"Yeah, Douglas isn't around anywhere that I can tell."

As they cleaned up and she removed the anal plug, she marveled at the pleasure she'd received from it. When she dressed Keira wondered what new things the night might still bring. Zane looked confident as hell, as usual.

When they left the weight room they took the sex toys with them. They may want them later. A secret smile touched her mouth as they approached the kitchen and dining areas. Zane stopped her in the hallway and backed her up against the wall.

She laughed as he slipped his arms around her and whispered in her ear. "The dining room, kitchen and living room all have hidden cameras. We can't search these rooms without disabling the cameras and that'll take too much time."

She whispered back in his ear, "What do we do, then?"

"Move onto easier territory for now. The hallways upstairs have cameras. We could test the doors to see if we can search any of the bedrooms. We'll need to act ridiculous. You know, drunk and disorderly. Play it up when we go up there so that getting into the other bedrooms doesn't seem odd. Then we better check out the basement. Even if there are cameras in there we may have to flirt, fool around just to keep it authentic."

She nodded and a flashed back to the hot tub in the conservatory. A wicked idea came to mind. "I know we're in a hurry, but that hot tub in the conservatory sounds like a nice place to wind down when this is all finished. I mean, if we don't find what we're looking for."

He nodded. "We are going to find what we're looking for. We don't have a choice."

She wanted to believe it, but as they wandered upstairs, she wondered. Perhaps Haan didn't keep *La Pasion* here. Or maybe the man didn't have them in the first place. At the top of the stairs they paused.

Zane dipped her and she let out a shriek and a giggle. "Zane!"

As he drew her back up against him, his eyes held tangible warmth that stirred new desire and a headiness she wanted to last forever. "I love you."

His gaze grew hot as he looked at her. Husky and filled with emotion, his voice sounded so sincere she drew in a ragged breath. *Easy, girl. He's just saying it for the cameras. Don't hyperventilate.*

She managed to say on a soft breath, "I love you."

Oh shit. Oh God. Her sentiment felt too real. She couldn't fall in love with him. She scarcely knew the man. Yet on some level she felt she knew him better than she'd known anyone before.

For a millisecond she saw his gaze flare, take on a deep, gut-level reaction to her words. She didn't know whether to be frightened or gratified by what she saw there. She couldn't know what he honestly felt for her, if anything.

Duty is what he feels, Keira. Don't confuse the mission with reality.

He drew her down the hallway and they laughed and put on the best show they could.

They bumped into some of the doors and he said, "I want to fuck you in each and every room." Hoarse and filled with lust, his voice spoke to ancient urges. "You want to be fucked in the ass? Strapped down on a table and have your pussy licked?"

A coil of heat spiraled in her belly at his blatant questions. She swallowed hard and answered. "Yes."

After they discovered the other bedroom doors locked, they weaved back the way they'd come and down the stairs.

He winked at her. "Let's check out the playroom downstairs."

She knew he meant the basement, and she feared what they'd find.

When they took the winding stairs down to the basement, she noted the plush navy carpet and the beautiful fern green leather chairs and sectional seating. A bar resided in one corner, a pool table in the other. All of it looked normal until she glanced to one side and saw the intriguing contraption near one wall.

"Oh boy," she said.

Zane tossed the sex toy bag on the bar. "Yeah."

The table, about as tall as a pool table, boasted a thick cushion on it with interesting modifications. A hole was cut out for an individual's ass to rest through. She guessed the hole had something to do with sex toy usage. At the arms and legs, straps and cuffs could be used to hold someone down. Zane opened a drawer in the side of the table and found another set of sex toys, including a vibrating butt plug and dildo.

"Interested?" He glanced around the room. She knew he scoped the area, hoping to find evidence of *La Pasion*.

"Yes."

The word popped out of her because she couldn't formulate a reasonable objection. Sure, she could claim all the sex made her sore. Maybe, just maybe the idea of making it on this table appealed to her in a wicked, unimaginable way. Well, she'd better start visualizing, because it might happen any minute. She decided to strip right away, to ruin her inhibitions about bondage by dropping her clothes before she could think.

Zane winked as a wicked gleam entered his eyes. He worked swiftly to remove his clothes. He no sooner shucked his pants when she saw he sported another huge hard-on. Tingling built in her belly and pussy at the sight of his cock burgeoning with new desire. She wanted to lick it, touch it, caress it within her mouth and feel his semen spurting down her throat. The steady ache in her body said she wanted to ride him and ride him and ride him until she couldn't take anymore.

The thought of strong cock pumping in her mouth spurred her to a new decision. "You get on the table."

"What?"

"Trust me. You're going to like this."

He stared at her for a few seconds, unsure he'd heard her right. She wanted him to get up on that bondage table?

Why the fuck not?

Two of his old girlfriends had experimented with bondage, allowing him to tie them up, but he'd stopped the minute he realized they didn't like it much. He'd never suggested to them that they could tie him up. Since then he'd been globetrotting too much to settle into a sexual relationship featuring something as intimate as allowing someone to tie you up.

"Well?" she said, her hands on her naked hips.

His gaze drank her in, appreciating curves. God, looking at her plump breasts and luscious curves made his heart race and his mouth went dry in anticipation. To hell with looking for *La Pasion* right away.

He needed this. "Hell, yes."

He climbed up onto the table and she set to fastening the buckles at his wrists and ankles, accommodating the straps for his big wrists and height. A shiver rippled over his body, but not because of cold. He liked this way too much with this woman; he'd fucked her twice already just that evening and should have it out of his system.

Momentary panic flared in his gut as she cinched the last buckle on his right ankle. Not because he believed she would hurt him, but because she might be hurt mentally and physically by what they'd experienced so far. Physically because this dangerous assignment wasn't over. Mentally because he knew she didn't trust easily and he felt she might now trust him.

Holy shit, Spinella. Are you a fuckin' idiot?

He almost told her to release him then and there. He almost told her they couldn't do this any longer; they *should* re-dress and continue this mission as if they hadn't screwed each other's brains out. They *should* pretend they hadn't invested any emotional time or entanglements. More than that, one thing stood out in his mind and demanded he back out of this unethical relationship right now.

He couldn't trust her. A woman with possible criminal ties.

Or could he?

On cue his erection started to fade.

Zane became more aware of the table under him. She'd positioned him so his ass filled the hole in the table, and he wondered with a jolt of lust if she planned to do anything about that convenient opening. He swung back and forth between wanting her to take him on the wildest sexual experienced of his life to yelling out for her to stop. After all, he always controlled situations, always knew which way to go...until this woman. Until she'd tied him down and planned to do who knows what.

Shit, shit, shit. I am the biggest idiot in the book. If she planned to skin him alive, stab him in the heart, or shoot him, she could do it and he would be a dead duck. Naked and bound, he felt his defenselessness. Like a seasoned pro she'd manipulated him toward this end where she could do whatever the hell she wanted.

Apparently oblivious to his angst, Keira reached for the new bag of sexy toys. She found the small bathroom close to the stairs. In an agony of indecision he waited. When she returned she'd washed a big butt plug and smeared lube on it. He almost told her to stop, but his mouth wouldn't seem to work. Instead he felt his erection return full force, his balls tightening, his cock burgeoning.

Whether his brain liked it or not, his flesh responded to her, not as a human who could choose to kill him any second if she wished. He remembered the tight, wet feel of her pussy and the way her face flushed and her body writhed as he skewered her deep. He wanted more with a fierceness that brooked no refusal.

Seconds later she crawled under the table, and his body tightened.

Then he said the stupidest thing he'd said in a long, long time. "What are you doing?"

She sighed. "Wait and see." Calm and unthreatening, her voice gave away nothing. "Um... I suppose I should have asked if you actually like your...if you..."

He helped her out, hearing the embarrassment crawling into her voice. "Yeah, I think I'm going to like it. A lot."

"You think?" Her voice sounded muffled.

"Yeah. A woman's never put a butt plug up my ass before. But my guess is it's going to feel great."

"Wow. And here I thought you were Mr. Experienced."

Her awed exclamation made him smile, and right then he wondered if maybe things would be all right. If not, he'd pay for his idiocy with his life. "I've been around the block a few times."

She laughed softly. "Spinella, you sound confident even when strapped to a table, helpless as a baby. Why does that not surprise me?"

It astounded the hell out of him. He shouldn't be this confident, and yet part of him observed the kinky proceedings as if he didn't have a care in the world. Just another fuckfest with his woman.

His woman.

Possessiveness swept over him, along with coils of deep longing. Whether he liked it or not, whether she meant to kill him in the end, he couldn't think of her anymore as a criminal. She meant more. So damned much more.

He felt her tentative touch on his ass cheeks, and the warm, tender touches on his skin made his cock surge and lengthen. With an accuracy that surprised him she wedged the butt plug into his crack and located his anus. She probed tentatively. A surge of heated excitement lit in his belly as she pushed gently.

"Is it all right?" she asked, her voice unsure.

"More than all right. Give me more. Give me all of it."

With a slow but steady pressure she inched the plug up his ass. He gasped as pleasure rippled over his body and his cock hardened even more. *Jesus, God, yes. That was good.*

"All right?"

"All right? It's fuckin' incredible."

With a final nudge she inserted the plug all the way, the flared base snuggling between his ass cheeks. He clenched on the instrument of torture, ready for whatever she did next. With a groan he savored the feeling of the plug, wanting her to bounce on his cock until he shot Keira full of cum. Now that would be the ultimate.

Strapped to a table, completely at this incredible woman's mercy turned him on more than any sexual experience he could think of before. Not even their two previous encounters tonight made him so hard, so ready to fuck like a madman.

An epiphany overcame him as she crawled out from under the table. He liked losing it during sex, just as he had in the tent and just as he had when he'd taken her against the wall. He'd loved keeping the fuck going at his pace, until he couldn't take the way her hot, wet pussy had flexed over his aching cock. Then he'd lost it, pounding into her like a madman.

Before he could think more about it, she took a feather from the assortment of toys. Then she acquired a shit-eating grin that said it all. He'd tortured her on more than one occasion, now she would take revenge. He swallowed hard.

"What are you going to do with that?" Zane asked.

A wicked, unrepentant grin touched her mouth. "Oh, just you wait and see."

As she crawled up onto the table and straddled his waist, her moist pussy nuzzled his belly. He groaned at little. It felt way too good. He could smell the sex on her and drew the scent inside him.

A pagan goddess. That's what she looked like. Her hair a bit mussed, her eyes golden with fire and passion, her full lips parted, she showed female power in high form. Nothing would hold her back from possessing him in every way.

Giving over to the realization made his cock harden almost painfully, his balls drawn tight. He wanted her so much. He couldn't imagine doing this or being anywhere else than with her right now.

He must be a fuckin' crazy man, but he didn't care.

The feather flicked over his right ear, sending a tingling into his stomach and straight to his groin. He moaned softly. His breathing accelerated, his heart rekindling a quick beat. Again the feather moved, but this time over his left ear. More tingles darted into his stomach. She worshiped his body with the instrument of torture, first drawing the feather down his neck, then over his pectoral muscles. He couldn't keep back the gasp and the way his muscles tightened as she teased with soft touches. As she tracked the torture device over his pecs and swirled small circles over his nipples, he gritted his teeth against another gut-wrenching moan.

Keira snaked the feather around his chest muscles, then scooted back so she could tantalize his stomach. He drew in a sharp breath as her butt touched his cock.

"You know," he said, "You could rise up a little and slide down on me for a ride."

She grinned, the warmth in her eyes full of teasing. "No way. You're not getting off that easily." She laid the feather on his chest and then leaned forward to press a smacking kiss on his mouth. "You're going to pay."

"For what?"

"For driving me insane since the first day I met you."

She made good on her threat. With attention to detail, she painted his body like a canvas expressing her desire. Long strokes caressed his cheeks, his lips, his pecs until his nipples stood pin-hard and needing the firmer touch of lips and hands. As her buttocks touched his cock again, he allowed his gaze to travel across her porcelain perfection. With earrings and necklace and wedding ring sparkling and the rest of her body bare for inspection, she symbolized a glorious fantasy. A woman this uninhibited, willing to try something new. Stubborn, yes. Amazing and tough and willing to go the extra mile. Yes, he'd give her all that and more.

Keira moved down to his legs, drawing the feather along his calves, then back up until she reached his thighs. With long, languid strokes she teased his inner thighs, so close to his balls and cock that his arousal tightened and throbbed with a combination of heady pleasure and ready-to-burst agony. She leaned over and pressed sultry kisses along his upper thighs until he twitched and gasped. Each soft contact made him want her that much more, to taste and lick and pleasure her as much as she did him.

She'd pay for this crazy-making sex. He'd see to it once he got out of these restraints.

Her eyes turned darker, a potent brandy as she eyed him with clear need. Oh, yeah. It felt good to be wanted like this. She licked his cock from base to tip. His cock jumped, as a jolt of excitement caused him to arch his hips. The feather moved, this time over his balls and up his length.

"Damn it," he said around a gasp of excitement. "That tickles."

She looked startled, then a smile covered her lush lips. She tossed the feather away. "Well, this won't."

She took him in her mouth, plunging down his length with a swift movement that encompassed him down to the balls. He couldn't hold back his verbal response. "Oh shit, yes."

As her tongue flirted with Zane's skin, licking and caressing his length, he felt the burn rise. His balls throbbed and as if she knew what he needed, she curled her small, delicately boned hand around the base of his cock. With satisfying strokes she milked him with lips and tongue, her grip on his cock firm. Swiftly and with a rhythm that curled his toes, she repeated the move with relentless fervor, her right hand pumping him from base to tip as she sucked him.

Hot and wet, her tongue and lips threatened to throw Zane off the edge. Lightning streaks of desire shook his body like a small earthquake. He lifted his head and watched her devour him with a frankness and enjoyment he couldn't recall experiencing. When she gently scraped her teeth over him once, he jerked and moaned.

His hands balled into fists and he arched his hips. "Ride it."

When she ignored him and released his cock, he thought he'd lose his mind. She enclosed his hard length in her grip, but this time she leaned down far enough to lick his balls. With her other hand she found the spot between his anus and balls and rubbed him. The combination about blew his head off.

"Shit. Ride, me," he said again, his voice hoarse. "Do it now."

It must have been his plea that did it. She released him long enough to straddle his hips.

Yeah. Oh, yeah. This is gonna be good.

But the little minx hadn't finished tormenting him.

She waited, gazing into his eyes with an intensity that left him breathless, as if she could read his mind and understood the urges roaring inside him like a pounding waterfall, a furious wind that rushed through his soul and imprinted on his psyche forever.

Then, like a seductress, she reached up and plucked her nipple. Oh, hell. She wouldn't, would she? Demand he watch while she got off in her own special way? He didn't think he could stand it, yet he wanted it more than anything.

"Do it again," he said, his voice rusty.

She not only did it again, Keira reached down and touched her pussy. Her middle finger began to stimulate her clit, and Zane thought his cock would blow right then and there. His mind reeled as his breathing came harsh and heavy. Her fingers went slick and shiny from her juices and she pinched first one nipple, then the next. Her tongue passed over her passion-swollen lips, her gaze riveted to his. Need grew in her eyes, smoldering and intense. He wanted to give her anything and everything she needed to climax, writhing and bucking on his cock like a woman gone mad with ecstasy.

"What do you want?" He arched his hips and his cock bumped against her butt cheeks again. "What do you need to get off?"

Her lips parted a little, her eyes widened as if his husky questions took her off guard. "I...I need to ride you."

"Do it, honey. Do it now and put me out of my misery." He'd never begged a woman to fuck him before, but he'd die if she didn't.

Without hesitation she lined up his cock with her pussy and moved down over him like a scabbard. Bliss vaulted up his spine and his cock and balls ached. As wet, heated flesh encompassed him, Zane gripped the side of the table with a vengeance. Sliding soft and wet, her flesh grasped him within an inferno he didn't know if he could survive.

A growl left his throat. "Come on, fuck me."

Trapped by the cuffs on his ankles and wrists, he could endure but not participate much more than to arch his hips the slightest bit. So he did. He pushed his hips upward that little increment and his breath hissed between his lips as her wet, hot passage caressed him.

As Keira started to pump up and down, she continued to pluck and pinch her nipples and manipulate her clit. Trapped in her pussy's sweet grip, all he could do was watch her pleasure unfold and enjoy the slick channel that embraced him.

As pleasure started to climb, he knew he couldn't last as long this time. She threw her head back and whimpered as she took him, slamming down on his cock with ever increasing movements of her hips. The added stimulation of the butt plug threatened to send him off any minute. He tightened his ass cheeks, determined to keep the butt plug firmly inside.

As their pleasure increased she mumbled an erotic litany. "Oh, yes. Yes, yes, yes, yes. Yes!"

Her body vibrated and he felt the twitching, the pull and tug as her pussy walls gripped and released him in rippling waves. Her shriek triggered the onrush. He aided her orgasm by grinding upward at the same time she jammed her hips against his.

Climax slammed him like a freight train and he groaned and his hips bucked with each screaming blast of cum. His body shuddered, shivering deep inside her as bliss spread through his veins, his muscles, his very skin. Pure ecstasy pulsed out of his cock as he filled her with spurt after spurt of cum.

Languid enjoyment sluiced through his body as she collapsed on him. He felt boneless. She nuzzled his neck and he sighed and savored the exhilaration buzzing through his head like the aftereffect of a strange tonic. She eased away, but not before sharing a hungry, deep kiss. As she released him she smiled.

Casually he looked to the left and his gaze snagged on an object he hadn't noticed before.

"I can't believe it," he said as his attention adhered to the strange statue on the corner of the bar.

She followed his gaze. "What?"

"I hate to break the mood, but look at that statue on the edge of the bar. What do you see?"

Her gaze narrowed and she sat up all the way and stared at the odd statue. "It looks similar to the figures we saw in the circle of stones in the jungle."

Dark wood rather than stonework, the foot-tall statue showed a man holding a woman in his embrace. The statue was missing an interlocking half showing the entire body of another figure, presumably the woman. Their lower bodies blended into the wood.

"It's beautiful," she said. "Is it broken in half?"

"Maybe." Clearly she didn't see what he did. "Look at the base of the statue."

Her eyes widened. "Oh my God."

Then he saw something over her shoulder that froze his blood.

Keira must have spotted the reaction on his face. She whirled and a gasp left her throat.

Chapter Fifteen

El Jaguar stood at the bottom of the stairs, his brown eyes intense and icy.

Ah shit. Zane almost groaned at the injustice. He was trussed up like a fuckin' chicken with this madman gawking at Keira's naked ass.

At first no one spoke, but then the rebel smiled. His gaze coasted over Keira in appreciation, but his eyes held no malice. Composed and calculating, and probably enjoying what he'd seen, *El Jaguar* moved closer.

"Undo me," Zane said to Keira.

El Jaguar put up his hand as she reached for the buckle on Zane's left wrist. "No, Keira. I think you should leave him there. He looks comfortable."

She didn't listen, thank God. She managed to get the left wrist undone before Zane heard the distinctive click of a weapon being readied. She froze.

El Jaguar aimed a small caliber pistol right at her head. Fear for Keira burned a path through Zane's veins like acid. His breath hitched in his throat.

"I said, I think you should leave him as is." The rebel gestured. "Get off the table and put on your clothes."

She slipped off the table and started to dress. Zane's heartbeat eased a little, but not by much.

"What the hell are you doing here and how did you get in?" Zane asked the rebel.

El Jaguar's smile held sarcasm. "Haan's security is not all it seems. He left an important hole when he took that hairy thug Douglas with him. We've disabled the rest of his guards."

Zane frowned and tested his other wrist, clenching his fist and pulling at the strap. "Did you bring your whole army with you?"

"Only part, *Señor*. Enough to get the job done."

Great. Just great. He stood here with his cock gleaming with pussy juices and cum and a butt plug stuck in his ass. If he wasn't so damned pissed he'd be amused. If this story ever made it back to SIA he'd be the laughingstock of the entire organization, not to mention kissing his career goodbye.

Keira could be hurt or killed all because he'd allowed his physical needs get in the way of the mission.

Son of a bitch!

By this time Keira slipped back into her rumpled wedding dress and the flush of embarrassment left her face. She glared at the rebel. "Let me undo Zane so he can dress."

"I do not think so, *chica*. He is much too dangerous. I think keeping him naked is a good idea for now."

She looked like she wanted to argue, but she stopped short of saying anymore about it. Instead she asked, "Why are you here?"

Keeping his weapon trained in their general direction, *El Jaguar* said, "To take the one half of *La Pasion* back to the jungle with me."

"What?" she asked.

"You heard me. *La Pasion*. What your people call the Octagon. They belong to the tribe. To my people. First they were stolen by the British and placed in a museum. They paid a terrible for their arrogance expecting *La Pasion* to comply in captivity."

"You make them sound like animate objects," she said.

El Jaguar chuckled. "Animate and ready to be of service, but only to those deserving. When they were put together in the museum, a terrible thing happened because those who put them together did not understand the forces within them."

"How did you know what happened in the museum?" Zane asked.

El Jaguar's smile held pure contempt. "I have sources in the museum that would see *La Pasion* returned to its rightful place."

Keira looked puzzled as she stood by the table near Zane's free left hand. "So why did one man survive the event in the museum and the other didn't?"

El Jaguar lowered his weapon and shoved it back into his shoulder holster. "You don't know who the man is that survived the situation in the museum?"

She shrugged, a wariness coming into those tawny eyes. "Should I?"

Sighing, the rebel took a turn around the table until he ended up on Zane's right side. His dark eyes glittered. "The man who lived was your grandfather. He is one of my sources."

Despite the SIA's extensive intelligence network, this factoid blew Zane away. The room went deathly silent, until Zane thought he could hear his heart beat.

"You're lying," she said.

"I am *not*, *Señora*. He has worked for us since he survived *La Pasion* being brought together. Because he is pure of heart and a good man, *La Pasion* would not harm him. It never harms innocence. Only those who are evil or unworthy."

She shook her head and Zane could see she didn't believe a word of it. Truth be told, neither did he. Makepeace remained guilty as far as Zane was concerned.

"We approached him all those years ago," *El Jaguar* said. "When he realized my people and I were sincere about saving *La Pasion* and bringing it back to the jungle of *La Selva Negra*, he vowed to assist us. He is a wise man, your grandfather. He knows truth from lies. He saw that our world would not be the same without the artifacts returned to us. Since *La Pasion* was stolen all those years before, the power of my people has diminished. We grow weaker each day."

"It took all these years for him to get the *La Pasion* out of England and into your hands?" Zane asked. "Then why is it here in Haan's house?"

El Jaguar paced to the end of the table, then back to Keira's side. "An extraction difficulty. When we smuggled it from the museum in Britain and then into the country, our source was killed by Haan's men and half the artifact taken."

"Then where is the other statue? Somewhere in the house?" Zane asked.

El Jaguar shook his head. "We have it. Two sources came into the country at different times to avoid such a problem. One half of *La Pasion* resides in the city in the jungle in its rightful place."

She looked puzzled. "There's a city in the jungle?"

Zane said, "You remember the legend we talked about? The lost city no one has ever found? That must be what he's talking about."

El Jaguar actually appeared relaxed, his hostility tempered by the telling of the tale. "*Sí*. It exists in *La Selva Negra* not far from where we first took you to our temporary camp. It seems you were well on your way to going there, *chica*, when you stopped by the waterfall and took a rest. A little while longer with the ring on your finger and you would have found the dark city. The ring protected you against anything that might harm you."

Her mouth popped open. Revelation hit Zane right between the eyes. "That's where Haan went when he took that trek into the jungle. He was after the second half of *La Pasion* and discovered the city in the jungle."

The rebel's dark eyes seemed to grow liquid, and for a second Zane thought he saw them shift, their size and color fluctuating. Zane blinked hard. It couldn't be. A man's eyes didn't change like that.

"Oh, yes, *Señor* Spinella. You could say that Mr. Haan learned there are greater mysteries in the jungle than he could have imagined. Things he didn't want to know about once he exposed them. He left the city without the male half of *La Pasion* because his expedition was decimated before he could reach it. His greed caused their demise. His hatred burns a hole in our land and *La Selva Negra*. Evil damages the jungle in more ways than one."

"Why would Haan give me the ring? Does he know what it does?" Keira asked.

"He knows. He sent a man to follow you in hopes the ring would take you to the city. Then the man could find the other half of *La Pasion*, take the ring from you and come back to Haan. You see, the ring was also stolen from my people, but many years ago. It has been in Haan's possession all this time. He finally figured out what it was for."

"Jesus," Zane breathed out. "A directional finder. A compass to help the bearer locate the city without harm."

"Exactly," *El Jaguar* said.

Part of Zane didn't want to believe it. Couldn't believe it. But he'd seen too damned many weird things in the last few days not to give *El Jaguar's* statements about the ring credence.

"What happened to the man who stalked Keira in the jungle?" Zane asked.

"Yes," she said. "What did happen to him?"

El Jaguar shrugged. "My men disposed of him. He would have harmed you. Not only did he mean to follow you to the city, he would have raped and perhaps murdered you once there. Haan's men have no regard for women. Unlike my tribe where women are revered and protected."

A long paused entered the room until Keira deigned to speak.

"Why didn't you come for the other half of the statue until now?" Keira clutched the side of the bondage table, her knuckles white.

The rebel smiled shrewdly. "We waited until the coast was clear, as you would say." He walked toward the artifact and lifted it. "And now I've claimed it, I will be going."

Zane drew in a breath. "Not with the statue."

El Jaguar's gaze went from soft to hard as his gaze swung back to Zane. "Oh, yes, *Señor.* I will be going with the statue. You see, I know you want to take it back to the museum, and I can't permit that."

"Son of a bitch," Zane said with a growl. "You know I have to take it back. It doesn't matter where you go with it, I *will* get it back."

A nonchalant smile eased over the rebel's mouth. "I think not. You are at a slight disadvantage, no? And I think when Haan returns and discovers you allowed me to take the statue, you will be in a very bad way."

Keira looked at Zane, her gaze hard. "You knew my grandfather was one of the sources at the museum but didn't tell me."

He shook his head. "I didn't know he was this so-called source for *El Jaguar.* I thought he was just a thief in league with Haan."

Pain entered her pretty features. "I guess I should have listened to you."

"Do not be harsh upon your grandfather," *El Jaguar* said. "He has sold nothing to anyone. Any other artifacts you've seen in Haan's home were taken by another thief, not by your grandfather."

She shook her head. "How can I believe you?"

El Jaguar put the statue back on the table. He reached out and touched her face, his gesture as tender as a lover's caress.

Jealousy and pure fear spiked through Zane. *El Jaguar* may claim his tribe didn't hurt women, but Zane didn't trust him. "Don't touch her."

The rebel laughed softly and complied. "She is a rare beauty and yet I'm not sure you deserve her, *Señor* Spinella. After all, you would take *La Pasion* back to Britain. I think she is more like her grandfather and sees the error in returning it to the museum. We've protected Aloysius Makepeace and his family from forces who would destroy him." The rebel's eyes actually looked gentle as he observed her. "We will do so for you."

Keira stiffened. Tears fell from her eyes and Zane's defensive urges rose up.

"You didn't protect my grandmother," Keira said, her voice hoarse with sorrow.

"Keira." Zane's throat tightened at the sight of her grief. Frustration and fierce desire to gather her in his arms made him say, "Damn it, *El Jaguar*, untie me."

"I think not."

She crossed her arms, her stance protective to her body and perhaps to her soul. "If you wanted to help my grandfather, why didn't you —?" She shivered. "It all goes together now. It all makes sense."

"Why didn't they what?" Zane asked. "Keira?"

Her gaze returned to Zane's. "You know. My grandmother was kidnapped while we were in Egypt. Hollister told my grandfather if he didn't deliver the second artifact my grandmother would be killed. When you saw us in the square that day, Grandfather was telling Hollister it would take time to get the second half. I had no idea what he was talking about because Grandfather refused to explain what the artifacts were. He simply said he'd have to make contact with someone in Puerto Azul and then the artifact could be delivered. Grandmother was murdered anyway when Grandfather couldn't guarantee delivery on time." She stomped toward *El Jaguar*, her face enraged with fresh pain. "Did Grandfather tell you what happened? Did he?"

To Zane's surprise he saw equal sorrow on the rebel's face.

"He tried," *El Jaguar* said. "We were deep in *La Selva Negra* when he attempted to contact me about his dear wife's situation. But it was too late. If we would have known, you may rest assured we would have done everything we could to help her."

"Even given up *La Pasion*?" she asked.

Slowly *El Jaguar* shook his head. "Everything but that. Even your grandfather knew we could not give up *La Pasion*."

Zane's soul ached at the pain on Keira's face. Did she feel her grandfather had sacrificed her grandmother in order to keep *La Pasion* safe?

Zane didn't give a fuck about statues. Nothing mattered but returning *La Pasion* to Britain and keeping Keira safe. No, if it came down to it, he would never sacrifice *her* for a statue.

What a ridiculous snafu this was. A goat-fuck of the first order.

Truth hit Zane like a slap in the face.

Pinned like an insect on this ridiculous table, naked as jaybird, he realized doing the job no longer meant anything to him if Keira fell into harm's way again. The SIA, the Chesterham Museum and the British government could go to hell on a rocket ship. The single precious thing in this room *was* Keira. Truth burned in his gut, drowning him in a tangle of feelings so intense he almost couldn't contain them.

He loved her.

Fuck me. I'm one hundred percent, out of my freakin' mind, crazy in love with her.

Zane vowed then and there he'd do anything for her.

He glared at *El Jaguar*. "If you take the other half of *La Pasion* now, you're putting Makepeace and his granddaughter in jeopardy this time. Haan will come after you."

"*Sí*. But we have already surrounded her grandfather with extra protection. We've been planning this since the limousine crash when we realized who she was. We contacted Eduardo and he is helping."

"Eduardo?" she asked, her voice thin with stress. "Wait a minute. He isn't just a driver, is he?"

Now all the cats had left the bag, Zane didn't see any reason to hold back. "He also works for the SIA. How did he know to trust you, *El Jaguar*?"

"We explained to him who we really are. He knows the truth when he hears it. He's contacted your…what do you call them?…the Special Investigations Agency and updated them on the situation."

Maybe, just maybe, if Zane didn't get his ass shot off, he could save Keira and *La Pasion*. "You'll have to return this statue and the other one in your city to Britain. Even if you stop me, there will be other SIA agents who come after you."

The other man shrugged and put his hands on his hips. "I think I will get away with it. Because you see, there are some things I'm willing to sacrifice for my people. The first, *Señor*, is you. The only reason why I do not leave Keira to the mercy of Haan is that I would not see a woman hurt. And she is Makepeace's granddaughter. I owe him a great debt."

"No," Keira said suddenly, backing away a few steps until Zane couldn't see her. "I won't go with you if you leave Zane tied to this table. At least give him a chance to fight Haan when he comes back. Let him dress and you can tie him to a chair."

A little relief moved through Zane. Maybe she didn't hate his guts after all.

El Jaguar thought about it way too long. The rebel took his gun from his holster and held in on Zane. "Very well. For you I do this favor, *chica*. Release him and he may dress."

Tired of holding onto the butt plug like a lifeline, Zane decided he'd gone way past embarrassment. He released the plug and it hit the floor. Keira must have heard the soft thud on the carpet, for as she worked to free him, she caught his gaze. A twinkle danced in her eyes and a smile twitched over her lips. He couldn't help responding. This screwy state of affairs would be damned funny if it weren't so serious. A few moments later she freed him and moved off the table quickly but not fast enough to alarm the other man. After he dressed, *El Jaguar* required Keira to tie him to a leg of the table with some rope *El Jaguar* dragged from a cargo pocket on his pants.

"Come," *El Jaguar* said to her. "We will gather your possessions and be off."

"Where are you taking me?" she asked, throwing him an alarmed expression.

El Jaguar lifted the statue in one arm. "We go to *La Selva Negra* with *La Pasion* to unite it with its twin."

As *El Jaguar* directed her to the door, Zane's feelings rushed to the fore. "*El Jaguar*."

The rebel turned enough to look at Zane but not take his attention off her. "Yes, *Señor* Spinella?"

Zane took a deep breath and the words came out gruff. "I swear to God, if you hurt her in any way or you allow her to be harmed, I will hunt you down and kill you."

El Jaguar's smile held no mirth. "Fair enough, *Señor*. Fair enough."

* * * * *

Rough road caused the fancy all-terrain vehicle to bounce over the primitive jungle road. Keira's body ached from the rattling ride. While she'd enjoyed the luxury of a limo, she'd never seen a vehicle as sophisticated as this one. She took in details, her mind racing as she unobtrusively searched the vehicle for a weapon.

Fat chance. El Jaguar is watching my every move.

They'd left Haan's complex with no trouble; she saw a couple of Haan's bodyguards lying dead along the perimeter once *El Jaguar* drove away from the complex. She wondered why they took the vehicle instead of going into the jungle directly, but she didn't bother to ask. Before they departed he'd allowed her to change into cargo pants, her hiking boots, and a camp shirt. She even wore a wide brimmed hat and sunscreen.

True to his word, he let her to pack her valuables and bring them with her. They'd bumped along this rotten excuse for a road for over an hour, the pace slow and monotonous. *El Jaguar* drove but no one else accompanied them. She imagined either he'd eliminated the guards at Haan's by himself, or his fellow thugs disappeared back into the rainforest.

She didn't relish the idea of going back into *La Selva Negra* at any time, but night scared her silly. The thought of crawling through the bushes with icky nocturnal animals didn't appeal. At the same time, she refused to let fear render her useless.

She remembered a more pleasant aspect of her journey.

Zane's hands touching her breasts, caressing her pussy, bringing her to screaming orgasm. One wonderful memory to take with her in case she never experienced his mind-blowing touch again.

Her mind whirled with the things she'd discovered about her family in such a short time and all the information about *La Pasion*. Stunned, she couldn't absorb much more. No matter how much it shocked her, Keira didn't know if she could be unhappy with her grandfather for being *El Jaguar's* source at the museum.

Then again, that would make him an accomplice to a thief, just as the SIA charged. Albeit not the kind of burglar they thought, but a crook nonetheless. Tears burned her eyes for the hundredth time since she left with *El Jaguar*. More than anything Zane's last words burned into her mind and gave her a little hope.

I swear to God, if you hurt her in any way or you allow her to be harmed, I will hunt you down and kill you.

She'd seen the fierceness in his eyes, the determination to kick ass and take names. If the raw emotion in his voice had been any indication, he would launch a rescue. She felt almost giddy at the prospect of him coming for her. Keira had made sure she kept his bonds loose enough he could escape. At least she hoped he could escape. Worry burned in her gut as she thought about Haan injuring or killing Zane.

Please, please let Zane be all right. She'd go anywhere with El Jaguar as long as Zane would survive.

"Don't worry about *Señor* Spinella, *chica*."

She frowned deeply and turned her gaze on the rebel, but said nothing.

"You left the bonds loose enough for him to escape, I take it?" *El Jaguar* asked, keeping his attention on the road.

"Of course. You're going to live to regret this, you know. Zane—"

"I know. He would give his life for you. That is obvious." He smiled.

Her mouth popped open, but she couldn't think of an immediate retort.

"Why didn't you let him come with us?" she asked after a significant pause.

"Because he would have resisted our plans and as an agent of the SIA, he is well-trained and dangerous. I think he and I would have to fight to the death."

"You'd kill him over a statue?" She heard contempt in her voice.

"If it comes to it, I would."

She didn't understand this mysterious man. While she hadn't noticed so much before, in close quarters with him now she acknowledged his virility. He might not be her type, but his tall, muscular body and handsome face probably captivated plenty of *chicas*.

She decided to talk about something else. "Haan didn't expect you to attack tonight. That's why he didn't have more security on his house, right?"

"Correct."

"Why now? Why didn't you break into his house before?"

"We tried. Haan's men killed several of our men at other attempts to infiltrate his property. We tested his defenses until we found a weakness."

"Why do you want me with you? You could have just taken the statue and left."

El Jaguar's right eyebrow twitched and he took his eyes off the road long enough to flick an amused glance her way. "Because with you as a hostage, I know Zane will be cautious."

He went silent and the all-terrain ate up the miles. Before long the motion lulled her to sleep. It seemed only a few minutes when she felt the big car come to a stop. Her heart racing, she sat up straight and looked around. They'd arrived at a dead end, but past the tree line she saw the camp.

"This isn't the camp where we were before," she said as he opened the door.

"Of course not. We move frequently."

Within seconds men appeared out of the bushes, their olive drab uniforms and painted faces acting as effective camouflage. It didn't take long for them to unload the vehicle, then one of the men piled inside and drove off.

Once they wandered into the village, she saw a familiar face right away. Christina. The young woman waved to her and smiled. Caught off guard, Keira took a little longer to respond. Genuinely relieved to see a welcoming face, Keira waved back. The girl disappeared into a tent.

They arrived at *El Jaguar's* tent and she reluctantly followed him inside. After putting the statue on a table, he turned to her. "We will rest a few minutes, then we will take the ring and be off."

The ring.

When he'd asked her about it, she'd lied and said she'd put in the backpack she'd taken with her. She'd left the ring back at the house and good riddance.

She glared at the infuriating man. Irritation, sadness and exhaustion nipped at her heels. "Don't you know where this mythical city is? Is the ring supposed to lead you there?"

"We already know where the city is and have been there many times. But we also could use the ring for protection. More specifically, you need it for protection."

"I won't put it on."

"Why?"

She explained what the ring did to her. "It will knock me out for part of the trip at least, if the last experience I had with it is any indication."

He nodded. "Very well. We'll take it along, but you won't wear it."

She pushed her hands through her hair and sighed with weariness, determined to finish this fiasco. If it meant going into some damned forbidden city, she'd do it.

She didn't want to ask the next question. "What are you going to do with me after *La Pasion* is returned?"

He drew beef jerky out of a container and passed it to her. "There is no need to fear us. You'll be returned to a safe haven after we have what we want. As Makepeace's granddaughter you are much revered here."

She didn't believe him, although the man hadn't proved to be dangerous to women so far as she could tell. After all, he'd made the statement about his culture respecting women. Macho country or not, she suspected his people were far more different than she imagined.

Her stomach growled and she ate the jerky without reservation. With the adventure ahead she wondered if it might indeed be her last meal.

* * * * *

Zane wrestled with his bonds like a madman. The skin on his wrists burned. He'd worked at the rope for some time, and at one point thought he might find freedom before *El Jaguar* took Keira out of the house or Haan returned from his party. It took longer than he expected. By the time he raced through the house he knew *El Jaguar* had left with Keira. He ran to their bedroom to grab supplies, taking enough time to rip off the useless suit and jump into serviceable clothes for the jungle.

Every motion proficient, he readied for a final showdown. He almost left when he saw the ring lying under the nearby dresser. An oversight? He picked it up and stuffed it in his pocket. It might come in handy later on, if what *El Jaguar* said turned out to be the truth. He grimaced. He hoped to hell *El Jaguar* had half the honor he claimed to possess. Maybe if he did, Keira would come out of this mess in one piece.

Right now, that's all that mattered.

Equipped for action, Zane hurried through the house. He didn't have much time. Haan couldn't be far behind. He ran through the conservatory, his personal weapon secured in his shoulder holster. He would have preferred the semiautomatic, but Haan had put that weapon back in the locked arsenal in the basement.

Sweat ran down Zane's face as he approached the tropical forest, well aware as night drew down on the land he took a terrible risk. A worse risk would be to allow Haan to tag along with him on this journey. If the bastard wanted to travel through the night with his cronies and try and find the ancient city and the second half of *La Pasion*, let 'em. Zane refused to wait around for a party.

Not when the woman he loved depended on him.

An ache entered his gut, sharp and staggering. "Be safe, Keira. Please be safe."

For the first time in years tears burned his eyes and he inhaled sharply. He would temper the fear and use it to fuel his power. He couldn't allow it to throw him off guard. Haan would follow and at night the land would be far more treacherous than during the day. Nocturnal creatures, some poisonous and some aggressive, prowled the night.

Zane almost made it to the clearing, the backpack he'd used in the jungle earlier hefted onto his back and flashlight in hand.

"Halt! Stop!"

He heard the warning before the shot came, zinging over his head with sharp accuracy.

"Shit," he muttered as he launched into the bushes, aware he might have to dump the heavy pack.

"Get him!" another voice said, this one clear as a bell. "I want Spinella! Get him!"

Haan.

Great. The jig was up and all votes cast. His ass would be grass and Haan the lawnmower if he didn't act fast. Zane turned off his flashlight, jammed it into his pocket and crashed through the undergrowth. He couldn't risk the light drawing their fire.

More shots rang out and he heard men entering the jungle behind him. If they kept up this pursuit he might be chicken droppings before too long.

No.

Keira needed him. He would survive.

He almost tripped over a liana, but kept on motoring. Training prepared him for running with a pack on his back, but he couldn't go on forever this way. Even with a much lighter load than what he'd taken the other day to locate Keira, the extra weight impeded his speed.

Zane remembered the ring. Drawing it out of his pocket, he decided he didn't have anything to lose. Perhaps *El Jaguar's* supposition about the ring being protective of anyone who wore it might come true.

Just as he slipped it on his pinky finger he heard a shot. Searing pain lacerated his upper right shoulder and he staggered. Darkness edged out his remaining vision and encroached fast. He fell and fell and didn't remember reaching the bottom of the night that swallowed him whole.

Chapter Sixteen

Keira flinched as a frond slapped her in the face. "Ow! Damn!"

"Shh," one of the men in the group of six said as they traversed the long path toward San Cristobal Plateau. Here on the rockier side of the plateau, their flashlights managed to stream down the hillside and penetrate thick flora.

Above her head a fluttering sound and a high-pitched squeak caught her attention. Seconds later dozens of fruit-eating bats sailed overhead.

El Jaguar looked back at her, his smile a mere flash of white teeth. The five men who accompanied *El Jaguar* and Keira into the wilderness remained grim-faced. The jackasses who harassed her and Zane at the limo wreck didn't accompany this expedition.

Exhaustion dogged her heels as she tried to keep up with *El Jaguar's* punishing pace. While he might respect women, he didn't appear concerned about her keeping up. She pushed forward, determined not to fall behind. He slashed at the jungle, when needed, with a machete.

Of course, when they discovered she'd dropped the ring at the house somewhere instead of bringing it with her, they might be pissed and decide to leave her out here. The pack they'd given her held marginal supplies. If they decided she was a burden, she could be dead meat in no time.

Worry for Zane also stressed Keira, and not a moment passed when she didn't think of him.

If I ever see him again…

What?

If she saw him again what would she say? That her feelings transformed from irritation and contempt to something that felt deep and warm and lasting?

Love.

She'd forced the word away earlier as they'd moved through the jungle. If she didn't admit to loving Zane, then the pain of losing him would be diminished. She could ride through this chaos without feeling the immeasurable pain of being foolish enough to love him.

Sex is not love. Remember that.

Yes, she experienced the most elemental, exquisite lovemaking she could imagine in his arms. It didn't mean he loved her or she loved him.

Besides, love didn't happen that quickly. Did it?

No, she wouldn't think about love…even the ghost of admiration, until this event came to a head, until the strangeness she experienced over this last week dissolved into nothing more than a bad dream.

Tired and thirsty, her head aching, she walked faster until she came almost abreast of *El Jaguar*. She grabbed onto his sleeve and he frowned down at her. "What is it?"

"How much…longer?" Her strenuous breathing puffed between her lips. "I need water…and rest."

El Jaguar called a halt and she sank onto a big rock and sighed in relief. If she'd been fresh from sleep and relaxation she might not be so damned tired now. Instead weariness hung around her neck like an anvil, heavier by the hour. She took a healthy sip of water and suppressed a yawn.

They hadn't stopped more than a minute when a low rumbling filled the earth beneath their feet. The men muttered in Spanish, their voices low with agitation. She knew from earlier experience it must be a mild earthquake. A murmur went up from the men, but since she didn't understand Spanish, she didn't know what they said.

El Jaguar glanced at her, his gaze unfathomable. "There is nothing to fear, *chica*. We have earthquakes like this all the time. My guess is the four-mile giant is awakening."

"The what?" she asked.

"The volcano twenty miles away. *Cerro de Fuego.* Fire Ridge. It slumbers no longer. We heard there is a possibility it will erupt."

As his statement penetrated her exhaustion-filled brain, she said, "Oh my God."

"There is no warning yet from the authorities in San Cristobal about imminent danger."

Apprehension snaked into her. "Twenty miles away isn't far enough if it decides to erupt."

He nodded. "This is why we need to push onward, *chica*. Accomplish this before anything else bad can happen."

She nodded, then thought of something she'd meant to ask him before but just now possessed the courage to say. "Why do you call me *chica*?"

His grin held a saucy overtone, and she wondered if he meant to flirt with her. "I have this weakness for beautiful women. I compliment them."

The last thing Keira supposed she should do is smile at her captor, but *El Jaguar's* attitude was almost as protective as Zane's. She doubted he'd hurt her. "Thank you."

"You are very welcome. I think I am glad *Señor* Spinella isn't here. He would be throwing darts with his eyes right about now."

"I wish you hadn't left him tied up like that. I'm worried about him."

El Jaguar chuckled. "He is probably free and following us right about now."

She wished she could be as certain. "When we get to this city, what do we do?"

"Replace the rest of *La Pasion*, of course. Where there was one, there will be two. Both sides of the coin."

She took another taste of water, then screwed the cap back on the container and handed it back to him. "What happens then?"

El Jaguar's happiness shone in his eyes, a light in his deep eyes. He rubbed his fingers over the stubble along his chin. "Our tribe will regain the power it lost when the statues were taken. We will once again influence things that happen in and to *La Selva Negra*. Perhaps we can save our destiny from permanent destruction."

"You honestly believe two statues will do that for your entire culture?"

El Jaguar nodded. "There are not so many of us. Our population in this country has dwindled down to what you saw in camp. Many of our kind live elsewhere in Central America. They moved away over the years."

Native populations, once introduced to modernization, often took other roads to prosperity. At the same time, they often lost what made them unique as a people. She couldn't fault him for wanting a return of power and good fortune to his people.

"Are the carvings in the city like those in the stone circle where Zane and I camped the other night?"

"They are. Does that disturb you?"

Disturbed, yes. But not in the way he might imagine. "They're very unusual."

He grinned, a low chuckle coming from his throat. "You mean the sexual content? The fact that they come to life when a couple lies inside their circle and makes love?"

"How did—?" Her lips twitched, and her cheeks flushed. "Uh...yes."

"Our people see sex as a sacred ceremony that must always be taken to our whole heart. We do not engage in it lightly. Our people use the ancient circle on occasion for ritual. Sexual ritual."

Interesting concept. "Sex is power. Your people understand that."

His broad smile held pleasure and admiration. "This is why when the statues are brought together the male and female power innate in sexual energy will be spilled over the land and vitality restored. Our balance will be complete. As of now, the male power dominates the region, and Haan is king."

"You believe your people are descendants of the ancient ones who lived in the city?"

"We don't believe it. We know it." He turned toward her slightly. "We will need the ring when we arrive at the city. One of us will have to place it on your finger and deliver the statue to its rightful place along the other statue of *La Pasion*."

Her heart started to pound, but she didn't have a choice but to tell him the truth. "I don't know where it is."

His bright-eyed enthusiasm faded, replaced by the frosty eyes of a man who didn't believe what he heard. "What do you mean?"

"I think I left the ring in my room at Haan's home."

He slapped his thigh and the resulting clap and curse made everyone in the group jump. "Damn it all. We need that ring."

Taking a deep breath, she managed to say, "I'm sorry. I didn't mean to cause a problem."

His eyes narrowed menacingly as he stood. "I am not a stupid man. You left the ring on purpose. Why?"

"You know why. I already told you my reaction to the ring and the dizziness it causes. I'm out of control when that ring is on my finger."

He sighed. "A natural process of wearing the ring. You would have remained unharmed within the temple."

Keira didn't care. She wouldn't be pushed into wearing that ring for anything.

He scrubbed his hands through his hair and stood, impatience now marring his features. He spoke in Spanish to the men and they stood and prepared to move out. They hefted their backpacks.

"The ring belongs in the temple along with *La Pasion*. All that is sacred remains in the temple."

She lifted one brow. "Even sex?"

He shifted his feet and retrieved his automatic weapon. He slung the deadly instrument over his shoulder. "There is a sexual ritual performed within the temple. It guarantees youth, happiness, and success to all who participate. It pushes the boundaries of what most people will do. It also ensures stabilization of the land."

She saw it in his eyes. He wanted her to ask. "All who participate? Is it an orgy?"

"Hardly. It is between one man and one woman."

She couldn't believe she was asking this, but what the hell? "What makes it different from plain bread and butter sex?"

"The couple must be in love. It provides protection against all dangers within and without the temple. And it must be witnessed."

"Witnessed." The one word didn't come out as a question, but surprised disbelief. "You're kidding right?"

"No. The sex must be witnessed by one or more persons." He started off. "Let us proceed. We must arrive there as sunrise approaches."

As she fell into step behind him, she wondered if she would see the next day alive or if the mysterious tropical forest would swallow her whole and she'd disappear forever. With every mysterious chattering and squeaking from the forest, trepidation nipped at her heels. She half expected a big cat to leap from the gloom and attack. Grateful for the company of so many, she tried to keep up.

It seemed they walked until hell froze over, until night relented and new sun spilled over the canopy stretching many stories into the sky. As light and heat warmed the land, sweat tickled her skin. Her muscles ached and wooziness fogged her brain after walking a good portion of the night.

As they rounded the corner of a rocky outcropping she wondered if her eyes deceived her. Tall gold and ivory pillars reached from the ground into the sky, their shape almost Grecian or Roman in design. The surfaces, though pitted from age, were remarkably preserved. Along each column sexual scenes decorated the stone. Fascinated, she walked toward one of explicit masts. Tilting her head back, she admired the tall stone as only an archaeologist could. Whoever worked this stone did a remarkable job, as they had on *La Pasion*. For once her fear of what would happen subsided, and she permitted her curiosity as a scientist take over.

El Jaguar gestured for the rest of them to hurry. "Not much longer."

They passed through the twin columns and walked into the thicket another half mile. Nothing prepared her for the beauty, the grandeur of the overgrown city nestled against a deeply cratered side of the plateau. The city huddled into the depression, sheltered from much but relentless morning sunrise. Covered by the never-ending life in the jungle, the accumulation of the centuries of neglect, the city owned an ancient beauty.

Despite the structures' age, she could see the jungle preserved what time and weather might have destroyed. Spires rose into the sky, none of them higher than the flora that sheltered them. Here kings and queens might have ruled and she almost imagined the sounds of hundreds of inhabitants enjoying their world, going about their daily business.

These buildings didn't look like photographs she'd seen of ruins in Guatemala, El Salvador, Costa Rica, or Honduras, nor did they appear like those of South American countries. As she stared at the buildings Keira saw a wide undulating swath of darkness pass over the ground near the foot of the ruins. She blinked, then blinked again when the mass writhed and swirled, moving by the buildings in a mad race.

One of the men muttered something. *El Jaguar* translated. "Army ants. I hope they pass quickly."

The column of ants passed by in a flash and continued onward. By this time her head hurt and her feet ached. How far they'd marched through thick vegetation, she couldn't be certain. Long enough for her to feel if she ever survived this she'd never go hiking again. When they reached the base of the city, she admired the huge buildings with awe. Her archaeologist colleagues would never believe this, and she didn't have a camera to take photos for proof.

The men proceeded ahead of her while *El Jaguar* took up the rear. She hurried forward, eager to see everything she could.

Before she could make a sound of warning a snake slithered into the path ahead, not three feet from her.

She froze.

She recognized the type of snake and her heart pounded furiously in her chest.

El Jaguar shouted a warning. "Fer-de-lance! Don't move."

She didn't plan on moving, but the snake raced toward her with a furious pace. She gasped, her heart surging into her throat as she realized she didn't have time to react.

The snake lunged, teeth bared. Teeth tore through her pants at the same time she started to run. Lacerating pain slashed her left shin and she cried out. Anger and disbelief gave her strength as she shook her leg and the snake flopped away into the dirt. A loud pop rang in her ears as someone took a shot at the serpent. It writhed and twitched, its death completed instantly.

El Jaguar grabbed her by the shoulders and then swept her off her feet. Stunned, she allowed him to place her on the ground. He ripped the rest of her pants leg down the seam. Blood marred her shin.

"¡*Madre de Dios!*" A rapid fire string of Spanish came from him as he dumped his pack and dug around inside it. "Damn it, *chica*. You've done it now."

"I've done it now?" she asked weakly, her stomach curling with illness as she realized the implication of what happened.

The panic, the outright fear wouldn't penetrate. It didn't need to. The stark fright in *El Jaguar's* eyes spelled the answer for her. She knew as well as he did what would happen. Too far from civilization, she didn't have a chance. A fer-de-lance's bite could be fatal within four hours without instant treatment, and even then, severe damage to nerves and tissue would be almost certain.

He ripped a shirt into shreds and tied a tourniquet above the point of the bite, a little ways under her knee. "We must get you to the temple now. It's your only chance." He gestured to one of the other men hovering nearby. "Take my pack. I must carry her. We go now! *¡Vamonos!*"

Again he swept her into his arms and ran for the temple in the near distance. She wanted, in that moment, for Zane to be the one cradling her in his arms. Before she could feel the intensity of her situation or cry out as pain lanced her flesh, a black cloud obscured her vision and she faded into shadows.

Before night approached for the second time in one day, she thought she heard *El Jaguar's* strangled cry. "*Chica*, don't do this! *¡Chica!*"

* * * * *

Dull throbbing in Zane's skull aroused him from a semi-stupor. Daylight greeted him as he forced open his eyes. He sucked in a breath and damp, hot air filled his throat. He choked on the feeling, gasping for breath. He swallowed painfully. As he shifted, disoriented as hell, pain rocketed through his right shoulder.

"Damn it." He groaned. "Damn it all to hell."

He lay flat on his face, his right cheek pressed into the dirt. Heavy weight pressed on his back. His backpack.

For a terrifying moment he couldn't remember shit, where he was and how he got there. As the ache in his shoulder throbbed, he peered into the jungle and tried to orient with his surroundings.

He sensed movement, furtive and scurrying. Insects. Small animals. Memory crashed into him full force. He'd been running from Haan's men, then one of them shot him in the right shoulder and he'd passed out. He should be a dead man. Instead he lay prone and pinned by his backpack. Maybe if he could get to his knees he could at least dump the pack and check his shoulder. It couldn't be too bad or he probably would have bled out by now.

Obviously he'd been out a long time. With daylight he could make his way with more ease. Even if it meant hiding from Haan's thugs would be a little harder. Why hadn't they killed him? They should have been able to locate him after he'd passed out. Stunned by good fortune, he decided conjecture could wait. Locating Keira remained top priority.

He wiggled out of his pack by rolling to the left. With a harsh, pain-filled breath, he clamored to his feet. He checked his shoulder and discovered the bullet hadn't gone through. He probed the stinging area and realized it amounted to more of a flesh wound, a long drag of the bullet to the right of his shoulder blade. Damned happy for the reprieve, he stripped off his shirt and dug into the first aid kit. After locating a tiny bottle of antiseptic, he poured about half of it onto his shoulder.

Pain seared his skin and he groaned. "Fuck! Hell! Shit!"

At this angle he couldn't bandage the wound, but he didn't think it bled copiously. He would have to live with it until he could get help.

Pack reloaded onto his back, he headed into the undergrowth. As he walked he became a little lightheaded, and he wondered if blood loss or if the strange ring had something to do with it. He walked very few miles before the dizziness threatened to tow him under. With a groan of anger he stopped long enough to take a breather. His legs felt like noodles, so he dumped his pack by a log and sat down. Long, deep breaths cleared his head a few minutes later. He slogged down water to assure he didn't become dehydrated.

While he waited to regain strength, the jungle around him came alive with sounds. A woodpecker assaulted a tree, and birds uttered high-pitch caterwauling. Dew dropped from the vegetation above. He shivered, damp and even a little cold. Deep in his gut new urgency called and he stood, ready for more jungle no matter how unforgiving or dangerous. He pressed onward, his pace relentless regardless of his exhaustion and injury.

Down to his bones he felt it. His woman needed him now.

Zane knew what he'd say when he found her again. She would know, without one doubt, that he loved her. He wanted her with him to the end of his days, his career be damned. If Keira would have him, he was hers.

As time elapsed it dawned on Zane he knew what direction to walk to reach the ancient city. He scarcely hesitated at the pillars where he'd made love to Keira the first time.

More than once he glanced back, still astonished Haan's men hadn't located him by now. Unless...unless they followed him with the stealth of wildcats, determined to locate the hidden city and regain possession of *La Pasion*.

No. He didn't sense them, and he'd always been bad-ass excellent at detecting the enemy approaching from any direction. No, they'd given up searching for him long ago and headed straight for the jungle city. He quickened his pace, blood rushing in his ears, his breathing fast, and muscles burning with exertion. All his resources, mental and physical, worked toward the ultimate goal.

Before too long he passed the waterfall area and headed deeper into the jungle below the San Cristobal Plateau. Sweat ran down his face and his shoulder hurt like hell if he gave it too much thought. His breathing became labored as he took the hillside with a vengeance, determination drawn into his skin and blood and bone. He would find her, no matter how long it took, no matter where they'd taken her. A litany ran through his mind.

Please keep her safe. I don't care what the hell happens to me. As long as Keira is all right, I don't give a shit about anything else.

He recognized exhaustion and hunger depleting his reserves and trudged onward even as he stuffed down a snack bar for energy. Granted it wouldn't heal his shoulder or dissolve fatigue like a good ten hours of sleep, but he couldn't afford to stop. In a way he understood the ring's part in keeping him alive and giving him the instinctual ability to scour the jungle for the mysterious city. Without the ring he might be dead now. Never in a million years did he imagine believing in supernatural occurrences, but he'd seen too many odd things in the last few days to argue.

He stiffened as rustling came from the deep thicket in front of him and the low murmur voices. A shout, muffled and desperate, issued from someone's throat. The male voice almost sounded like *El Jaguar's* but he couldn't be sure. Moving faster, he plunged through the thicket. Covertness at this point wouldn't bring him nearer to reaching Keira.

He came to a parting in the jungle. Tremendous pillars decorated with strange symbols and carvings came into view. *Yes! God, let this be it.* He implored whatever gods inhabited the area to help him find Keira unharmed. He dashed toward the pillars and continued through them, running with sheer resolve. Keira must be close. He sensed her.

Fear rocked his body without mercy. Danger made his blood turn icy, his skin prickle with chills and his heart pound. He didn't understand how he knew it, but Keira must be in horrible danger. He felt it like a sickness deep in his gut.

As he rounded an outcropping he could see across a grass-grown sunken area. A granite city turned golden by morning sunlight, wrapped in the vines of age, a testimony to a mysterious people's hard work and long vanished history. From here he couldn't be certain, but it looked like mortarless stone masonry, with most of the buildings reaching twenty to forty feet high. The city looked vast, but he couldn't be certain of exact size with rainforest covering a good portion of the area. For a breathless second awe struck him down and refused to let him move. Low city walls crawled along the ground, as if they didn't need to defend themselves against an enemy.

The earth shifted under him and he grunted as the world swayed and rocked. It stopped almost as fast as it began. Yet the magnificent stonework in front of him looked undamaged by human occupancy, war, or natural disaster. How many earthquakes in eons of time had rocked this place?

Jerked out of his admiration for the structures, he remembered how much Keira needed him.

And there, with perfect timing, he saw several figures making their way across the grass-strewn tangle covering a sunken plaza. One of the figures was being carried in *El Jaguar's* arms. The body looked delicate. Feminine. And unconscious.

Oh, Jesus. "Keira." He wanted to cry out to her, yet he bit back the impulse. *Hurry, hurry, hurry.* "Hang on, Keira."

Aware the anxiety in his voice matched the ache in his heart, he worked his way through the vegetation and down the steep hillside. Zane almost expected *El Jaguar* and his men to hear his pursuit and turn to face his attack. Instead they continued their frantic pace toward the city.

Run, run, run. His feet picked up speed. Running with the backpack and the injury sent waves of heat and sickness into his battered body but he disregarded the misery. Fury steamed his blood along with fear and kept him moving.

He followed at a discreet distance as the men hurried toward the apex of a large building in the center of scarred, scattered ruins. The great basalt and sandstone pyramid resembled, in a superficial way, some designs he'd seen in Tiahuanaco in Bolivia. He estimated the size around a two-hundred-fifty-foot square and almost forty-foot high. In this case the pyramid appeared to have been built right into the side of the plateau.

The men ran into the pyramid and disappeared. He dropped his backpack outside on the ground and followed, plunging into the slender entrance and following the glow from bobbing flashlights. As they meandered deeper into the primitive structure, he didn't dare turn on his flashlight and alert them of his presence. If he kept back they might not see him until too late.

Growls reached his ears, as if somewhere in this maze wildcats lived.

But no. That wasn't possible, was it?

Narrow passageways, right angles, and cul-de-sacs riddled the pyramid. When they skirted a corner and stepped into a larger chamber, he peeked around the corner. How much farther did they plan to go?

His answer came when the reached a chamber with a fifteen-foot-high barrel-vault ceiling and two stone altars in the middle. Behind the altars stood a strange statue carved with images of a snarling god with fangs like a big cat, claws on hands and feet. Along the walls a few low-relief carvings survived. Like the circle of stones these images featured women and men in a variety of sexual escapades, along with paintings of people engaged in dancing and playing flute-like instruments. In a blinding instant he remembered a place he'd seen in a Shiva temple in India. He'd seen a holy shrine of *garba-griha*, literally, the womb house. In the womb house a *lingam*, or phallic symbol, was encircled by the *yoni*, or vulva. *Lingam* and *yoni* represented the creative energy of the universe. The power of sexual union completed the universe. Perhaps this room proved a similar belief in its long-dead people.

Behind the first altar stood the male and female halves of *La Pasion*, so close but not quite touching. No one yet attempted to put the stones together.

Shock rippled through Zane as he spotted five jaguars pacing near the altars and the statue in a wide circle. All of the men had disappeared except for *El Jaguar*. The men couldn't have passed him and no other passages led out of the room.

Holy shit. They couldn't be…no, it just couldn't be.

All signs said *El Jaguar's* men had turned into big cats and now guarded the rebel and Keira.

Zane's blood pumped through his veins at an alarming rate, his heart slamming in his chest as he fought weakness and a terrifying realization of the supernatural staring him in the face. His legs felt shaky, his senses striving for clarity.

El Jaguar placed Keira on the first altar. Her eyes were closed, her face pale and one pant leg torn almost off. A tourniquet was tied below her knee. Worry sculpted the rebel's face, as if he also feared her death. Not the face of a man bent on sacrifice or harm. A small hope energized Zane.

"Come out now, Zane, and help me with your woman," the rebel said.

Not surprised the rebel knew he was there, Zane drew his weapon from his holster and stepped from around the corner. He started to walk toward the altar when the five jaguars turned, their vibrating snarls echoing in the room.

El Jaguar waved his hands at the cats and spoke in Spanish. All five jaguars backed away but stayed nearby. Zane half expected to see them pick up discarded automatic weapons in their paws. Instead they watched with fierce eyes. Any wrong moves and they'd tear him apart before he could run or fire his weapon.

"Get away from her," Zane said, his voice hoarse with anger as he pointed his weapon at *El Jaguar*.

"No."

"I said—"

"There's no time to lose! She's been bitten by a fer-de-lance. Give me the ring. It is the only way to save her."

Bone-melting, overwhelming fear plowed through Zane's psyche. "What?"

El Jaguar paced toward him, his eyes fierce. He put out one hand. "It will save her from the poison. We will put the stones together and the poison will not harm her any longer."

El Jaguar continued toward him, as if he'd fight tooth and nail for the ring. The jaguars growled again, perhaps sensing the struggle to come. Tempted to fire on the rebel, Zane's finger twitched on the trigger.

"Stop right there!" A voice rang out, German and harsh. Zane whirled to see Haan standing at entrance with Douglas. Streaked with mud and dirt and evil smiles, their expressions anticipated victory. "Give me the ring and both sides of *La Pasion*."

Zane had several choices, but none of them guaranteed survival. Fanaticism etched Haan's face, his gaze so certain and controlled. The man would do anything to achieve his goal.

"After we cure her. We'll give it to you after that," Zane said.

Douglas brought his hand gun up and pointed it straight at Zane. He looked ready to fire any second. Zane kept his own weapon pointed at Haan and his sidekick.

"I don't think so," Haan said. "We want that ring and *La Pasion* now."

Haan paced toward the altar but the jaguars stopped him, their feline bodies walking toward him and his bodyguard with slinky menace.

"The cats will not allow you close to us and firing upon them will do you no good," *El Jaguar* said. "They are not ordinary jaguars and cannot be harmed by bullets."

Douglas laughed and shot at one of the big cats. The cat didn't flinch and a plinking sound hit the air as the bullet dropped to the floor in front of the jaguar.

"Shit," Douglas said, eyes wide. He turned his gun on Zane again as if to fire.

Zane shot back and as the bullet hit the thug in the chest, Douglas went down like a ton of bricks.

Haan bared his teeth in a feral grin. "You think that's going to stop me?"

Zane returned the asshole's smile. "Looks like it already has."

Zane gave the ring to *El Jaguar* without another hesitation. Zane had nothing to lose but her, and he'd be damned if he'd let that happen.

El Jaguar slipped the cabochon ring on her left hand. "Be prepared, Zane. What happened to her grandfather back at the museum all those years ago will probably happen to you."

Before Zane could say another word, Haan shouted, "It's mine! Both of those are mine! You can't take them from me!"

Disgusted and damned tired of the incompetent, lily-white asshole, Zane almost turned and shot him, too. "Watch us."

Zane put his gun back in his holster and moved around the altar until he stood next to her. His heart ached with pain as he saw her leg, now swollen and obviously pumped full of poison. He leaned down and listened to her breathing as he put one hand over her heart. Swallow breaths parted her lips. He swallowed hard in relief when he felt her heart beating strongly.

"Ah, Jesus," he whispered. "Honey, I'm sorry I got you into this." He leaned down and kissed her forehead. "Can you hear me? Please don't leave me, Keira. I love you. Do you hear me? I love you."

Behind him Zane heard *El Jaguar* take a deep breath. "Hold on tight to her."

Zane slipped his arms around her upper body and drew her close. Cradling her in his embrace, he drank in the feeling of holding her and prayed like he'd never prayed before. "Please save her."

"No!" Haan's agonized voice called out as he started to run from the temple.

Too late.

El Jaguar brought *La Pasion* together with a click of the stones as the octagon bases linked. In a flash the room turned a blinding white.

El Jaguar's voice rang out. "Where there is love and life, there can be no death!"

Zane hoped with his next breath that if he died he would awaken to heaven in Keira's arms.

Chapter Seventeen

Heat and hardness embraced Keira in comfort and security. Peace inside her brought the greatest paradise and warmest love. She tried to remember when she'd last felt this wonderful. *Yes. I know. When Zane held me after we made love.* She longed for him with a deep, powerful ache. Foggy and disoriented, she didn't want to wake from the light-as-a-feather feeling. *If this is heaven, I'll stay here.*

"Keira, can you hear me?" The deep male voice sounded frayed, almost broken with grief.

Did she imagine it? Zane? She licked her dry lips and tried to speak. "Zane? Is that you?"

A quick inhalation, a heartfelt groan and his lips touched her forehead with total reverence. "Thank you, God. Please open your eyes. Please."

Energy seeped slowly into her limbs, and she did as requested. Zane cradled her tenderly in his arms and pressed the occasional kiss to her forehead and nose like she might be the most precious commodity in the world. Elation leapt inside her when he smiled, his eyes sparkling with joy. She hoped this beautiful situation didn't dissolve like a dream.

"Are you all right?" he asked.

"Yes. What—? How—? Where am I?"

"Easy. You're in the temple in *La Selva Negra* city. *El Jaguar* and his men are here. You're safe."

Safe? She shifted, wanting to sit up, and he allowed her. He kept his arm around her shoulders. With a start she remembered the horrible bite wound and looked down at her pant leg. Her leg, other than slightly bloody, showed no sign of the poisonous infection.

"The fer-de-lance," she said hoarsely.

"*El Jaguar* put *La Pasion* together and with the help of the ring, it saved your life." He shook his head. "Don't ask me how, but I don't really care. All I care about is you're okay."

His voice held the deepest reverence and she cupped his dear face in wonder.

As she perused his handsome countenance, she saw the red stain splattered on his shirt. "Is that blood? You're hurt."

"A shoulder wound. Haan's men shot me."

"Zane," she said in alarm, "let me see it."

He caught her searching hands against his chest. "It's already healing. When *La Pasion* came together, it worked for me, too."

Wanting reassurance, she slid off the altar with his help. "I don't care. Let me see it."

That's when she spied the six jaguars pacing near the entrance to the temple.

One came toward them and she gasped a warning, "Zane, there are jaguars in here."

Another smile touched his lips, this one unrepentant and a little teasing. "No shit."

As the cats approached she cringed and his arm went around her again. She watched, stunned, as the jaguars morphed. Their spots stretched as they lengthened, bodies transforming with rapid movements into—*El Jaguar* and the other five men.

If she'd been the hysterical type, she would have screamed or maybe run. As *El Jaguar* walked toward her and Zane, his smile sincere and maybe amused, she laughed softly.

"You don't believe your eyes, eh, *chica*?" *El Jaguar's* grin held mischief and relief.

She shook her head. "So your name *is* who you are."

One of the men cleared his throat and spoke in soft, broken English. "We are the descendants of the werejaguars who built *La Selva Negra*."

She couldn't wrap her mind around the paranormal concept. "This is beyond incredible. I can't believe this truly happened. We both should be dead."

Zane explained to her what happened when she left Haan's complex with the rebel and how the ring made him invisible to Haan's thugs. "If I'd been wearing the ring earlier they probably couldn't have seen me at all. I wouldn't have gotten shot."

She glanced at *La Pasion*. The figure of the man and woman kissed into eternity and beyond, locked together by love. A radiant glow pulsated from the joined statues, lighting the entire room.

Walking into the glowing circle surrounding *La Pasion*, the rebel said, "Haan and his other men have escaped. But we will hunt them. The power of the ring and *La Pasion* will claim them."

"The power of man and woman together?" she asked.

El Jaguar nodded, his gaze intent on the statues. "Creation of life and all that is sacred is the energy of man and woman together. Haan wanted that power for himself, but even if he'd obtained both statues they would have destroyed him."

"This is unbelievable," she breathed in wonder. "Absolutely incredible."

El Jaguar's nodded, turning his hand this way and that in the glow. "It is warm. Warm with love."

A gentle rumbling filled the room and she looked up at the high roof with worry.

"Do not fear the volcano." *El Jaguar* turned his back on *La Pasion*. "The volcano had cooled. Now that *La Pasion* reclaims the land, there is no imbalance." He looked toward Zane with critical eyes. "Unless you mean to try and take *La Pasion* back to the museum."

She held her breath, nervous for a moment that Zane might insist upon it.

Zane's arms tightened around her and he kissed her forehead. "*La Pasion* gave Keira's life back." As he looked down on her she saw the love stirring there with a force as powerful as the earth. "It gave back *my* life. It may cost me my job, but I won't betray your people or her grandfather. What you have here is more important."

El Jaguar's relief showed clearly as he sighed, the burden of ages released. "Thank you. Never fear about your job. We will carve two replicas for you to present to the museum. They will never know the difference."

Keira frowned. "With carbon dating or other methods they could tell."

The rebel strode around the statues, his attention sealed to the glowing statue of the lovers. "Trust us. We'll take care of that." He clapped his hands. "Men, let us go outside." He smiled. "You know what I said about the altar? It must be done now, *chica*. The energy of the lovers will give you strength and the love between you and Zane will complete the circle."

A little nervous, she said, "Now?"

"Now. We will celebrate in camp tonight!"

The men cheered and filed out behind their leader.

Zane turned toward her, his eyes more tender and warm than she'd ever seen them. "Zane Spinella, you're incredible." Tears touched her eyes and she cupped his face. "Did I hear you say you love me?"

Husky with emotion, his words told her all she needed to know. "Yes." He clasped her wrists and smoothed his fingers over her skin. "Any chance you might feel the same about me?"

She gave a laugh that almost sounded like a sob as tears poured down her face. "Yes. Yes."

With a sweet tenderness that went all the way to her heart, he smiled. A primitive stirring deep in her loins reminded her of the passion yet to come.

She cleared her throat. "Um... *El Jaguar* said for this place to be truly energized and sanctified, a couple must make love at this altar. With witnesses."

His eyebrows went up. "With witnesses?" He dragged her against him, renewed passion in the love-filled darkness of his eyes. "Whatever you want, wife."

She twined her arms around his neck. "Only you, husband. Only you."

His mouth took hers, the power of her ardor for this man rocking her to the foundations. Immediately she felt his cock rising hard against her belly, telling her where danger no longer ruled, sex now did. As his tongue slipped inside and tasted with rough, wholly sexual thrusts, leftover adrenaline streaked through her battered system. She burned eagerly in the fires she knew they could create. Energized by the frantic craving, she understood they'd become like the werejaguars, responding to the primordial, the glow of *La Pasion* as it smoldered behind them.

The circle was complete.

Epilogue
Two weeks later
Chesterham Museum
London, England

Late afternoon closed in on the museum as Keira and Zane left the drizzling rain and stepped into the cavernous building. She walked hand in hand with Zane toward the cubicle where the fake *La Pasion* resided. Strong emotions sheared her to the bone.

Happiness. Completeness. And not just because the man she loved more than anything on earth walked beside her.

She should feel guilty; the part she'd played in returning the counterfeit *La Pasion* could have sent them to jail for many years. Instead she reveled in the knowledge *El Jaguar* and the people of *La Selva Negra* now lived in the peace and harmony they'd been without for so many years. Her grandfather's peace of mind was restored knowing *La Pasion* would be safe forever in the temple pyramid.

They'd recovered from their ordeal with a few days rest at the rebel camp. Zane sent word through Eduardo to Mac Tudor that they'd completed the mission. They knew much of their adventure would never be reported; despite the strange cases SIA worked on every day, some things Zane and Keira couldn't share. It remained too amazing, too personal.

In less than a week they'd be married again, in the United States surrounded by friends and family.

"Do you think they'll ever find Haan and his men?" she asked after they paid their admission and wandered through the maze of hallways to the cubicle.

"No. I think *El Jaguar* was true to his word. Haan will never be seen again."

They found the small space with the plaque that said, *La Pasion, 12th century carving from Puerto Azul.* Nestled in the cubicle and under secured glass, *La Pasion* sat under the gentle glow of an overhead light. She knew the real *La Pasion* remained in the temple, the glow from its continuous energy illuminating the *Selva Negra* Temple.

Zane slipped his arm around her shoulders. In a soft voice that no one else could hear him but Keira, he sang the words of the song he'd serenaded her with in Puerto Azul.

As the words flowed over her, tears came to her eyes. He stopped singing but she could hear the melody in her head and heart. Slipping into his arms she kissed him with all the love building inside. Over the last two weeks they confessed so many things, their nights filled with glorious lovemaking beyond anything they could have imagined. One of the side effects of making love in the temple proved to be a tremendously high sex drive. It could strike any time.

Anywhere.

When he stopped kissing her, a smile tipped his carnal mouth. "Do you feel what I feel?"

"Love?" she asked, teasing him.

"Definitely that. But there's something else."

She liked playing this game with him. "Oh, *that* something else."

"Yeah," he said his voice rough with desire.

His eyes twinkled with an unholy fire that also came from mating in the temple. She knew the glow danced in her eyes, too. She took his hand and led him toward a more secluded area, a place only she knew about and where they wouldn't be disturbed.

About the author:

Suspenseful, erotic, edgy, thrilling, romantic, adventurous. All these words are used to describe award-winning, best-selling novelist Denise A. Agnew's novels. Romantic Times Magazine called her romantic suspense novels DANGEROUS INTENTIONS and TREACHEROUS WISHES "top-notch romantic suspense." With paranormal, time travel, romantic comedy, contemporary, historical, erotica, and romantic suspense novels under her belt, she proves her gift for writing about a diverse range of subjects. (Writing tales that scare the reader is her ultimate thrill.)

Denise's inspiration for her novels comes from innumerable sources, but the fact she has lived in Colorado, Hawaii, and the United Kingdom has given her a lifetime of ideas. Her experiences with archaeology have crept into her work, as well as numerous travels throughout England, Ireland, Scotland, and Wales. Denise currently lives in Arizona with her real life hero, her husband.

Website: http://www.tilt.com/authors/deniseagnew.htm

Email: danovelist@earthlink.net

Denise welcomes mail from readers. You can write to her c/o Ellora's Cave Publishing at 1337 Commerce Drive, Suite 13, Stow OH 44224.

Why an electronic book?

We live in the Information Age—an exciting time in the history of human civilization in which technology rules supreme and continues to progress in leaps and bounds every minute of every hour of every day. For a multitude of reasons, more and more avid literary fans are opting to purchase e-books instead of paperbacks. The question to those not yet initiated to the world of electronic reading is simply: *why?*

1. *Price.* An electronic title at Ellora's Cave Publishing runs anywhere from 40-75% less than the cover price of the <u>exact same title</u> in paperback format. Why? Cold mathematics. It is less expensive to publish an e-book than it is to publish a paperback, so the savings are passed along to the consumer.

2. *Space.* Running out of room to house your paperback books? That is one worry you will never have with electronic novels. For a low one-time cost, you can purchase a handheld computer designed specifically for e-reading purposes. Many e-readers are larger than the average handheld, giving you plenty of screen room. Better yet, hundreds of titles can be stored within your new library—a single microchip. (Please note that Ellora's Cave does not endorse any specific brands. You can check our website at www.ellorascave.com for customer recommendations we make available to new consumers.)

3. *Mobility.* Because your new library now consists of only a microchip, your entire cache of books can be taken with you wherever you go.

4. *Personal preferences are accounted for.* Are the words you are currently reading too small? Too large?

Too...**ANNOYING**? Paperback books cannot be modified according to personal preferences, but e-books can.

5. *Innovation.* The way you read a book is not the only advancement the Information Age has gifted the literary community with. There is also the factor of what you can read. Ellora's Cave Publishing will be introducing a new line of interactive titles that are available in e-book format only.

6. *Instant gratification.* Is it the middle of the night and all the bookstores are closed? Are you tired of waiting days—sometimes weeks—for online and offline bookstores to ship the novels you bought? Ellora's Cave Publishing sells instantaneous downloads 24 hours a day, 7 days a week, 365 days a year. Our e-book delivery system is 100% automated, meaning your order is filled as soon as you pay for it.

Those are a few of the top reasons why electronic novels are displacing paperbacks for many an avid reader. As always, Ellora's Cave Publishing welcomes your questions and comments. We invite you to email us at service@ellorascave.com or write to us directly at: 1337 Commerce Drive, Suite 13, Stow OH 44224.

Discover for yourself why readers can't get enough of the multiple award-winning publisher Ellora's Cave. Whether you prefer e-books or paperbacks, be sure to visit EC on the web at www.ellorascave.com for an erotic reading experience that will leave you breathless.